"Why are you keeping me here ...   e-
manded.

His lazy eyes were warm with humor and a deeper,
more intimate heat. "I should like you to be my
mistress."

Her eyes widened with shock and fury; then she
gazed at him with a calm, gauging look that had him
off balance. "Why me?" she said finally. "You undoubtedly have all of London to choose from."

"My sweet, you do yourself no justice. You are
every man's desire—beautiful, mysterious, and even
dangerous. The ladies of the town are as shallow as
their imaginations and are insipid beyond belief. You
have my interest, and that is no easy accomplishment."

"And when your interest wanes, what then? To
gaol? Back to the gutters? You offer a showy sleight
of hand, a bit of flashy trickery with no substance."

"I offer you more than you can dream of." His pale
blue eyes were glittering now like ice on fire.

Tempest drew a shaky breath, feeling an insane
urge to accept what he proposed.

"I will give you all the time you need, but I will
have you. Get used to the idea. I always get what I
want."

"Perhaps it is time something was denied you, my
spoiled aristocrat," she countered smoothly. "Not
everything has a price . . ."

SWEET TEMPEST

BY LAUREN GIDDINGS

ZEBRA BOOKS
KENSINGTON PUBLISHING CORP.

ZEBRA BOOKS

are published by

Kensington Publishing Corp.
475 Park Avenue South
New York, NY 10016

First printing: August 1987

Printed in the United States of America

For Julie and Marla
for insisting I get on with it.

Chapter One

Travel beyond the turnpike at Hyde Park Corner through Knightsbridge was dangerous folly after dark, but the need for discretion outweighed the risks. A fast-moving closed carriage braved that ominously shadowed thoroughfare, harness tracings and whirling spokes punctuating the quiet of the deserted road with echoing clatter. On top, the eyes of the driver scanned the sheltering darkness, his apprehension unfelt by the two couples in the plush interior. The two elegantly garbed women could be easily recognized as wives of prominent political figures. The fact that their escorts were not their husbands necessitated the chancy avenue.

The pleasures far surpassed the consequence, thought Lady Loretta Martel as she snuggled against the exquisitely unyielding chest of her dozing companion. Her movement woke him with a slight jerk, and his arm tightened reflexively about her shoulders. With a sigh, she tipped up her head to receive his kiss, warm and tasting pleasantly of the brandy that had made him so relaxed and good-tempered. Taking

7

advantage of his mood, she murmured huskily, "When will I see you again?"

"How greedy you are, my lady. Weren't tonight's pleasures enough to satisfy you for a time?"

The generous red mouth tightened as she frowned. If Connor Amberson had been one fraction less gorgeous to behold or even minutely lacking as a lover, she would not have tolerated his often sardonic humor. The idea that a man would find her passion amusing was not in the least flattering. But Connor Amberson was faultless both in bed and out, and his biting wit she would bear to keep his attention a while longer. Not that she couldn't replace him in an instant. She didn't really want to. Their arrangement was so agreeable, and even though she could not flaunt him publicly, the whispers linking their names bolstered her vanity. Her closest confidants were positively green when she coquettishly discouraged but never denied the handsome lord was often in her company when the elderly earl was absent. Though she appeared smug and confident, she was not fool enough to take her pretty lover for granted. He had a notorious reputation as a rake with a restless eye, and even now, she wondered how long she could keep him from straying.

Diplomatically, Loretta gave a soft chuckle and kissed him long and lingeringly until sufficiently reassured by his response, then sat back to observe his shadowy features in the carriage's dim interior.

"You are a most aggravating man, Connie," she scolded mildly. "I sometimes wonder why I indulge you so."

"Do you?" he drawled, his fingertip tracing from

her soft cheek down to the deep valley of her bosom so scantily held in the brief silken bodice of her gown. "When would you like to see me?"

She gave a shaky laugh that trembled with desire. "The earl has a late dinner on Thursday eve. I am certain Priscilla could invite me to a small rout that night."

Connor smiled lazily. She played a good game, the lovely deceitful lady, and he knew it was from long practice. He was not the first or the last of her illicit affairs, and he was thankful for her experienced caution. He had no desire to face the aged earl over her jaded honor. Luckily, Loretta's cousin, the Lady Priscilla Standhope, was of a similar disposition. He glanced across the coach to where the lady reclined very much in the arms of his best friend, George Morley. The ladies used each other to cover their trysts with clever aplomb, and theirs had been a comfortable foursome for nearly five months. Had George not been so enamoured of the Lady Priscilla, perhaps he would have left Loretta some weeks past, but the situation was so convenient he had let it continue out of simple habit. Loretta was fair enough, even though well past him in age, and, lord knew, she had a youthful exuberance in appetites of the flesh, but she had begun to irritate him with her wheedling demands for adoration. Quite bluntly, she had begun to bore him. He supposed it was time to cast about to see what wayward wife he could entertain to replace her.

The Lady Martel was happily ignorant of his thoughts as she lay her head against his shoulder with a soft sound of contentment. Her languid memories of their evening at the intimate inn made her blood warm in anticipation of Thursday night.

The well-sprung carriage gave a sudden lurch, the unexpected halt nearly spilling George and his lady from their seat. Connor's attitude of leisurely repose was instantly overtaken by alertness as he thumped the roof with the head of his cane.

"What is it, Ivan?"

"We've been set upon, my lord," came the muffled reply.

"Oh, no," squeaked Priscilla. "You cannot let this happen, George. How am I to explain the loss of my pin money? This brooch was my anniversary gift from the viscount. I mustn't lose it."

"Steady, Pris," George soothed her absently, but his gaze was keen as it met that of his friend's. "Conn?"

"Sit easy until we find out what we stand against. I've no wish to have my throat cut over a replaceable bauble."

George nodded at the wisdom of that as he patted the hands of his protesting lady. Before she could argue indignantly, the door of the carriage was jerked open, and a rough voice commanded them to step out.

The carriage had been waylaid beneath a dark nave of trees, its shadows lying deep and threatening as it cloaked their accosters in anonymity. The time of night on the uninviting road guaranteed that there would be no traffic to bear witness or aid. One man sat on horseback holding two weighty pistols, one leveled at the wooden-faced driver and the other on the richly dressed couples. Their aim was unwavering. A second masked man was afoot, apparently unarmed. That man approached them and thrust out a canvas bag.

"Empty your pockets, lest we be forced to harm you. Nothing you carry is worth your lives," growled the husky voice behind the cloth.

"Do as he says," Connor insisted softly. There was a steely edge to his tone that made George tense and ready.

Coin, rings, jewelry all fell into the bulging sack, Priscilla's brooch the last to be begrudgingly surrendered. Satisfied, the footpad gave a mocking bow and trotted to his waiting accomplice. The whole matter had taken only a few seconds. He swung easily up behind the other man and relieved him of one of the pistols so the reins could be plied to wheel the stocky horse about.

Calmly, Connor drew a primed pistol from the folds of his great coat. Sighting down the barrel at the rapidly disappearing figures, he squeezed off a shot but was prevented from another as Loretta reeled against him in an ill-timed swoon. Cursing, he let her fall unceremoniously to the dusty road in a crumple of costly silk.

His single shot was well placed, for there was a short cry as the second thief tumbled from the saddle. The horseman drew up, hesitating a moment before the sight of the pursuing figures urged him to spur on his mount.

Pistol trained on the sprawled body, Connor knelt down, features harsh and without mercy. Only once had anyone ever robbed him. That occurrence had found him reeling drunk, and a blow to the head had

11

left him senseless in a muddy gutter all one cold night. He had little sympathy for the man he had laid out, remembering that instance with a feeling of well-deserved revenge.

The bullet had struck the footpad in the shoulder, leaving a darkening circle on the crude coat. Cautiously, the assailant was rolled over, but he remained motionless. Dispassionately, Connor pulled open his coat to view the bloody exit his shot had taken, then put down a hand over the blackguard's heart.

With a rattly breath of surprise, Connor drew back in some confusion.

"Conn? What is it?" George insisted, crouching down beside him. "Did you kill the wretch?"

Somewhat reluctantly, Connor reached up to tug loose the mask, then said hoarsely, "Damn, George, I've shot a woman!"

"What?"

Even in the darkness, there could be no mistaking the fragile cut of the pale face. Their attacker wasn't yet a woman but a youthful girl, who lay bleeding before them.

"Gad, Conn. What are we going to do with her?" George muttered in shock, but his friend made no reply, his thoughts quite arrested by the angelic face. George continued, "We can't just leave her here, and we can't compromise the ladies by going to the sheriff."

His stunned trance finally broken, Connor bent and lifted the unconscious figure carefully in his arms. In spite of the bulky concealing clothes, the light form was definitely feminine. Wordlessly, George followed as Connor strode back to the carriage where their companions stood hugging each other fearfully.

"Ivan, to my house as quick as you can," he snapped to the driver, then climbed into the carriage with his cradled bundle without an explanation to the gawking women.

"Connor, what madness is this?" Loretta demanded as she sat next to him, keeping a wary distance.

"Light the lamp," was his brusque reply.

As the coach spun on at a rapid pace, the mellow glow of the lamp lifted the gloom of the interior, and Loretta gave a strickened cry.

"Connor, that's a girl!"

"Be quiet, Loretta," he said coldly. "I know that."

"You are taking that creature to your home?" she gasped in horror. "After she tried to rob us?"

"If you are so afraid, I can have Ivan leave you off here," he warned her gruffly, but he spared her no glance, his eyes on the white face and faintly moving shirtfront. With a jerk, he pulled free his immaculate cravat and wadded it into a crude bandage to press to the oozing wound.

Taken back by his abruptness, Loretta stayed silent, but there was a tightness to her expression as she watched her handsome lover tend the wound of the dainty highwayman. She didn't like the misplaced concern she saw there and felt a threatening chill of warning.

When the carriage stopped outside the Ambersons' ample house on Grosvenor Square, Connor gathered the injured woman beneath the generous folds of his

13

coat.

"George, see the ladies home," he ordered briefly as he stepped out onto the thankfully deserted street.

"Do you want me to send a doctor or the sheriff?" George offered, curious but unwilling to challenge his friend's behavior.

"Not tonight."

"I'll come by in the morning."

Without so much as a nod or farewell to his companion, Connor walked quickly up to his door. It opened instantly, and he pushed by the rather stunned servant to hurry upstairs.

Rogers had been with his lordship since he was in short pants, and his expression never altered when he saw his master turn into the bedchamber with the still and bloodied body of a young woman in his arms. He pulled down the bedcovers to receive the slack figure and only then ventured a brief question.

"Are you hurt, my lord?"

"No," was the curt reply. "Fetch me some clean linens, some water, a bottle of anything handy, and turn up the lights."

"Right away, my lord."

As his manservant rushed to comply, Connor eased the limp figure out of the tattered coat, then after a brief pause removed the stained shirt as well. The sight of the firm, barely covered breasts beneath a worm chemise distracted him for a long, hard beat of his heart. With a dry swallow, he turned back to the nasty wound.

Bullet wounds were no stranger to him, his own scarred flesh bearing witness to that. He was not unfamiliar with dressing them after serving as second to several secretive duels. As he began to mop away the frightful amount of blood, the girl's head moved restlessly on the pillow as if the pain reached her even in her unconsciousness.

"That will be all, Rogers," he said absently to the unquestioning servant.

"Call if you need anything, sir."

Alone with his pretty captive, Connor liberally cleaned the wound front and back with harsh rum, grimacing with empathic discomfort as the girl twisted and groaned. The worst done, he bound her shoulder snugly, then eased her down on the fat pillows. With a damp cloth, he gently sponged off the dappling of perspiration from her brow and neck, then drew up the sheet to her chin in defiance of his desire to ogle her shapely figure. Having done all he could to see her comfortable, he sat at the bedside and waited for her to return to awareness.

Connor took a long pull on the bottle of rum, repressing a shudder at its bite after the smooth brandy that had flowed so freely all evening. As he studied the still form, he was aware of a strange breathlessness. His pulses were hammering with a thrill of excitement and anticipation, feelings too long dormant within him. That this unlikely turn of events could trigger such emotion brought a twist of amusement to his lips. He had been uninspired for too long and now felt alive, challenged by questions and provoking curiosity. And, more strongly, by desire.

The girl was beautiful. Connor couldn't help but stare with a lustful fascination at the lovely enigma, a woman dressed as a man and undertaking such a dangerous occupation. He had been completely fooled by her ingenious disguise. The rough clothing on her tall frame, the low gravelly voice so heavy with menace, had been misleading. She didn't look fearsome now. Her face was almost as pale as the linens she rested upon, and her titian hair formed a close-cut halo of riotous curls about her oval face, its brightness making the pallor of her flawless skin still more apparent. Heavy lashes lay in a sweeping crescent beneath fine arched brows. There was no hint of baseborn coarseness in the thin nose with its impertinent tilt or in the chiseled cheekbones. The softly parted lips were full and inviting with an innocent sultriness that made his gaze linger long and wistfully; he wondered if he would have occasion to taste them. The rest of her was equally tempting from what he had seen. Had he found his replacement for the Lady Martel in the mystery-cloaked maid? He grinned to himself when he thought of the self-possessed lady's fury at being supplanted by a footpad. What a lively scene that would be, for the lady thought herself quite superior to all other forms of female enticement.

His amused smile still lingering, Connor relinquished his struggle against the lull of the rum and let it calm his fanciful musings. He shifted in the well-padded chair until moderately comfortable and let sleep steal him away from the image of ripe lips and wispily clad breast.

He slept unaware of the bright feverish eyes that flickered open to wander the room of dark unfamiliar shadow in vague puzzlement. Seeing the indistinct

16

silhouette of his figure at the bedside woke only a distant feeling of alarm in a world too full of pain to recognize fear. The dazed mind labored in that heavy fog of hurt to make sense of her surroundings and find a cause for the crippling hurt that made breathing an agony. Fragments of memory returned, piecing together a sketchy sequence. Dinner with her family in the warm, noisy kitchen. Slipping out into the cool darkness, a pistol banging with an ominous weight against her hip as she ran. The long wait in silent shadow until Eddie's hand tapped hers. His had been cold and slick with sweat, but the approaching carriage had distracted her from that observation.

The carriage had been a fancy one, pulled by a sleek pair. In the blackness, Eddie's teeth had flashed white in a hopeful smile before being masked by a rough cotton square. She had known his thoughts. Let it be a rich take.

The fine garb of the coach's passengers had seemed to bear that out, and her heart had begun an excited race as a wealth of coin was offered up. So much, she had almost moaned gratefully. It would go far toward meeting the dangerous debt.

She had made a silent pact with her conscience never to look upon the faces of those she robbed, to concentrate instead on the goods that weighed down the sack. This night, she had glanced up unwittingly and had known the folly of it. Her pulses had given an odd jump at the cool stare bearing down into her own. It had been too dark to discern more than a shadowy outline, but an odd play of light from the coach's lanterns had glinted off that piercing stare like sunlight on cold, bared steel. She had shivered

17

uncontrollably, then had run back to where Eddie waited nervously.

As their ancient nag bore them away with its bone-rattling gait, she had caught another silvery flash. Then the world had exploded into vivid spots of color, flaring to engulf her senses. Then blackness. The pain had seeped into that deep well of nothingness, nudging her relentlessly and gnawing with sharp, eager teeth. She had tried to cling to the darkness that held the hungry beast at bay, but it was persistent, stealing beneath that protective cloak to nip and torture her until she groaned aloud.

A cool hand lay upon her damp brow, pushing away that merciless creature. Out of the rising mists of unconsciousness came a voice, its low, soothing tone a balm to ease her back into blissful numbness. With a grateful sigh, she let the silky flow of words carry her from the gnashing jaws of torment to the cool quiet where nothing reached her.

Chapter Two

The world Tempest Swift woke to was so strange, she was certain she was still in some fevered dream. She closed her eyes, but when they opened again, nothing had changed. She was not in some filthy gaol or paupers' hospital but in a huge airy room so elegantly furnished she could only gape in astonishment. Never had she seen such fabulous surroundings, the rich burgundy and gilt trappings exuding a comfortable wealth that was as foreign to her as the bed holding her slight weight in a sumptuous embrace. It was large enough to accommodate her entire family. The bed linens were fine enough to be satin, so smoothly did they lie against her skin. Where was she?

Trying to sit up was a mistake. Fiery pain lanced through her shoulder, causing her to drop back with a muffled groan. It was several minutes before it had ebbed enough to allow her to open her eyes again. She had been shot. She remembered that much but noth-

19

ing after that would give any clue as to how she had come to this opulent room or who had brought her. Casting a glance about, she saw her coat and shirt draped over the back of an armchair. They looked so dirty and coarse against the fine damask, she cringed over her own appearance. Endless questions made her head ache, but she could find no answers in the empty apartment. Why wasn't she in gaol? Where was her guard? Where was Eddie?

That last thought made her tremble. Eddie had to have escaped. He couldn't have been killed. She wouldn't even think that. But if he had indeed escaped, where was he? He wouldn't have left her gravely wounded on the roadside.

Her frantic doubts were put to a quick end as the door to the spacious room opened. Shutting her eyes, she feigned sleep as she heard the approach of two sets of bootsteps.

"I'll own she's a fair piece, but what are you going to do with her, Conn?"

There was the sound of a heavy sigh and a low, pleasant voice that played soft upon her memory. "Can't say I know, George." He gave a laugh. "The possibilities are intriguing though."

Tempest forced herself to breathe evenly as she felt a presence grow near. She choked down a gasp as fingertips lightly grazed along her cheek. Feeling trapped and helpless, she lay as still as a cornered hare, hoping the charade would fool them. Surely they could hear the panicked race of her heart.

"You can't think to keep her here?"

"And why not?" was the arrogant reply. "I must say, I've never been so taken with a woman to my recall. Who's to tell me I cannot?"

"Loretta's quite out of countenance with you over this lark, so be warned lest she take your head off."

Connor gave an indifferent shrug. "That doesn't signify. She's grown tiresome of late. Now this little miss, I'll wager she's no boring work."

George groaned at the speculative look on his friend's face. Connor's impulsive moods could prove hazardous. "More likely she'll slit your throat than thank you."

"It may be worth the risk," he mused, unable to keep himself from touching the pale cheek a second time. It was unnerving how the chit stirred his blood, and he had yet to see the color of her eyes.

"And what will the marquis say when he finds out you're keeping house with a criminal, pretty though she may be?" The careless lift of Connor's brows didn't fool George.

"The old man thinks me a fool and a wastrel anyway. Why should this be any different than any of my other scandals?"

"He's fair to disinheriting you now, Conn. You'd best walk a straight and narrow path till he cools over the Westham matter."

Connor glowered. The mention of that unfortunate, distasteful episode pricked him sorely. Killing the man hadn't been his intention, especially since he hadn't really been at fault. He had merely been testing the waters around the fair Constance Westham, and to be called out, having never taken the full plunge, had been plagued annoying. He hadn't meant for his shot to be mortal. He had even let the outraged husband fire first and took a nasty furrow in

21

his arm. He had aimed for the other man's shoulder, sighting coolly and unerringly. He couldn't be faulted because the fool had broken in panic and jumped straight into a fatal shot.

Peevishly, he snapped, "Afraid you'll have to find someone else to leech off of, George?"

George was silent for a long beat, time enough for Connor to regret the sharp, hurtful words, but before he could stammer a hasty apology, his friend announced smoothly, "I suppose I could snag some heiress with my charming appeal. Having a lady instead of you pad my purse would have obvious benefits."

Connor grinned in quick relief, but his tone was contrite. "You would be far better off. That was churlish of me. I do beg your pardon, George."

George tossed off the apology. He could never begrudge Connor his occasional acerbic outbursts, because he was always so sincerely distraught afterward. "I should not have broached the subject."

"The old man couldn't think any worse if I was out robbing coaches. He is quite disgusted with me, you know."

"That's not so, Conn." It was an oft-heard rebuttal.

"It is. The only thing the old tyrant wants is for me to come to heel with some dreary wife to populate the nursery at Amberly."

"Isn't that what you want as well?"

Connor gave a frustrated sigh and murmured truthfully, "Well, yes, but I'll not crawl back like some beaten hound to beg a place in my own home. Damme, George, he knows he's provoking me into running these crazy circles, and he's enjoying it. I cannot go back under his terms. I'll not hang my head as if ashamed of all I've done."

"You should be, you know," George pronounced not unkindly, seeing his friend's shoulders slump.

"I know. I'm not a very good fellow. I'm grateful you tolerate me. I've given the old man no reason to respect me. It's his game, and I cannot but lose. If only these stakes weren't so high."

"You're a fine friend, Conn. Have I ever said different? I'm not just trying to fob you off to get a taste of that hearty cognac you had sent over. And being such a good friend, I'm sure you planned to share it with me."

George Morley skillfully maneuvered him from his brooding temper. Though he said it to cajole a smile, the words were true enough. He couldn't ask for a better friend than Connor Amberson. Looking at him objectively, he had often wondered how that could be, the two of them such unlikely complements. In all the years they had known each other, George had never felt even a twinge of envy toward his friend, who on the surface seemed to have everything a man could desire. Perhaps because he had known how shallow that image was. Connor's life was not to be envied.

Purpose was what his friend lacked, the simple, elemental drive that made each day an individual joy. Quite frankly, Connor Amberson didn't care. Not about anything. Not about his reputation, not about his money, not about those around him. He was titled, rich, handsome, accepted and sought after in every circle. His education and natural charm made him the perfect companion, and his assets the perfect

23

match for scheming mamas seeking a secure future for their daughters. But there was something about Lord Amberson that made those around him uncomfortable. In spite of his wealth, matrons steered their darlings away, and men, while eager to share a game and a drink, were reluctant to open their homes to him. He was reckless, and that indifference to caution made him an affable companion but not a friend. Even with every advantage to cushion his life, he chose to do things just because they were difficult.

As a boy, it had been a rampant wildness that had sent him home from prestigious schools countless times, but he had always been taken back because of his family's purse and his own untapped potential brilliance. He had sailed through his studies, learning coming too easily to hold his interest. Everything in his life had come too easily. His name had opened the doors of society. His wealth had gained him any desire, and his face, any woman. What seemed an enviable blessing had been to him a curse. The easy availability of all in life had cheapened it for him. By the time George had met him, sixteen-year-old Connor was already a hardened cynic. Because he could buy everything he saw, both things and people, he held all in similar disdain. That outlook had only deepened with age, making a hard, calloused man of the disillusioned boy. He had indulged himself scandalously, taking anything he fancied and crushing it, once it lost its appeal, with an uncaring ruthlessness. His indifference had made him carelessly bold, living as if tomorrow held no promise, risking fortune and often life in chancy gambles as if neither held any consequence. Some thought Connor Amberson dangerously unstable. Others thought him simply dangerous.

Just how George had become a confidant to the daring, aloof lord was a mystery to George. He had no fortune, no social connections, no fair face or similarities that would draw them close. The Morleys had an old name but little else to rely on. Poor George was the third son with no hope of a title or inheritance. When he had latched onto the flashy, flagrantly rich Connor, his peers had sneered that he rode on the other's coattails, sponging off the lavish spending and capitalizing on his social acceptance. It had also appeared that Connor had bought his friendship, taking the near penniless George to the best clothiers in London to fit them both in high style and making staggering expenditures on gifts from horseflesh to pleasures of the flesh. Though George was often embarrassed, Connor was amused by the importance others put on his wealth.

In Connor, George had the ideal companion. He was outrageously generous and wildly entertaining with his impulsive schemes. The cool barriers of haughty disdain were lowered for the sake of their friendship. His devotion to his friend was a steadfast and serious matter to Connor, who often bemused George with his sudden demonstrations of unashamed affection, fierce protectiveness, and a dogged, almost desperate need to please. For his part, George's kind, gregarious nature proved a conducive foil for the moody, taciturn lord. He was the loose tether that kept Connor from plunging into willful harm. If there was any good in Connor Amberson, it was only because George forced it out from the hoarded emotions guarded more zealously than his coin.

Together, the two friends toyed with London society, wasting time and money as if it was a respectable occupation. George was always nonplused that Connor had no need for a bevy of followers. He, alone, was spared the casual contempt and thoughtlessness that met all others. While he didn't understand it, he treasured it far above the guilelessly tendered gifts. Now, as he watched the strange play of expressions flit over the handsome face as his friend stared down at the unmoving girl, he felt a jealous threat to their private world.

Uncomfortable with the selfish prickles of doubt, George forced a smile and demanded cheerily, "Is it your plan to let me thirst while you drink with your eyes?"

Connor laughed and with an arm about his companion's shoulders insisted, "Help me sample a bottle, George."

Once the footsteps had receded, Tempest let out her breath with a noisy rush. She had felt dreadfully uncomfortable being privy to their private conversation and was grateful to be alone once more. She looked about in a desperate effort to work some plan to free her from what could prove more dangerous than prison. There was but one door and where that led, she didn't know. Wandering unfamiliar halls could cause her to be confronted by her faceless captors. She was in a corner room, for there were full-length casements on two walls. The view of the clear

26

summer sky told her dishearteningly that she was on the second floor. She had to get to the windows to see if they offered any hope of escape.

Determinedly, she edged to the side of the immense bed and slid her feet from under the covers. Her oversized boots were gone, and bare toes peered through worn holes in the often patched wool socks. Gritting her teeth to hold in an involuntary cry, she sat upright. The room swayed in great dizzying swoops, leaving her faint and nauseous, but she forced the weakness down, concentrating on the dozen or so feet of polished floor between her and whatever possibilities lay beyond the many-paned glass. Rising up with grim purpose, she lost consciousness. The fall seemed endless.

Tempest had no idea how long she had lain senseless on the floor. Awareness lapped back in a slow tide of sickening hurt from the steady throb of agony in her shoulder. The room swam before her teary eyes. The distance to the window could well have been a hundred miles and as impossible as the climb back into bed. Her thoughts were hot and confused, and when she heard the door open, she felt a wild panic. With a desperate cry, she scrambled awkwardly toward the window in a frightened bid for freedom.

Hands caught her about the waist and lifted her easily despite her squirming struggles. Strong arms held her firmly, her only discomfort coming from her own thrashing movements.

A low, soothing voice reached her even in her

fevered distress. "Shh. Shh. Easy now. I'm not going to hurt you. You are safe here. Don't fight me."

"Please. Please let me go," Tempest sobbed, twisting in the close embrace until weakened by the swamping pain. Her flushed face was trapped in a gentle hand. A kiss stunned her into submission, the brief powerful gesture draining her of fight with a soft moan of bewilderment.

"There now. That's better. Calm yourself. You'll only do more damage. You've my pledge you'll not be harmed," the steady voice continued as she was carried in a near faint to the bed and carefully stretched upon it.

Tempest writhed on the cool sheets, clutching at the seeping bandage. Crimson from the reopened wound stained her fingers. She couldn't contain the hard weeping or the panting pleas as her fingers tore at the sheets, then held tightly to the larger hand that encompassed hers.

"It hurts so," she cried brokenly, her eyes squeezed shut. "Please make it stop."

"I know it does, sweet, and I am sorry. Drink this down. 'Twill ease the pain some."

Obediently, she gulped down the tumbler of smooth liquor he held to her lips, then lay back, kneading his long cool fingers convulsively until its numbing strength carried her adrift.

Relinquishing the small slack hand reluctantly, Connor pulled the sheet up over the fitfully sleeping girl and resumed his watch from the side chair. What indeed was he going to do with her? Surrendering her to the authorities was no alternative. Did they hang highwaymen? He didn't know. Would the fact that she was a woman make her judgment more lenient? He thought not. London was too full of poor, desperate people, and the law had long since hardened its heart to their plight.

No, he would not turn her loose. His mouth still tingled pleasantly from the impulsive kiss. Her soft lips had been wonderfully yielding and warm beneath his. The stolen gesture had awakened all manner of urgent feelings, settling his mind to his plan of action. He had never kept a woman before, but the thought of it now filled him with an eager anticipation. He would not let her leave his rooms, and soon, she would not want to.

Connor was still plotting along these lines some time later when he became aware of calm eyes staring at him steadily. They were blue, a clear bright sapphire that regarded him boldly with no trace of alarm.

"Hello. Feeling better?" he asked cordially with an offered smile.

"All things considered, tolerably well." Her voice was deep and a bit husky, but he was pleased to note she was well spoken. "Who are you?"

"Forgive me for not making the proper introductions on the road last night. Lord Connor Amberson, your servant. And you?"

She ignored his question, eyes flashing about. "Where am I?"

"At my house."

She raised a fine arched brow. "Are you my gaoler, sir?"

"No, indeed. Consider yourself my guest."

"Do you often shoot people in order to drag them

29

to your house to entertain them?"

Connor chuckled. She was delightful, better than he had dreamed and certainly better than Loretta Martel. "You are the first," he assured her.

"I rob you; you try to murder me, then ask me to feel comfortable in your home. Am I to assume I am closeted with a madman?"

He laughed again, a warm, throaty sound. "I have been called such, I do apologize for your discomfort. I am usually an excellent marksman, and I meant to kill you but an inordinate amount of brandy unsettled my hand."

"I am to be thankful that you are a ginfish then," she replied wryly.

"As am I. It would have distressed me to have missed this opportunity to make your acquaintance."

"Why am I here?" she challenged directly, regarding her host with a suspicious eye. The touch of his hand on her cheek and the heat of his mouth were much too prominent in her thoughts. She tried to sit up, then remained still when the sleeping beast in her shoulder threatened to wake.

"You would prefer prison?" was the cool response.

"I am not sure." Her voice was cautious, but there was no anxiety in her gaze.

"Are you frightened of me? I have assured you I mean you no harm."

"Short of trying to kill me, of course."

"That was before I discovered what lay behind your mask."

No, she wasn't afraid of him. His touch had been too gentle for her to think he would harm her. But what then was his intention? She asked him forthrightly.

"Your company, of course," he answered smoothly. "You will be well cared for until you are stronger and on the mend."

"You'll release me then?" There was a faint tremor of doubtful hope in her tone that tugged at his conscience.

"We'll talk of it then," he concluded. His gaze said plainly that until then, she would remain where she was. "Is there anyone I can notify of your safety? Your family?"

Tempest hesitated. She desperately wanted to ask after Eddie, but how could she trust this silken-tongued stranger? Finally, she said, "No, there is no one."

As if he read her worried thoughts, Connor said quietly, "Your friend escaped harm."

She gave a heavy sigh, her eyes closing briefly. Then she regarded him again. "Thank you for telling me."

"Can I have some name to place you?" he asked simply.

"Tempest."

"For tempestuous?"

"Perhaps," she conceded, returning his broad smile.

"Would you care for some lunch with me, or would you prefer to rest?"

"I am quite famished, if it is no trouble."

When he returned bearing a heavily laden tray for two, Tempest gave Lord Connor Amberson an appraising look. In a word, he was magnificent. The well-tailored clothing showcased his tall, straight bearing, his fine coat measuring broad shoulders and cut off at a lean waist. The snug trousers displayed an excellent leg, long and well muscled, proving him no idle dandy. He moved with an easy confidence, strong, graceful—an avid sportsman she concluded correctly.

Though his form was admirable, his face was arresting, his features so perfect and unflawed they were sure to set any maiden's heart to pulsing. Tempest was no exception. He wore his hair cropped shorter than was the fashion and without the curls and waves that were often artificially produced. He brushed it back from a high, noble brow to affect a windswept bristling as dark as midnight. Black brows made an arrogant arch above haughty features set in an expression of smug conceit from heavily-lidded eyes of pale gray-blue to imperiously straight nose and full, rather pouty mouth. Sun-bronzed skin stretched tautly over prominent cheekbones that formed lean, intriguing shadows that tapered to a firm, masterful chin. Even his hands were beautiful with long well-shaped fingers that could to her experience be both strong and tender. She marveled at the smooth feel of them; her own were rough and cracked. He sported a single, heavy gold signet on his smallest finger. She remembered seeing him toss it into her cache. Apparently, the fruits of their labor had been for naught.

Noting her scrutiny and confident she had not found him wanting, Connor grinned. That quick gesture altered his vain image entirely. His smile was a mile across, creasing the lean cheeks with deep dimples and displaying a shocking amount of teeth. His front two were slightly crooked, spoiling the flawless facade with an endearing boyishness. Tempest was at a loss before such overwhelming charm and flushed uncomfortably as she struggled for composure.

"I hope this will be adequate," he was saying, enjoying her flustered embarrassment. "I fear my larder is sadly lacking. I rarely eat in."

"If you've made other plans, pray do not let me detain you," she said coolly, recovering from her unsettled awkwardness.

"I assure you, I find the company more appealing here."

Tempest looked skeptical, but she made no reply and eyed the savory feast, her stomach rumbling impatiently. Connor lifted her carefully and propped several pillows behind her to support her back. Her grimace brought an immediate light of concern to the pale eyes.

"Can you manage?" he asked softly.

His conciliatory attitude made her reply rather brittle. "I do not need your help. You did not cripple both arms."

With that crisp rejoinder, she launched a barbaric attack on the luncheon tray, making short messy work of the kidney pie, biscuits, and fruity wine. Connor observed her ravenous devouring in appalled silence, for though his attitude toward others was rude and lacking, his own personal manners were impeccable. He had seen hunting hounds make neater disposal of their meals. Though her speech was good, her habits were atrocious.

Cringing inwardly, he finished his portion slowly with dampened appetite, losing it completely when

33

she noisily licked her fingers. He removed the tray thankfully and poured them generous glasses of wine. She met his eyes unblinkingly with that bold questioning look he found so refreshing.

"Now, sir, to business," she began brusquely. "Why are you keeping me here? Since you have admitted your intent to kill me, I do not think you to be a soft-hearted reformer, and since I am for the most part still decently clad, I assume your motives are not of a depraved nature—unless you were waiting for me to be a more responsive victim to your lusts. So what is it then?"

Connor laughed, leaning back in his chair to observe her with a quizzical smile. "Gad, you are famous. What a delightful creature you are."

Tempest did not share his amusement. "I am waiting, sir. I demand to know your purpose."

The lazy eyes were warm with humor and a deeper, more intimate heat. "I should like you to be my mistress," he told her bluntly.

"What?" It was nearly a shriek as her eyes widened with shock.

He continued easily as if she were not on the verge of an apoplectic fit. "I will not force you, of course. It must be your decision, but I beg you to consider it seriously. Surely you can find no displeasure in my appearance or manner or in these surroundings."

"Only in your monumental conceit. I am a thief, not a harlot, sir, and your offer is more insult than flattery."

She was so sincerely outraged that he chuckled in appreciation. "Come, come now, sweet. You are no gentle lady, and I am sure you are well versed in more basic worldly affairs."

"You, sir, are no gentleman. I find you a pompous jackanapes so full of your own airs you cannot believe a lady would not swoon at such an offer."

"Most would," he replied candidly, then went on to say, "If not overwhelmed by my charm, consider what I can offer materially. I could give you anything you desire, clothing, jewels, the finest foods, the best entertainment. Convince me if you can that you live so well that what I propose is not tempting."

She was silent for a long minute, rage replaced by a calm gauging look that had him off balance. "Why me?" she asked finally. "You undoubtedly have all of London to choose from, so why direct your attentions to one so unworthy?"

"My sweet, you do yourself no justice. You are every man's desire, beautiful, mysterious, and even dangerous. The ladies of the ton are as shallow as their imaginations and are insipid beyond belief. In your place, they would be prostrate with anxiety, not fencing with their eyes and wit as you do so superbly. You have my interest and that, my sweet, is no easy accomplishment."

"And when your interest wanes, what then? To gaol? Back to the gutters? You offer a showy sleight of hand, a bit of flashy trickery with no substance."

"I offer you more than you can dream of." The pale eyes were glittering now like ice on fire, cool and hot and full of promise.

Tempest drew a shaky breath, feeling an odd constriction in her chest and an insane urge to accept what he had proposed. Being kept by a wealthy lord was no disgrace in her circle. Indeed, most would

35

have called her mad for even hesitating. She had to keep him at bay so she could think reasonably. Even in the huge room, his presence seemed to fill it with a suffocating closeness.

"Please, my lord, I beg time to compose myself. Your suggestion has me quite nonplused," she pleaded frailly, eyes canted downward so she could watch his expression through the heavy fringe of lashes.

"Stuff," he pronounced with great amusement. "I will give you all the time you need, but I will have you. Get used to the idea. I always get what I want."

"Perhaps it is time something was denied you, my spoiled aristocrat," she countered smoothly. "Not everything has a price."

"You are wrong there, sweet. There is always a price, not money alone perhaps. By the time you are well enough to leave, you'll beg me to stay." His smile was confident, his eyes challenging, and Tempest shivered.

"I think not, sir," she answered boldly. "If I had a price, you could not meet it."

"Name the price and we shall see."

The exchange was so charged and intense, Tempest felt drained and dizzy. The bright head fell back on the fluff of pillows, eyes closing to the sudden swirl of lights. Seeing her sudden weakness, Connor was instantly solicitous.

"But we've time to talk of this later. Rest yourself now, my lady Tempest, and dream of me."

Tempest snorted at his silky suggestion but offered no resistance as he held her up, then eased her back on a single pillow. His fingers touched her cheek, but she lacked the resolve to turn away, her lids sagging over tired eyes.

"Sleep, my sweet. I will be here when you awake."

Chapter Three

He was true to his word, for when Tempest stirred hours later to find the room in lengthening shadow, Connor was there at her bedside, seated in the comfortable chair. He watched her with veiled eyes while sipping brandy. His look warmed immediately when he saw her awake.

"Good. I had hoped to see you before going out this evening. I have some things to attend to, dreary business but it shan't keep me all night."

"You needn't concern yourself, my lord. I'll not pine away your absence."

The tart reply made him grin broadly at her return to wry humor. It was a sign she was feeling better. Having to watch her suffer placed him in an awkward position of feeling both justified and guilty. "I'll have my man bring a tray up for you. Is there anything else you require? Will this room be satisfactory?"

His genuine concern made her purse her lips saucily. "I suppose I can make do." The condescending tone implied he was quite ridiculous to think she would find her opulent gaol wanting.

"I would like to talk with you for a time if you are not too tired."

It was a request, not a command, and gave her an unexpected sense of control over the situation. Strangely, she didn't want him to go. To subdue that complex yearning, her answer was dry and touched with amusement.

"On what subject would you like to converse, my lord? I am sure we have much in common to discuss."

Connor was not put off by her manner. He settled back in the chair as if in no hurry to leave. In all seriousness, he asked, "Why did you take to thievery?"

Somewhat surprised by his interest, she searched for an explanation that would betray no information about herself. The less he knew about her, the more secure she would feel when her time came to flee.

"To survive, my lord, strange as that may sound to you. I have no one to bring me meals on a tray."

He actually flushed, the slight warming of color making her catch her breath. His looks were stunning. "But surely there are other means, less dangerous ways. I almost killed you. You must own that makes for a hazardous day-to-day profession."

"You are naive, sir," she bit out, sapphire eyes hard and brilliant. How could the likes of him ever understand what one did in desperation. "The risk I take is my own and far preferable to the alternatives."

"Being what?"

Her reply was blunt and shockingly descriptive. "Lying on my back each night for any dog who has a few coins. My fine lordship, do you see that as a better way?"

"No," he said, his voice very quiet. He imagined that life for one in her standing would be far different than the comfortable elegance of the Cyprians he had occasion to visit. He leaned forward, his light eyes intense and earnest. "Tempest, let me make things better for you. I can, you know. I would treat you very well. You would never have to take those risks or hold yourself cheap."

Her tone was harsh. "What difference is one man or one hundred? I am not a whore, sir."

He was annoyed and looked it, his black brows sweeping down to furrow his brow. His words were stiff with irritation. "You are a prideful fool, madam. What is your objection to me?"

Tempest regarded his indignant pout coolly. "I do not love you, sir."

Of all the reasons she could have given, that one astonished him. He blinked at a loss for a long moment, then blurted out, "I should think not. You don't even know me. What has love to do with anything?"

"Everything," she concluded, watching primly as he frowned and glowered in search of an argument to her claim.

"Now who is being naive? I do not ask that you love me. I'm not asking you to marry me or to devote yourself to me or any such nonsense. All I ask is for an agreeable arrangement from which we can both profit."

"You ask me to be intimate with you, and that is not agreeable. You are a stranger, sir. I do not know you. Why would I give you the only thing I have of any value? You do not know me. You do not care about me."

His annoyance was wiped away with the appearance of a small smile. "But I like you. Very much. That is more than I can own for most of my relationships with women. And I want you. Do you find me unappealing? Do you fear me? Do you think I would hurt you?"

"No," she answered to all three in a soft voice.

"Then why protest so much? Have you a husband or a lover?" he asked a bit tightly as if that would displease him greatly. He thought of the man who had waited on horseback, the one who had left her. Did he have some claim to her emotions?

"There is no one."

"Then why not me?"

"I do not want you."

He considered this; then a slow smile spread across his handsome visage that made Tempest clutch the sheet up to her chin warily. "And if you did, would you relent?"

"That will not happen," she assured him, meeting his heated stare with all the cool indifference she could command.

"A wager I will enjoy," he said to himself. He stood abruptly, causing her to shrink back in alarm but he came no closer. He grinned down at her with a disconcerting confidence. "I must leave you now, but we will continue this talk another time. I warn you of my persistence."

"And I warn you of my determination."

"I am forewarned. Have a good evening, my sweet.

My thoughts will be with you. And yours?"

"I have better things to consider," she snapped frostily.

Connor bowed with an encouraged grin and left her to her musings, which contrarily were filled with him.

What nerve, she steamed. What incredible gall. She was no common tart to leap between his sheets on his fleeting whim. Tempest shifted restlessly in the massive bed, then blushed deeply, realizing for the first time that it must be his. She glanced about uneasily at the bold, richly masculine furnishings. This was his room, his bed she was sleeping in. Well, she would sleep in it alone, she vowed fiercely. She was no simple-witted chit who could be swayed by pretty speeches and an even prettier face. She was sure his handsome lordship was used to having his way with women—but not this one.

Having settled that in her mind, she nestled under the covers with a sigh. How comfortable it was, how yielding and accommodating. She thought wryly of her own worn tick so flat the texture of the warped floor could be felt through it. If she had to be laid up for a time, there were worst places, in gaol, for instance. So far, she felt safe here, but if Connor Amberson chose to be less agreeable, her position was extremely vulnerable. She was sure he was not above trickery, but force didn't seem to be his style. He was too smug in his own self-image. Well, let him crow and strut and preen, for naught would come of it. One thing Will Swift had instilled in her was her own worth, and as long as she had her self-esteem, all trials could be born with pride. To sell herself would shatter his belief in her and hers in herself. He had not kept her shielded from male attention in her mannish garb only to lose her to an arrogant lord used to buying and discarding people callously. Let the swaggering poppinjay woo her sweetly with promises. She could endure his attentions until she was well enough to escape them.

She tensed warily when the door opened before a man carrying an ample tray. He was short, dark, and compactly built, broad to the point of straining his fine attire. He observed her with expressionless dark eyes, but she sensed his displeasure behind the schooled features.

"I am Rogers, madam," Lord Amberson's valet. He bade me to see to your comfort in his absence. Is there anything you wish?"

His silky voice with its proper tone of reproof made her bristle. "I assure you, sir, I did not request this attention. The meal will suffice. I would not want to put you out."

"Very good, madam. And I am Rogers, madam, not sir." That was said with less formality, and Tempest relaxed her antagonistic pose. Her avid stare was drawn to the delicious fare he set upon her lap. Without being asked, he helped her sit up with a bolster of pillows.

"Tell me, Rogers, is your lordship always so—so trusting to harbor criminals in his home?"

The heavy brows raised elegantly. "Lord Amberson is of decidedly good nature when it suits him and quite blind to that he wishes not to see. He relies on others to see to his interests."

"Such as yourself."

"Yes, madam."

43

"And in his interest, I am sure you've counted all the silver."

The narrow lips twisted involuntarily. "Of course, madam. Enjoy your meal."

"Thank you, Rogers."

Tempest admired her dinner of rice-stuffed game hen for a long awed moment before surrendering to her hunger. As she wolfed down the feast, she pondered the heavy sterling. It would bring a fine price. She couldn't believe people could be so casual about their belongings. She fingered the oval tray with its raised sculpting of delicate scrollwork. She doubted that his lordship ever looked at this single piece with any appreciation. Why, the large square napkin was made of finer fabric than any garment she ever owned. How she would have liked to gift her mother with a gown half as rich.

No, Connor Amberson took all things for granted, as he would her if she allowed it. But as he had noted, she was no gentle lady, and if he thought to dominate her, he was in for quite a tussle.

Smiling, Tempest cleaned her plate, then saw to her fingers.

Connor Amberson was a frequent patron of St. James's Street, his carriage often seen before the best gambling clubs, White's, Boodle's, and Brook's. This night it was Brook's. He was greeted familiarly at the door and told that Mr. Morley awaited him upstairs in the gold saloon.

George Morley was easy to spot in the largest of crowds, for he sported a full head of the most outrageously bright orange hair. Aside from the flaming hair, there was nothing above average about him. He was of medium stature and of plain, unexceptional looks with soft hazel eyes, rather prominent nose, and pointed chin. Only when he smiled did anyone notice him, for it was so contagious, one couldn't help but respond. He grinned when he saw his handsome friend and waved him over.

"Evening, George. How's your luck?"

"Dreadful, Conn. I've yet to win a hand," he mourned, folding the one he held in weary concession.

"You'd play more carefully if you had to work for your money," Connor chided.

"And you'd be more stingy in your lending if you did."

Connor grinned and hoisted his friend up by the elbow. "Come on, George. Let's get a bite to eat and wait for Lady Luck to grow more compassionate."

"I'm for it."

As they headed down to the dining room, Connor asked casually, "How much are you down?"

"Five hundred. What wretched cards."

Connor counted out that amount, doubled it, and pressed the notes in his companion's hand. To refuse him would have angered him; to thank him would have insulted him; so George took it and said nothing.

Dining on the rather dull fare of boiled fowl, oyster sauce, and apple tarts, George puzzled over his friend's high animation. Rarely did he look so self-satisfied and content, and George was reluctant to name its source. Finally, he gave way and asked about his guest.

"She and I are getting on famously," Connor boasted happily. "I've asked her to be my mistress, and she's so choked with gratitude she'll most likely feed me my heart."

George laughed somewhat nervously. He had seen Connor on the hunt of a new pigeon many times, but this brilliant-eyed, edgy excitement was novel. "Careful, Conn, that she does not snare you," he warned, earning a chuckle.

"Oh, George, do I sound that rattled? Perhaps I am. I'm not used to being run such a race, but the victory cannot be but the sweeter."

"So sure, are you?" George scoffed. Sometimes his friend's vanity was impossible.

"Of course. Why wouldn't she give in to me? Aren't I a likeable fellow?"

George laughed at that, shaking his bright head. "In your own conceited way, I suppose."

Connor's smile grew suddenly rigid and alarmed; George followed his steely glare across the room.

"What's he doing here?" George grumbled in annoyance, seeing the ruin of the evening with the appearance of Tyler Amberson, Connor's only cousin. As the two possible heirs to the vast family fortune, there was no affection between them.

Connor smiled through gritted teeth as Tyler approached them. He was taller and more slender than his cousin, his air foppish and affected from the fastidiously curled coif of auburn hair to the excellent cut of his puce coat. His handsome good looks were of a delicate, almost feminine mold with no resemblance to Connor's strong, angular features. There was no blood between them. Connor's father had died shortly after his birth, and his mother had married into the Amberson family. Though Connor legally was a member, Tyler always made a point of treating him as an interloper.

"Good evening, Connie," Tyler began with false pleasure. Only he and Lady Martel called him by that hated bastardization of his name. "George," he added as an afterthought.

"Tyler. Sorry we cannot invite you to join us, for we were just finishing," George said smoothly, eager to separate the two before tempers began to heat.

"That's quite all right. I'm joining friends." His tone stated they weren't considered among them.

"What do you want, Ty?" Connor demanded coldly.

Tyler examined his shapely white hands and replied nonchalantly, "Mother and I have moved to Amberly at Grandpapa's invitation. He wants me to try my hand at managing the estate. I wanted to ask if you desire your belongings stored or sent to Grosvenor Square."

"Leave my things where they are. It will take a better man than you to move them." The threat was clear, and Tyler took a cautious step back.

"I don't believe you have any say in that, Cousin. A Lord Smythe spent a good part of the day with Grandpapa's ear, and I daresay the old gentleman did not appear pleased by the conversation."

Connor showed no emotion, but inwardly he groaned. It had seemed like high amusement at the time when he and George had crashed the Smythes's exclusive rout in the company of two outrageous

Cyprians, the four of them foxed to the nines and quite a spectacle. Apparently, Jonathan Amberson was not amused.

"Tell the old man I shall be on hand shortly," he said with forced calm.

"Do be good enough to drop a note so we can have a room readied."

Connor came up in a rage that widened the narrow dark eyes with surprise. George stood as well, putting a cautioning hand on the tensed forearm. Connor's words were deep and throbbing with fury. "My rooms are always there for me, and it will be a cold day in hell before I need your permission to stay in my own house."

Startled, Tyler recovered and smiled nastily. "Things change, Connie. You might find an invitation from me the only way you'll be welcomed."

As Connor sucked in a breath, George turned him about and gave him a hard shove toward the door. He then looked up at Tyler with a friendly warning.

"It would not aggrieve me to stand as Conn's second, so be careful how hard you prod him."

Tyler sneered at the smaller man in unconcealed contempt. "Don't lecture me, you pathetic parasite. Just because Connor treats you like a lavish mistress does not mean you are of any consequence. If you were prettier, I daresay there would be talk of a most vile nature about you and my fair cousin."

George's smile only widened, but the usually warm hazel eyes were dangerously hard. "If you value your own girlish looks, you best not cast such idle talk loosely."

"You would foist your fight on my cousin?" Tyler

48

jeered.

"Oh, no. I would want the pleasure for myself. Good evening, Mr. Amberson."

Connor was standing out in the cool night, staring off aimlessly. When George put a hand on his shoulder, he felt a shiver of rage beneath it. The light eyes that turned to him were shimmering with fury, hatred, and, more strongly, fear.

"Get me out of here, George, before I break something. Or someone."

Once inside George's fine carriage, Connor collapsed on the seat with his head in hands, moaning in despair. "Oh, George, what am I to do? To lose it, to lose Amberly to that weak, mincing poor excuse for a man. I'd rather kill him or myself than let him take it to ruin. I never believed the old man would actually cut me out. I cannot bear it, George. I swear it will quite break me."

George pulled down the unsteady hands and said firmly, "I'll tell you what you'll do. You'll go to Amberly tonight and beg and grovel before that old tyrant. You'll swear that you've become a model paragon of virtue."

Connor jerked free, his expression a desperate mix of hurt and anger. "No. No, I won't. I won't slither back like a spineless toadeater. I won't. I can't. How could he do this? He knows what it means to me."

"You'll lose it, Conn. All of it," George cautioned him softly.

Connor sat back, panting hard, and pounded a fist into his palm. "Damn him! He thinks he has me well trapped. There must be a way around it. I won't eat bitter crow unless there's no way out. Damn him!"

The room was dark and silent as Connor slipped in to take his place in the large chair. He took a long pull from the bottle he carried and listened to the soft sounds of heavy slumber from the slight figure in his bed. How he wished he could curl up beside her, make love to her, and lose himself to the gnawing worries. He was cornered and helpless and at a loss with such emotions.

He took another long swallow. He had two options, and neither suited. He could turn his back on Amberly and break the old man's heart as well as his own, or he could humble himself to the patriarch's wishes. That would mean taking a respectable wife and retreating under the wing and hawklike eye of his grandfather. How he would hate that, but what of the alternative? Could he see Tyler and his sly mother holding the reins? He knew he could never go there under those conditions. True, he had enough of his own wealth to live regally in London, but that wasn't what he wanted. He wanted Amberly. He had always pictured himself there, lovingly seeing to its care with a woman at his side. But he had found no woman he could tolerate, let alone respect enough to share his shrine, and being alone on that great quiet estate would be too monastic for his healthy, virile male appetites. He knew his grandfather would allow none of his roving, short-term affairs beneath its roof.

There would be no answers on this night, he finally conceded with a sigh, but what if none came tomorrow? Or the next day? How long would he have before the axe fell, severing him from his place in the family? His grandfather would not relent. The lines had been drawn at their last volatile meeting. What was he going to do?

Chapter Four

"Good morning, my lord."

Connor turned from the window to offer a smile of greeting to the girl who stretched gingerly between the sheets. The intriguing contours outlined by that supple movement held his interest for a brief moment, then he looked back out on the waking street below.

Tempest frowned slightly and studied the clean, exquisite profile set against the soft pastels of morning. He looked tired and pensive, his moodiness making him aloof. How unlike the playful flirt of their prior meetings. She much preferred that light-hearted gaoler to this brooding stranger.

"Something troubles you, my lord?"

Connor glanced around in surprise. George was the only one who usually paid attention to his moods. He looked long into the bright blue eyes, puzzling over the concern in them. His smile was easy and affected.

"Nothing really."

Her eyebrows arched in disbelief, making him shift awkwardly.

"Nothing for you to worry over, sweet, though the

idea of your interest pleases me. Dare I hope your cold heart is softening toward me?"

Tempest smiled at that but knew his teasing banter was for her benefit and only half-hearted. Something was distracting him with weighty consequence. "If you like to think so, my lord," she replied without the prior day's tartness. "You have been too kind to me for me to wish you so disturbed."

"Indeed? Have I?" The preoccupied glumness was gone, his eyes growing warm and heavy as they held hers. "I should like to be kinder still."

His smoldering suggestion brought the fiery snap to the sapphire eyes and returned her caustic humor. "I prefer your chivalrous hospitality, sir."

His grin was genuine. "For now I will concede to that." How good she was for him, how crisp and refreshing, lightening his spirits without an effort and making his difficulties ebb to a manageable proportion. "If I am to be a considerate host, I shall have to check on the progress of your wound. You've my word I'll derive no unseemly pleasure from it."

Tempest pursed her lips but offered no resistance when he came to sit on the edge of the bed to lift her up and carefully undo the saturated bandage. She concentrated on one of the oils on the far wall, forcing her breath to remain slow and even as he cleaned the wound with a harsh ointment. The burn was fierce to the torn flesh and brought tears but no sound. He bound her shoulder with a practiced hand while speaking in a low, admiring voice.

"It looks very good. No sign of infection. Luckily, the bullet went through cleanly. Any daring gown will display a most intriguing scar."

"Not likely since I own none," she countered in a strained tone. She was very pale.

"I will remedy that. I should like to see you in silk." His eyes lowered, making her aware of how scantily she was clad. The worn chemise offered little in the way of modesty. The sheet came up defensively, bringing a smile, then a look of deeper warmth. "You have much courage, sweet. It moves me to great feeling."

"I fear it takes little to stir you, my lord," she commented dryly. He was sitting much too close, and her heart was racing at a frantic tempo. The way he was looking at her, light eyes so aglow and unwavering, made her uncomfortably aware of him as a man. More alarming was the fact that she enjoyed those giddy feelings. He was going to kiss her, and she realized in forlorn panic, she was not going to stop him.

"I hope you are not in too much discomfort," he was saying huskily, the warmth of his breath brushing her face. "That thought distresses me deeply."

His eyes began to drift shut, and she gave a slight gasp as his mouth pressed over hers. She knew she shouldn't have allowed it, but curiosity and a wonderful breathlessness held her as his lips moved upon hers in a slow, unpressuring caress. It was her first real kiss, and she wanted to savor it, but all too soon, he leaned away.

Arrested by her sultry beauty, sparkling eyes languid and lips softly parted as if asking for more of the same, Connor was perilously close to losing all control, something he never did. His forefinger stroked lightly down her flushed cheek to tap her beneath the chin. Not trusting himself to speak, he stood and walked purposely from the room.

Tempest lay back, trembling with a strange shivery weakness. The tip of her tongue slid over her damp lips to dreamily taste the feel of his kiss. The hurt in her shoulder was forgotten as her frazzled imaginings toyed with what it would be like to become his mistress, to share more than his kiss. For all her unsavory background, she was frightfully naive about the interaction of man with woman. Her father protected that veil of innocence zealously, allowing no wayward behavior. Bawdy jokes and suggestions were the closest she had ever come to a relationship with the opposite sex. Eddie had often teased with cruel accuracy that she was Will Swift's sacred virgin, too precious for mortal touch. She often chafed under that yoke, stirred by natural curiosities where men were concerned but having never met one worth going contrary to her father's wishes. Until now. She wished fervently that she had some experience to lessen the impact Lord Amberson had on her sensibilities, some comparison that would make her less vulnerable to these new, exciting feelings he provoked with such powerful sensuous suggestion.

She was relieved but also oddly lonely as the day crept by without his making another appearance. After a sizable breakfast, she slept again until the annoying throb that ran the whole length of her arm woke her. After a light lunch, she managed to rest in short stretches, feeling ill and uncomfortable. But when Rogers removed her untouched supper tray and brought in several boxes of varying sizes to set beside her, her low spirits lifted.

"His lordship begs you to pardon his neglect but promises to return soon," the manservant relayed with stiff formality.

"What is all this?" she asked in confusion, curiosity getting the better of her misery. She struggled up and put a hand on the top parcel. "From his lordship?" she asked faintly, both pleased and alarmed by the gesture.

"I would assume so, madam," was the crisp reply. Seeing her unhappy hesitance, Rogers relented with a quiet, "I am sorry you aren't feeling well this evening, madam. If you wish a taste of something later, please let me know. It will be no bother."

She gave him a wan smile, then continued to stare at the boxes after he had gone. She had never received a gift before except for simple tokens at Christmas time. Gingerly, she drew the top package onto her lap and removed the lid. Pushing aside the colorful tissue, she gave a soft cry of awe. Her hands trembled as she held up the delicate linen chemise with its intricate needlework adorning the neckline. Beneath it was a single petticoat of equally fine detailing. Eagerly, she opened the next bundle and was again speechless with delight on discovering a white muslin gown with drawstring bodice and tiny cap sleeves. She had seen such graceful confections on the ladies of ton and wondered how it would look on herself. Reluctantly, she replaced it and went to the last box, childishly excited as she tore open the paper.

She never imagined anything as beautiful as the silken nightdress of pale blue sapphire, a color so close to her eyes she knew he had picked it himself. The cut was simple and surprisingly modest with a cord to wrap Grecian style to contain its fullness. Hands trembling, she touched the matching dressing gown, its ivory silk stitched to match the cool blue. She held it up to her cheek and began to cry. She couldn't contain the unexplained tears that choked her, overwhelmed by gifts the likes of which she had never seen. Weeping softly, she rubbed against the smooth fabric. How glorious such raiment must feel against the skin. How would she look in such finery, a cart horse putting on the trappings of a Thoroughbred?

Sniffing loudly, Tempest replaced all the lids and pushed the boxes aside. Such affectations would not change what she was. Silk was not meant to be worn on a frame suited for rough cloth. How foolish she would appear in the foreign garb. Did he think to buy her affection with these flagrant, inappropriate gifts? Frowning, she turned away from them to remember who and what she was.

Connor found her still brooding, eyes red and mouth thin with upset. Observing the closed boxes and the shabby undergarment she still wore, he frowned uncertainly.

"What is it?" he asked in bewilderment. "You weren't pleased with my gifts? If they don't suit you, you can exchange them."

"No," she blurted out in a tone so harsh he blinked. "I cannot accept them."

The handsome face clouded with a moment of confusion; then he understood at least part of her dilemma and was quick to explain. "You must take

57

them. They are yours with no conditions. I ruined your things. Please allow me to replace them."

She gestured toward the boxes with a strickened look. "Those are hardly a fair exchange for what I owned. My lord, you are too lavish."

Connor brightened considerably and urged, "I wanted selfishly to see you in silk. Please don't reject my gifts. It pleases me to do things for those I like."

Tempest couldn't meet his eyes as she caught her lower lip between her teeth. How could she explain to someone who took such luxury for granted? Timidly, she said, "I fear I am not fit for these fine garments."

Choosing to misunderstand her, Connor laughed agreeably. "Why didn't I think of that? Of course, you'll want to bathe first. I'll see to it. That will make all the difference."

Before she could protest that a good scrubbing would change nothing, he hurried out. Sighing helplessly, she watched as an assortment of servants brought in a metal tub, folding screen, plush towels, and endless pitchers of steaming water. A kindly woman, assisting her from the bed, frowned at seeing her attire.

"Child, what be a pretty miss doing in such garb?" she scolded and, without leave, stripped the offensive garments from her, then helped her into the deep tub.

Tempest drew a sharp breath, then settled into the near scalding water. The rising steam carried a delicious scent as clean and fragile as a spring morn. She didn't think to question why a man would have such a scent on hand. With a soft sound of reluctant pleasure, she surrendered herself to the older woman's care to be washed with tender hands from calloused foot to bright head with a fragrant glycerin soap that had none of the harsh abrasiveness of the homemade stuff she was used to. Pampered shamelessly, she relaxed in the soothing water, her thoughts adrift with fanciful dreams. Imagine being treated with such regal difference all one's life. How simple it would be to relent to the indulgent spoiling. Was that what Lord Amberson was trying to slyly convince her of?

Her skin silken and scented, Tempest was dried and helped into the night dress. Its flowing lines caressed her with a scandalous clinging like loving hands running the length of her body. She shivered as a hushed voice spoke from behind her.

"That will be all, Grace. Thank you."

Tempest stood stiffly for a long moment, then, hating her cowardice, turned slowly. Let him see for himself how unfitting the sumptuous fabric was upon her.

But Connor realized no such thing. His eyes swept over her in a lingering appraisal, his throat tightening until he could scarcely breathe. "You are beautiful," he managed to rasp, dizzy at the sight of her trim figure in the revealing cloth.

Tempest smiled nervously, toying with the lengths of cord. "I'm afraid I'm at a loss over what to do with these," she confessed quietly, unsettled by the intensity of his stare.

"Let me help you."

She realized her mistake when he came to her, taking the silken strings, crisscrossing them beneath her bosom, then winding them behind her. She could feel his closeness at her back when he drew in the cords until the fabric was molded to her firm young breasts. She gave a startled cry as his mouth burned against the tender flesh of her neck. Before she could bolt, his arm clasped about her waist, trapping her flush to his unyielding frame. His hot lips continued to scorch her throat until she was panting in a swirl of confused panic and unwanted delight.

"Oh, sweet, you smell so good. You taste so good. You look so good. Tempest, I must have you. We were meant to be lovers. You feel it too. I know you do. Let me make love to you. I know you want me to."

The throaty words battered her sensibilities, destroying her defenses until she clung to a final thread of resistance.

"No. No, I don't. Please," she moaned hoarsely as his kisses nibbled along her shoulder until she was quivering with raw emotions she didn't understand.

"Then why do you tremble so?" he argued, licking around her tiny ear until she feared she would swoon. "Why does your heart beat as though it would burst?"

His hand slid up to cup her breast in bold possession, that shock riding hard upon the next as he pressed to her. The full state of his arousal was startlingly apparent through the thin silk of her gown.

With a shriek of rage, she twisted to face him. He expected a slap but not the well-placed fist that struck a stunning blow on his chin. He had taken softer blows from many a man.

They regarded each other for a long moment. Tempest was breathing hard, her temper as flaming as her short locks while she watched him rub his jaw in amazement. Then his features split with that imperfect grin, and he pulled her to him for a sound, forceful kiss.

She had been shaken earlier by his tenderness, but this shock of passion had an intoxicating taste. She lay limply on his chest in a whirling daze. The intrusion of his questioning tongue between slack lips woke her from her stupor. She tried to wrench away with an angry muffled cry, but a hand behind her head anchored her for the perusal of her mouth. Deeper and harder his kiss became until a feverish panic blotted out all else. My God, she was enjoying it.

With a desperate wail, Tempest pulled free of him, stumbling in her urgency. Just as anxiously, Connor grabbed for her, having sensed surrender in those last seconds and rushed to recapture the moment. He caught her with a clumsy roughness as she turned, provoking a sudden twist of her body.

Her sob of pain froze his ardor as she slipped to the floor in a fog of hurt. As her head swam, she felt him lift her carefully and, sitting in his chair, cradle her in the loose circle of his arms. His voice heavy with anguished guilt, he spoke softly as he held her damp face to his shoulder.

"Forgive me, sweet. I never meant to hurt you. I'm sorry. I forgot myself in the heat of the moment. It won't happen again. I promise you. I'll never cause you another moment's pain. Never. Please forgive me. Please, my sweet."

His long fingers cupped her chin and tilted it up so he could lose himself in the swimming seas of her eyes. Helplessly, he sought her lips once more, this time with a searching gentleness that wrought a slow, building response.

Hurt and confused, Tempest gave way to the budding emotions spurred not by his desire but by his quiet. She had no defense against that. She felt his breath falter when she touched his face. His cheek was warm and slightly rough, but the dark hair was pure silk sliding through her fingers with a glorious smooth caress. Unbidden, they clenched in it to hold him close. Her lips parted shyly in uncertain offering, but suddenly, he found he could not take it. Her vulnerability had touched on a conscience he didn't know he had. He turned away, breathing unevenly and his eyes tightly closed. Later, he would curse himself many times over for his restraint, but for now he knew it was the right thing to do.

Tempest lay her head upon his broad shoulder, grateful for his unexpected retreat, for she had felt no compunction to slow the race of feelings that galloped along on the frantic pulse of her heart. While he kissed her so sweetly, she could form no objection to halt the growing sensation of need and want, and that was frightening. What was he doing to her? She had never known a moment's weakness in her character, but he had uncovered a vast, deep store of emotion that made her helpless and indecisive, and she didn't mind that failing. Clinging to him was its own reward. How strong he was, she marveled as her inquisitive fingers tested the hard line of his shoulder and upper arm. His embrace tightened gradually, and she shivered in anticipation.

She wanted more than his kisses but was wise enough to know that now was not the time. He was far from relaxed, his body tense and his heartbeat hard and fast against her breast. He would not hold back if her offer was made again, and the thought of what would follow the ardent kisses made her hesitate. The woman he had stirred in her was eager for discovery, but the cautious nature of her will kept her from plunging into deeper water than she could tread. She dared not push his self-restraint too far, fearing she couldn't or wouldn't stop him from the conclusion he seemed to know was inevitable.

Would that be so bad, her desires argued slyly? Would surrender to this man be so wrong? He had promised she would enjoy it, and the response prompted by his determined mouth seemed to confirm it. No, she concluded fiercely. She could not yield to the desires they were both tempted by, for once breached, there would be no return to innocence, and the knowledge he would bring her would change what she was, stealing away part of her independence. Her resolve would have to be unshakable.

"My lord," she began quietly, "I am very weary. I should like to rest now."

"Are you uncomfortable here?" he challenged gently.

She stiffened as his cheek rubbed against her tossled curls and forced down the answer he wanted, that he expected. "I do not feel well and should like to lie down." That was no real untruth, for she felt overly warm and dizzy with conflicting wants.

"As you wish, my sweet," he murmured.

It was a struggle to lay her upon the cool sheets, a seductive vision in icy blue, and straighten again, but he managed. To touch her now would bring ruin to his noble vow of restraint. There would be no sitting at her bedside on this night. He knew he would find no rest in the guest rooms, but he could find no peace so close to what he wanted so urgently.

"Good night, Tempest," he said huskily. "Sleep well."

"And you, my lord."

He gave a wry, doubtful smile and made a quick retreat before nobility of purpose was cast aside.

But Tempest found no quick escape in slumber either. She shifted restlessly in the darkness, her body and thoughts vividly awake with strange relentless yearnings. Submitting to Connor Amberson would be grave folly. She had only to look to her own wayward confusion for proof of that. She had none of his experienced detachment to cling to. All he showed her was new and fearfully exciting, and she found herself eager for more, not just more of the titillating sensations but of the man himself. She was in danger of losing more than her virtue to the sleepy-eyed libertine. There would be only pain in loving a man like him. Though his intention would not be to hurt her, she would be crushed by his self-interested existence, too filled with his own greedy, changeable wants. She could not afford to give him leverage to cruelly bend her will to his own purpose, then to be carelessly tossed aside. A taste of what he offered would sour too quickly. Better to chance no unwise sampling. His world was not her own.

Chapter Five

That was painfully apparent when he appeared after breakfast. She cringed when comparing herself to this coolly elegant man. He was of a different cut of cloth, one of the unreachable set she envied from afar. Freshly groomed and achingly handsome, he was a fashion plate of high style in a tailored coat of darkest blue, long tails squared out behind his knees and cut short in front to reveal several inches of a tasteful waistcoat. In contrast, his shirt was a shock of white with its immaculately tied cravat and high points. The hugging trousers were tucked into "highlows," the popular ankle boots of glossy leather. She could not scoff at him for being an affected dandy, but his carefully planned elegance was a testimony to his wealth and standing. How could she have ever dreamed they could find some neutral ground between them?

"Good morning," he called warmly, his eyes taking their fill of her as she sat propped against the fluff of pillows, her burnished hair complementing the creamy glow of her skin and her bright eyes holding him momentarily mesmerized. He found it hard to believe that he could ever tire of such a sight. The lustful fleeting passion for her had unintentionally become ingrained upon his heart, but blissfully unaware, he thought only of the present. "You are looking much better and, if possible, more beautiful."

Tempest flushed with an awkward pleasure. The heat in his gaze made her uncomfortably aware of what had passed between them, and she couldn't quell the quickening of her naive desires. It supplied an excited tension that had before been a teasing banter. She tried to restore some of that easy antagonism, but her humor was stilted.

"Oh, stuff, sir. I do feel fit, though I am not sure if I should blame you or thank you."

Connor laughed, but he could sense the subtle change as well and wasn't certain how to proceed. His night had been one of agitated sleeplessness, and it had been a difficult struggle not to rush in at first light to see if her softening to him had been but an illusion. This morning she was a confusion of mixed signals, her bright eyes beckoning, her smile typically cynical, and her posture wary.

"I'm glad for your recovery. I had hoped to take you out for some air this morning in my carriage, but it looks as though a storm is brewing."

Her eyes darted to the window anxiously. "Does it?"

"Perhaps tomorrow. It would please me to show you off on my arm."

Tempest gave him a long, assessing look and frowned slightly. "Why would you want to do that?"

The look of cool arrogance sharpened his features

as he smiled at her ignorance. "I like to be seen in the company of a beautiful woman, and you will far outshine any in the past."

"You roast me, sir. I would prove quite an embarrassment to you. You couldn't mean to let your friends see me with you."

He was puzzled by her stiff, almost angry tone. "And why on earth not?"

"They would consider me a rare joke, and you an uncommon fool."

"Why should I care a rip what anyone thinks? You please me, and that is enough." His brows had lowered into a scowling line, for he did not understand her complaint.

Tempest wanted to shriek at his denseness. How could he fail to see how she would fare in comparison with the lovely ladies he had been with on the night they met? "I should mind, my lord," she cried. "I would not like to be laughed at."

"Who would laugh? Gad, woman, I don't plan to escort you out in your trousers and mask with a pistol on your hip. Dressed as a lady, who would know you not to be one?"

Tempest colored at his mild criticism, her eyes sparkling dangerously. He didn't know her well enough to be wary of that sudden brightness. "I would know, and so would you. You are ashamed of me as I am, and I am not inclined to dress a sham to soothe your vanity."

Connor was taken back by her blunt attack and said in disbelief, "You think me a snob?"

"Of the first order, my lord," she accused him hotly. "Pray how would you introduce me to your

67

hobnob acquaintances? As a beggerly robber you shot, then took a fancy to, and have closeted in your rooms to seduce with your silky charms?"

He displayed that wide expanse of teeth and chuckled. "Yes, I think I will. That would stir quite an on-dit."

Her displeasure only grew. "You would humiliate me so for your own amusement? You, sir, are a heartless cad, and I do not think I like you at all."

Connor's humor fell before her blistering summation, his expression becoming contrite. "You are right, my sweet. I am a miserable fellow with faults too many to number, but I would never make sport of you. I respect you too much. I wanted you with me because I enjoy your delightful company. I've insulted you, and I beg your pardon."

Her fierce glower lifted slowly. His humbling honesty moved her strangely, exciting a sudden surge of feeling for him that she could not put a name to, and before she could stop the words, she blurted, "My lord, I should like very much for you to—" She caught herself and blushed in acute dismay.

"You should like what, my sweet?" he prompted softly.

Tempest's eyes dropped to study her trembling hands. She could feel him waiting for her to go on and managed to say in a constricted voice, "I should not mind so very much if you were to want to kiss me."

There was a lengthy pause until her gaze rose to meet his uncertainly. He looked surprised but not displeased, as his husky reply attested.

"I cannot recall wanting anything more."

He came slowly to sit on the edge of the bed, making his movements leisurely while inside his blood pounded in wild abandon. Her eyes never wavered, holding his with that bold frankness that unbalanced him so pleasantly. She shivered when his fingers brushed her cheek but didn't draw away. He was reminded of a timid foal eager for a gentle touch but bunched and ready to bolt.

Tempest's breath caught as he leaned forward, but his lips only grazed her forehead. That sterile gesture far from satisfied her anxious desires. His light kiss on her cheek only heightened that eager impatience. She turned to capture his mouth with a soft, urgent sound. It was spectacular. He remained still while her avid lips roved over his in a curious hunger, seeking to taste and experience to the fullest degree until no mystery remained. When his mouth opened, she was drawn into its warm darkness in innocent exploration. A moan of hapless wonder came from her as the tip of his tongue fenced briefly with hers, then pursued it into her private recess. This time, he found no objection and played about unhurriedly until he heard her whimper pleadingly either to stop or to continue. He asked quietly which it was to be.

Tempest was dizzy with a feverish chill, her thoughts reeling while thousands of fluttery emotions trembled through her insides. His kiss was firm and knowing, teaching her unbelievable pleasures. Her breasts tingled where they pressed against his fine coat, and shamefully, she wanted to feel his hot mouth there as well. More alarmingly was the deep, intense ache, pulsing and insistent, for what, she did not know. She was sure he would have the answer. He

69

had no inkling of how unspoiled she was as she received his touch, how like a delicate peach, fragile enough to be bruised by careless handling. Her body and heart were untried morsels, sweet and far too delectable from the brief taste he had been given. He did not know that the first sample was his or that his husky question rattled her with an uncertain might.

"Do I go on, sweet? How far do you want to take this? If you mean to stop me, do it now."

Go on, she wanted to beg, but her words said, "Please stop." She couldn't met his searching gaze, afraid he would see her dilemma. With difficulty, she opened the fingers that had risen to clench his lapels and let her arms fall to her sides.

He gave her one last lingering kiss and stood quickly, as awkward as an untried suitor. He was desperate to escape from the befuddled state she held him in and stammered, "I must be off. I'm late as it is."

Tempest said nothing, praying fervently that he would go quickly to release her from the binding pressure his presence caused. Once alone, she collapsed on the pillows, weak and drained. Her lips were wet and pulsing from his kisses. Moaning in despair, she scrubbed her hand across them. She didn't want him to make her feel this way. She didn't want to crave the taste of his mouth like a most addictive sweet. She had to flee this dream before it was too late to realize how far from reality she had strayed. He was a spoiled, pampered nobleman, used to being indulged. He would take her, use her, then tire of her. To him, she was but a cheap distraction. He would go unthinkingly from her to the next conquest, and where would that leave her? She wouldn't be used like that. Her pride would not allow it, and her emerging emotions could not bear it.

With a set determination, she went to the window. Movement provoked a steady pain, but she could manage it much easier than those she would know with Connor Amberson.

There was no escape from the first window, a two-floor drop to the street, but a large spreading oak grew in the shadow of the house on the other side, close enough for a desperate woman to reach as an avenue to freedom.

Anxiously, she looked at the darkening sky heavy with swollen gray clouds. It was going to rain. She would put off her escape another day. In the morning she would be gone, and soon thoughts of her handsome lord would be but a wistful memory.

Of the St. John Street gaming clubs, Waiter's alone prided itself on its cuisine that earned for it a following bored with the bland fare of Brook's and White's. Macao was the house game, and Connor and George played amiably after many a luncheon. On this day, Connor lingered over his meal, picking disinterestedly at the food before him.

"Still brooding over Amberly?" the brilliant-haired man asked in quiet sympathy.

"What?" Connor looked up from his dissected meal with a vague question, then gave a heavy sigh. "No, actually I had quite forgotten about it."

"Forgotten—?" George stared at him in disbelief. What could possibly have more importance than

Amberly? "Conn, what the deuce is wrong with you today?"

He toyed with the fragile stem of his wineglass, looking unhappy and bewildered. "George, have you ever wanted something so badly you were afraid to take it, lest you be disappointed?"

"We're not talking about Amberly here, are we?" George stated uncomfortably, then frowned when his friend shook his dark head. "What do you expect from her, Connor? What is it you're looking to find?"

"I don't know," he admitted glumly. "Something more. Something different and better, good. She's like no woman I've ever known."

"I take it she's yet to succumb to your noted charm."

Connor fidgeted for a moment, then blurted, "Oh, damme, George, she's so available, willing, and waiting. What keeps me from just taking her? You know me. I'm not one to hesitate when there's something I want. I grab it. I'm not one for caring a straw for a woman's feelings. Just thinking about her— For God's sake, feel my hands."

They were ice cold and clammy with sweat.

George sat back in his chair to ponder his friend's predicament. "Could it be you're in love with this girl, Conn?" he asked quietly.

Connor gaped at him, then gave a hearty laugh. "Be serious, George."

"Oh, I am, or rather you are. What do you plan to do with her? Keep her locked in your house indefinitely? What happens when she wants to go?"

"She can't! I mean, she's not fit to yet." The idea of her leaving him incited a nagging panic that brightened the pale eyes with a sudden fervor.

"Are you hoping to convince her to stay?"

"Yes," he mumbled, his eyes dropping away.

George scratched his carroty looks in wonder. "You don't have to put her up to bed her, you know."

"I want her there," Connor protested in his defense, then spread his hands wide as if asking for understanding. "I like her, George. I like being with her. There are so few people I can say that about. Most I find a dreadful bore, and the rest cannot tolerate me."

"If it's companionship you want, get a big dog. They're friendly, loyal, and take easily to a leash."

"Don't quiz me, George," he grumbled with a smile.

"Do you value my opinion?"

"Mostly. You can be quite brilliant at times."

"Sleep with her, and get her out of your system," he said bluntly. "The chase is what has you so caught up. Once you have her, the attraction will fade as fast as the others."

"I fear that will only make matters worse."

George was at a loss for a moment. He had never seen the fickle, skiddish Lord Amberson in this light. Mostly he was flashy surface charm that could chill with cruel abruptness. He was shy of entanglements and phobic of close bonds. He pursued married women alone for that reason, saying he would rather face a cuckolded husband over a brace of pistols than an outraged mama screaming that he do the honorable thing. With this girl, he was breaking all his own rules.

"If you have a care for this girl, let her go and

73

quickly. She has no place in our set. She'd be lost in the life you lead."

"That's just it," he argued, pouring them both more wine and gulping his down hurriedly. "I can do for her, give her things she could never have otherwise. I want to do that."

George's expression softened, but his words were spoken dryly. "Always taking in strays, turning the mongrel into a pedigree." He was speaking of himself, of course, and Connor looked uncomfortable. "Conn, she's not like me. If you cut me loose, I'd not sink. I've my own name and the freedom to move through the best parlors. If you take this chit in and show her the fabulous things life affords you because you can afford it, you are doing her a grave disservice. It would be cruel to let her sample such things and then abandon her. Don't do it, Conn."

"I wouldn't abandon her," he protested earnestly, appalled by the idea. "I'd—"

"What? Support her for life? What if, after turning her out as a fine lady, you find she no longer appeals to you? You are not famous for your kind treatment to your castoffs. You would break off as quick as possible and not look back. And where would that leave the unfortunate creature? She'd have no choice but to return to the gutters. I'm not bluedeviling you, Conn. I just know you too well. Trust me in this. You do her no favor by showing her what she cannot have."

"You think she's better off now?" Connor scoffed.

"Yes. Yes, I do. She belongs in that world, not in yours." He sighed, seeing his friend's turmoil. "That is my opinion. You need pay it no mind."

That was small consolation.

Connor moped through the rest of the day, forcing himself to stay away from his own house and the company he longed to keep. He tried to concentrate on the problem of Amberly, but his thoughts kept straying. Amberly. He would take her there and make it an Arcadian paradise for the two of them. Glumly, he recalled that not only his grandfather but aunt and cousin were there to shadow that dream. He knew George was right, knew it but didn't want to believe it. He had no wish to hurt Tempest, but he was too selfish to forgo his own needs. What was wrong with wanting to shower the poor girl with gifts and pamper her outrageously? There could be no harm in it. She was a sensible creature not likely to be overwhelmed. She would recover herself without difficulty when he ended their affair, and the time in between would be for them to enjoy without ties or promises. He didn't like promises, for he felt so bad about breaking them. And he always broke them.

He would give himself until Tempest's shoulder healed before deciding what to do. He had her for at least that long, so why cloud the interval with unhappy brooding. He would not fall in love with her or her with him. Convinced of that, he was able to hurry to where he was eager to be.

Chapter Six

Tempest looked up in relief as Connor came into the room. His coat was splotched and his hair was gleaming from the cloudburst that had caught him as he trotted up the walk. He shook his head and ran quick fingers through the damp hair to restore some order before giving her a broad smile. The sight of her gladdened his heart and spirit.

"It's really wet out there," he commented as he stripped off the sodden coat. Mistaking the cause of her nervousness, he didn't go to her but crossed to the window to pull back the drapes. In the distance, the sky flickered with uneven flashes of light too far for the sound to reach them. "Oh, I say, this is going to be quite spectacular. A good night to be indoors."

"Please close those."

The small tight voice made Connor turn in surprise. In the soft lamplight, Tempest looked decidedly pale. Her eyes were screwed shut, and her hands clutched at the bedcovers. She looked terrified.

"They are closed, my sweet. What is it?"

"The storm. I do not like them. They—unsettle

me," she told him in the same faint voice as her eyes slitted open cautiously.

"Perhaps some brandy would help," he offered, to which she nodded gratefully. As he reached the door, the first rumble sounded, and she called breathlessly for him to stay. "I'll be but a moment," he soothed her.

"Please, my lord. Connor, don't leave me."

The use of his name startled him but not as greatly as the mask of fear that distorted her features. He closed the door, saying gently, "I won't."

"Come sit by me, please," she begged, her huge shimmering eyes holding his in a desperate entreaty.

No sooner had he settled on the edge of the bed, then there was another rolling grumble. Tempest was instantly molded to him, her face burrowing into the warm hollow of his throat and her trembling hands lost in the fabric of his shirt. Her muffled voice was quavering.

"Hold me. Hold me close."

His arms circled her slight figure obligingly, encompassing her while she shivered fitfully. "It's all right, sweet. I have you. You're safe here. Nothing will harm you. It's just a little noise, is all."

"Make it stop," she moaned in anguish.

"I'm afraid I haven't that kind of standing," he chuckled soothingly. He was amazed by the violence of her childlike fear, but comforting her was no great chore. His senses were tantalizing by the fragrance held in the springy curls, and his body by the urgent press of her small, firm breasts. Closing his eyes to lose himself in those delightful sensations, he hoped the storm would be of long duration.

How badly he felt about that wish when he realized how truly afraid she was, her quick frantic breaths becoming a heartrending sobbing until his shoulder was soaked with her tears. Quiet reassurances were instinctively murmured while his hands stroked her soft hair and rubbed the curve of her silk-clad back. It was like trying to convince a child on waking that the horrors of a nightmare could not follow into reality.

A clap so sharp it sent the windows shivering brought a panicked wail of distress. Tempest tore from the haven of his arms to roll away, her body hugged into a defensive knot and her fists pressed to her ears. A piercing sizzle rode on a flash of lightning so close the current electrified the air. Even the damask at the windows couldn't blanket its vivid illumination. The sound that followed was deafening. Tempest screamed into the roar, writhing in torment.

Unable to bear her distraught weeping, Connor leaned over with the intention of hugging her tenderly, but she came to him with a sudden fervor. Her arm wrapped about his neck, pulling him down half across her. Her mouth seized his with a hard bruising inexperience, impatient, slanting and devouring in a mindless hunger. Once he mastered his shock, he was quick to respond, and for a long minute they clung to one another, lost to passion.

As the fury of the storm heightened, so did her urgency. Her questing lips were hot and avid as they scorched over his face and throat, sending him into a wild tumult of desire. Soon his emotional state was as shaken as her own. He tried to catch her tossing head, to still her for a long kiss, but she wouldn't be calmed. With each rumbling peal from the heavens, she quaked and clutched him tighter.

The windows rattled as a pelting hail beat upon them, the thunder echoing in fiercesome wrath until it became a steady growl through the blackened sky. Desperate to find a means to blot out her terror, Tempest panted hard against his parted lips, "Connor, make love to me. Make the sound go away. Please. Please, take me now. Please love me."

His reply was a rough groan, heavy with untapped emotion. "Ah, sweet, I do love you. I love you and want you so."

Instinct, not understanding, directed Tempest's artless movements. When he would have paused, shocked by the proof of her innocence, she pulled him even closer . . . and he was lost. She was so intense, so demanding, that he was excited to a frenzied pace that wrought an abrupt quickening of sensation, chilling, burning, shivering through him to force a conclusion of shattering strength.

Dazed and drained, Connor tried to hold her close until her restlesness eased, but still she would not be quieted.

She sought his mouth, trembling in agitation. "Love me again," she pleaded fiercely. "Connor, please. I need you. Love me some more." She could find no peace within herself until the violence abated outside.

"I'm sorry, sweet. I wish to God it was so, but I cannot. Give me a little time—"

"No, now. Why not now?"

"You've taken my strength, love. Give me a minute to recover it," he explained huskily. How odd he felt, shaken to the core and awash with a rare contentment. Usually, that would have satisfied him, but with this one, he wanted more, frustrated by his inability to give as much as he had received. He had never had a woman make love to him before, and he had to admit he had been no match for the fiery whirlwind that snatched up his sensibilities, swirling them to a hot airless plane and sapping him of all his virility with an insatiable hunger he couldn't, for the first time, meet.

"Connor, hold me close," she whimpered, taken by another spasm of weeping as gusts of gale-force wind seemed to shudder the very foundation of the house. "Don't let me go. Hold me until it's over."

"I will," he promised, tightening his embrace until he could feel the frantic tempo of her fear pounding against him in a desperate race. Both of her arms were about him in a crush; her upset so great, she felt no protest from her injury. The sound of her frightened moans ebbed as the fury of the storm played itself out. By the time it had become a gentle rain, she was limp against him, deep in an exhausted sleep.

Connor dozed for several minutes, hours, he didn't know. As long as she was safely tucked in at his side, he wouldn't care if weeks sped by. Time had no importance. Nothing else did. He lay his hand gently atop her bright head as she began to stir, wanting her return to awareness to be a secure, easy one. When he felt her body stiffen with surprise, his arms relaxed to give her leave to draw away.

When great blue eyes rose to meet his, there was no fear or alarm in the sparkling depths, only a bewildered question. "My lord?" she mumbled faintly. It was as if she had woken from a dream to find nothing real about her.

"It's all right, sweet. You're safe."

She believed him. Though puzzled about the hows and whys, she was not dismayed to find him lying with her. Slowly, more things came into focus, the fact that her night dress was wound up to leave her half naked and the curious, not unpleasant, aching of her body.

"We made love." It was not a question as she looked to him for confirmation.

The gray-blue eyes darkened with a smoky warmth. "Fabulously," he attested, not daring to touch her while her look was so uncertain. More softly, he added. "I can lay no claim to that though. I fear I was quite a disappointment to you."

The faintest of smiles etched her face, making her beauty ethereal. "I cannot believe that, my lord." With a flush of color, she tugged her gown down to cover her hips, then looked at him shyly. "I could truly use that brandy now."

He quickly pulled together his clothing and left her briefly. She took advantage of his absence to try and assemble her composure, straightening her night dress and drawing the sheet up to drape about her and hide the apparent signs that spelled the loss of her virginity. That she suffered no remorse over that fact was a puzzle as was the sudden overwhelming need for her host, to feel his presence, to look upon his splendid features, to experience the comforting heat of his body close beside her. The details of their intimacy were lost in the dark swirl of terror, but some of the impressions remained, that of being enveloped by his protective strength and of how wonderful that feeling had been.

Connor paused inside the door, wistfully observing the childlike figure huddled in the vast sea of his bed. She looked so young, so vulnerable. So stirringly beautiful. Had her impassioned loving been spurred by a desire for him or just in frantic response to her fear of the storm? Had she but used him for a distraction? He studied the delicate features, the soft lips still swollen from taking his. That thought wounded him deeply, not in the fragile ego, but somewhere closer to the heart of him.

Tempest looked up to see his brooding features heavy with displeasure and wondered anxiously what she had done. Now that he had what he wanted from her, did her presence no longer please him?

Connor shook off his melancholy and advanced into the room. Her wary eyes held him at bay, keeping him from joining her in the bed they had shared. He stood at the night stand and poured them both a generous glass of the cognac George had raved about. When he handed her one of the snifters, her fingers slipped over his. She relieved him of the glass with the other hand, holding his as her gaze lifted. He complied to the gentle tug and sat beside her. Both of them were nervous with their own expectations as they sipped the warming liquor in silence. Finally, he took her empty glass and set it aside, turning back to hold her direct stare edged with question but no shame.

"My lord," she began, then with a faint smile amended that. "Connor, you claim that what passed between us was fabulous. I had always dreamed it would be, but now that moment has come and gone, and I feel vastly cheated that all was out of my control. I had wanted it to be so different, a time of sharing, not desperate taking. Might I impose on you to show me again?"

He was so still, she wasn't sure of his reaction; then the pale, sleepy eyes grew heavy and smoldering. His long fingers brushed over her cheek, slowly drawing her to him until their lips became reacquainted with unhurried thoroughness. He gave a slight start when his shirt was pushed from his shoulders, unaware that she had unbuttoned it. As he reached around to cut the light, she stayed him.

"Leave it on," she said softly. "I should like to see you." At the widening of his eyes, she teased, "If you do not mind. I had not thought you to be shy."

Amazingly, he could feel a warm tinge of color invade his cheeks as she leaned on her elbow to calmly wait for him to undress. How absurd, he thought with a snort. What was he being so timid about? She had been the virgin, not himself. Under her unwavering scrutiny, he stripped down to tanned flesh, then lay back with a slightly defensive frown as if daring her to find him wanting. She didn't.

"You are incredibly beautiful, my lord. You indeed have much to boast of. I never dreamed a man would look so hard and fine and sleek."

His answering kiss was achingly sweet, and this time she refrained from the insistent urge to plunder the tantalizing pleasures of his mouth. Relaxing beneath the possession of his lips, she let the warmth and brandied nectar of his kiss arouse a lazy passion that uncoiled and stretched until it filled her to every extreme. She didn't open her eyes as the silken sheath was drawn over her head, feeling the heat of his stare scorch over her skin. She trembled unwittingly at the first touch of his hand, his smooth palm rubbing small circles over her flat belly and curve of her torso until his thumb etched light revolutions about the tender peak of her breast. As the tightening crest responded to his encouraging play, delightful chills of sensation quivered through her until she moaned helplessly.

"Oh, Connor," she breathed in hushed amazement. "It is fabulous." Then words and thought and the very world around them was lost to the fiery maelstrom brewed in torrential fervor between them, releasing a flooding sweep to carry them to a quiet sated peace.

Hearing her soft mutter of complaint as his head rested on her injured shoulder, Connor shifted to the mattress beside her. She needed no encouragement to cuddle close, her arm looping about his neck and her fingers twining in the midnight silk of his hair.

"If only this feeling could last forever," she sighed contentedly.

"But it can," he protested, hugging her with a possessive strength. "It must. Oh, sweet Tempest, I can never let you go now."

There was no reply as her cheek burrowed against his sturdy chest. After a moment, her breath became deep and soft, and her hand was still upon his head.

Connor could find no rest. His emotions spurred his mind to urgent thought. No, he couldn't let her go. He couldn't lose this unexpected joy. He untangled himself from her embrace so he could lean on his elbow and watch her sleep, a calming tenderness swelling within his chest. To think that this sweet-faced innocent was the demanding lover that built him to such a towering passion. She looked so angelic in sleep, her delicate features warmed with the flush of pleasure he had given her. Her body was aglow with it, all creamy, smooth satin and smooth, gentle curves from small, impudent breasts to long, slender limbs flawed only by a tiny strawberry mark atop one shapely knee. She was perfection, and now she was his alone.

Smiling softly, he pressed a kiss to the titian curls and drew her near until, soothed by the heat of her and the steady rhythm of her breathing, he was unable to sleep.

He was still slumbering blissfully in ignorance when the pale silver light of predawn betrayed the silent figure that slipped from his bed and hurriedly dressed in tattered, bloodied rags, leaving the fine silks and linens untouched. His mouth curled softly as his dreams touched on the very one who was about to flee him.

Tempest pushed open the long window. The night air was crisp with the lingering sweet scent of rain, and the damp streets below were black, slick, and empty. Though her mind was urging not to look back, a quieter voice made her turn and stand at the bedside, to gaze down on the still figure of the man who had shown her and brought her love. The seren-ity of slumber made his face painfully glorious be-neath the crumple of untidy hair. She wanted to touch him and feel the warmth of his skin, to kiss him and delight in the sweetness of his lips, but she couldn't

85

risk waking him. She would never see him again, and this was how she wanted to hold him in her memory. Looking at him now, she saw only a man, but once he awoke and donned his fine apparel, he would become Lord Amberson.

"Thank you, my lord," she said in a hushed voice. "I shall always carry you in my heart."

The sturdy limbs of the oak seemed twice the distance away as she stood poised on the casement. Holding onto the sash, she leaned out, stretching as far as she could, but her questing fingers fell inches short. Sighing with frustration, she gathered her courage. After a moment of fierce concentration, she leaped from the sill into the darkness.

Chapter Seven

Connor lingered in the heavy luxury of sleep. He let his thoughts drift while his weary body lay inert, the musings bringing a smile to his face. Today he would have the best clothiers in London prepare an enviable wardrobe for his lady. When he presented her on his arm, she would look like a queen. Of course, that would not be today. Today he had plans only to lounge in bed, the bed he would share with her from now on. They could idle away the time exploring the boundaries of each other's passions and perhaps find time for a meal.

Eager to see if the lady in question was agreeable, Connor stretched out his hand. His eyes flashed open.

"Tempest?"

A quick inventory proved the room empty. His glance darted to the door, then fell on the open window. He was off the bed in an instant, dashing across the cool floor while his mind presented the image of her broken body sprawled below. He leaned out in a chill of panic, but there was no crumpled figure. She was gone.

A shout from below made him aware that he was standing naked before all Grosvenor Square. He pulled back and sat heavily on the edge of the bed. Distractedly, his fingers toyed with the silken cords of the night dress. She had taken her filthy clothes and run from him, taking nothing of his, not his fine gifts, not the wadding of bills on the dressing table carelessly torn from his pockets. Why, his mind and heart cried in anguish. What had he done? What had prompted this unexpected desertion? His thoughts searched back, recalling with a dull edging of pain the beautiful love they had made together, the passion and submission she had displayed. Had she been planning to flee even then? Even as she kissed him and encouraged him with the thrust of her hips and soft cries of his name? Even as she heard him profess his love for her?

Damn her! Connor flung the gown in blind fury. Love her? No, never. He was not that big a fool. No deceiving tart could trick him into surrendering his heart. Torn out and fed to him. Wasn't that what he had jokingly told George. Quite the joke. No, he would never speak of love again. Never again would he weaken his spirit to this shredding hurt. No, never.

That evening George Morley looked at his friend curiously. Something was very wrong with the man who smiled in greeting, the gesture never reaching his glazed eyes. It was yet early, but Connor was quite foxed as he studied his cards in a blurry concentration. He played the hand badly and was convinced by George to leave the table for a bite of supper.

After watching him push around pieces of his untasted meal while drinking steadily, George finally asked, "How's your pretty highwayman, Conn?"

The fork paused in its indiscriminant stabbing, but Connor didn't look up. His reply was offhand and airy. "Gone. For the best, as you said." Before the barrage of questions could start, he shifted topics. "I've a race tomorrow against Waterston's new grays. Care to ride with me?"

"Of course," was the expected response. Connor was an expert at handling the ribbons, but his reputation for recklessness would have made most cry off from such an offer. "Heard rumors that those tits set a pretty fair pace."

"You'd best hope that isn't the case, or we'll both be looking for someone to pay for our supper."

George asked softly, "How much have you bet?"

"Only £100,000. Waterston wouldn't go any higher."

The casually mentioned sum made George wheeze. "Are you mad?"

"Quite probably," Connor agreed, tossing down another glass.

It took George a moment to gain his composure; then he urged, "If you've wagered that much, shouldn't you be home so you'll have a steady hand tomorrow?"

Connor lifted his drink with a lopsided grin and proclaimed, "My steely nerves are right in here. Don't worry, George. I'm fine."

"Are you?"

The blunt question edged behind the affected banter, and for an instant, George had a glimpse of what was hidden by the flashy smile. That briefly exposed truth of raw hurt set him back in surprise, but the look was gone in the blink of an eye, and Connor's carefree attitude was back in place.

"Why wouldn't I be?" he challenged with a laugh. "Come on. Let's take a turn at E.O. and lose some money while we still have it."

The rest of the evening was spent in hard and fast gambling. Connor shied away from any conversation with a desperate good humor, his laugh too frequent and loud and his eyes evasive. He was persuaded to leave after midnight, but instead of going home to his empty bed, Connor insisted they stop at Brook's to try the new faro dealer.

Still later, over breakfast, he mapped out the course of the race to a yawning George. He didn't look at all tired or drunk with his steady hands and hard, brilliant eyes. And when the time came for the race, he sent his light racing curricle flying on the heels of his perfectly matched chestnuts, and none could argue he was not at top form. He handled the pair boldly, taking chances that would make the most experienced driver blanch, and several times George closed his eyes, sure they were about to be killed. But miraculously, they didn't overturn.

Waterston's horses were fleeter of foot, but the advantage of a daring hand at the reins proved a balance. As they careened around the final turn, Connor made a risky bid to pull ahead, passing and cutting in front of the other with inches to spare. To avoid a nasty spill, Waterston was forced to draw up and break his grays' stride. When he greeted the winner, he was full of curses and complaints, but

Connor merely smiled as he accepted the man's paper and remarked that one shouldn't play when one wasn't willing to win at any cost.

Leaving their sore-spirited competitor harping on his loss to any sympathetic ear, Connor and George adjourned to Waiter's where again the dark-haired man indulged in a liquid lunch from a glass. He was soaring high on adrenaline by this time and scoffed at his friend's suggestion that he slow down his fevered pace. He was, in fact, afraid that if he slacked off, the present would catch up with him, and he didn't want to think about that or the emptiness of his future. It was better to keep pushing blindly ahead.

And so he did with a fierce determination for the next two days. Neither food nor sleep eased the steady influx of drink. He drifted from one club to the next, unaware of where he was nor of the huge sums that came and went across the green baize tables. George, finally conceding that he couldn't sway Connor from this strange suicidal bent, went home for some much needed rest.

It was short-lived for he had scarcely lost himself to dreams when an urgent message came to him from Mackleroy's. Sleepy-eyed, he followed the man to a second-floor saloon where an incredible sight greeted him.

Connor Amberson was sitting cross-legged atop one of the tables, his boots resting carelessly on a stack of bills and a bottle between them. He held a primed pistol in one hand, aimed unwaveringly at a very uneasy Lord Jacob Whitingham where he sat sweating in a chair opposite to him.

"What's happened here?" George asked the manager quietly.

"That madman accused Lord Whitingham of cheating and is threatening to kill him."

"Was he cheating?" George inquired reasonably.

"I don't know and I don't care. Just get him out of here before I call the sheriff." The man was distraught and very serious.

"I'll see no harm is done and repay you for any inconvenience."

"You can be sure of that."

"I suggest you clear this room of the curious for their own safety."

The tight-lipped manager nodded and went about it with admirable tact.

George advanced slowly through the nearly abandoned room, an easy smile fixed on his face while his thoughts raced in a panic. The eyes that flashed up to his were wild and dangerously bright.

"Hello, George," Connor called warmly. His head lolled slightly, his expression losing its sharpness; then it jerked upright, all edgy excitement. Drink and exhaustion had pushed him far beyond the brink of reason.

"What a spectacle you're making," George chuckled softly. "Give me that gun and come off there." He had stepped behind Whitingham's chair. Placing a hand on the quaking shoulder, he said to him quietly, "Don't move. He's not himself, and he might just shoot you."

"I'm going to kill him, George," Connor said in slurred tones. "The scoundrel tried to cheat me, thinking I was too drunk to see it. Imagine that." He laughed, a strange chilling sound. "Step away,

George." His eyes focused in a hard, unblinking stare, his breathing coming in quick pants. Wherever he was behind that glassy stare, George wasn't sure he could reach him.

"You can't shoot, Conn."

"Why not?"

"In your condition you might miss and hit me. Think how badly you'd feel about that in the morning," he stated calmly.

"Oh, I shouldn't like that at all," he agreed.

"Let him go. We can always find him later when your aim is better."

Connor nodded, his barrel dipping. His eyes did a slow loop.

"Get out fast," George hissed, shoving the terrified man. "Mind whom you cheat next time."

Lord Whitingham bolted like a startled hare.

Expelling a heavy sigh, George stretched out his hand. "Come on, Conn. Let's get you home."

The pistol jerked up defensively. Connor stared at him through dazed, souless eyes, all flat, glittering brilliance. "No, George. There's nothing for me there. Nothing for me anywhere," he mourned. The muzzle tipped up, and he leaned his temple upon it. "I'm so tired, so tired of it all."

"Don't do this, Conn," George moaned in a strickened voice, his insides clutching in a hard icy knot at the thought of his friend pulling the trigger before his eyes. "I'll take you home, home to Amberly."

The glazed eyes flickered briefly, and his expression grew dreamy. "To Amberly. Yes. I'll feel better there."

"Give me your pistol then. You wouldn't want it to

misfire and make a mess of your new coat."

"No. Cost me a fortune," he muttered.

George held his breath and put his hand over his friend's. He drew the pistol down without resistance and eased it from the slack fingers. Only then did he breathe. "Come on," he urged, helping Connor to crawl off the tabletop and wobble uncertainly on his feet.

"You're a good fellow, George. You take good care of me," he burbled fondly, wondering why his ankles seemed to be suddenly made of water. He clung to the carrot-topped man for balance in this abruptly confused world.

"Someone has to, you fool," George agreed. He began to tow his uncoordinated burden toward the door when he pulled up short.

"My winnings," he slurred.

"Leave them for the house," George suggested, nearly dragging him. He gave the frowning manager a broad smile that had no effect. "No harm done."

"I don't want him back here," the man growled.

Connor was all smiles, lost in his own daze as he addressed his hostile host. "Thank you for a most enjoyable evening."

George redoubled his efforts, but Connor dug in his heels in objection.

"I've forgotten my hat, George. Where's my hat?"

"We'll get it later. Come on."

Appeased, Connor stumbled along obediently, bowing with awkward politeness to acquaintances they passed and laughing to himself. With a great deal of pushing and tugging, George was able to get him into his carriage and then sat opposite his weaving friend.

Bleary eyes opening, Connor gave an unhappy frown when he observed his companion's disapproving glower. "I say, George, you're not angry with me, are you? George? I could not bear you to be put out."

George shook his head with a long-suffering grin. "No, I'm not put out."

"You're a great friend, George," he concluded, his eyes sagging closed then popping open in distress. His color had altered drastically. At his meaningful groan, George kicked open the door of the speeding carriage and thrust him halfway out, holding on to his coat collar to keep him from tumbling beneath the wheels. When the hoarse sounds of sickness finally ended, George pulled him back in, but Connor chose to remain slumped on the floor of the coach, his head resting on its plush seat, oblivious to all else. Insensible, he was carried by George and Rogers to his room where awareness ebbed back, his mood low and disspirited. Flopped across the bed, he spoke of his misery while George wrestled with his boots.

"Why do they all leave me, George, everyone I care for? I don't mean to be the way I am, you know. I try. I want them to like me. What does it take to get them to like me? You're my friend, aren't you, George?"

"I always will be, Conn. You know that," George assured him soothingly, paying no heed to the depressed ramblings. He had heard the unhappy wailings on several occasions, prompted by too much drink, and knew the morning would bring a new outlook and no memory of it. As he listened to the broken lamentations, he loosened his friend's cravat and shirt collar, then raised a brow at the scattering of vivid bruises that made a discolored ring about his throat.

"Gad, Conn, what got hold of you?"

Connor brightened instantly, his smile soft and his eyes wistful. "Oh, George," he sighed. "She was fantastic. I would trade anything I possess for her. Why would she leave me, George? I don't understand. I would have given her anything. I told her I loved her, and still she ran from me. Why? Why, George?"

So that was it, all this madness over that chit of a girl. George said nothing, and in the silence, Connor finally slipped away into deep, heavy slumber. While he snored noisily, George sat in the side chair, his lips pursed thoughtfully. He loved her? Thank heavens she was gone then. An unscrupled jade could have easily taken everything he owned, then left him flat. It was better this way. Once at Amberly, Connor would forget the unsuitable fling, and that would be the end of it. Love a low-born creature of the streets? George shuddered in horror. It would ruin his life. He would be disinherited from his precious estates, and all the doors of ton would close to him. Much better he be isolated at Amberly until his blood had cooled and the fiasco of this evening was forgotten.

It was his birthday. He was thirteen years old. The sloping lawns of Amberly were lush and silent, the wild pack of schoolboys that had scrambled over it having gone home. He was stretched out on his back, his head resting on his fingers laced behind it and his bare toes dug deeply into the cool, thick grass. His daydreaming was interrupted by his impish five-year-old cousin, who flopped down uninvited at his side and began a noisy chattering. He shushed her and coaxed her to lie quietly beside him. Together, they watched the clouds wander idly across a peaceful expanse of blue, making up stories about what they saw, a battleship, a castle, a dragon, a naked lady. Holly giggled at that. Entertaining children, especially girls, was something he usually shunned, but it had been a glorious day with all his schoolmates and family about him. His father had given him a Thoroughbred and a promise that while on vacation he could join him on his tours of the vast estate. Even more exciting, his mother had given him the best gift, sharing with him before any other the fact that she was carrying a brother or sister for him. The day couldn't have been more perfect.

Until Tyler appeared and spoiled everything with his usual aplomb. He had been pouting all day in the shadow of his cousin's celebration and was looking for an opportunity to vent his pettish slight.

Holly gave a loud wail as her favorite doll was wrested from her grasp. She leaped up and began to pursue the gleefully taunting Tyler. Her stubby legs tangled in petticoats were no match for the lanky boy. Her sobs of hurt and upset as she fell hard on a cobbled walk provoked a quick intervention. Tyler was knocked down with one well-placed blow that sent him blubbering to the house with a split lip. With the unfortunate bit of fractured porcelain in his hand, he scooped up his young cousin and carried her to the house. Her arms were tight about his neck as she sobbed as if her heart were breaking. He washed away her tears and examined the skinned elbows and knees with a promise to see the toy made whole or replaced.

The tears stopped and huge, china blue eyes rose to his, surprisingly bright with a snap of fury and maturity. No, she vowed, she would see Tyler paid for shattering the poor Sally or Junie or Betsy or whatever the doll had been christened, and she kissed him warmly on the cheek, calling him her Sir Galahad.

He blushed awkwardly with a happy satisfaction that was short-lived. For his rough behavior he was confined to the house for the remainder of the holiday while a smug, swollen-lipped Tyler rode out each day with his father. He had wept bitter tears over life's unfairness and a lesson he would never forget.

Connor woke with a jerk to the darkness of his room, George's hair glowed like a beacon in the dim light where he slumbered at the bedside. With a heavy sigh, he lay back and closed his eyes, but the strange dream or rather memory would not leave him. It was odd because he rarely recalled a dream or thought about his childhood, especially around that time when everyone he loved had been torn from him. What had brought on the all-too-vivid recollections, he mused; then all traces of restfulness fled. With a gasp, he sat up, his mind churning at a frantic pace.

"I've got it."

The jubilant shout snatched George rudely from his sleep to confront what could well have been a madman. Connor was laughing in a frenzy.

"Oh, George, George, I know how I'm going to do it. I know how I'm going to have Amberly. Oh, this is too perfect. I'll have it all, and the old man won't be the wiser."

"Conn, are you indulging in lunacy, or are you still drunk?"

"Neither. Just listen to me. Then tell me my plan isn't brilliant."

George listened and had to admit it was brilliant, all of brilliant, but also cold, calculating, and risky. And he didn't like it at all. At first he flatly refused to have any part in the bold deception, but Connor cajoled and pouted and played on his every sympathy until he reluctantly assented.

With a shout of delight, Connor rebounded from a darkest despair to a new hope for his future. His greatest wish he hadn't mentioned to his good friend, but it was the force behind his quick, wide smile and eagerness to put his plan in motion. He called for breakfast and a bath, and together he and George began refining his scheme.

Chapter Eight

The next few nights Connor spent on the shadowy roads and in twopenny taverns searching for a clue to his lady highwayman. Though his coin was lavishly scattered, he could find no one who admitted knowing her or her whereabouts. His elegant clothing made him suspect, but hopes of fleecing his purse were halted by the pistol he carried nonchalantly.

Exhausted and disheartened, he was about to return home after another fruitless scouring of dirty inns and sewerlike taverns when a quiet voice called to him from the shadows. Cautiously, he tied up his horse and advanced into the foul alley. He had only a whisper of warning as a heavy cudgel struck the base of his skull, rendering him unconscious.

Movement was impossible without waking all manner of agonies in this throbbing head, so Connor sat very still and reached out with his other senses. He was seated on a straight-backed chair, his wrists lashed together behind it to hold him uncomfortably upright. The smell of alcohol and muffled laughter from many celebrants came from somewhere near. He tensed when he heard movement very near followed by a searing voice.

"Come on, fancy face. I didn't hit you all that hard."

Gritting his teeth to hold in a groan of complaint, Connor lifted his head. It took a moment for the swirl of bright dots to fade enough to see his tormentor. He was a boy of some fourteen summers. It was hard to judge. His features were very youthful beneath a rumpled shock of dark hair, his cheeks innocent of any fuzz, his blunt upturned nose, and his dimpled chin, but the dark eyes observing him were hard and aged well beyond the pixyish face. He sat on the edge of a sturdy table at a wary distance. The rough cut and cloth of his clothing placed him as one of the city's many poor. For a time, they eyed each other assessingly then Connor demanded sharply, "What do you mean by this treatment of me?"

"I'll be asking the questions," the boy stated coldly. "I ain't impressed by your fancy airs and fine duds."

"What do you want?" Connor snapped. His head ached meanly and did little for his temperament.

"The question be, what do you want? You been asking about a certain lady. Why?"

"That's between me and the lady."

"You're wrong there. It's just you and me."

Connor's eyes narrowed as his features set in arrogant lines. His voice was very cool and derisive. "I do not plan to discuss my personal affairs with a rude little boy. What I have to say is for the lady alone."

The boy's face went white with rigid insult; then he

smirked, "You weren't near so cocky last time we met."

That was a surprise. "We've met?" Connor frowned, searching his memory.

"Not formally. You might say we passed in the night."

Connor gave a soft laugh of understanding. "Ah, of course, her accomplice. Done in by two children. My pride can hardly bear it."

The dark eyes sparkled. He hopped off the table, and in a single stride, the back of his hand struck with surprising force, rocking Connor in the confines of his bonds.

"That's for shooting her. If your aim had been better, you'd be dead," he snarled fiercely.

Connor glared at him, anger replacing all else. "You display a great deal of concern for someone who left her on the side of the road to save your own neck."

The boy flushed darkly, his lips thinning into a tight line, but he wouldn't be goaded. "I ask you again, why are you trying to find her? What do you want?"

"What concern is it to you?"

"She's my sister."

Connor sat back. Another surprise. He looked closely at the slight figure but could see no similarities except perhaps in the plucky attitude. "I only want to talk to her. I mean her no harm. You've my word on that."

"Your word?" he sneered.

"I am not the one who robs people and attacks them from behind in dark alleys."

Connor's starched shirtfront was gripped in a rough hand, and the boy drew close, his eyes black with hatred. "I should kill you. I want to very much, so mind how you speak to me."

Connor was not intimidated. "I'm in no danger from you. Tempest would not like me harmed."

The boy's expression grew even fiercer. "What makes you think she gives a damn about what happens to you?"

"Ask her."

The boy shoved away from the confident man and began to pace in agitation. The calm, ice blue eyes unnerved him, made him feel awkward like a child, and he didn't care at all for the man's bold claims to know his sister's mind. "I'll ask you one last time, what be your business with my sister?"

"I've come to see to her welfare."

"Oh? How do you plan to do that? She already told you she wouldn't be your whore."

Connor was taken aback. How much had she told him? Not all, or the angry-eyed boy would have slit his throat. "I want to see she has a future, which is more than I can say for you. You're her brother, and yet you let her risk her life over a few pieces of coin. What kind of man puts a woman in danger?"

The boy blanched, then went crimson. "I don't like it. I never have. What do you know?"

"I know I value her more than that."

"It's her doing, not mine," he protested, off guard and on the defensive. "If there was another way—Our father owes a lot of money to some very bad men."

"Eddie, you don't need to excuse yourself to him."

The low, crisp voice sent a shiver through Connor as he strained around to get a glimpse of her. Had she been there all along? She came out into the light, and his breath caught painfully. Even in the mannish garb, she stirred his emotions with a mighty force of desire. It was a struggle to keep his expression composed while inside he was a-jangle.

"Hello, my lord. I had not expected to see you again." Her words were smooth and detached as though speaking to a stranger. In these harsh surroundings, she looked hardened and wary, not at all the woman who had asked him to love her.

Confused and stung by her aloofness, Connor's reply was curt. "Had I known you were in such a hurry to leave, I would have seen you to the door. There was no need to risk your pretty neck jumping from the window."

She shrugged, wincing at the gesture and bringing a look of concern to his eyes.

"How is your shoulder?" he asked quietly.

"Much better, thank you."

Eddie had been watching the exchange with a curious alarm. "You mean no thanks to him," he growled.

"Eddie, mind your manners," Tempest scolded, earning a glower. She rarely dressed him down, but the appearance of Connor Amberson had her quite out of countenance. When she returned to her family, she had tried to convince herself that nothing was any different. Now here he was, proving how wrong she was to think she could put him out of her life. Just seeing him had her heart beating with a crazy panicked rhythm. Why did he have to appear so soon after their parting before she had a chance to purge him from her system? His very appeal made him much too dangerous.

"So, Lord Amberson, what is it you want of me?"

"I have come to propose an arrangement that we will both profit from handsomely."

Tempest's face flushed with a brightness that rivaled her hair. "I have already told you I won't be bought as your mistress, not at any price."

The heavy distaste in her tone wounded him with a thrust that hit home, and he was quick to retaliate in kind. "What I propose is of more importance than a brief dalliance between the sheets."

Her face lost its high color in a draining rush, and she snapped, "State your business."

"Untie me." It was an order, not a request, and she balked with a rebellious pout. "Come now. You cannot think me such a threat that I need to be so trussed."

Still frowning, she tugged at the ropes, feeling him stiffen at her cool touch, her fingers brushing over his hands. Once she had freed him, she stepped quickly away while he rubbed his chafed wrists tenderly.

"Now," he continued regally, "I should like to speak with your father if he has any control over you two incorrigible children."

Eddie made a quick movement, but it was intercepted.

"Go find Papa, Eddie."

"But—"

"Do it."

After shooting Connor a withering glare, he stalked out of the small room. Connor started to stand but was quickly subdued by a blinding stab of pain in his head. His involuntary sound brought Tempest to him. Placing a hand on his shoulder, she forced his head down between his knees until the nauseous ache began to recede.

"I'm sorry you were hurt," she was saying in quiet sincerity. "Eddie didn't know who you were and got a bit alarmed when he heard you asking for me." She lightly felt the lump on the base of his skull, then before she could stop herself, let her fingers glide through the dark silk of his hair. It was a brief caress, but it brought his eyes up to hers in a searching question.

"Why did you run from me, Tempest? Were you so afraid of me you had to sneak out in the night without a word?"

Yes, she wanted to cry, but she forced a laugh. "Little frightens me, my lord. I thought it was time to go, is all."

"The things I gave you were yours to keep."

Again the laugh and a wry smile. "As you can see, my life has few occasions for silk."

"At least you would have looked like a woman instead of a grubby boy."

She bristled at his criticism and stood away, her thoughts of how much she wanted to taste his mouth replaced by the desire to slap him.

Will Swift was an older version of his son, his features perpetually boyish despite the generous iron gray in his hair. He was openly awed by the elegantly attired man who rose to greet him with an extended hand.

"Will Swift, my lord. What service can I be to

you?"

"We can be of service to each other, Mr. Swift. Please sit down."

Tempest and Eddie rankled at their father's toad-eating manner, and the quick, expectant way Connor Amberson took advantage of it.

"Eddie, fetch the gentleman and meself something wet to ease our throats while we talk a bit."

"Yes, Papa," was the muttered reply.

"You was saying, my lord?"

Connor sat back, confident in the hand he was about to deal. Will Swift would be no problem. "Mr. Swift, I understand you've some problems with creditors."

The older man looked stunned. "The children told you, did they? Well, I tend to gamble on the ponies a bit and not too good." He chuckled with embarrassment, and Connor supplied a smile to ease it. "I keeps thinking my luck will change, but she can be a stubborn jade when she wants to be."

"How far are you in?"

Will glanced uncomfortably at Tempest, then leaned closer to the sympathetic gentleman. "Near to £60,000. I know that ain't but a drop to you, but the interest alone is about to bury us."

Connor nodded. Moneylenders were greedy parasites that sucked dry those they could latch onto. "Mr. Swift, I am a wealthy man, very, very wealthy."

Swift's eyes widened appreciatively at the emphasis.

"It would be no strain on my pocket to cut you loose of these bloodsuckers." When Swift's dark eyes became hard slits, he assured him, "I'm not talking

107

about charity. I've little use for that myself. I expect payment of a kind."

Tempest went rigid. Would he dare name her as his price? How she would enjoy seeing her father take down the snooty Lord Amberson a peg. In spite of her outrage, she couldn't help the tingle of expectation that arose in her.

But Connor's choice of payment was very different.

"While I have an extensive inheritance, I am about to forfeit my properties to a cousin I loathe, and I find the situation quiet intolerable. That is where you, or should I say your daughter, can help me."

"How, my lord?"

"I am second in line to the estates. My cousin Holly was originally the heir, but she was lost in a tragic accident that took the lives of her parents. Despite all evidence to the contrary, my grandfather still believes her to be alive, and I am about to produce her."

"I don't understand."

"Holly was about six when she disappeared. She'd be about Tempest's age now and of similar coloring. She also had a peculiar birthmark above her left knee like a ripe strawberry." He paused when he heard her draw a sharp breath.

"How did you come to see such a mark on my daughter?" Will demanded tightly.

"Oh, quite innocently, I assure you." Connor said soothingly to quite the ruffled parental feathers. "She took a spill from her horse in front of my carriage several nights ago."

"When she twisted her shoulder."

"Quite," he agreed, his eyes sliding to a very calm

108

set of blue eyes. "Well, I got a glance of the mark, and it set me thinking. That's when I came to you, sir. I would not contrive such a plan without your consent."

Swift puffed up with importance. "What do you want with my girl?"

"Just an innocent deception. No harm will be done, and nothing illegal. The properties are mine, and I only mean to see they are."

Eddie pushed a mug of ale at him with a venomous look that only intensified when he was cordially thanked.

"Spell out your plan, my lord."

Connor went over the details he and George had labored over. Tempest would pose as the long-lost Holly who was discovered living in anonymity brought to the bosom of the family by her loving cousin. She would claim her rightful inheritance, then after an interval name Connor as its executor, and subtly disappear.

"When Tempest goes with me to Amberly, I will clear your accounts with all your debtors and, in addition, see you have an ample income for life."

"An ingenious plan, my lord." Eddie made the title sound like an insult. "But who is going to believe Este here be some fancy heiress?"

Tempest colored hotly under Connor's appraising stare. "She's bright enough, and if she works hard, I think I can transform her into a passable lady of quality."

Before she could make a scathing reply, her father interrupted, "How do we know your intentions be honorable toward my little girl?"

"My only interest is in claiming my lands, not in seducing your daughter. You've my word she'll return to you unchanged from the way she is right now."

Tempest shot him a sour glance he calmly ignored.

"When the estate is in my hands, she is free to do whatever she pleases. I mean to use her only to those ends."

Tempest glared at him, angered more by his casual dismissal of her than by his blatant advances. In her budding woman's heart, she had hoped he had come to her to make an entreaty to lure her back into his bed. She wasn't sure she would have put up much of a struggle. But here he sat, practically ignoring her, talking about her as a tool to be discarded when its usefulness had ended, boldly courting her father's vanity with silken half-truths to fire his desperate greed. How sure he was, dangling his wealth before the peasants. How she hated that smugness in him as much as she desired the gentle passion she also knew he possessed.

Will Swift sat back in a daze. It all seemed so easy, the perfect solution to all his troubles. No more threats, no more fear for his family's safety, no more worry his inn would be taken. Like some gift of providence, it had been offered to him, but as much as he wanted it for himself, the decision was not his to make.

"You are being most generous, my lord, but I cannot accept."

Connor's features froze in disbelief. "What?"

"It be up to Tempest. I cannot tell her to do this for my sake. It will have to be her choice, for it's her help you need, I but benefit from it."

Connor's eyes shifted to the brilliant stare that seemed to burn right through him. She looked so angry. He had found her price and had met it, her family's welfare, and it was nettling her sorely to give in. "Well?" he asked mildly.

Tempest regarded him in silence for an endless moment, basking in the beauty of his face with a cold, unhappy enjoyment. Her pride demanded she say no, to throw it back in his self-assured face. Her intuition warned her to stay far away from him, that he would hurt her terribly. Her loyalty insisted she think of her family, of easing her father's fears, and of keeping Eddie from any harm on their daring midnight raids. And more subtly, her emotions whispered, go with him, don't let him get away, he might be made to love you.

In a firm, determined voice, she answered. "I will play the game, but I want no ties. I want to be free to go whenever I see fit, once all are convinced I am who I pretend to be."

"Done," he agreed quickly.

Will gave a great sigh of relief, but Eddie was suspicious. "Get it all in writing, Papa, that way he can't fob us off."

"You're a bright lad," Connor said begrudgingly with a smile.

"Right. All ready for Eton," the boy sneered.

"A document is a good idea. Can any of you read?"

Eddie flushed beneath the cool stare, then boasted, "Este can."

"Some," she admitted. "Make the wording simple." She said this quietly, hating to confess to igno-

111

rance before him.

"That is an accomplishment you should be proud of. Few women can do more than sign their names at their dressmakers."

The unexpected warmth in the gray-blue eyes flooded her with a confusion of thanks and emotion that he would consider her feelings. Then he looked away, and the brief closeness was gone.

The papers were drawn up and signed, a copy to each of them. Then Connor stood.

"Are you ready?"

Tempest was in a sudden panic. Her reply was a sputter. "Now? No. I have to have time—to gather my things, to say my good-byes."

"Oh, of course." He dismissed her reasons with a condescending impatience as if none was of importance. "My coach will come for you tomorrow and take you to my friend, George Morley. You'll stay with him."

"Not with you?" she asked in a small voice.

"No." He didn't tell her it was because he could trust her with George, but not with himself.

"I will be ready."

"Tomorrow then."

And he was gone.

The following eve she waited at the door of her father's inn, worn bag in hand and back rigid with determination. She wouldn't let herself think of what lay ahead or what she was leaving behind. It was too late for that. She was not of a fickle mind, and she had given her word. Her parents had said their reluctant good-byes, and she had kissed the children as they lay asleep in the shared bed. Now only Eddie remained silent and disapproving at her side. She put an arm about his shoulders, and after a bit of feigned resistance, he hugged her tightly.

"I don't like this, Este," he said in a rush. "I don't trust him. I swear if he hurts you in any way—"

"Eddie, Eddie, calm yourself. I've nothing to fear from Lord Amberson."

"He ain't no gentleman!"

"I didn't say he was. In fact, I know he isn't, but I do trust him and know he would do me no harm. Please don't worry so," she pleaded, holding tightly to him. "If he can keep us from having to steal to stay alive, then you should thank him, not curse him."

"I don't like the way he looks at you," he grumbled.

"How's that?" she prompted, trying to curb her eagerness.

"All hungry-like, the way the coves ogle the fancy women. I don't like it. I don't think he's—safe."

She laughed fondly to ease his fears, though she knew he had cause. "Little brother, you don't like any man to look at me at all. I can't hide in britches all my life."

"Well, you don't have to look back," he muttered.

"What do you mean?" she demanded, meeting the dark accusing eyes.

"He ain't the only one who looks hungry."

"Eddie Swift, you are imagining things."

"Is that why you're so angry?"

"I am not—" She broke off and began to laugh. "Oh, Eddie, you're the only man in my life."

"Until he gets you out of your britches." He turned away and, after a silent pause, said in a constricted tone, "What he said about me leaving you on the side of the road—"

"Don't think of that," she protested, feeling his pain and upset.

"Oh, Este, I was so scared. I thought he'd killed you, but I couldn't shoot. I couldn't. So I ran and just left you there."

"Shh. Don't. You did the right thing. If you'd been caught, you'd have been hanged. I wouldn't have been able to bear that. That's why I'm so grateful we can put aside the masks and guns. We have a chance now, and we have to take it."

"Don't let him hurt you, Este. If you need me, I'll be there. You know that."

"I know, and I love you."

They embraced for a long moment. Then the elegant coach came to take her away from all she knew.

Chapter Nine

"Lord Morley?"

The timid question came from a beggarly ragamuffin in the foyer. Had he not been expecting a young woman, he would have thought it some urchin boy who stood there so uneasily, cap pulled low over wide blue eyes and figure swaddled in baggy male attire.

"It's George. I've no title and no pretensions, so let's not be formal. Come in, Tempest, and welcome."

The wide, somewhat reluctant smile beneath the shocking tuft of hair made her nervousness disappear. George Morley was no threat. She followed him through the small house to her room upstairs. The dwelling wasn't as grand as the Ambersons', but in Tempest's overawed eyes, it was a palace. It was so spacious and so clean. And smelled so good. That was perhaps the best. There was no stale, lingering odor of ale, smoke, and unwashed humanity.

Her room was simply furnished with just necessities, a guest room that had never been used for

Connor had never made it beyond the couch when he had occasion to stay. She laid her tattered bag upon the bed and turned to her host a bit shyly.

"Connor—Lord Amberson is not here?"

George's reply held a defensive edge, as if she posed some danger. "Conn will be by after breakfast."

She shifted beneath his disapproving eye, not understanding the complaint. Very meekly she ventured, "I thank you for allowing me to stay in your home. I've no want to be a burden. I have no money, but I'm willing to work for my keep. Perhaps I could clean or cook—"

George's hearty laugh cut her short, bringing a flush to the grimy face. She thought he was making sport of her, but his warm grin relieved that worry. "No wonder Conn—no wonder he is so taken with you. I don't expect my guests to pay me, and that's what you are here. Get settled in, Tempest. I'm across the hall, so if you need anything, let me or my staff know." He chuckled to himself over that. His "staff" she was to discover consisted of an elderly housekeeper and a woman who came in to tidy the rooms twice a week. It was far different than the endless crew who bustled about his friend's home.

Alone in the airy room, Tempest unpacked her bag. It contained her most precious belongings, a change of masculine clothing, a thin night shift, a pair of sturdy walking shoes, a nearly bristleless brush, a cake of pungent soap, and a tarnished locket. Tears prickled behind her eyes. How meager they looked compared to the rich surroundings, a glaring contrast just as she must be. What a fool she was. What was

116

she doing here amid all this splendor?

She gave a loud sniff and dashed the wetness from her cheeks. Enough. Her father hadn't taught her to be ashamed of what she was. Poverty was a circumstance, he said, not a choice, and one could rise out of it and above it. The only difference between her and the Ambersons and Morleys of the world was they were born with their advantages and she would have to make her own.

When she opened the huge armoire to house her set of clothes, she was surprised to find it partially filled with gowns of brilliant silk and opalescent muslin. She simply stared at them for a moment, thinking it must be George Morley's mistress's wardrobe, then pushed her tattered garments far into a back corner. As she began to close the cupboard, her eyes fell on the shimmer of icy blue silk. Were these things for her? She drew the gleaming night dress out almost hesitantly, then crushed it to her cheek, assailed by memories and feelings that left her shaken. As she slipped it on, the caress of the fabric reminded her of another touch, warm and possessive on her skin. Trembling, she climbed into bed and extinguished the light. But her thoughts could not be so easily snuffed out.

Why had he placed her here instead of in his own house? Had his professed ardor been satisfied with one sampling? Had he already tired of her now that she had a more important use? She wasn't sure it was relief or distress she felt at that thought. Connor Amberson was no greenling. He was a rake and a libertine of the first order. She would do well to remember that and why she was here, not because he

117

wanted her as a woman but because he needed her as a pawn in some game of wealth and power. She meant nothing to him, and she could not, would not let herself be deluded into thinking his interest would last longer than the moment. No woman would claim Lord Amberson, and she was sure many better than herself had tried and failed. She didn't want to be listed among them.

With a heavy sigh, she closed her eyes and waited for sleep to free her from any further doubts and treacherous hopes.

Tempest awoke with a start to find the room's east exposure bathing it in a shock of sunlight. She rose quickly, as she was wont to do, and dressed in her own clothes. After a moment of hesitation, she ventured from her room and down the carpeted stairs where the sound of voices directed her to the rear parlor. The deeper of the two gave her pulse a hasty skip. She hadn't expected to see him so soon. With a deep bracing breath, she sauntered into the room in the middle of the conversation. George gave her a warm smile of greeting, but Connor's gaze merely touched on her as he continued with what he was saying.

"Aunt Kate and Tyler will most likely be apoplectic at first, but they won't be easily fobbed off. We have to make it very difficult for them to check on Holly's whereabouts these last few years. They're not going to be tossed off the throne without a fuss. Everything has to be perfect. They can't have any doubts."

Tempest glanced about awkwardly, waiting for

118

some direction. When they still ignored her, she poured herself a cup of tea and curled up with her feet tucked beneath her on a settle to devour a sweet cake.

"She's going to have to know everything about your family and, of course, about Holly," George was saying.

"That won't be hard. I can tell her all of that. It was a long time ago. She won't be expected to have a perfect recall. The hard part is turning her into a convincing lady. She talks well enough, thank goodness, but it's still going to take a great deal of work. She'll have to know how to dress like a woman for a change, how to conduct herself in public and in private. We'll have to do something about her hands and that dreadful haircut. And oh, yes—that."

Connor's disdainful gesture caught her, with her mouth stuffed full, about to polish the sugary glaze from her fingers.

"She has to learn to eat in a manner that won't make everyone who sees her ill."

Uncaringly, Tempest licked her fingers clean, her eyes bright with rebellion. Her temper flared even hotter when he waved an elegant hand.

"Stand up. Let's see you walk," he demanded.

Feeling her cheeks warm dangerously, Tempest uncoiled her legs and under their critical eyes did a quick turn about the room. Her step was light with promised grace, but it was more a rolling swagger than a feminine sway.

"That would do well on the deck of a ship but not in a drawing room," Connor observed bluntly. "She has no ladylike graces at all. We'd have better luck changing *you* into a woman, George."

"No, thank you, Conn. You would make a prettier one. It'll take time, but I'm sure she can be taught."

"And who is going to teach me?" Tempest interrupted, her color high and her tongue fierce. "How can the two of you teach anything about manners when you are so rude as to talk about me as though you were buying a saddle horse."

Connor smiled in amusement, eyeing her with unflattering boldness. "My sweet, I would not have such a poor-looking horse in my stables."

"Oh!" she shrieked. Her hand closed on a heavy paperweight and sent it sailing at his head followed by a string of descriptive words that would have caused a well-bred lady to perish in shock.

Before she could lay her hands on any other missile, Connor caught her wrists, laughing as she cursed and tried to strike him. She was pleased when he winced at a well-placed kick on the shin.

"If you are going to act like an ill-mannered roughneck, so you will be treated," he vowed, slinging her over his shoulder. When she wriggled and kicked, he smacked her bottom sharply. "Come along, you little termagant. Let's get you washed and into some proper clothes. I never want to see these rags again."

George shook his head with a doubtful grin as Connor carried her shouting and pummeling his back up the stairs. It would be interesting to see who taught whom manners.

In her room, Connor set her down and stepped back quickly but not fast enough to avoid the sharp crack of her hand upon his cheek. She was plainly furious, panting hard, and with blazing eyes.

"I will not be treated that way," she said fiercely. "I will not be talked around and made sport of. I am as much a human being as you are, my fine wealthy lord. I have feelings, too, and you will not trample on them. I am not a well-bred gentle lady, nor do I pretend to be. I know I have much to learn, but you'll find I respond better to patience than ridicule."

"So I remember."

His softly spoken words took her off guard, dousing the heat of her furious tirade with his smoldering look of warm apology.

"Please forgive me. I will not make that mistake again."

"You are forgiven," she replied testily. She turned away from his languid, appraising eyes in a riot of confusion, trying to cover it with a calm she didn't feel. Going to the armoire, she looked inside at the extravagant finery with a wry comment. "How am I to wear such things if I don't know how to get in them."

"I'll show you. I've undressed enough ladies to know the routine fairly well."

His boast stiffened her spine, but she made no retort, fearing her words would be conceived as jealous spite. Which would have not been far from the truth.

"A bath's been drawn for you," he went on casually. "Why don't you soak for a bit while I find something for you to wear?"

Tempest went behind the trifold screen, then peered back at him suspiciously but he was busy rummaging about in the closet. Without further encouragement, she shed her brother's clothes and sank

121

into the soothing water. The scented soap made a spectacular lather, and she indulged herself lavishly, scrubbing until her flesh protested. Finding a large plush towel, she climbed from the tub and wrapped it about herself. When she peered around the edge of the screen, Connor grinned at her.

"Don't tell me you're shy," he teased, making her blush and step boldly out in her saronglike covering. The sight of her slender legs made him pause to struggle with an abrupt influx of desire. His voice was unintentionally gruff. "I'm sure you can figure out how to get into these."

She caught the linen chemise and knee-length drawers and made a face at him before disappearing once more. The fine fabric did little for the sake of modesty but was quite comfortable. When she reappeared, she could feel his gaze scorch the bosom of her undergarment. Hungry, Eddie said. Ravenous was more apt a description.

"What now?" she queried, breaking his lustful concentration.

"Sit," he instructed curtly, then knelt before her to lift one small foot. The thought of her calloused heels and jagged nails tearing through silk stockings made him grimace. "Do you bite your toenails as well?" he asked sarcastically, dropping her foot. "We'll do without stockings for now."

Tempest stood at his prompting and wriggled into a white muslin gown cut so narrowly it hugged her like a cocoon. "How do you walk in such a thing?" she gasped in dismay.

"Like a lady," he told her, ending any further complaint. He observed her closely. The willowy figure was perfect for the vertical line of fashion, slender enough to do without stays, yet ripe enough to give the drape a sinuous appeal. Even in her stiff uncertainty, she far surpassed the beauties of the day. How envious they would be and how proud he would feel to have her on his arm.

"That will do," he announced. "Now to work."

And work it was. She spent the morning traversing the house for what seemed endless miles in the binding gown while her every move was critiqued and corrected. The welcome break for lunch proved an ordeal of a worse sort. Each mouthful rose under watchful eyes. For the most part, Connor was silent, his expression pained, while George instructed her in table etiquette in his more tactful manner. After that lengthy trial, it was more walking, sitting and standing, bending and turning, folding and unfolding hands until she felt like a puppet with too many strings pulled at one time.

Dinner was easier, mostly due to the wine; then the three of them retired to the cozy study. George supplied her with a half-dozen copies of *La Belle Assemblée* and *The Lady's Magazine* to leaf through to obtain an idea of the current fashion. While she sat back on the couch, Connor took up the other end and pulled her bare feet onto his lap. At her surprised look, he merely smiled and began to pare her ill-kept toenails and pumice the tough layers of callus. Quite content with his administrations, she lounged back and thumbed through the journals.

The French in *La Belle Assemblée* was far beyond her understanding, but there were many interesting illustrations. She followed most of the reading in the other magazine and became engrossed in the foreign ideals of high style, smiling to herself in amusement at the rigors women went through. The foot massage was relaxing, Connor's hands warm, and his touch gentle. The peace of the moment made the day's turmoil fade into insignificance.

Once satisfied that the soles of her feet were smooth enough to cause no damage to the sheerest stockings, Connor took a moment to admire them, so nicely shaped and small enough to fit in the length of his hand. His appraisal rose higher to the trim ankles and slender calves, his thoughts traveling further than his eyes could see. What a devastating effect she had on him.

"Conn?"

He looked up almost guiltily at the soft call of his name, then followed his friend's nod to find Tempest fast asleep, a journal still open upon her bosom. In the simple elegance of the white gown, she could well have been an angel trapped in earthly guise, and it took a force of will for him to wrest his eyes away.

"I'll take her up," Connor said quietly. "Pour me a brandy."

Connor found himself lingering after he had laid her down on the bed, unable to just walk away. He sat carefully on the edge of the mattress, his thoughts and passions deep and still as a light fingertip traced over her soft lips. Why, his heart ached once more. Why hadn't she wanted to stay with him? How frustrating and hurtful it was to know she was only here because of his bribe. She hadn't come to be with him, to bask in the love he longed to shower her with. She had made it bitterly clear that this situation was temporary, that as soon as her price was paid she would be gone, this time forever, for he would have no reason to stay her or bring her back.

Would she fight him if he was to come to her on this inviting bed? Would she reject his kisses or demand them with that impatient greed? Tonight was not the time to seek those answers. Perhaps once she grew more comfortable in his world and used to him—he would have to wait. His vanity wasn't used to being uncertain of a woman's reaction to him. It was aggravating but at the same time exciting, challenging. Perhaps that was her attraction. There were no certainties, no predictability. She was fresh and different, and he was trying to mold her into the same tedious cast as all the others. Part of him hoped he would fail.

"Good night, sweet," he said softly.

The next day was much the same with endless drilling. Her walk, her poise, her table manners. They practiced the exchange of greetings, being seated and assisted by a gentleman, having one's coat put on. It seemed the ladies of ton did very little for themselves. She worked on balancing a teacup on her knee, grateful the cup was empty for all her clumsiness. Connor was short-tempered, and they clashed time and again over his exacting demands with George interceding before any more of his belongings were damaged. The sharp, acidic words slashed at her confidence until her nerves were rubbed raw.

After the cup and spoon had taken a tumble for a countless time, Connor threw up his hands in exasperation. "Gad, woman, can't you do the simplest things? Must we go over and over this? Are you deliberately refusing to learn?"

The saucer followed its counterparts to the floor as Tempest surged to her feet. "Sir, I am not a circus pony for you to crack your whip at."

"A good thing, for you would find yourself with a good many stripes. Sit down and do it right."

"I will not. I have had enough browbeating for one day. I am going to my room." As she begun to turn, his terse command stilled her.

"I have not said we are finished."

Slowly brilliant blue met cool gray, and the sparks were instantaneous.

"You are mistaken, sir. We are finished." Her reply was so curt it brought a flush to his face. With every grain of her newfound poise, she revolved on her heel and walked away from him.

Infuriated beyond reason, Connor shouted after her. "If you leave this room, you may as well put those rags back on and go back to your sewers. I've done with you."

Tempest never hesitated, and with her head held high she climbed the stairs.

With a roar of frustration, Connor shattered the delicate cup with a swift kick of his polished boot and then ground his heel on the saucer.

"If you are quite finished destroying my tableware, I would like a word with you."

Connor looked up in surprise at the coolly uttered words, then hung his head, ashamed of his childish rage. "I am sorry, George. I'll replace it, of course."

"Get control of yourself before you break something you cannot mend or replace."

He gave a pouty frown, then sighed. "It's useless, George. This will never work."

"You are wrong, Conn. Did you see how she left the room? With the dignity of a lady. She's doing fine. You are expecting too much. Go home. Let me calm her. Go home," he stated again more firmly to quell any protest.

"I'm going," Tempest growled as she heard the soft tap on her door, but when she whirled around ready to do battle, it was not the expected foe. "Oh, forgive me for snapping at you, George. Tell his royal lordship that I will be packed and out of his life in a moment."

George smiled and said soothingly, "You need go nowhere. Remember this is my house. He cannot toss out my guests, and I sent him packing."

"Did you?" She returned his smile and collapsed on the bed with a shake of her curls. "Is he always such a—a—"

"An obnoxious, overbearing child?" George supplied mildly. "When he thinks he can get by with it. He's really the best of sorts when you let him know you'll not be gudgeoned."

"What does that signify? He's done with me anyway. He sees me as a three-legged cart horse."

George chuckled at her chagrin, wondering what she would say if she really knew how he saw her. He sat beside her on the bed, still smiling. "That's because you don't know him. If you didn't matter, he wouldn't waste his temper on you."

Tempest sighed, only partially convinced. She directed a sidelong glance at her companion and took a chance. "Have you been friends long?"

"Forever, it seems. We fell in at school because no one else would have us. I was without money and a bit of an odd-looking duck with this blazing head of mine, and Conn was so pushy and brash no one could stomach him. We sort of took each other in out of necessity."

"Forgive me for saying so, but you seem to make an odd pair of friends."

"Because he has such an abundance of everything, looks and money, and I don't?" It was the closest he would ever come to sounding peevish.

Tempest flushed and was quick to say, "That's not what I meant at all. It just seems so one-sided. You've such a warm, giving nature and are so—nice. Connor isn't at all nice to people. He loves only himself and his money. You seem to have a poor bargain as a friend."

"Don't ever say that, especially not to Conn. It isn't at all true. Conn can be high-minded and heavy-handed and so arrogant you want to choke him, but that's not all there is to him. He doesn't care for people because all they want of him is his pretty face, prestigious name, and fat bankroll. Of course he's a snob, but how many would take in someone like me or you who have nothing to offer him? Don't criticize Conn to me. I know his multitude of faults, and yet I can think of no one I'd rather have stand beside me in a tight spot or at a gaming table. He is my best friend, and if you hurt him, I will not think kindly of it."

There, it was said, the unspoken warning she had seen in his eyes since they had met. Tempest's brows shot up in an arch of disbelief. "What on earth could I do to hurt a man like Connor Amberson?"

George gave a cryptic smile. Didn't she know she already had? "Don't fail him. Amberly is the one thing he's always wanted, the one thing out of his reach. It's not just a house to him, Tempest, it's everything. It changes him. You'll understand when you get there; you'll see the change and know why he needs it so."

"Is that why he's so angry with me?"

"Not at all, at himself for treating it so lightly. Now he's afraid it might be too late."

"I'm trying, George."

"I know."

"I will learn. I will do this and not just for him but for myself. I may never be a grand lady, but I'll never be so terribly ignorant again. Now, help me master that cursed cup."

What George Morley's house lacked in size was compensated for by the walled private garden in the rear. It was a secluded jungle in the heart of London with trickling fountains and exotic greenery. Tempest was nearly swallowed up in that lush tropical darkness of evening. Connor gave a soft chuckle as he watched her balance the porcelain cup with a fierce concentration. She started at the unexpected sound, and the fragile piece splintered on the brick walk.

"Don't worry," Connor assured her. "I most likely will be held accountable for replacing the whole set."

Tempest frowned in annoyance, both at his comment and at the sudden palpitations of her heart as he stood in the doorframe, a tall elegant figure silhouetted against the lamplight.

"If you've come to be mean, sir, I'd advise you to put up your guard," she warned him smartly.

"Oh no, quite the contrary. I'm here with the noblest of intentions."

"Harrumph," she snorted and turned away, watching him covertly from the corner of her eye. Her anger with him had long since faded, eased by her talk with George and by her own inability to carry grudges, but she didn't want him to know that. Her pride demanded a pretty apology, and from the look of him, she would have it. He came toward her with his confident stride, his smile and light eyes warm and hopeful.

"May I join you?" His voice was a silken caress.

In answer, Tempest slid over on the stone bench. Though it was of good length, he sat very close, close enough to hear her breath catch, then grow light and quick.

"I brought you a gift," he announced softly, leaning nearer still until her senses were swimming with the intoxicating male scent of him.

"By way of an apology?"

He grinned at her tartness, then his sleepy eyes held hers for a lengthy search. She shifted uncomfortably, sure he could read her deepest thoughts with so intense a gaze.

"I was rude to you, and no fancy bribe will ease my conscience, but I want you to have this token of my appreciation for all your hard work and tolerance of

130

my knavishness."

She took the flat box apprehensively, still held by his plunging stare. To break that mesmerizing claim, she smiled ruefully. "If this is a book on etiquette, I am going to force you to eat it."

Connor laughed, looking well pleased with himself as her fingers tore open the wrapping, then lifted the hinged lid. For a moment, she sat perfectly still; then the box snapped shut.

"No, I cannot accept this." Her voice wavered frailly as she pushed the gift back at him. "Please, my lord. It is too much."

Unperturbed, he opened the box and lifted out the sparkling collar of silver and sapphires. She gasped as he laid them about her neck, sitting stiffly while the clasp was fastened. His hands lingered warm and familiar on the gentle slope of her shoulders.

"Connor—"

"They look beautiful," he interrupted, then added huskily, "You look beautiful, and I'm going to kiss you whether you mind or not."

Tempest didn't mind. In fact, she wanted him to desperately. His kiss was met with eagerly parted lips followed more slowly by the circle of her arms about his neck. Encouraged, his embrace tightened, bringing her up to his chest to pin her there while the intent of his mouth grew more demanding and possessive.

Tempest was drowning, unable to draw a breath to clear the fog of confused desire from her spinning head. She would never be unaffected by his kiss no matter what she might pretend, but his bold, assured touch at the fastenings of her gown was enough of a surprise to shock her from her heady dreams. With a sound of protest, she forced her hands between the crush of their bodies and pushed mightily.

When he refused to relent, Tempest said in a constricted tone, "Please, my lord, you hurt me."

She was instantly freed. Scuttling back, she panted in an effort to recover herself. The jeweled necklace was chilling against her heated skin. When he reached out to her, she knocked his hand aside with a mutter of denial.

"Why do you stop me, sweet?" His voice was a rumbling caress, low and persuasive. "Don't say no to me when I can see yes in your lovely eyes and taste it in your kiss."

Her sudden amused laugh brought him up short with a pouty frown.

"What is this, my lord? Afraid your expensive gift would not be enough to assure my cooperation?"

Connor blinked in confusion.

"You do not need to woo me sweetly with your convincing charms," she continued, taking advantage of his bewilderment to stand and put a safe distance between them. She had to play it carefully lest he see how unnerved she was by his touch. "You have my word and my signed pledge that I will see your charade through."

His petulant mouth tightened with frustration. "Tempest, one has naught to do with the other. I wanted you long before this idea came to mind."

"Oh la, sir," she challenged brightly. "The thought of profit only adds heat to the fire." She had to get him angry or amused, anything to sway him from the passionate bent she had so little defense against.

"You tease me like a green girl. Your payment is more than adequate for what I am doing. I ask for no more."

He hesitated. Was she serious? Then his heavily lidded eyes lowered so the blue was a pale glitter in the moonlight. "Ah, my sweet, but think of the advantages of working with me day and night."

Inside, she trembled at his throaty promise, but her smile was wicked and her tone full of taunting. "So you would quiz me in your bed. And would you be so uncharitable in your lessons there? Is it your plan to teach me how a lady conducts herself between the sheets? Do you think I will be put to the test there as well? Perhaps so. Perhaps I will take advantage of the situation and trap myself a titled husband or lover, but you, sir, flatter yourself if you think I need your schooling. I can seduce a man without your instruction, but I suppose you wish to be convinced of that."

Pretending a casual experience she didn't have, she bent down, fingers gliding into his midnight hair. She heard him draw a quick raspy breath. She kissed him hard and full and with an abandon drawn from a vivid imagination, but she gave him no chance to respond before stepping away.

"Good night, Lord Amberson."

Connor sat in the garden for a long while, his senses so out of balance he was afraid to move. He knew if he stood, he could not control his need to rush after her, and that would be great folly. He did not love this intriguing girl. No, it was not love that made his desires gallop and his emotions fall into a panic at her nearness. He didn't love, he wouldn't love her, but he would have her. He had tasted surrender in her lips, just waiting for the right time to submit. He would look only to that goal. It would have shocked him to discover she had already trapped her titled paramour.

Chapter Ten

Conversation ceased when Tempest appeared in the doorway, and both men rose reflexively to their feet. She hesitated in wonderment that she would cause such a stir, then advanced into the room. The looks she drew told her she had chosen well after long deliberation in front of the closet and mirror. Her crepe gown had a subtle stripe of rose and olive with a straw-colored spencer over it. Every detail of her appearance was perfect, down to the decorative clocks on her stockings and the dainty ribbons of her silk slippers that tied across her instep. She had discovered both these methods in her extensive memorization of the fashion tabloids.

"Good morning, George, my lord. May I join you for a bite of breakfast if my presence is no intrusion?"

She paused behind a vacant chair, her brow arched in a question. George was quicker to return to his senses and drew out her chair.

"Please do. Our morning meal has never been so graced."

Tempest tapped his hand while fluttering her

lashes, coquettishly. "Pray do not tease me, sir. I do not believe I am the first to have sat across from either of you at the breakfast table."

"Quite true, but you are the fairest to my recall," George amended nicely. She did look remarkable, he thought to himself, after most likely staying up the better part of the night. He had seen the light beneath her door when he had retired in the early hours of the morning, and it had still burned when he awoke.

She continued the light, playful banter throughout the meal, nibbling delicately from her buttered muffin, then daubing her greasy fingers with her napkin. She was enjoying the look of astonishment on the arrogant lord's face, for he could find no fault with her appearance, dialogue, or manner.

Finishing her last sip of tea, she met that puzzled stare directly. "Well, my lord, what ordeals have you planned for me today? I feel quite capable of passing any test thrown at me. Shall I show my gait like a pampered filly or balance my table service upon my knee, nose, or head like a well-trained circus seal? I am at your disposal, sir."

Connor remained unprovoked by her sugary gibes, but George chortled into his napkin in appreciation.

"This morning we shall train only your mind. You need to know everything about the Ambersons."

"Sounds like fascinating fare. I'm sure you rarely tire of talking about yourself."

Her dry comment earned a cool glance but no more. Apparently, Lord Amberson was firmly in check this morning.

George cleared his throat with an amused smirk.

"If you will both excuse me, I have things to attend to this morning." He gave Tempest a conspiratorial wink and grinned to offset his friend's suspicious glower.

Connor led her out into the sunny garden. In the wash of daylight it lost its exotic romance and was merely a thicket of oversized, overpowering greenery that crowded the paths. In the heat of the morning, the huge blooms were in full flower, and their fragrance hung heavily on the air like perfume applied too enthusiastically.

"I've often told George all he needs is several gaudy squawking birds and a monkey or two to make this jungle authentic," Connor observed as he sat her on the bench they had shared the previous night.

"You treat your friend poorly. You are lucky to have one at all," she snapped, rankled by his unkind criticism of her genial host.

Connor looked slightly surprised, then said in all seriousness, "I have George, and he is all the friend I need. I would never do anything to cause him any hurt. I would give him anything I own or even my life if he asked for it. I am very loyal to those I care for and would do anything for them. I would care for you that way if you would let me."

His sudden quiet declaration caught her off guard. Before she could gather her startled thoughts, he was sitting very close, her hands captured in his in an earnest pressure.

"Tempest, I would be so very good to you," he vowed huskily.

She struggled to suppress the weakness in her that would believe him and smiled, simply saying, "No, you wouldn't, my lord."

"Now you are treating me poorly," he bemoaned, but he was smiling, and the danger of the moment was past. "How is your shoulder, sweet? You seem not to favor it quite so much."

"It causes me some discomfort, but I can move much easier now." She saw no reason to tell her it pained her so greatly at times she wanted to scream.

"I should like to see how it is healing if you've no objection. Your health is my responsibility in this case. I promise I will take no unfair advantage." He grinned. "Unless you want me to."

"Just see to the wound, my lord. The rest is not ailing."

"So you say," he mused. His touch was very gentle as he pushed aside the sleeveless coat and tiny cap sleeve of her gown to peer beneath the fresh wrapping. Satisfied with its progress, he let his fingers rub the smooth flesh of her shoulder. That satiny texture cartwheeled his thoughts to ignite a simmer of passion.

Tempest gasped as warm lips brushed along the line of her shoulder to mix with the wet tracings of his tongue. The shivery sensation stirred a deeper need that surged up bold and insistent. The hand that tangled in his ebony hair to pull him away merely turned his head so she could seek his mouth. Their kiss was heated with a hurried desperation until both were breathless and impatient for more.

Holding the titian head between unsteady hands, Connor tore himself away. The sight of her closed eyes and willing lips made speech extremely difficult, his words a hoarse whisper.

"Don't deny me, sweet. I want to make love to you.

138

Now."

The bright eyes flew open with a reluctant protest. "Here? In George's house?" That idea seemed somehow unsavory and impolite.

Connor kissed her deeply then, to reassure her embarrassed sensibilities, and murmured, "It will not be the first time, sweet. George will not be unduly shocked."

Tempest had not believed anything could put a halt to the crazy hammering of her heart and the rage of her desire, but his confession was a bath in ice water. The flashing blue fire in her eyes was chilled.

"There will be no first time here for us, my lord," she stated frostily. "I suggest you bring us some cool refreshment before we begin our work. You seem quite overheated."

Connor had two choices: he could force the issue or he could retreat. After a search of her frozen features, he gave a wan smile. "With good reason, I had thought. My mistake."

"Yes," was her clipped reply.

When he returned with two glasses of chilled wine, he took a neutral position on the adjacent bench. His manner cool and aloof, he started right in with the history of the Amberson family.

Jonathan Amberson was the family patriarch and autocratic ruler, Connor told her. As an only child, he had inherited the huge estates that had been a feudal grant to some past relative. A good marriage had increased his financial larder twofold. At two-year intervals, he was presented with three sons, Jeffrey, Samuel, and Thomas. The youngest, frugal Thomas, married Katherine Fulbright, a penniless girl of good parentage who gave rather quick birth to a son, Tyler. Practical and dogmatic Samuel was captivated by a pretty young widow and rushed her to the altar, dutifully giving his name to Jillian Garrett's five-year-old son, Connor. Jeffrey, the eldest and most like his father, took a long time to find a wife, being too wedded to the land to be distracted, but when Sarah Middlebury tossed her auburn head and sassy smile his way, his future had a new priority, Sarah, and within a year, a daughter, Holly.

Thomas broke away from Amberly, making his own home in the next county, a small unassuming estate that didn't require much of his guarded wealth for maintenance. The other sons lived in the rambling family home. Father and sons saw to the land and its tenants religiously.

"I rarely saw my father. He was always closeted away with the books or out on some far corner of the grounds. I was shipped off to school so Amberly was like a vacation spot rather than a home. Oh, I don't blame Father. He was always good to me. He saw I went to the best schools and tried to make extra time when I was home for holidays."

Connor paused for a moment, drawing a long sighing breath. His eyes were miles and years away. Resolutely, he shook himself out of his daze of recollections.

"Holly was much younger than I, about eight years, I think. She was a naughty little thing, always tagging behind me like a pup nipping at the ankles. She was Grandfather's favorite. I was too wild, and Tyler too sly. He thought the sun rose and set on her. He was like a man possessed after the accident. Uncle

Jeffrey, Aunt Sarah, and Holly were returning home from spending Christmas day with Aunt Sarah's relations. Their carriage was set upon by highwaymen. Uncle Jeffrey was shot and killed. The horses bolted, and the carriage overturned in the river. Aunt Sarah was pinned inside and drowned. Holly's body was never recovered. Grandfather had them search for weeks. All they found were her shoes and coat. He posted a fabulous reward and hired scores of men but never turned up a trace. Holly was to be his heir. He had made no secret of it. She was the child of his eldest son. He never accepted her death. He made me his successor with extreme reluctance."

"What of your parents and your other uncle?"

"Uncle Thomas died some years before that, shot by one of his tenants who'd had too much to drink. Aunt Kate and Grandfather disliked each other intensely so she wasted a huge sum setting herself up in London. My parents are dead." He said it quickly and emotionally, then hurried on. "Grandfather raised me at Amberly or rather at school. He's a tyrant, that man, and it always irritated him when he couldn't manipulate me the way he had his sons. Oh, the rows we used to have. Finally, I moved to London, and he stays at his fortress gnashing his teeth over all my exploits. For years he's been threatening to cut me out in order to bring me to heel. I always thought the old man was bluffing until he had Aunt Kate and Tyler come to Amberly. He must be playing a serious game to bring a woman he despises under his roof. The old man is getting on, and if he should die, the way things stand between us at present, I would have a difficult time getting control, not being a blood

141

relation, even though I have legal title. I can't see him deeding it to Tyler. I just can't. He wants to make me squirm, but the joke will be on him when I produce the long-lost Holly."

Tempest regarded him uneasily. His handsome face was sharpened into hard belligerent lines of pettish revenge like a mean, spoiled child. She didn't like the man she saw and said as much.

"It seems a cruel joke to play on an old man's grief."

Connor looked at her as though that was a novel thought, then frowned. "I suppose it is, but the old martinet left me no other choice. He's the one who made the stakes of this stupid game so high. He knows I can live well off my real father's wealth without a penny from him. Damme, I don't want his money. I want my home. He cannot keep that from me. I don't care what I have to do."

"Including breaking your grandfather's heart?"

Her soft question brought up his eyes to meet hers. They cut through her with a harsh fury. "Don't preach to me, you little thief. Your hands are far too dirty to judge anything I put mine to. You are nothing, so do not try to impress me with your self-righteous sentiments."

Far too angry to notice the effect of his searing words, Connor stalked into the house. He paced the hall in ill-tempered outrage for several minutes, then looked back toward the garden and the slight figure sitting so still in a soft halo of morning sun. His upset turning in on himself, he went back outside to sink down on the bench beside the motionless woman. After observing her lovely profile for a long second,

142

he launched into a hasty apology.

"Forgive me, Tempest. I misspoke myself. This trickery is not to my liking, but I am quite desperate. I have no call to turn on you so roguishly."

"No, my lord," she interrupted quietly. "You owe me no apology. You were correct. I am of no importance in this. You are paying me to do your bidding, not to find fault with your method. As a lowly pawn, I have no right to an opinion of the bold knight's moves. I was taught that thievery and lying were equal sins. I am too ignorant to understand that deception is a common practice among my betters. Forgive me for acting as an equal. I may pretend, but that will not change what we both know me to be."

Her head was bowed, her eyes meekly downcast, so Connor had no notion of the anger that flamed in them. To him, she appeared humble and subservient, and that groveling manner made him feel the lowest of curs. No apology could relieve his guilt at bruising her fine spirit with his thoughtless words.

Very gently, he cupped her delicate chin in his palm and turned her face up toward him, but she would not raise her eyes. Pensively, his hand stroked along the fine line of her jaw.

"Ah, sweet, I wish I was your equal. Then perhaps I would not be trapped in such an unpleasant situation."

The quiet voice brought up the large blue eyes, now empty of all ill-feeling. She stared long into his unhappy gaze. George was right. How much more there was to Connor Amberson than the brash surface betrayed.

"We have much to do, my lord. Shall we continue?"

They spent the rest of the morning on Holly Amberson. Connor related what he could remember of the tiny sprite and then quizzed Tempest to see what she had retained. The quickness of her mind reassured him that all would go as planned.

"But where has Holly been all this time and why hasn't she—haven't I contacted the family?"

"That bit of the story I'm working on tonight," he answered evasively. "If all goes well, we go to Amberly the first of the week."

"Four days?" she cried in dismay.

Connor smiled to soothe her alarm. "We need not stay there long; then we can return here. I will be with you if you need any prompting. It will go just fine."

She was not convinced, her hands wringing in her lap. "I am not going to fool anyone. They are all going to know exactly what I am."

"What you are is a beautiful woman who is well spoken, graciously mannered, and intimately acquainted with the Ambersons, with one of them anyway." He grinned hugely at her vivid blush. "No one will see anything else. You are Holly Amberson, my cousin, and soon-to-be heiress. The old man is the only one you have to convince. Sway him, and the others won't matter. He has to name you in his will, otherwise Amberly will be lost." He looked so fierce, so intense, his exquisite features saturnine even in the pure bright of the morning.

"I will do all I can," she promised quietly.

The dark shadowy mood lifted instantly as he smiled at her. Her tiny hands were caught up in his and peppered with quick kisses.

"Thank you, sweet."

The evening crept by. Her hands slathed with a softening cream inside gloves, Tempest played an awkward hand of whist with George and practiced conversation, discussing the prominent figures and affairs she should be familiar with. When she asked him the time as she had so frequently all evening, George smiled.

"He won't be back tonight, Tempest."

She looked as though she might protest that Lord Amberson wasn't the subject tormenting her concentration, then decided against it. She had no reason to deceive George. He was perhaps her only friend in this new frightening world.

Laying down her cards, she looked directly into the calm hazel eyes. "What are your feelings about all of this, George?"

He took a moment to answer; then he did so carefully. "I would support Connor in any venture whether I agreed with him or not. I owe him that much. I tried to discourage him from this pretense. He could well lose everything. The stubborn lout won't recant; so I have to go along with him and hope for the best."

"Is his grandfather the ogre he paints him to be?"

Seeing her nervousness, George squeezed her gloved hand. "Not at all. I fancy you'll like the old tyrant. He comes on a bit gruff, but he has a kind heart. He's always treated me famously."

145

"Then why do he and Connor hate each other so?"

"Hate each other?" George shook his bright head. "Oh, no, quite the opposite. They couldn't love each other more if they were true kin."

"I guess I don't understand."

"You would not be the first. I don't think they do either. They love one another but just cannot be in the same room. The marquis is quite fond of his power. He's used to having his own way, and as long as you let him believe he is having it, there are no problems; he's a sweet old man. But Conn, you may have noticed, is a bit of a headstrong brat. He hasn't a speck of diplomacy in him. The two of them would argue over the day of the week, just to be contrary, and neither would care who's right. They want the same thing, but they cannot get together on it. Conn's always wanted to be at Amberly, but he just won't compromise. He moved here to spite himself just to make the old man miserable. It's a game they play, but I cannot see that either of them ever win at it."

"If Connor loves him, how can he play such a terrible trick on him? Is he a bad person, George?"

"No, Tempest. Not really. He doesn't mean to be. He has a good generous heart, but if he looked twice at one of my sisters I'd warn him off with a pistol. He doesn't trust and can't be trusted. I don't know why, but I suspect it has something to do with his parents' death."

"What happened to them?" she asked softly, remembering the way the pale eyes had dropped off when he mentioned them. She wanted to understand the man who moved her heart so strangely with

146

tenderness one moment, only to provoke her ire the next with his hateful conceit.

"I don't know. It was before I met him. Very close to the time Holly and her family were lost. It must have been one hell of a shock to him. He's never spoken of it, not once, though he's always been full of questions about mine. Be careful, Tempest. Don't let yourself become vulnerable to him. He'll take advantage of it, and you'll be hurt. He won't plan to, but he will. Don't fall in love with him."

Connor leaned back from the very thorough kiss and murmured softly, "Well, what is it to be, yes or no?"

"Connie, I must think on it. You ask a great deal."

"But aren't I worth it? Don't you want to help me? I would be so very grateful."

The husky words made Lady Martel tremble. She really couldn't concentrate when she was aching for him to touch her.

It had been on Loretta's mind to brusquely chastise her errant lover when he arrived at her home, but those thoughts fled at the touch of his urgent kiss. The great house was silent, the earl away and the servants dismissed for the night. Now Loretta lay back on the cushions, mussed and dazed with passion as Connor asked his favor. She wanted more than his kisses, but so far those were all he would grant her.

Regarding her flushed face dispassionately, he urged, "An answer if you please. If I mean anything to you at all, do this for me."

The languid green eyes rose to his, stirred by the

intensity she saw there. He must have been quite desperate to let his countenance so slip. To have Connor Amberson in her debt would have its value.

"You know how much you mean to me, Connie," she vowed.

"Then help me. Please."

Loretta lay back. Her mind was working now, quickly and slyly. She would never have a chance like this again. "You know I would do anything for you, but you realize the position you put me in. You must make it worth my while."

The scheming tart, he thought angrily, but he smiled and kissed her jeweled hand. So sure was Connor of his power over his fawning mistress, he overlooked the control he was placing in her greedy hands, hands every bit as vicious as his own, capable of closing about his neck to choke the life from all his carefully drawn plans. If he had looked beyond the simpering facade to the cold, hard glitter of self-interest in those cat's eyes, he would have seen the danger. But it was too late. She was the only choice of accomplice he had. George was too well known as his friend and loyal compatriot. It had to be someone beyond suspicion, someone supposedly uninvolved. His habit of alienation left few to pick from. He could handle Loretta's tantrums, he assured himself with confidence.

"What do you want of me, love?"

"Just you. I want you, Connie. When all is done, I want you to be my lover until the earl favors me and dies. Then I want to become Lady Amberson, your wife."

Connor smiled, then said silkily, "You have my

promise." When Amberly was his, it would be no great feat to convince Loretta that she didn't really want him; so he wouldn't really be breaking a promise. Bestowing a final, tantalizing kiss upon Loretta's waiting lips, Connor made his exit, that confident smile lingering on his face.

Chapter Eleven

It was early afternoon before Connor appeared at the Morley house, grinning complacently as he placed a box in Tempest's lap.

"By way of apology?" she remarked wryly. She couldn't help but smile in return at his expectant exuberance. "If I continue to provoke your temper, I will need a clothier to tend my gifts."

Connor refused to acknowledge her gibe as he waited anxiously for her to open the box. Her gasp of delighted surprise filled him with a rewarding warmth.

"Oh, Connor, it's beautiful," she cried, lifting the pelerine from the tissue. She buried her face in the fur collar, sighing rapturously.

"Stand up," he hurried her. "Let's see it on you."

He draped her shoulder cape about her, admiring the way the rich sable accented her coloring. Impulsively, his fingers curled in the lapels, drawing her up to him for a hastily stolen kiss. He set her back before she had time to protest.

"Thank you, my lord," she said a bit breathlessly.

He gave a reckless laugh. "For the cape or the kiss? Or both?"

"You are incorrigible, sir," she pronounced, but her taunt couldn't overshadow the way her eyes glimmered so brightly as she nuzzled the luxurious fur. She noticed George's slight frown as he watched their playful exchange.

"George, a brandy and a toast," Connor called cheerfully. "All is taken care of. Amberly is going to be mine."

"Loretta agreed? I thought she was quite put out with you."

"You underestimate my power of persuasion," he boasted. "I charmed her out of her annoyance. She agreed with some conditions. I'm not concerned with them now."

Tempest took off the beautiful cape and folded it carefully. Loretta? He was with a woman all night. She put away the extravagant gift, wondering now what motive had prompted its giver. She looked covertly at the tall, exquisitely made man, wondering why the thought of him with another woman twisted in her belly like cold bitter steel. She could still feel the warmth of his mouth on hers, and he was crowing about his prowess with another. She dropped the box on the seat beside her. So much for Connor Amberson.

The next few days were frenzied with preparation. Connor was always present, filling her with endless details until she felt her head would burst. He called her Holly, insisting that she respond to it naturally, but that was the only response he got from her. His advances were cut cold with a chilly stare or biting remark, demanding they concentrate on their business. Perplexed, he kept a reluctant distance, chafing at the cool treatment and hating going to his solitary room each night. He ached for a glimpse of her teasing smile or twinkling eyes.

Tempest endured the final touches with stoic acceptance. Her hair was reshaped, her nails manicured, her measurements taken, and her body became a mannequin for an endless parade of clothing. She was quizzed and critiqued from morning until night and even then had no rest, for she was haunted by the pale blue eyes with their icy fire always upon her with that unasked heated question she had to deny.

Tomorrow would be her test. Tempest paced her room in agitation, her mind cluttered with facts and snippets of information. How could she ever remember it all? By morning she would be a knotted mass of doubts after fretting away the night with constant repetition.

"My lady?" A voice interrupted her thoughts.

Tempest looked up in surprise to see Rogers in the hall. "Yes?"

"His lordship sent me to bring you round."

"Did he?" How calm she sounded when all her emotions were in a panic. "Did he say what for?"

"He did not confide in me, madam," was the prim reply.

"Of course not," she returned with a smile.

The house on Grosvenor Square was overwhelming, huge, and elaborately decorated, making George's seem quaintly shabby in comparison. Having only been in one room before, Tempest was at a loss in the maze of rooms. Rogers cordially took her pelerine and steered her into an intimate salon.

The room was aglow with the soft gleam of candlelight that created an inviting halo about a small table set for two. Tempest couldn't help but smile at the trouble he had taken in order to impress her with his thoughtfulness. He could be quite sweet when it suited him.

"Good evening."

The low voice startled her but not as much as the sight of him in the muted candlelight. Quite simply, he stole her breath away. The luminescent light cast his face in dramatic shadow contouring the well-defined cheekbones and sparking a brilliance in the languorous blue eyes beneath the heavy sweep of black lashes and brows. He was dressed as always with unaffected sophistication, the dark clothes lending him a Byronesque air of forbidden romance, deep, dangerous, and exciting.

"Good evening, my lord. You sent for me?" Her voice sounded oddly stilted, as she struggled not to betray that if he wanted her on this night, he would have her.

"I thought you would be pacing at George's probably as nervously as I am here and decided it would do us both a bit of good to forget what tomorrow brings over a glass of wine."

"I would like that."

Her easy compliance gave Connor an unexpected chill of anticipation. He had wanted only her company, but he would happily conquer all the ground she would allow him.

"I have some affairs to finish up if you could kindly excuse me for a few moments."

Tempest's smile became a rigid grimace at the sound of a lilting female voice.

"Connie? Where did you disappear to? I am most anxious to finish our conversation."

Lady Martel paused in the doorway. It took her a moment to recognize the urchin in the shimmering silks, but that discovery alarmed her. This was whom she was helping Connor to be with? What kind of a fool did he think her?

Tempest was just as dismayed. She also recalled Loretta from the darkened road, but in this flattering light, she was stunning. Though nearly twice her age, the woman's face and figure were perfection, golden ringlets capping an ivory complexion and the most brilliant green eyes she had ever seen. Her beauty alone would have been enough to disconcert the inexperienced girl, but the woman's poise had her shattered. This was a real lady, and the difference between reality and Tempest's pretense yawned wide and glaringly apparent to her. Then there was the way

154

the woman put her hand on Connor's dark sleeve, so intimate and possessing.

If Connor could have made a hasty retreat without being labeled a coward, he would have rushed to do so. He had hoped to keep the two from meeting, but here they were, both as rigid and wary as scenting cats. As smoothly as possible he introduced them.

"Of course," Loretta purred. "Our first meeting was brief but quite memorable."

"For me as well," Tempest parried. "Is this one of your unfinished affairs, my lord?" She took note of the wedding band with its gaudy flash of precious stones and added pertly, "A poor choice of terms, I see." Then it made sense to her. What a dolt she was. The candlelit meal was not for her but for his regal paramour. Feeling humiliated and acutely ridiculous, she murmured quickly, "I can see I am interrupting your plans. Thank you for your offer, my lord, but I am quite fine and ready for tomorrow. You need not trouble yourself on my behalf. I can see myself out."

Before he could protest, she was gone, not even pausing to retrieve her cape or to wait for the carriage.

Bounding up George's front steps, Lord Amberson looked far from the usual dignified caller.

"Where's Tempest?" he shouted to a startled George, then raced up the stairs at his friend's gesture. The door to her room stood open, and the room was empty. The only trace was the silken sheath she had been wearing left on the floor like a discarded cocoon.

"She's gone," he mumbled in shock. He turned to George, his expression blank with disbelief and panic. "My God, what am I going to do?" He wasn't thinking about Amberly or all his well-laid plans but of the unbearable emptiness without her.

Hurt and upset, Tempest had only one thought—to return home. She needed to get in touch with who she was, not the fantasy she was living. She had begun to think she was the part she played and that Connor Amberson might come to love her one day. That nonsense had to be quickly forgotten. She needed the refreshing starkness of her own surroundings to clear the fanciful cobwebs of dreams from her head.

Nothing had changed. All the tension of the past week was gone the moment she stepped into her mother's kitchen. She was in her own element and comfortable with who she was, no pretense, no pressure, just a quick welcome acceptance.

After being joyously greeted by her parents, she was pulled into a crushing embrace.

"Oh, Este, what a sight you are. I was sure you'd forgotten us."

She cuffed the rumpled dark head fondly with an exclamation of, "How could you say such a thing to me, you terrible boy?" She kissed his smudged cheek until he was quite crimson. "Have you been keeping out of trouble?" she asked in a low aside.

"I wouldn't try anything without you. You have the brains between us," Eddie laughed. Then he was all big eyes and seriousness. "Are you here to stay?"

She shook her head sadly, bringing a look of dejection to the elfin face. "No, just for the night."

"You're still going with him then?"

His petulant expression softened her heart. "In the morning. I don't know when I'll be back."

Eddie frowned and shuffled his feet. "Has he treated you well?"

"Very well."

He looked even more uncomfortable before stammering, "He hasn't tried—of course he's tried. Have you let him succeed?"

"No." Not this time, she added to herself. "I should like to see the children before they go to sleep. I'll be down shortly."

She had just finished tucking in her youngest brother and sister when a sudden premonition made her turn. He stood in the doorway regarding her with veiled eyes. She wasn't surprised. Shushing him with a finger to her lips, she placed a quick kiss on each dark head and joined him in the hall.

After she closed the door, Connor asked, "How many are there of you?"

"Four. Jesse's six and Jack is eight."

"And the other one?"

"Eddie's fourteen."

"A lot to feed," he mused.

Tempest's reply was sharp and cynical. "I'm sure you are not here to discuss my family's living conditions. Did you fear I had left you?"

"It had crossed my thoughts," he said simply without expression.

"Don't concern yourself, my lord. I had no plans to desert you. Have you come to fetch me back? I was not aware that I was your prisoner."

"You're not," he said tightly. "You left so abruptly, is all, and I had no chance to explain."

"Explain what?"

He winced at the cold remark but plunged on determinedly. "About Lady Martel."

The sapphire eyes blazed with suppressed fury. How she wanted to strike him, to deal him some hurt to compensate her for the pain he had given her. But what was the point of letting him know how vulnerable she had been. Very coolly, she retorted, "There is nothing about your mistress that needs explanation, and believe me, I am not at all interested in the intimate details of your life. They do not concern me just as my private affairs are not open to you. I am a thief, not a liar. You have my word I will be ready to go with you tomorrow, but tonight I wish to play no games. I want to be myself and among those who prefer me that way."

"I won't interfere," he promised. "I'll wait to see you back home."

Tempest laughed at him. "Home? I *am* home. This is my home. Believe me, my lord, I have much less to fear here than you. I do not need your escort."

"Then perhaps I need yours. Just let me know when you are ready to leave."

She shrugged, then turned to go downstairs, pausing when his hand curled under her elbow. It was a natural gesture for him, one of politeness and gentility, but here in this world it seemed odd and disturbing just as he, himself, was.

"Don't," she insisted softly, pulling away. "You need not pretend I am a lady. Everyone here knows what I am."

He looked after her with a frown of perplexed slight, then followed more slowly.

Will Swift's inn was a tavern with a half-dozen rooms rarely used for more than an hour at a time. The taproom was filled with a motley assortment of the Southside's dregs there to get drunk for a penny or dead drunk for twopence on Madame Geneva, Strip-Me-Naked, or Blue Ruin. Will provided only the space and the gut-twisting liquor, not the prostitutes. He wanted nothing to do with that dangerous underworld operating in Coal Hole or Cyder Cellars in Maiden Lane. He tried to keep his place as honest as he could, cheating no one and discouraging those who would. He looked up from the bar and blinked in surprise to see Lord Amberson in the midst of his unruly patrons. The man stood out like a sleek Thoroughbred among braying donkeys. Catching his eye, he waved him over urgently to give him a warning.

"Good evening, my lord. Forgive me for saying as much, but you don't rightly belong here."

Connor raised an elegant brow as if he was not already well aware of that fact. "Are you saying you won't serve me, Swift?"

"No, of course not, my lord. Only advising that you stick close to the bar and keep you hand on your purse."

"I will take your advice, sir." He looked curiously

159

at the murky liquid in his glass, then bolted it down. His teeth clenched, and his eyes squeezed shut as the noxious stuff tore down his cultured throat. It was awful, bringing tears and most likely eating his stomach with a corrosive strength. "Leave the bottle," he wheezed.

Glass in hand, Connor turned to search the smoky room for Tempest. He frowned to see her flitting between the tables, exchanging pleasantries with the riffraff who squeezed her roughly and slapped her trouser-clad bottom in ribald humor. The crude fondling made his teeth grind and his temper heat. But Tempest seemed not to mind. Apparently, it was only his touch she took exception to. She laughed at the amorous attempts to steal a kiss from her and, when she felt the need, dished out a vigorous cuff to the head to mollify an overzealous entreaty.

Will Swift was no fool to keep his daughter in baggy man's attire, for if this pack of wolves got a scent of the yielding curves beneath them, they would be on her like a tender meal. Dressed as she was, she could move about them, unthreatened and playfully joking. She was teased and occasionally propositioned, but as long as the scantily clad women were available, she was in no danger.

Connor had no way of knowing that. She had been untouched when she came to him. Now that he had taken her innocence, would she find herself turned out among the painted charmers who weaved their way between the tables like underfed alley cats? Every fiber of his being recoiled against that thought as he watched the hands that fell familiarly on her slender waist and hip, imagining in horror how those same pawing hands would cruelly misuse her body.

So deep was he in these glum thoughts that an unexpected hand on his chest startled him and made him leap back.

"Don't worry, me love. I ain't gonna hurt ya. No, sir. What I gots in mind is something else altogether."

Pressed back against the bar with no retreat available, Connor leaned back as the creature rubbed against him, straddling his thigh suggestively. Struggling to keep the look of distaste from showing, he turned his face away from the overpowering smell of her. The combination of cheap drink, rotten teeth, and unwashed body was enough to make his stomach knot in protest. There was no subtlety in the bold avaricious eyes or in the rough groping of her hand. He was too stunned to react for a moment, then pushed her away. She was molded to him again, her insistent hands sliding beneath his coat.

"What say, me love? Time for a quick tumble for a good price?"

"No thank you, madam," he managed with no little effort. "I am flattered by your offer, but I am not in the market."

The dirty face twisted in a sneer. In a strident voice loud enough to draw attention, she railed at him, "Ain't I good enough for you? 'Fraid you'll catch something?"

Her hands were pulled away, and Eddie Swift whispered in her ear. She looked up at Connor with a contemptuous smile and moved quickly away.

Connor looked at Tempest's brother with reluctant

161

gratitude, but the boy merely glowered at him.

"I told her your tastes didn't run toward women. None of 'em will be wasting their time on you."

"Thank you for that bit of ingenuity," he said wryly. "How nice of you to protect my virtue."

"I was saving your neck, idiot," he snapped. "These birds may be trash to you, fancy face, but they're angels to these coves. If you insult them, you're risking more than a dose of the pox."

Angrily, Eddie shoved the weighty purse he had retrieved from the whore's nimble fingers back at his lordship and strode away.

Connor could never remember being truly afraid for his life, but looking about at the hard narrow eyes that assessed him harshly, he was aware of a profuse sweating. He didn't belong in this place among these people. They knew it too. His appearance was like a slap, and he could taste their hatred. Some were thinking of killing him for his money, some just for the enjoyment of it. He had never backed down from a fight, no matter what the odds, but he would find no honorable match here. He cursed himself for being so unprepared. In his haste to follow Tempest, he hadn't taken his pistol. He was fair with his fists but not fool enough to think he could square off against any of this brutish lot. As he tossed down another glass of the potent rot, he noticed several men muttering as they eyed his arrogant stance and expensive apparel. One of them fingered a narrow-bladed knife lovingly.

Not seeing Tempest in the threatening room, Connor began a tactical retreat. He took another drink, then slipped out into the night, jogging quickly down the street and turning into the first alleyway and then the next.

The world he found himself in was a dark, seamy maze, a nightmare he couldn't believe existed. The face of the Southside was ugly enough, but its heart was foul and rotten. He wandered the narrow alleys in wide-eyed shock, his way lost, and stunned by what he saw. It was a world unto itself, an open sewer from which every manner of pestilence bred and thrived. The streets were mired with rubbish and waste. The shadows seethed with corruption, pawnbrokers, vendors, prostitutes and their sly-eyed pimps, pickpockets, and the crippled who lined the gutters with begging tins. The children were the worst, roaming about like starved animals, their eyes hollow and desperate, their skinny bodies covered with sores, and their chests rattling with the sounds of tuberculosis. Skeletal hands clutched hopefully at his coat until he doled out a fistful of coin. The flash of silver and copper brought them out of the darkness like a hungry pack, their palms outstretched and voices whining. In claustrophobic alarm, he cast the contents of his pockets onto the dirty cobbles so he could escape them.

Dazed and panicked, Connor reeled against a cold grimy wall, leaning there while he fought down the bitter gorge that rose in his throat. His mind was afloat in a slogging of warm rum that fuzzed the edges of the too harsh reality. He jumped as something black the size of a well-fed housecat scurried across his boots. The smell, sour and putrid like a slow, lingering death, made his head ache.

There Tempest found him.

"My lord, this is not a very safe place to take a midnight stroll. Come back with me, and I'll see you to your carriage."

The hand Tempest lifted was cold, his fingers curling about hers with the desperation of someone drowning.

"My lord, are you all right?" she asked quietly.

He shook his head and looked up. Even the sky had a dusky, coarse cast. "How can people live like this?" he asked hoarsely. "How can they stand it, to exist like—like vermin?" He gave a hard shudder, the urge to retch rising strong in dizzying waves until his face beaded with sweat.

Tempest smiled wryly at his distress. "Welcome to my world, my lord. Would you take us all in? Would you invite us all to your fine house to live? Would you see us all in silk? I think not. Did you think just because you never saw it when your carriage hurried by with your lacy handkerchief over your nose that it didn't exist, this cesspool of the poor?"

"I had no idea," he choked out, his eyes closing as if he could make it all disappear.

"I'm sure you didn't," she said softly, rubbing the well-tended hand that clutched hers. "This is what I am, Connor, where I come from. How could you ever understand me when my existence turns your stomach inside itself. You'd best return to your clean streets and neat, pretty houses where everyone looks nice and smells good. You can pretend this was all a bad dream. I wouldn't expect you to know how to relate to this. It's much easier to look up than down, and you cannot look any farther down than this hell. Go home, my lord, where you belong. Pretty manners and a title will not serve you on these streets."

"Will you come with me?" he asked, his words still constricted and unsteady.

"No, my lord. These sights don't offend my eyes, just sadden my heart. I mean to enjoy my evening. It's not all as horrible as it must seem to you. There is life here if you know where to look and what to see."

He took a long breath, then looked at her steadily. "Show me."

"My lord," she scoffed, "this is beneath you. Don't dirty your manicured nails or soil your expensive clothes."

Connor's jaw squared, and he regarded her calmly, in control now. "How shallow you must think me. I'm really not. Ignorant, granted, spoiled, definitely, but not fragile. Show me how to live in your world."

Tempest looked up at him warily, but the blue-gray eyes were fired with sincerity. A smile touched her lips, bringing a beauty to her that no grimy clothing could disguise. So he would walk in her shoes for a while.

"All right, my lord. Let's make you a little less presentable."

She stripped him of his fine coat and waistcoat, putting the heavy gold jewelry in her pockets. To loosen his look, she tore off his cravat and rolled up his shirtsleeves. With a critical frown, she looked him over, aping the manner he had used with her. There wasn't much she could do about his proud bearing,

165

but with a gleeful grin, she reached up to muss his sculptured hair. His disgruntled pout made her laugh. "Now you could almost pass for working class."

"Should that please me?" he asked doubtfully. She caught his hand as it rose reflexively to tidy his hair. His glower only increased her enjoyment of the moment, and quite unexpectedly, she stretched up to press a quick kiss on his mouth.

"You still look upper ten. All the dirty and shabby clothes on the Southside couldn't change that. Come along, my lord. Let us hobnob with the poor."

Reentering Swift's tavern was like going into the lion's den twice in one night. This time when Connor took her arm, Tempest had no complaint. She could feel the tension in his grip. How well she knew those feelings of displaced isolation.

To his chagrin, she picked a crowded table surrounded by burly men, seating him elbow to elbow with a hairy mammoth and fitting close against his other side. She introduced him simply as Conn, for that seemed more palatable than his lordship, less priggish than Connie, and without the pretensions of Connor.

Connor offered a wan smile of greeting that was met by a ring of hard flat stares. I'm dead, he thought to himself as he tossed back the drink poured for him. He was too anxious to notice its fiery burn, and that won him a few begrudging nods. The glass was refilled, and between the liquor's soothing fog and Tempest's nearness, he began to slowly unknot. A deck was produced, and he joined in an animated game, playing loosely so he lost more than he won. Soon he saw just men intent on their game, and his smile came easily. Through it all, he was acutely aware of the fingers that rubbed over his and teased at the nape of his neck. The crush of her bosom against his arm was much more intoxicating than the countless drinks. When he glanced up at her, he puzzled over the look that softened the bright eyes to a sultry simmer.

Will Swift smiled to himself behind the bar as pleased as Eddie was enraged by his daughter's relationship with her quixotic nobleman. He could dream of better things for her, couldn't he?

Chapter Twelve

Tempest looked long and silently at the man seated across from her in the carriage as he watched her just as intently from beneath heavy lids. There was a companionable ease between them that was pleasant, yet vaguely disturbing. Sitting there in his shirtsleeves, smelling of cheap drink and smoke, he almost seemed approachable as if this distance could be spanned. Or could it?

Impulsively, Tempest joined him on his cushion, leaning across his chest to kiss him for the second time that night. The taste of the awful liquor didn't detract from the sweetness of his mouth.

"You surprised me, my lord. I expected you to turn green and run for the sanctity of your palace, but you didn't."

"I was sorely tempted, sweet. Believe me." Casually, his arm curved about her, drawing her yielding form into the warm hollow he created against his side. "Does this mean you no longer see me as a pompous, pampered snob?"

168

Smiling, she pillowed her head on his shoulder and replied lightly, "Oh no. You are still all of that. I just think I've found a soul in you. It took a good deal of courage to step off your pedestal into the muck of humanity."

"Please. Now you're roasting me," he chuckled.

"Where are we going, my lord? To George's?"

"Not tonight, sweet. I promised you a bottle of wine, and it has breathed long enough."

She felt a quiver of anticipation as his lips brushed her burnished crown, but her retort was brusque and searingly pointed. "You must be hungry as well since you had no time to have your meal. I apologize for spoiling that intimate scene."

"As well you should. I could hardly dine once my guest had run off without giving me an opportunity to tell her how beautiful she looked."

Tempest was still as her breath caught in numbed surprise. Slowly, her wide eyes lifted. "It was for me?"

Connor frowned. "Of course it was for you. Do you think I invited you to sit and watch me eat?"

"But I thought you and—"

He blinked, than gave a snort of disbelief. "Now, I see. I told you you would want my explanation. I had no idea she would arrive like that. She wasn't expected. And she wasn't welcomed."

"Oh," Tempest murmured meekly, but she was smiling as she snuggled into his shoulder.

"Am I forgiven?" he asked a bit testily.

"No gift this time, my lord?" she teased, her fingers lacing behind his neck in an easy embrace.

"What would you like?"

She gave a soft smile. "I will let you know."

Connor lifted the fine crystal goblet to fill his nose with the exquisite bouquet, then took a swallow, swishing it about like a gargle to rinse away the abhorrent taste that seemed to permeate his senses so disagreeably. How gloriously it slipped down his much abused throat.

He turned to extend a glass to his odd-looking companion. Tempest took the wine with a veiled smile and set it untouched on the table.

"I find I am no longer thirsty but hungry instead."

Her abrupt kiss was charged with an urgent passion, rooting him to the spot. Unconsciously, the glass fell from his fingers as his hands rose to hold her. She was instantly molded to him, stealing his breath with the blatant desire in her greedy lips. Panting between the eager kisses, she insisted gruffly, "Make love to me, Connor. I've been able to think of nothing else all night."

He gave a shaky laugh. "Had I known that, I would have cut our evening much shorter."

She stepped away from him, her face flushed and her eyes sparkling like precious jewels. The husky timbre of her voice made him tremble. "I don't know how to find your room unless it's through the window."

"The stairs are safer. And quicker," he added more deeply. He brought her small hand up for a light kiss, his intense stare never wavering. "Come with me."

His room was dark, but this time she protested the light.

"I don't need it," she told him softly. "I can see every inch of you in my memory."

"Oh, sweet Tempest, I've wanted you so," he cried hoarsely into her kiss.

They rid each other quickly of clothing then, the only thing between the frantic beating of their hearts being warm, willing flesh. When he would build her passion slowly beneath a caressing hand, she pushed it aside, her words hard and demanding.

"No. Later. Take me now, Connor. I need you now."

She welcomed him with a small cry; then the only sounds were their ever-quickening breaths. She burned beneath him like a consuming fire, engulfing him in a pyre of heated passion that seemed endless, that demanded he surrender totally to its searing flames. And he became lost in the swirling vortex of her intensity. After a small broken whisper of his name, her energy ebbed as she savored the gift she wanted from him, then was recharged and, more vital than before, surrounded him, flooding him, rushing him until the pricelessness of what he had given was returned.

Breathless and strangely afraid, Connor listened to the sound of her fractured breathing in the darkness as they lay side by side. It was he who put the distance between them, and he could feel her puzzled stare. A cautious hand reached out to brush her

171

cheek. She turned into his palm, her lips nibbling at his fingers. That tender gesture only tightened his apprehension.

"Tempest, promise me," he began in a shaky whisper.

"What, my lord?"

"Promise me that when I wake I won't find you gone."

She wished she could see him, to look into his eyes. His husky plea made her smile lazily as she touched his face, his breath quick against her skin. "Were you planning to fall right to sleep, my lord?"

Her teasing insinuation failed to lighten his mood. "I am serious, Tempest. Don't leave me."

"Rest your fears, Connor. I've no wish to shimmy down your tree on this night. I'll not leave you. I'm not done with you yet."

To prove her point, she rolled up tight against him, her palm and knee rubbing over his hot flesh while the tip of her tongue painted a wet tracing across his throat. It didn't take much of this treatment to bring his arms up, his fingers clenching in her riot of curls.

"Can I coax you to stay awake for a time?" she crooned into his ear.

"You'll find I'm easy to persuade if you ask the right way."

She did. He was.

George paused in the doorway. He had expected to find Connor restless with agitation, not slumbering peacefully on his side. How he hated to wake him with the news that Tempest had not yet returned.

The blue eyes slitted open, and there was a sleepy murmur of, "Good morning, George."

Before he could begin his unpleasant task, George was halted by the sight of a small hand that glided up over Connor's bare shoulder, then down to curl against his cheek. His eyes closed, Connor made a soft sound of contentment and kissed the motionless fingers.

Flushing over his blundering intrusion, George stammered, "Don't bother to get up. I can wait downstairs until—whenever."

"Be down in a while, George. Don't wait breakfast," was the dismissing mutter.

Connor dozed languidly, feeling lulled and secure and wildly happy, all due to the warm figure fitted snugly to his back. He was prompted by no desire to move until she began to stir; then the desire was there, but the purpose different. He rolled over with the warmest of intentions, only to be stilled by the wary gaze that met him. Inwardly, he groaned. Would he have to start all over again?

"Good morning, sweet," he offered gently.

"My lord," was her quiet response. He could read nothing in her expression to betray her thoughts. She was so beautiful, all freshly waked and tossled.

Cautiously, he leaned forward to touch his mouth to hers with a slow, searching movement. Her lips were yielding, even encouraging until his hand slid up to cup her breast. She was off the bed before he could blink, her sheet wound about her and her posture defensive.

Flustered by his puzzled look and the sight of his body's obvious intentions, she blurted quickly. "We shouldn't keep George waiting. We've a long day ahead of us."

"And a long night after that," he said hopefully. Her reaction was less than inspiring.

"Let's see to the day, my lord."

Without awaiting comment, she wriggled into her ragged clothing behind the sheet and fled the room like a startled virgin.

"Good morning, George," Tempest called awkwardly, a bright color flooding her face when he turned. What would he think, discovering she and Connor were lovers, or had he already known? She felt the urge to apologize and beg him not to think less of her.

George's greeting was uncharacteristically cool, his disapproval carefully concealed, but she felt it in the absence of his usual warmth. She could read the warning clearly in the hazel eyes—don't hurt him.

Her discomfort worsened when Connor appeared, his haste apparent in the hastily donned clothes, bare feet, and rumpled hair. He paused for a long exchanged look across the room, his eyes holding hers in silent question. Finally, hers dropped away, her evasion his answer. His shoulders rising and falling with a heavy sigh, Connor ran a distracted hand through the bristly black hair.

"We should be on the road soon. It's a long ride to Amberly. George, take Tempest back with you and see she's packed and ready. I'll be by after I get myself together."

174

Tempest was ready and nervously waiting beside her baggage when Connor's well-sprung carriage arrived. When Lord Amberson stepped down, her spirits flagged, for there was no trace of her jovial companion in the arrogantly postured nobleman. He gestured for his driver to load the luggage while he cast a gauging eye over her. He could find no fault with the fashion plate she presented. Nodding, he turned to George Morley.

"George, I couldn't have managed this without you," he said quietly.

Smiling, George put out his hand. "Good luck, Conn. I'll see you at Amberly."

Connor ignored the extended hand and crushed his friend in a quick, hard embrace. "Thank you, George."

Shaking him by the forearms, George stepped back to caution him. "Mind yourself with Tyler. I won't be there to keep you from each other's throats."

"I will mind my manners. I promise."

"Promise? Now I can rest easy." The carrot-topped man grinned wickedly. "Just have a care until you can throw his prissy rump down the front steps."

"A most pleasant thought. Good-bye, my friend."

The ride was indeed long and tiring, both physically and mentally. The carriage was heavy with a stilted silence. Connor sat opposite her, staring out the window, his handsome face set in brooding lines.

175

He offered no conversation, and Tempest could think of nothing to say to him.

It was her fault, Tempest realized. She had let him think their relationship had taken a more personal turn and was obviously pouting when that had proved false. How could she possibly apologize or explain why she had let him draw that conclusion? How could she blurt out that she loved him so deeply she thought her heart would explode from the mounting pressures of desire and need. Oh, the passion had been seeded from the first touch of his lips, and his looks had won an instant infatuation, but as they spent the evening together in her father's tavern, she had become aware of these new and powerful feelings. Perhaps it was because she had seen him more clearly in that grimy setting, discovering a man behind the fancy figurehead, one of rare vulnerability, sensitive and warm with a tempering strength. And so exciting. The man she discovered, she wanted desperately.

Even now as she glanced at the fine profile, she battled the urge to nestle close to him, to let him hold her and kiss her and do all the things he longed to do, for she wanted them as well. But Connor Amberson had made it very clear from the start—she would only be a temporary fancy. While the promise of exhilarating nights was a mighty temptation, the reality of their ending sobered her. These budding feelings would not be of a fickle nature. She could not toy lightly with them. To submit to the craving of her flesh would mean a shattering of her spirit. Her love was not of a fleeting passion but of binding commitment, and that she would never have from this man.

Being his mistress would mean fine treatment and ample loving, but it also would leave her subject to his whim. That she could not endure. Her emotions could not be turned off at a moment's notice because his desire had cooled. They were too important to be so carelessly handled. Better to leave them unexplored than to wake something too powerful for her to control.

The discovery that George was not going with them was an unpleasant shock. Now there would only be Connor in the web of deception he meant to weave. How could she maintain a distance when forced into such close proximity? How much of his presence could her weakening will deny? Last night had been a dreadful mistake, confirming that loving Connor Amberson was a sweet heaven. Even so, she didn't regret it. She had wanted him, and it had seemed so right. On waking, that illusion had disappeared. Only the wanting remained.

Miserably, she twisted on the seat to find a comfortable spot and closed her eyes to the sight that so tormented her. She directed her thoughts instead to what lay ahead and to what she was leaving behind, perhaps forever.

For his part, Connor risked losing the long-suffering petulant image he was cultivating by giving a sidelong look at the opposing seat. Tempest was crooked awkwardly on the cushion, sound asleep. With a sigh, he settled back in his seat. There was no purpose in pouting prettily for his own benefit. As he stared at her, he wanted to summon anger or indifference, but he couldn't. He could manage only warm memories and the hurt of rejection. What moved her to run so hot and cold, to make her hunger for his kiss but flee from his touch? She had found as much pleasure in the shared bed as he had. She had come boldly to him both times, so it was not a question of unwillingness. What then? He had no past experience to draw on. He was not detached and uninvolved with this one. He was in grave danger, and he knew it; yet he wanted her still in spite of the risk. Bedding her had only deepened the fascination, an added attraction, where in other cases the bedding had been the only one.

Telling himself it was only because she looked so cramped and uncomfortable, he switched seats and gathered her gingerly in his arms to afford her an easier rest. The bright head burrowed into the pillow of his shoulder, and her slack hand fell carelessly into his lap. That contact brought an abrupt response, and without being aware of it, Connor's breathing became light and fast. He lifted her unknowing hand from his tortured loins and curled her arm about his neck, enjoying this contrived embrace for the contentment her closeness gave his frayed emotions. Cuddling her close as if she was a willing lover, he shut his eyes to the passing countryside, and he, too, slept.

Waking was a pleasant experience, all warm and secure. Tempest let herself linger in that safe haven while her thoughts slowly gathered. Beneath her cheek, she could feel a slow steady pulse, a rhythm as soothing as the light message between her shoulder blades. Her own fingers were twined in the finest of silk, black silk she mused dreamily. Oh, how good it all was. From somewhere in her past memories, she heard low hushed words whispered against her mouth.

"Ah, sweet, I do love you. I love you and want you so."

Connor? When had he said that to her? In a dream?

Startled, she jerked back out of his circling arms to regard him suspiciously. How had he come to be her cushion? But Connor wasn't looking at her. His pale eyes were held—no, mesmerized—by something outside the carriage.

"Connor?" she questioned softly.

He glanced at her only briefly; then his rapt stare turned away. "Amberly," he announced almost reverently.

Curious to see what had him so shaken, Tempest leaned across his knees to peer out the window.

Amberly was breathtaking. No description could have prepared her for the sight. Set on a small knoll above parklike grounds, it was an imposing three-story mansion with a long commanding face marked by the strong vertical lines of Gothic styling. Built of rose-red brick dappled with black by Cotswold masons, the forbidding front was broken by arched doorways and paneled oriels. Expansive mullioned windows topped by transoms promised a well-lit interior. The lengthy roofline was interrupted by numerous pointed gables and fine chimneys of brick with stone cornice caps.

179

"Oh, Connor, it's spectacular," Tempest proclaimed in awe. Its size alone at that distance impressed her beyond words. To her limited scope of life, his London house had been overwhelming, but this—this was monumental. "No wonder you love it so."

"It's mine, Tempest. If not by birth, then by right, and no one's going to take it from me." He sounded angry and almost fierce. She lifted her eyes to meet the intensity of his. "You can get it for me, sweet. I need you. Don't fail me. Secure Amberly for me, and I'll give you anything you desire. Anything."

She was still practically lying in his lap, so he had no great distance to draw her to his chest. His hand cupping her cheek, he bent his head, his smoldering blue eyes open and intent until the instant their lips met. Hers parted in forlorn submission to the unhurried probing of his tongue, as she let the conquering emotions possess her completely. He continued to kiss her slowly, deeply, hungrily, his mouth warm and tempting her to yield to its tender persuasion. Fearing to caress her lest she end this tantalizing feast, he merely held her close as they kissed, and for this moment, that was enough. She returned his kiss, not with an urgent passion but with a soul-wrenching sweetness that seized his heart ruthlessly. Unable to maintain his restraint, Connor chose to release her rather than to risk her rejection. She sagged weakly against his chest, making no effort to withdraw.

Neither could find a voice to speak, nor could they relinquish the fiery heat they drew from one another. Finally, reluctantly, Tempest straightened, meeting his eyes with caution.

"You are so beautiful," he murmured thickly. "Thank you, Tempest."

"For the kiss or for being beautiful? Or both?" she tossed back at him.

His ear-to-ear grin broke the tension of the moment, and the easiness was back between them. He pressed a warm kiss to the back of her hand, then turned his attention back to his fast-approaching home.

The familiar markings of Lord Connor Amberson's coach quickly caught the attention of the household. They expected his tall dapper figure but not the young lady he handed down with such diffidence.

Up close, Amberly was engulfing, the soaring lines rising straight up to the heavens. Tempest unconsciously clung to the proffered arm, her grip tight and a bit fearful.

"Are you ready, sweet?" asked a low voice. "You still have time to recant if you wish."

The bright blue eyes rose to meet pale fire, and her bearing stiffened. "I am ready, my lord. I gave my word. I will not be intimidated by a bunch of stuffy gentry."

His expression didn't alter, but his eyes sparked with amusement. At that moment, he wanted to hug her bold saucy self tight and tell her he loved her for her tartness and irrepressible spirit. Then his eyes were drawn to the figure in the door, and his thoughts froze.

Jonathan Amberson was not at all a fearsome figure. He looked like a balding, portly old gentleman that age had slowed from an energetic overseer to a content squire. There was no similarity between him and Connor, but then, Tempest recalled, they weren't related by blood. The marquis' florid face was heavily jowled and lined by the laughter and sorrow of the passing years. One of the greatest sources of both was before him now. For a moment, his eyes misted with fond welcome; then they narrowed into hard slits.

"Connor, I cannot say I am surprised to see you," he rumbled in a gravelly bass timbre.

His grandson's mouth twisted wryly. "No, I'm sure you thought your latest ruse would bring me running, tail between my legs and whining." Though his words were disrespectful, his tone was not.

"I am not sure I would welcome a whimpering cur, but here you are."

"Not because of your tricks, old man," he boasted with a proud lift of his chin.

"Why are you here then? Certainly not to pay homage to an old man in his failing years."

Connor grinned at his acidic remark. How he loved the irascible old goat. "In a way I have." He paused, waiting for the shrewd eyes to betray interest. "I have brought you something of great value. Something you lost that you held dear."

Jonathan frowned, following Connor's glance to the young woman at his side. Looking at her for the first time, he was surprised. She didn't seem the type for the dashing young Amberson lord. But then he had never laid eyes on any of his many women. This was the first he had ever brought to Amberly. She was fresh and pretty but with none of the frivolous nonsense of the younger set. She seemed more of an innocent, a combination of fair face and direct eyes. He liked her at once for that. He had seen enough of the devil-may-care in his grandson. But that didn't explain why she was here. Unless—could Connor have brought a bride? His heart leaped with anticipation.

"Grandfather, I want to present you with Holly Amberson."

Jonathan didn't move, sure he had misunderstood. Then the girl stepped forward, her hand outstretched.

"Hello, Grandfather. It has been a long time, and it must be a shock to you, but it is really me."

In a daze, he took the small hand. "Please come inside where we can talk," he mumbled. His gnarled hand was squeezing hers unwittingly as if he feared to let go. Once inside the great hall, his eyes feasted on her as if begging himself to believe the unexpected miracle.

"How can this be?" he asked unsteadily, his confused eyes lifting to his grandson's. "How—Where? After searching all these years . . ." His voice trailed off, thin and quavering.

In all his careful planning and sly plotting, Connor had never prepared himself to face the strength of the old patriarch's emotions. The sight of tears welling in the faded eyes had his conscience writhing and twisting his heart into a guilty knot. His mouth opened of its own accord to proclaim the falseness of the scene when a sudden intruding voice made it snap shut with resolve.

"Well, well, well. The return of the prodigal," Tyler

boomed. "What did I tell you, Mama?"

Katherine Amberson regarded her nephew with only mildly disguised dislike. She had been an attractive woman before her figure settled thickly and her own disposition soured and tightened her features as if they had been too snugly screwed. She was tall, like her son, with the same affected bearing. Her disparaging gaze went from the tall man who met her eyes unblinkingly to the chit at his side. Tempest winced at that stare that labeled her all manner of unspeakable things.

"Shall I have rooms prepared for you and your— lady friend, Connor, or is your visit going to be thankfully brief?" she asked frostily.

"We will have our own rooms, dear Aunt, and the duration of our stay may be quite permanent."

Still smarting under the woman's cutting appraisal, Tempest stepped forward boldly. "I cannot see that you have changed greatly, Aunt Kate, but Tyler has added a foot or two. Tell me, Tyler, do you still taunt little girls and make them cry?"

The narrow, dark eyes met hers in cool annoyance. "Who the devil are you? I don't know you."

"Let me present your cousin, Holly," Connor said smoothly, a pleased close-lipped smile etching his face as the other man's jaw loosened.

"What?" Katherine nearly shrieked. "That is impossible. Connor, what nonsense is this? Who is this chit you are trying so cruelly to foist upon us?"

Again, Tempest spoke up, her tone crisper in the defense of the man at her side. "Connor is not at fault here for returning me to my rightful home. Liar

184

is a term I cannot condone, so let me lay at rest your accusations from the start. If you recognize the mark, you'll know I am who I say I am."

Before their shocked eyes, she pulled her skirts and petticoats thigh-high to display an attractive pair of legs with a unique rose-colored birthmark. After a moment of gawking silence, Connor tugged down the gown.

"That will do, sweet," he whispered tightly, uncomfortably stirred by the lithesome display.

Jonathan Amberson gave a low chuckle. "Even if I had not seen the mark, I would have recognized the temper. Come here, Holly. Welcome home."

She stepped into the old man's embrace, and the deception began.

Chapter Thirteen

And so the story was told over brandy in one of Amberly's many salons. Connor was an adept tale-teller, relating the harrowing experiences of a young Holly's fate at second hand, sounding properly shocked and surprised and totally believable. Tempest interrupted as if to correct a fact from time to time to keep the eloquently woven fairy tale plausible.

Connor told how a half-drowned child had been pulled from the river by Cecil Martel. He had noticed the small bundle clinging to some bobbing driftwood as he had steamed toward the ocean for a passage to the Colonies. The child had been in deep shock and had cleaved to him in desperation, sobbing that he not leave her. His rough seafarer's heart had been touched by her tears, and he had seen to her safety. All he had managed to learn was the name Holly and that her parents were dead.

Unable to delay his voyage, Cecil had placed the child in a convent where he was assured she would be gently nurtured and better cared for than at the abominable orphanages. Quite content under his wing, Holly had become his ward. Between his lengthy trips abroad, she had stayed with him and, in his absence, had made a home with the sisters at the convent. Her memory before the night she had been found did not return.

Holly had been not yet of age when word had come of Cecil's death at sea. While the sisters were kind and understanding, they could not keep her at the nunnery unless she chose their life. When it was apparent she was not suited to become one of them, a letter had been sent to Martel's kin, informing them of the situation. Though previously unaware of her existence, Loretta Martel had sent for the girl and, after learning of her sad plight, had generously opened her home to the nameless waif. Connor had difficulty expounding on Lady Martel's saintliness with an unaffected countenance.

At a small rout, young Holly had met an acquaintance of the Martels and had been unable to dispel the nagging feeling that she knew him. She had followed him about until she gathered the courage to confront him. Then it had all returned to her, the tragedy of her parents' death and the existence of the family she had forgotten.

After carefully verifying her claim, Connor had brought her back into the fold of her loved ones, and here she was.

"A pretty tale, Connor," Katherine said smoothly, her eyes fencing with the cool blue-gray pair. She was too wise to denounce him while Jonathan was obviously of a mind to believe the creative imaginings; so she would proceed with caution. "I'm sure it can withstand a thorough investigation."

"Oh, I quite insist on it, Aunt Kate," Tempest interjected calmly. "Please treat me as you would a guest and a stranger until you are convinced of who I am. I will not feel comfortable as long as there are doubts."

"I have none," Jonathan affirmed, taking up her hand and pressing it fondly. "Only many questions."

Connor stood, a light touch falling on Tempest's shoulder. "Could the questions wait, Grandfather? It has been a tiring journey, and I'm sure Holly would like to get settled in and have a good night's rest, as would I."

Taking her cue, Tempest said quickly, "I am truly exhausted."

"Of course, child. How thoughtless of me not to have considered you, but I confess my old eyes are so hungry for the sight of you, I am quite selfish about letting you go. Good night, dear Holly."

Again, Connor suffered the wrenching of guilt, but this time it was not so severe, and without hesitating, he offered his arm to Holly with a gallant insistence that he see her up. He led her out leisurely, but once out of sight of the others, he had her nearly running up the stairs to match his long strides. In the shadow of the upper hall, he spun her into a crushing embrace that cleared her feet from the expensive carpet.

"You are brilliant, my sweet," he said in excited relief, settling her back on the floor but not releasing her.

"And what of you, my lord?" she teased, caught up in his jubilation and giddy after the strain. "I swear I heard angels weeping at the deliverance of your speech."

Laughing softly, their eyes met and held. The light amusement faded before a slow sweep of deeper emotion. His long fingers caressing her upturned face, Connor vowed warmly, "We make a good pairing, do we not? In all things." At that husky conclusion, his mouth lowered to seek hers but found only air.

Tempest leaned away, immediately bracing her hands upon his chest. The intense thunder of his heart was alarming beneath her palms.

"No, my lord. Please do not complicate things. We are supposedly just met and related. How would it seem if we were found groping each other like familiar lovers?"

" 'Tis what we are, is it not?" he argued petulantly, but she knew she had touched his reason for he hesitated. If he had managed to kiss her, she feared she would have been lost.

"Not here, my lord. Not in this house. I will play your game, but we must play to win. That means no unwise gambles. Good night, Cousin Connor. Practice some restraint."

A slow grin of concession touched his lips as he looked down at her fair, inviting face. He brought her hand graciously up for a kiss, then seared her knuckles with a featherlike stroke of his tongue.

"For the moment. Just for the moment," he agreed. "It might well be that poor, cloistered Cousin Holly was so captivated by her sophisticated relation that she could not help but fall into his arms." He stopped in front of a door and pushed it wide for her.

"A pretty tale, my lord," she taunted, her eyes sparkling with sassy laughter. "But I think not."

With that, she slipped inside and closed the door behind her.

"We shall see," Connor said with quiet conviction. Smiling confidently, he continued on to his own room.

Tempest had expected to fall quickly to sleep in the pretty, little girl's room with its lingering scent of dusty disuse, but her eyes remained open and her spirit restless. It was not due to the churning emotions provoked by a dark handsome lord or to the unfamiliar surroundings. It was the silence, a deep seeping quiet that crept in to lie heavy and oppressive like a smothering blanket. Having never been out of the city, she missed its constant throbbing pulse of sound. Amberly was like being in church. Or a grave. She shivered.

How isolated were they here on this country estate? She had slept for most of the ride, so she had no idea of direction or distance. How difficult would it be to escape this family fortress should the need arise? And could she trust the man who had brought her here to see to her safe return? No, said her mind. No, said his best friend. Trust him, said her heart.

Opening her window wide, Tempest let in the warmth of the morning breeze. She leaned out on the casement and filled her lungs with it until they ached. After the foulness of the slums, this was like a fragrant perfume, heady and rich and intoxicating and so crisp it almost burned. How wonderful to wake and stir the senses with so exquisite a fuel.

Clad only in her night dress, she perched upon the sill, her bare feet tucked up and her chin upon her knees. As far as she could see, it was green and lush and huge. Everything was so vast she felt lost and insignificant. And frightened.

Then a solitary figure caught her eye, and all things returned to manageable proportions. She watched in perplexity as Lord Connor Amberson strode across the sloping green lawn. His presence alone was startling enough, for he was not an early riser, but his appearance made her smile. Coatless and barefooted, he looked no proud aristocrat. While she looked on in bewilderment, he sprawled out full length on the grass, his eyes closed and his arms flung wide. He lay like that for some time, then flopped onto his stomach, his chin on his hands. As his gaze lifted, he grinned.

Tempest smiled when he motioned to her to come down. She shook her head. Undaunted, he blew her an elaborate kiss that made her chuckle as she left the window to see to her dressing.

Amberly. Connor sighed happily as he lay upon the ground. The heavy dew quickly saturated his clothing with a wet chill, but it felt so good. Everything about Amberly woke his dormant senses, making him feel and taste and breathe. And live. Plying the damp thick blades with his toes and fingers, he felt as though he was drawing strength and life from beneath him. He had always felt it, this unbreakable link, the earthy power that drew him back home. To Amberly.

Here his restlessness eased, and he could find some peace. Perhaps it was only because he never stayed long enough to tire of it. Tire of it? No. Never.

Then he had rolled over to admire the dusky rose building, his home, his sanctuary. As if his dreams had been breathed into life, Tempest had been there. Even after she had left the window, the image lingered, and so did his fanciful musings. Tempest and Amberly. Could these two things he wanted with such painful urgency become one? Could both together hold him here and still his idle wanderings? He thought of the contentment of waking with the heat of her body conformed closely to the line of his and of that deep joy of this morning upon opening his eyes to find himself in the room he so loved. What more could he possibly ask of life, a place to belong to and a woman to love him.

With a sudden wry chuckle, Connor got to his feet. What a dreamer. Tempest was not remaining to become Amberly's mistress or his own. She had insisted upon her release once her part was done, and he had agreed to it. She professed to hold him and his way of life in contempt, so what could possibly hold her to either? She didn't love him. But then perhaps he was underestimating himself. Hadn't he boasted that he always got what he wanted? And would this time as well?

His damp clothing changed and his grass-stained feet clad in Hussar boots, looking again like the stylish Lord Amberson, Connor trotted down the wide solid staircase. His fingers caressed the smooth balaster, as he recalled images of a boy sliding down the rail, whooping wildly to hear the endless echoes of his voice. Still smiling wistfully, he started toward the breakfast room and then pulled up in alarm when he heard two voices, Tempest's and Jonathan's.

Furiously, he hurried ahead. The little fool. She had promised to wait for him, not to meet with family members alone, especially not the old patriarch. How could she take such a careless risk after chastising him?

The scene he came upon stilled his anger. The two were seated at the table, a small hand closed within a wrinkled one atop the linen cloth. They were laughing over something one of them had said. Everything looked so natural, a doting grandfather with his favorite grandchild stealing a quiet moment alone while the great house slept. All a lie, Connor thought miserably as he looked upon the aged face with its happy glow. What he wouldn't give at that moment to render up the real Holly, even at the cost of Amberly.

The sharp eyes lifted, and the wrinkled face permitted a cynical smile. "Connor? At this hour? I'm more inclined to believe you had yet to retire than that you have woke at a civil time."

"Good morning, Grandfather. Holly. It must be all the clean air purging the corruption of the city from the lungs."

"It would take more than clean air for that impossible task."

Connor grinned at the insult. "Can't we breakfast in peace this once, old man?"

"I cannot recall our ever breakfasting together, you lazy cub, but join us, and I will attempt to be

193

amiable."

"That, too, will be a first," he mused, then more seriously asked, "Have you and Holly been getting reacquainted?" He flashed Tempest a stabbing glance of warning.

"Oh, just going on about things," the elderly man said with a soft smile. "I'd almost forgotten how to laugh, but then no one could coax it from me like this little minx. Others were too busy making me frown." He gave the dark head a mock cuff, but his tone was somber. "We have some things to discuss, Connor."

"I know, sir. I am at your disposal."

The quiet of the unexpected reply took Jonathan by surprise. Mollified, he said, "In an hour in my study then."

"Yes, sir."

"I've some things to see to, so I'll leave you two to each other's company."

Alone, Tempest glanced at her companion, puzzled by the solemnness of his expression. Did the idea of her meeting with his grandfather disturb him, or was it something else? "Connor?"

The pale eyes rose, startled. Then he gave a wan smile. "Sorry, sweet. You were saying?"

"Are you all right, my lord?"

He sighed. "Just not resting very well on the bed I've made for myself."

"Come in, Connor, and close the doors."

Doing as he was bid, Connor advanced into the darkly paneled den of the waiting lion. As always, his defenses were cloaked in arrogance worn in a casual

194

fashion, but his grandfather was never fooled.

"It is good to have you here, cub, for at least when you are in my sight, I am not bedeviled by tales of what you're doing."

"I'm flattered by your interest in my activities," was the dry retort.

"Activities? Adultery, gaming, whoring, murder? I have no interest in hearing of these things. Do you do them just to torment me, or do you find real pleasure in such unworthy exploits?"

"You flatter yourself to think that I would live my life just to annoy you, old man, though I'm sure it does. Let's hear the list of foul deeds and get it over with. I'll let you know if you've left any sordid detail out."

Jonathan's florid face grew even darker, and his deep voice rumbled, "Do not make a joke of my concern. When will you take the task of being a man of your position seriously? Is there nothing in your shiftless existence that you hold dear?"

"Yes."

The earnestly spoken reply made the older man pause in his typical tirade. It was a scenario they played each time they were together, but this was a new twist.

"What?"

"Amberly," Connor told him with candid urgency. He was weary of the game and would have it over. He had to know how things lay in his grandfather's heart and mind. "I want Amberly. I want to move back home to stay."

Jonathan's eyes gauged the younger man skeptically. How intense he looked, how sincere. But he knew his grandson.

"No, Connor."

Connor winced as if he had been unfairly struck. For once, his expression was void of all pretense. "Why?" he insisted in anguish. "You cannot mean for it to go to Tyler. He has no love for Amberly, only for himself. I want to come home. It's all I've ever wanted."

The old man permitted a heavy sigh as he observed the other's distress not without compassion. "Connor, I have given you chance after chance to come home, and you've thrown it in my face each time. I'm old. I'm not well. I want to see Amberly safe before I die. I will not split up the land between my heirs. It will have one rule by one capable hand. It will not be yours. You've not shown yourself worthy."

Connor stood stiffly, held by an influx of anger, hurt, and despair until his protective insolence returned. "Fine," he said with a haughty sneer. "I'll see that my business is none of yours. This place is no longer my home. I'm done trying to earn my way into this family." With that, he wheeled about to leave the room.

The sharp bark of his name checked his brash retreat.

"Don't walk away from me with words like that," Jonathan ordered firmly. "Turn around and face me. Now!"

Rigid with upset and his eyes hotly challenging, Connor spun about. His anger seethed as sharply as the breath between his clenched teeth.

Jonathan Amberson pointed a finger in warning. "Don't you ever say that. Don't think it and don't feel it. I have never, ever thought of you as anything but a part of this family. From the moment your mother married my son, you've been as much a grandson to me as Tyler. Have I ever made you feel unloved or unwanted here in this house? Ever?"

The fierceness left the pale eyes as his gaze dropped away. "No, sir. Never," he mumbled.

"If you look for blame because of what has befallen you, place it correctly. You've led a hard and hellish life, and I've seen no indication that it will change with more chances or more years. You are reckless, defiant, and too unstable to succeed me. I am weary of the heartache you've caused me, Connor." Jonathan sat down heavily, and for the first time, he looked the old man he claimed to be.

Quietly, his grandson said, "Is all the blame mine? You could have made it easier for me."

"No," he disagreed flatly. "Someone had to make it harder."

There was a long silence. Then Connor asked, "What happens to Amberly? And to me?"

"Amberly will always be your home. You may live under its roof any time you choose, but nothing will be deeded to you. You've the Garrett fortune to sustain you so I know you'll not be in the cold. If you do manage to gamble your way through it, an allowance will be provided for you. I do this out of love for you, not in spite. You understand that, don't you?"

"Yes." It was barely a whisper.

"Amberly will not be Tyler's. I plan to leave it to Holly under the protection of a guardian until her twenty-first year or her marriage."

The light eyes lifted, bright and hopeful. "I could

be that guardian. Would you trust me that far?"

"Should I? Would you in my place?" he asked shrewdly.

"No, I would not."

Jonathan smiled ruefully. "I am always at a loss with you, cub. Do not make me regret this. I've committed nothing to paper yet, so until that time, it is up to you."

"I won't fail you, Grandfather."

"Don't worry about me. Don't fail yourself."

Tempest gazed questioningly as the tall figure emerged from the study. She returned his wide smile with relief.

"Come, dear Cousin," he announced, lifting her up from the bench she had been waiting on. "Let me give you a tour of your new inheritance."

Arm in arm, he escorted her through the endless maze of rooms, sketching out a history of each in high humor. His warm, witty anecdotes lessened the ominous overshadowing she felt within the cavernous halls. He made her see it as he did, through loving eyes, cherishing details and scoffing at its stuffiness. As he went on and on, Tempest watched him closely. Yes, she could see the change George had told her of, a softening, a quieting, an easing of his usual brusque speech and body tension. She had had a fleeting glance of that look before when she woke to find his eyes upon her.

The floors they traversed were alternately of marble and parquet, their footsteps muffled by scatterings of finely woven rugs. The interior was rich with decoration, the lower walls lined with wainscot paneling and the ceilings ornamented with delicate carvings. The artwork and statuary were all priceless and meticulously maintained. Besides the huge main hall, there were countless salons and drawing rooms, one leading to the next, a solarium, and even a small family chapel that had seen the marriages of all three Amberson boys. The second floor was mostly unused guest suites. The ones she peered into curiously were shrouded with dustcovers and smelled stuffy. One of the rooms, a long airy chamber lined with mullioned windows, was empty of all but dust.

"The nursery," she stated with certainty.

"Yes. How did you guess that?"

She advanced into the bright room to kneel down on the scuffed floor. "You can still see little heads bowed over their play here among the sunbeams. It must have been a cheery place when it was furnished."

"It was," he admitted, glancing about remembering. "Of course, I was too old to play here by the time I came, but I remember Holly sitting on my knee as I read some dreadful children's story over and over to her. It's been empty for a long time."

"Will your children play here?"

The question was innocently asked, but when she looked up, her expression so pure and lovely, her skirt and palms smudged with dust, his heart gave a sudden shudder. Our children, its frantic tempo seemed to insist.

"Come, there's one more place I want to show you," he said, his voice a trifle strained. How would he ever rid these rooms of her shadow once she had gone?

Tempest stood, brushing off her skirt and ignorant of the inner heat firing the pale eyes as they caressed her so thoroughly. "Lead on, my lord."

When he opened the final door, she started inside naively, but one glance about warned her of her mistake. She recognized the bold taste in furnishings and the toiletry items on the bureau top. Stepping back quickly, she bumped into the solid barrier of his body, and when she whirled, she was in his arms.

"The best for last," he murmured huskily as his mouth fastened hungrily upon hers. Through the sudden roar of her blood, she heard his heel thud against the door, closing off her escape.

Smashed against his chest, Tempest didn't struggle, but neither did she respond to the demanding probe of his kiss. Not that he needed encouragement. She finally managed to twist her head away and gasp for air and reason.

"My lord, is this the way you end all tours of your home?" she panted.

"This is the first, but I am quite enjoying it." His lips nibbled along the slender column of her throat.

"I had not thought there were many first times left in your jaded life," she pursued, trying to distract him from his purposeful course.

"A few," he admitted between hot kisses about her neck. "I've saved them for you. Would you like to know what they are?"

"Yes—no. Stop that." She slapped at him as his lips dipped lower, brushing the creamy swell of her breasts.

"I cannot help myself," he muttered thickly.

"Indeed, sir. I think you help yourself to much too much. Must you always act as thought I were a mare and you a fancy stallion out to stud?"

His laugh was warm upon her skin. Then he straightened, the crisp fire of his eyes burning into hers. "I need you, Tempest."

"For what? For how long?" Her curt reply cooled the heat in him with a chill of rankled vanity. "My lord, what you offer I can find anywhere, though I must admit not so prettily wrapped. I will not be played with for your amusement. Your need can be well met any number of places, so why choose my unworthy and unwilling frame?"

He looked so angry for a moment she feared he would strike her. His growling voice delivered a hard enough blow. "As you wish. I will not beg you."

Abruptly, she found herself in the hall and the door between them slammed shut. She was too startled to do more than blink. Then she chuckled to herself. The bold peacock did not react well to an attack on his male pride. What a humiliation it must be for so vain a lord to have a lowly pauper spurn his lavish advances. It would be well he got used to that feeling. She could not soothe his ruffled feathers by telling him what a difficult trial it was to walk away when all she desired lay within the room. But walk, she did.

For the next two weeks they skirted each other with frosty civility while Tempest settled into the role of Holly Amberson.

True to his vow, Connor behaved superbly, even with Tyler, though that politeness caused much gnashing of teeth. His grandfather noticed and approved of his efforts, but the elderly man was too taken by the reappearance of his heir to offer much encouragement. To him, Holly had brought new life, and he couldn't spend enough time in her delightful company. Anxious to show her off with the pride of ownership, he planned an extravagant gala in her honor, the guest cards posted totally over three hundred.

Close watch was kept on the reborn Holly Amberson by others as well. Tyler eyed her with interest, seeing her as a means to the vast Amberson wealth, but his mother surprisingly opposed that idea.

She, alone, knew it was not Holly. Holly Amberson was dead.

Chapter Fourteen

The loud growl of thunder woke Connor from his sleep as it rattled the panes of his casements. With a sleepy mutter, he rolled over and sank deeper into the warmth of his covers to enjoy the lulling sounds of the storm. He was nearly asleep when the awareness came to him of one who would find no peaceful rest as the raging elements shook the glass and howled about the weathered brick.

Thoughtful, he turned onto his back to wait. Surely this storm would bring her to him when nothing else seemed to. After long minutes stretched out, he began to frown, then was up, tugging on trousers and padding barefooted down the dark silent hall. He hesitated outside her closed door. Just a peek to see if she was all right, he told himself. She couldn't roast him for that. He wouldn't even go in.

A gust of frigid air brought goose flesh to his bare chest as he opened the door. The windows stood open, the curtains flapping inside as they were bandied about by torrents of slashing rain. A flash of lightning confirmed an empty bed.

Shivering in the cold and damp, Connor hurried to pull in the windows and latch them securely against the force of the wind.

A low plaintive moan sounded in the darkness.

"Tempest?"

Another flash of light outlined a huddled figure crouched in the corner by the dresser. Connor knelt down behind her, putting a gentle hand on her shoulder. She was trembling and soaked through. His touch made her knot more tightly in her defensive ball, the whimper becoming a wail of fright.

"No. Don't hurt me. Please."

"Tempest, it's Connor. It's all right. I'm here with you." He dragged her like a cowering animal from her protective lair and cradled her closely. She was freezing. "I have you now. Nothing can hurt you."

"Please don't hurt me," she sobbed in a tiny child's voice that cut through to the quick of his emotions.

"Who would hurt you, sweet? Name a name, and I promise you'll have nothing to fear again," he urged fiercely, but she would say no more, lost to terrified weeping.

Carefully lifting his unresponsive burden, Connor carried her from the icy dampness into the comforting warmth of his room. She seemed not to know him, taking no assurances from his voice or presence, making no effort to cling to him as she had before. She was in a world of her own, a dark, awful place where there was no escape or safety.

After stripping the sodden night dress from her, Connor tucked her beneath his blankets and crawled in after her. He sucked in a quick breath at the first encounter with her cold flesh, then drew her slowly to him until her trembling figure met his full length. The tender curves kindled a deeper more insistent heat.

Curling his fingers beneath her chin, Connor tipped up her face and began to kiss away the salty tears. His mounting ardor steered a path to the slackly parted lips.

"Please," she whimpered, eyes tightly closed.

"Please what, my love?" he asked softly. "Say yes or no to me."

"Please don't hurt me," was the broken reply.

With a resigned sigh, Connor drew the damp head to his chest, pillowing his cheek atop it. "You're safe, my love. I could never hurt you. I can wait. There will be other times for us. You can trust me for this night. After that, no promises."

Sipping her strong tea, Tempest stared out over the brilliant lawn of Amberly, bright and fresh after the rain. From her serene expression no one would guess the confusion of her thoughts.

To wake in Connor's room, pressed close to him in his bed, her night clothing tossed to the floor, had been a shocking revelation. That he hadn't touched her was a puzzling one. Searching her memory, she could find no explanation for waking in his embrace. She had slipped out of that warm refuge before giving way to the urge to kiss him awake and now was anxiously searching for a way to ask him what had happened.

The approach of a carriage interrupted her thoughts, making her follow its progress curiously. A glare of orange against the morning pastels brought a sound of happy welcome as she rushed to the door. Her exuberance was checked when she recalled the chilliness of their parting.

"Hello, Mr. Morley. How good to see you again," she said with smooth formality.

George's expansive grin encouraged one in return, and with a squeal, she was hugging him tightly.

"Oh, George, I've needed a friend in this huge old mausoleum. I'm so glad to see you here."

"And this is by far the best welcome I've had at Amberly," he chuckled.

Over a light breakfast, she told him conspiritorially of their progress. He confessed he hadn't been able to suppress his curiosity another day until Holly's ball, so he had arrived early to satisfy himself and have his pick of the guest rooms. She couldn't have been more thankful for his timing, for George would be a buffer between her own waning will and Connor's pressuring.

When George mentioned the ball, Tempest confided a new worry. "George, I don't know how to dance, and I'm sure it will be expected of me."

He stood, bowing low over her hand. "Honor me, Miss Amberson. Your servant begs permission to give you a lesson."

Tempest laughed at his affected humor and curtsied deeply. "Tell me, Mr. Morley, do you often give lessons at the break of dawn?"

"Not in the ballroom arts, I own, but no time like the present."

She grinned at him and followed his lead. For the next hour, they moved about the quiet parlor. Anyone observing them would have been puzzled to see them step to the sound of no music while the masters of the house slept above. Tempest quickly grasped the staid movements of the formal dance, all repetition and slow predictability, but she was awkward in the waltz, unable to catch the fluid rhythm. She gave a gasp as her hand was taken from George's.

"Let me. George, give us a count."

As George called out the time, Connor turned her easily about the room. He held her close, the heat of his hard body and the intensity of his eyes making her forget the dictates of her feet as she glided with him in instinctive grace.

"I expected to see you a bit sooner this morning in more private surroundings," he whispered huskily. "I shall have to learn to be a lighter sleeper."

"Perhaps you can explain how I came to be in such surroundings, sir," she replied in equally hushed tones.

He grinned at the bold challenge in her eyes. "Did you think I abducted you from your pristine bed with mean intensions?"

"If so, what kept you from them?"

"Disappointed, sweet?" he teased; then his expression sobered. "What are you afraid of, Tempest? Who is trying to hurt you?"

"I don't understand, my lord."

Her sincerity was not affected, but he pressed on. "During the storm, you were begging not to be hurt. You were so frightened you didn't even know me."

Her steps faltered. Frowning, she answered, "I

have no idea what you speak of. No one threatens me but an occasionally overzealous lord with too high an opinion of himself."

The gibe failed to bring a smile, and he stopped the dance to search her expression. "What frightens you about the storm, Tempest? What is it you fear?"

Her breath quickening in agitation from a source she didn't understand, Tempest pulled free. "I don't know. I don't know, my lord."

With those constricted words, she fled the room, leaving him to look after her in silent concern. He would find out if her fears were real and, if so, put an end to them.

Tempest watched the endless line of coaches come up the drive with a growing apprehension. Hiding behind the drapes of the front parlor like a child, she had an unobstructed view of the fine guests come to welcome her return. No, not for her but Holly.

Pulling the door quietly closed behind him, Connor smiled at the picture she presented, her knees upon the window seat and her face pressed to the glass.

"You can see better from the hall."

She turned with a guilty flush, then scowled. "Don't tease me, Connor. I am quite cowed by the thought of facing this mob."

"Nonsense. You will dazzle them all. Stand up and let me see you."

Tempest Swift glittered like moonlight on still water. Though of simple Grecian style, her gown was anything but plain. Ice blue tulle shimmered with sequins, making her sparkle almost as brightly as the brilliant stones about her neck. The gown's snug lines emphasized her lithe figure, and the hip-length stays enhanced the look, thrusting up her bosom to present an almost scandalous display in the scant inches of gathered fabric between the drawstrings at her neck and under her breasts. Gloves of the same hue rose nearly to the tiny cap sleeves. She was coolly elegant, but what the sight of her stirred was a brazier of desire.

He stared for so long, she asked hesitantly, "Do I look presentable?"

"Almost," he said tightly. He came to her slowly and opened a flat case. She stood motionless as he draped her in sapphires. They dripped from her tiny ears, made a circle of fire around her slender wrists, and flashed amid her tossled curls. "Perfect."

Putting a gloved hand to his cheek, Tempest stretched up to touch his lips briefly with hers. "Thank you, my lord."

Though he didn't pursue the kiss, he held her near so that his words were a tingling caress against her moistened lips. "While you wear them, think of how very much I want you." He straightened and calmly crooked his elbow. "Shall we greet your guests, Cousin Holly?"

The great hall was ablaze with light and vivid with the colors and scent of thousands of cut flowers. On the raised dais where the feudal lord and family once presided over their vassals, the Ambersons greeted their guests. The polished marble floor was soon

209

swept with the finest silks, satins, and taffetas, and the best shoe leather. Screens on an upper level at the lower end opened to a minstrels' gallery overlooking the distinguished company, where musicians plied the sounds of raptured harmony in an invitation to dance. Buffets, refreshments, and gaming tables were arranged in adjoining salons for the pleasure of the guests.

Jonathan Amberson oversaw all with a regal pride, hoarding his precious grandchildren about him like the richest treasure. They made an impressive group, the marquis staunch and gloating, the grandsons tall and sleekly elegant, Tyler all polish and suave perfection and Connor darkly handsome with his dangerous magnetism. Amid all the masculine strength, Holly was a fragile flower in budding bloom. She seemed endearingly nervous, clinging trustingly to the old patriarch's arm and bestowing shy smiles on all she greeted. None could find fault with her pretty manners and delicate grace except two women, one who had eyes for the Amberson fortune and one who wanted Connor Amberson.

Excused from his duties, Connor made a quick escape from the smothering politeness to find George and a strong drink. As they sipped their cognacs, George raised his in a toast.

"You've outdone yourself, Conn. She's magnificent. It's as if she's always been Holly and Tempest never existed."

That comment haunted him. Moody eyes followed the guest of honor as she was shepherded about by a strutting Tyler and led out in countless dances. She looked the pampered puppet, responding to every cue by rote with shallow coquetry, timid and teasing with bold inviting eyes and pretty giggles. He roamed through the crowd in solitary ill-humor, thankful for a reputation that allowed him to behave so rudely. No one expected courteous congeniality from Lord Connor Amberson unless it was to his advantage. For his grandfather's sake he did make an effort, speaking with several neighbors and acquaintances of long standing. All the while, his gaze never faltered.

What had he done, he brooded. Had he completed his work too thoroughly? Tempest seemed just another insipid miss, and that thought appalled him.

A light hand on his arm broke his glum thoughts.

"Our little impostor is creating quite a stir," Loretta Martel said frankly. Her eyes were not the only thing green about the lady.

"Yes, she acts as if she was born to all this tedious toad-eating," he grumbled. Why wasn't he pleased by that? It was what he wanted.

"Your dear aunt does not seem too content," Loretta summed up astutely. "If you promise to thank me generously, I will soothe her curiosity."

Connor looked down on her with a slight frown. Everything was beginning to have conditions where Loretta was concerned. He was growing uncomfortably aware of what refusal would mean. He had entrusted her with a damming amount of information when enlisting her help, but regrets now would change nothing. He had never thought of the jewel-eyed countess as an enemy, and his shoulder blades felt disagreeably vulnerable. Unwisely or no, he had made her a part of his plot, so he would use her to his best advantage. Consequence could wait.

Still preoccupied, he nodded to her terms and continued his unhappy reflections.

For Tempest, all was not as easy as it seemed. She was conscious of her every move and word, thoughts flying frantically to recall the right responses and proper gestures. She was too busy counting steps to enjoy the dancing. The pompous Tyler proved a thankful guardian, his banal speeches rescuing her from the effort of searching for something to say. Her feet throbbed in the flimsy slippers, the stays bit painfully beneath her breast forbidding a decent breath, and the struggle to remember names and faces and facts and manners and dance steps—oh, how her head ached with it.

Worst of all, Connor had abandoned her, making no attempt to be her buffer against mistakes and lend his supportive presence. She saw him here and there through the crowd, chatting idly. So why wasn't he with her to help her through this miserable ordeal?

Abruptly her hand was caught up in strong fingers that pulled her close to a familiar frame. He didn't speak as he guided her through the soaring turns of the waltz. Slate-colored eyes held hers as if puzzling over some worry. For the first time, she forgot the count, forgot the others about them, forgot the part she played, and relaxed in the loose curve of his arm. How simple it was to follow him. Theirs was indeed a good pairing for they moved with the same rhythm. She longed to close the distance between them, to lay her cheek over his heart and feel his breath stir her hair.

Alarmed by the strength of those feelings, she began to chatter frivolously about the excitement of the night, the fabulous clothing, the impressive guests in attendance, and oh, wasn't the music divine?

That was it. Enough. Connor could bear no more. Clasping her wrist tightly, he pulled her through the crowd, marching her at his side until they were close together in the humid, fragrant darkness of the solarium. Moonlight washed through the glass dome overhead, sparkling on the brilliant sapphires, both jewels and uplifted eyes.

Connor's anger was monumental, sharpening his angular features and his words. "What was that little display all about?" he demanded curtly.

"Connor, I don't—"

He cut off her bewildered reply gruffly. "Don't ever play me like that. Don't act the proper, dainty debutante. I know you, Tempest Swift. I know what you were before I found you, so don't pretend with me. Don't enjoy the pretense too much, for it will last only as long as I see fit."

"Enjoy it?" she echoed in disbelief. "Sir, you are mistaken. This has been the worst night of my entire life, surpassing even the one that brought me to you. I would end this pretense now if I were free to. How dare you trim me for doing as you told me. How dare you be so mean when I am so miserable. Go away, you boorish oaf. I think I quite hate you."

Unexpectedly, Connor grinned. She was so surprised, she didn't resist when he crushed her to him.

"You don't know how good it is to hear that,

213

Tempest. I've missed you sorely."

Before she could demand an explanation, he was kissing her.

Tempest's arms came up to curl about his neck, her fingers seeking the sleek satin of his hair. There was no hesitance in her response, her lips opening in eager acceptance, her body becoming liquid to conform to his. There was no reality save the strength of her love and the power of her passion, and she could summon no reason to deny them.

The neckline of her gown suddenly sagged, and his mouth was a burning brand upon the tender, aching flesh. She said his name with a strange sobbing urgency that sent a current racing through his veins.

Plundering the sweet surrender of her mouth, Connor cast a desperate eye about the unaccommodating space. To get to his room would mean threading through the guests. He would have to take her here, but damn, he couldn't help it. He had to have her. His body and brain were flaming with insistence. He couldn't wait. He was near to exploding as it was. There was no choice but to make the best of her yielding promise in this cursedly awkward place. He couldn't let the moment slip by him.

Moving as if in some languid dream, Tempest let Connor guide her down upon a low stone bench. The chill of the marble only made her flesh burn hotter. The sounds of muffled music and laughter were drowned by the frantic pulse of her blood, fierce, impatient, primal. Her breath came in short tortured pants, fractured with desire.

Connor bent down on one knee, touching her gently, almost in awe as if she were some moon sacrifice laid out on a pagan stone. His fingers traced over her flushed face, then down to cup an impudent breast so he could savor its perfumed softness, continuing on to rustle through her skirts until they were pushed high enough for her thighs to gleam whitely beneath the jeweled night sky. His lips brushed over that firm pale skin until she writhed in feverish complaint.

"Connor, please. Hurry."

"This won't be very comfortable," he warned, breathing so hard his words were rough gasps.

"I don't care," she cried passionately. "I know it will be wonderful."

"I will try to make it so," he promised, but the angle was awkward, the bench too narrow and unyielding, the binding clothes a nuisance. Then the welcoming heat of her body closed about him, and he could remember no faults in this sudden paradise.

Shaking with the tremendous force of her bursting desire, Tempest let the sensations build and flare within her, striving for the rapture she knew awaited. Her senses reached out for it, straining, stretching until suddenly a voice called out.

"Connor? Holly?"

With a black curse, Connor rolled them both from the bench to the shadowy walk where they fumbled to arrange their attire.

"Here, Aunt Kate. What is it?" Connor's voice was harsh with annoyance as he helped Tempest to her feet. The interruption left his thoughts quite scrambled.

Katherine swept the two of them with a judicious eye. She was not fooled by their feigned innocence.

215

"Jonathan is looking for you, Holly and Connor. A lady has been asking after you, a Lady Martel."

"Thank you. We shall attend to them," he replied brusquely. Their gazes locked in direct challenge; then Katherine smiled, amused by her obvious poor timing.

Once they were alone, Tempest sat heavily on the bench. She was breathless and trembling with unmet needs. Oh, how she had wanted him. Connor knelt before her, her name soft on his lips. She twisted out of his embrace.

"No. No, my lord," she insisted faintly, tottering to her feet and reeling away.

"I'll come to your room tonight—"

"No."

"Then you come to mine—"

"Connor, no. No."

"Dammit, don't do this to me. Tempest—"

"I'm sorry."

With a sob, she fled from him.

Stalking the room like a sleek, dark panther, tensed and ready to strike, Connor searched the blur of faces until finding the one he sought. She was standing with his grandfather, smiling serenely and so beautiful; his coiled frustration took a tighter turn. Aside from the high blush of color in her lovely face and some suspicious creases in her gown, he would have had difficulty believing this respectable sophisticate had been minutes before wrapped about him in hot urgency.

"You look as though you are about to devour

someone, Connie."

He looked in annoyance at the older woman, in no mood for her coy taunts.

Loretta was wise enough to recognize the ugly stirrings that darkened his eyes and switched her tack to one of seriousness. "Be careful of your aunt. She plied me with quite blunt questions. I don't think she is fooled."

His laugh was bitter. "No, I do not think she is. Katherine is of no consequence as long as the marquis is deaf to her serpent's tongue. Thankfully, he has little use for her. The old man is quite enamored of sweet Cousin Holly."

"And you, Connie? Are you enamored as well?"

The pale eyes narrowed into slivers of ice, and even she feared to push for an answer. Again, she altered her course. Her smooth fingers rubbing over his, her green eyes lifted, smoldering.

"The earl had to leave already, so your grandfather was kind enough to offer me lodgings for the night. You did promise to be grateful for my help."

Connor stared at her dispassionately for a long moment. "What room?"

Tempest glanced up from the punch cup she had been studying with fierce concentration and unluckily happened on a scene that froze her heart. Connor and Lady Martel were in intimate conversation that concluded with a small smile from the lady before she walked away. After a pause, Connor followed nonchalantly out of the hall.

She gasped at a sudden chill and looked down to

see a vivid stain down the front of her gown from the full cup tipped by numbed fingers. Excusing herself hurriedly, she escaped the stuffy confines of the hall. Seeking the sanctuary of her room, she raced up the broad staircase and turned into the upper gallery. Voices sounded low and intense, bringing her up short and making her nearly moan in recognition.

"You won't be long, will you, Connie?" cooed a throaty voice, followed by a murmur too low for her to hear and a feminine laugh. "Make sure it is cold, and you are warm."

Tempest lingered in anguish among the shadows until she realized in dismay he was coming toward her. There was no time to flee down the stairs. With a deep fortifying breath, she stood tall and continued on.

Seeing her, Connor drew up, his eyes a murky confusion of desire and pricked vanity. Had she seen him leave with Loretta and followed? Had she heard them plan their tryst? The brilliance of her eyes against her parchment skin made him wonder.

"My lord," she said with cool civility. "I fear my dress is ruined. I must change at once. Please excuse me."

She swept past him regally, leaving an icy wake. Connor winced and unclenched his hands. His palms stung from the deep furrows dug by well-manicured nails. The scent of her wafting perfume wreaked havoc on his system.

"Damme," he growled. "To hell with them both."

He marched down the stairs to seek out George, and after sending a magnum of champagne to cool a lady's passions, his only intent was to waste away the

218

night in amiable companionship.

Lovingly returning the winking jewels to their velvet cases, Tempest wiped the diamond wetness from her cheeks. She shouldn't waste tears on a man like Connor Amberson. How could she possibly love him? He was arrogant, conceited, lying, and totally unscrupled. He had gone from her arms straight to another's embrace, seeking only his pleasure and indifferent to the source. How could she listen so naively to his honeyed words when she knew they had no substance?

"I do love you," whispered his husky voice in that detached dream.

She hugged her arms about herself as her eyes squeezed shut. Liar, her heart screamed back.

Chapter Fifteen

Rising unusually late, Tempest was surprised to find the dining room filled with people who, due to the hour or the amount of drink, had remained as Amberly's guests. Connor and Lady Martel were not among them, nor was George, so she was treated to Tyler's solicitous attention. He served her from the cold buffet and seated her at his side, his brown eyes warm and flattering as he told her of the latest on-dit from London. Caroline Lamb had dramatically slashed her wrists at Lady Heathcote's ball, having suffered a long rejection from Lord Byron. Tempest expressed proper shock and murmured about the extremes of love while her heart lay heavy. Tyler's following words lost all meaning as Connor and George entered the room, dapperly dressed if a little bleary-eyed. She looked away determinedly to hang on Tyler's anecdotes with much amused laughter.

Seeing her in such objectionable company, Connor's humor blackened. His stare would have split Tyler Amberson in two had its edge substance. Tyler's hand covering the smaller one possessively, his dark-eyed gaze lifted, and a smug smile provoked even more murderous intentions.

"I've an idea," Tyler called out loudly, drawing all eyes. "Since so many of us are up and about and the day is so promising, what say you all to a shoot?"

A chorus of agreeable interest sounded as Tyler's eyes bored into his cousin's. "How about you, Connie? You'll join us, won't you?"

"No. I don't hunt. You knew that."

The quiet response made George look up in surprise. His friend was an avid sportsman and an admirable shot, yet with all the lush land at his disposal, he could never recall Connor taking up a gun in sport or attending any of the countryside shoots they had been asked to. He had never though it odd until this moment.

"Make an exception, Connie," Tyler goaded. "You're always crowing about what a deadly marksman you are. Let's make a it a wager, shall we? £1,000 per bird? Let's make it interesting for our guests."

The group murmured in appreciation, but Connor's answer was the same.

"No."

George was aghast. He couldn't believe Connor would forgo an opportunity to outshine his despised cousin. Or refuse an easy wager. "Go ahead, Conn. You are sure to clean him out," he urged. He prodded the silent figure and found him rigid as stone.

"Afraid of being bested, Connie?" Tyler continued, the silkiness of his tone not quite concealing his contempt. "Or could it be you don't want to be second best in the eyes of our dear cousin Holly?"

Still angered and hurt by his roving behavior, Tempest smiled with condescending sympathy. "Don't tease him, Tyler. He obviously knows his limitations." She took Tyler's arm with an admiring flutter of her lashes. "When can we start? I am quite excited by a challenge."

His teeth grinding in frustration and reluctance, Connor growled, "Have your money ready, Tyler." Ignoring the bravos from the room's company and George's pat on the back, he saw only Tyler's cold vicious smile. Turning on his heel, he strode quickly from the room.

There was a loud crowing and flap of wings as the ring-necked pheasant took to the air. Connor's shot was a clear miss, but Tyler's clipped the colorful bird from its flight, dropping it to the ground for the dogs to retrieve.

"I say, Connie, that's four for me, and you've yet to hit the mark," Tyler mused. "Are your sights off perhaps?"

Connor didn't respond to the gibe, wiping his hands again on his nankeen trousers and following silently with their jovial entourage.

Of the dozen of them that marched through the sweet-smelling field, only five of the men were shooting, the others coming along for the enjoyment of the sport or just to enjoy the conflict between the two Ambersons. Tempest was the only woman willing to brave the lengthy jaunt and tangled brush. She was thankful that George had forgone the shoot to provide an arm for her as she stumbled about in the cumbersome cashmere skirts and half boots. He chuckled as she confided her wish for a pair of britches and a well-balanced gun.

As another bird was flushed, again Connor was the first to fire and was wildly inaccurate. He had scarcely bothered to aim. He walked away without even noticing whose shot claimed the prize.

"Conn, what the deuce is the matter with you?" George insisted, hurrying after him with a reluctant Tempest in tow.

"Just not a good day, I guess," he explained vaguely, avoiding their curious stares.

Tempest took the rifle from his unresisting grip. Its smooth polished stock was slick with sweat. As a bevy of quail scattered against a backdrop of cloudless blue, she sighted expertly and fired, wincing at the recoil against her shoulder.

"Nice shot, Holly," Tyler called. "Obviously it's not the fault of the gun."

Frowning, Tempest offered it back to Connor, but he wouldn't take it. His expression was taut and distressed as he turned away.

"I'm no longer interested in this bet," he stated flatly.

"Only in losing it," George protested. "Conn, that's £4,000."

"It's not your money, George," he growled in warning, still not meeting the confused hazel eyes.

"Perhaps he thinks it is," Tyler chuckled. Though he was overheard by all, no one else dared find his comment amusing.

George looked quickly to his friend, but Connor seemed in a daze as if he hadn't heard the remark. In

223

his own defense, George snapped at Tyler, "You are a fine one to worry. Why concern yourself with Amberson money? You'll not see a shilling of it."

Tyler's fine-chiseled features paled, then flushed hot with fury. "You are worse than a parasite, Morley. You are my cousin's spineless eunuch."

If Tyler had had any notion that George had been a boxing enthusiast at school, he would have guarded his tongue more zealously. George's punch caught him squarely on the chin, clicking his teeth together and sending him staggering. George had begun to turn away and never saw the snarl of rage that congealed the other's expression. The butt of Tyler's rifle struck him above the eye, dropping him to the ground.

With a fearful cry, Tempest fell to her knees to draw the carroty head made even brighter by the fiercesome bleeding into her lap. George's eyes flickered and rolled, then finally began to focus. He put an unsteady hand to the gash in his forehead and glared indignantly at his assailant.

"That was a low shot, Tyler," he complained, then stopped. Tyler wasn't looking at him, his eyes narrowed and glittering like something poisonous and deadly. George followed his stare and said anxiously, "Conn, are you all right?"

The question seemed to echo and distort down a long tunnel, but all Connor could see was crimson slowly fading to black. His sense of time warped back, giving way to a feverish sickness that seared his thoughts. His vision dimming at the pressure of that engulfing surge, he reeled, then fled from the blank stares of astonishment.

That evening Tempest had no appetite for the savory meal prepared for the family and its few remaining guests. One of them, Lady Martel, seemed as concerned by Connor's empty chair as she was. Loretta had appeared soon after the shooting party returned. She was unbecomingly warm and eager to find the absent lord. But he didn't appear. No one spoke of what happened, George explaining away his cut temple as clumsiness when Jonathan asked worriedly after him. In a manner it was, for he would never be so foolish as to take his eyes off Tyler Amberson again.

Troubled by the image of Connor's face so twisted in horror, Tempest began a slow ascent of the stairs in the muted glow of lamplight. Suddenly, she paused and turned. She knew where to find him.

She entered the family chapel where the setting sun streamed through the stained glass oriel to form a kaleidoscopic rainbow of prismed colors down the single chapel aisle. She was about to withdraw when she noticed a pungent smell mingling with lemon oil and candle wax. Bourbon?

"Connor?"

The low mutter brought her quickly to the front. She hesitated when she discovered him on his knees hugging the gleaming altar rail. Then she scowled. An empty bottle lay beside him on the parquet floor. He was not kneeling, head bowed in prayer, but simply holding himself up. He was blindly drunk.

"Connor, how could you come to this holy place in such a state? Have you no fear of God?" she hissed, casting a reverent glance at the altar crucifix.

"Why? He has no love for me," he slurred thickly.

"Hush. That's blasphemous," she whispered, more than awed by this quiet sanctuary. She bent down beside him to tug on his arm, but he pulled away.

"He won't give me peace. He won't forgive me. What use is He?" His tone was loud and belligerent, echoing in the vaulted room.

"Connor, please. Don't talk like that."

"Afraid for my soul, sweet?" He laughed a bit crazily. "I'm already damned, so don't waste your concern." He raised his head to glance at her. He looked terrible, his puffy eyes an angry red and his face blotchy with feverish color. Had it not been for the liquor on his breath, she would have thought he had been crying. Losing his precarious balance, he sat heavily, braced up on his palms. He grinned at her obvious dismay.

"Did you drink all of that?" she demanded.

"And the better part of several others, but I can't seem to recall where I laid them."

"Get up, my lord. We have to get you out of here and to your room. I don't think Grandfather would be pleased to find you in here like this."

"You sound as priggish as the old man. I have no interest in moving. You may carry me if you like." With that, he dropped onto his back, his eyes closing.

Thinking he had lost consciousness, Tempest began to stand, but his constricted voice held her.

"Is George all right?"

"It was just a small cut. He has a royal headache, but he's quite fine. Connor?"

To her disbelief, he began to weep, the sounds he

made low and mournful.

"How could he do that to me?" he moaned. "He had to know. He was there. Why can't I forget? Why can't I be forgiven?" His words trailed off into a vague rambling as he rolled onto his stomach.

At a loss, Tempest ran for the only help she could think of and returned quickly with George. "Oh, George, I just didn't know what to do. He's so strange and far from himself."

George knelt down beside the recumbent figure, his words quiet and reassuring. "He's just had too much to drink and not enough sleep. I've seen him like this before. He'll be all right. We shouldn't have stayed up till dawn playing dice."

"Connor was with you. For how long?"

"All night. Why?"

"No reason," was the faint reply.

George shook the still figure roughly. "Conn, wake up. Let's get you to bed. You can't lie here all night, and I'm not about to drag you up a flight of stairs."

Connor grumbled to himself and drew his knees up under him, but that was as far as he could manage. George hauled him up by the shirt collar.

"Hello, George. I knew I could count on you. There's a good fellow." The dark head lolled forward on a boneless neck. His voice abruptly deepened with emotion. "Forgive me, George. I don't know what happened. I just couldn't get it out of my head. All that blood—on my hands. I just couldn't get it out of my head. They all left me, George, everyone I cared for. Don't leave me, George. You're my only friend."

When the blindly groping hands caught in the lapels of his coat, George turned him into his shoulder, holding him in an embrace of easy affection until the tormented words began to dwindle down. His reply was warm and light. "Never fear for that, Conn. I won't. Who else would support a spineless eunuch?"

Connor laughed wearily and rocked back on his heels, wiping his face on his coat sleeve.

"Come on, Conn. On your feet. Let's get you tucked in safe, so I can get some well-deserved sleep. My head's fair to splitting."

With George on one side and Tempest on the other, they struggled to steer a straight and hopefully unobserved path up the stairs. Connor began stripping off his clothing at the top of the stairs, and by the time he crawled into bed, he was down to his boots. George pulled those off and pulled a cover over him.

"He'll be all right once he sleeps through the night," George assured a still apprehensive Tempest. "He starts feeling blue-deviled, and the drink gets the better of him. He's one of the lucky ones who wake up with a clear head. I wish I could be convinced I was the same."

"What was he talking about, George?"

"I've no idea. I really don't. He gets started on it when he's like this, but he never finishes. I started to ask him once. I never will again. I'm going to put some ice on my head and some brandy in my stomach. Care to join me? You can put your ice in a glass."

"Thank you, George, but I think I'll stay a moment to make sure he's all right."

George smiled softly with a resigned sigh and nodded. "He's my friend so I'll mention none of this

228

in the morning."

"Nor will I. Good night, George."

Tempest went to sit gingerly on the edge of the bed, drawn to him by the ragged weeping that had begun again.

"Connor?"

He winced away from her touch and curled up tighter into himself, his voice muffled and heavy with anguish. "Leave me alone. Go away."

"I cannot leave you like this, my lord," she told him softly.

"Why? You don't care about me," he accused her. Then he lamented, "No one cares about me."

"What a fool you are, my fine arrogant lord. I care. George cares. Your grandfather cares. You are a lucky man. You have everything, position, money, your fair face, a wonderful friend, these beautiful grounds, yet you wail and moan like the most unfortunate of paupers. What right do you have to feel so sorry for yourself when you have so much?" Though the words were critical, they were spoken in a kind tone that lessened the sting.

"You know nothing. I have nothing," he cried in torment, rolling onto his back and staring up at her in hostile defensiveness. He looked no handsome lord, his hair a dark bristly disarray, his eyes swollen and murky with grief, and his mouth pulled into a pout. "I want—Oh, never mind. Just please go. I don't want to talk of this." His forearm was braced over his eyes, but the glistening trails that seeped from beneath it caught at her heart.

"What, my lord? What would it take to make you happy?" As she spoke, she stretched out beside him on the bed, leaning on one elbow. Her other hand clasped his arm lightly, feeling the muscles tense and tremble beneath her touch.

"Closing my eyes to see only darkness. Sleeping without dreams. To be able to forget that picture. To be able to look at myself without seeing—" His voice broke off into hard sobs. He was very drunk, and Tempest was afraid he was no longer aware of what he was saying.

"What is it you see?" she asked gently, wondering if she really wanted to know.

"The blood—so much of it—everywhere. It got all over my hands and clothes when I lifted his head into my lap. I tried to stop it and—the rest from pouring out, but I couldn't. I couldn't. It just kept on and on. Tyler started screaming and ran and left me there alone with—with him." He took a long shaky breath to steady the hiccuping words.

"Who, Connor?"

"My—my father. He wouldn't listen to me. He never listened to me. I—I tried to tell him it was an accident. But he didn't hear me. I begged him not to leave me. I begged God not to take him. No one listened to me. I knew if I could get him home—to Amberly, everything would be all right. He was so heavy, and I got so tired. It was dark, and I was so scared, so scared."

His arms lowered slowly from eyes as round and glassy as marbles. They squeezed tightly shut, and in a small faltering voice, he whispered, "He was dead. I killed him. I shot him. I killed my father."

"Oh, Connor, no," Tempest cried in horror, her heart breaking for the pain in his words. Thinking only of easing that raw hurt, she hugged him fiercely, pulling the dark head to her bosom. He lay stiffly, his body tightly knotted and his quick breaths shivering noisily. "It couldn't have been your fault. Surely no one blamed you."

"I did. It was my fault. My fault. Oh God, I didn't mean for it to happen."

"Oh course you didn't," she crooned tenderly, more than a little shaken by this unexpected outpouring of emotion. "Who would think such a thing?"

"They all do. All of them. They won't forgive me." His voice rose to a high frantic pitch."

"Connor, the only one who hasn't forgiven you is you."

"I can't. I can't," he moaned, then was silent, only the sound of his rapid catching breaths punctuating the silence of the night. Abruptly, his arms circled her in a desperate embrace as he cried with a quiet hoarseness, "I can't make it go away. I'm so tired, but I can't close my eyes. It's all right there waiting in the darkness of my mind, and I don't want to see it again. I didn't want you to see me like this. I just can't seem to stop shaking. Oh, damn Tyler. He had to know what it would do to me. When I saw George with his head all cut and bleeding—I'm sorry, Tempest. I know you must despise me for being so weak-spirited."

Her hand stroking the glossy black hair, she said simply, "No, quite the opposite."

"I'm a bluff, a disappointment, but I guess Tyler proved that to you clear enough."

"The only thing Tyler proved was that he is vindictive and hateful. If anything, I think more of you, my

231

lord. I would not have thought the opinion of a lowly footpad could so wound a loftly aristocrat."

The teasing words brought up his gaze, still rheumy but with a warmth that stirred a sultry haze in them like the heat of day misting cool still water. "More deeply than I would ever let you know," he replied in hushed earnest.

Tempest kissed him. It was meant to be a quick consoling gesture, but when his lips parted with a quiet sigh, she gave way to a wash of instincts so urgently protective, demanding that she comfort and possess him to share her strength while his was flagging. His breath trembled as her tongue touched his shyly, then slid over it in a bold silky caress. When she leaned away, his eyes didn't open.

"Please stay with me," he asked quietly.

Her words were tender with concern and a love she couldn't confess. "In my fear and confusion, I once asked you to hold me to take away those feelings, and you did. I would do the same for you now if you would let me. Connor, let me help to ease your hurt."

Her lips moved gently upon his, not seeking to enflame but to calm with their leisurely message. He almost relented, then pushed her away, rolling onto his back, the glistening eyes staring up at the ceiling.

"I'm sorry. I can't seem to manage," he said thickly.

"Shh, my proud fool," she insisted, turning his face back with a light touch of her fingertips. "I don't ask anything but that you let me hold you and be close. That's all I want, so relax yourself in my hands."

Her palm rubbing his chest, her lips pressed briefly to his before brushing over his cheeks and eyelids, wiping away the salty moisture with their soft full-ness. He sniffed loudly and tried to control the shaky breaths, but it was useless. The tearing sorrow had made him painfully sober, and the mental strain of emotion and memory was excruciating.

"Oh, Tempest, it hurts so bad sometimes. All I can think is why him. Why couldn't it have been me? It would have been no loss then. My life is so wretched, so pointless."

"Hush now, my lord. Such decisions were not yours to make, so do not torment yourself over them. Your life is pointless by your own making. That you can change. For now, just rest your thoughts. Empty your mind of all but quiet." Her fingers made small firm circles against his temples as she continued the soft rhythmic crooning of her voice. "Let yourself find some peace for a moment. Grief can only be dealt with that way, just a piece at a time, and with each piece, it is reduced. Let go of the hurt, and think only of rest. Sleep, Connor, and let tomorrow come quietly of its own accord while the past slips away."

The rise and fall of his chest had slowed and deepened, eased into slumber by the gently coaxing words. She knew she should leave him to that rest, but she couldn't. There was a mesmerizing hold on her that she could not break, the appeal of his defenselessness, of his trusting confidence in her. In this moment while he was lost to the world, Tempest could ease her pose of indifference. Her features softened as she beheld his face so strongly and mascu-linely beautiful. She wanted to bask in that sight, wanting no other to replace it before her adoring eyes. Knowing she was safe to do so, her fingers weaved through the ebony silk of his hair, its texture as cool and pliant as his flesh was warm and firm. What a magnificent work he was and though the only example she had seen, she knew a masterpiece without needing comparison.

Sighing wistfully, she lay at his side, her cheek finding a suitable pillow upon his shoulder. She loved him. That would not change, but could she be with him, share the kind of life he led, risk the dangers being in love with such a man would mean? She was certain there were many more Loretta Martels in his past, but what of his future?

"Oh, Connor, I wish mere love could be a strong enough bond to hold you," she whispered softly. "If only you would give me some reason to hope I could claim your heart, I would find a way to deal with the rest."

Chapter Sixteen

Tempest murmured sleepily at the warm insistent nuzzling of her neck. The tantalizing nibbles stirred a shiver of lanquid desire to spread slowly and seditiously through her waking senses, lulling her defenses with purposeful intent. Her hand rose to lie atop the dark head, not in protest but in contented affirmation. His weight created a convenient dip that drew her against him, and beneath the sheet, the full arousal of his manly form contrasted with his unhurried overtures.

"Good morning, my sweet. This is an unexpected delight. Why did you stay?" The blue ice of his eyes held hers in question while he waited, making no move to touch her.

"Because you asked me to. And I fell asleep." She smiled almost shyly.

"I've asked you to stay on countless occasions. Is it pity that held you? The truth. You have seen me at my lowest. I am at your mercy."

She placed a hand upon his rough cheek, closing his eyes briefly. "Your reasons for asking then were quite different. And as for the other, I don't pity you, my lord. You supply that in ample quantity. I feel for your pain, and if my presence could ease it, I could not go. Why would I think less of you because you have a heart? I was beginning to think that was not the case."

Connor smiled ruefully, catching her hand for a quick kiss. "You are not very kind to me," he complained mildly.

"Would you have me smother you with insincere sympathies? That is not what you need."

"But it might be nice. And what do I need in your learned opinion?" He was relaxed now, leaning on an elbow to look upon her with a warm, amused gaze.

"A sharp kick to get your attention and a short lead to guide you away from the reckless path you've chosen."

He examined her imprisoned hand for a long second, then met her eyes with a directness that unsettled her. "And are you willing to do that for me?"

With matching candor, she replied, "I don't know if I have that much strength."

"Tempest, could you ever love me?"

She drew a shaky breath from a chest that seemed painfully tight. His eyes probed straight into her soul. She dropped her gaze in alarm. Cornered and nervous, she replied, "We are too different, my lord. Neither of us can move in the other's world. What point is such a question?"

His forefinger tipped up her chin. "You did not answer me."

"Nor will I, my lord."

"It would please me to have you say yes," he encouraged silkily, his eyes compelling and his finger following the line of her determined jaw.

"You would not want me to love you, Connor. Make love to you, yes, but be in love with you, no. They are very different things."

"Why should I not wish you to love me? Why not have both?"

"So greedy. Would you break my heart, my lord? Would you have me miserable, knowing you would never love me in return?" She made her questions teasing so he would not guess the truth in them.

"What makes you certain I would not? I have loved you, fabulously, as you have said." He frowned petulantly when she laughed.

"That is not love, my lord."

"And you are so experienced to know the difference and correct me," he jeered in a pique, but his fingers played with the ties of her gown, their movement distracting.

"Oh, I have not your long list of conquests, sir, but I probably know more of love than you."

"Hah!"

"Tell me how many of your lady loves you have you been in love with. How many of them have inspired feeling in you above the waist? How many of them have tormented you with thoughts of them when you were apart? A dozen? Ten? Five? Even one?"

Connor said nothing. He could in truth think only of one, and he would not tell her as much.

"No," she concluded. "I thought not. Men like you don't give their hearts to women like me. I have seen

237

it oft times enough to know. You buy what you want, use it until it no longer pleases you, then cast it off. I would not be used by any man. If I give, I want in return."

"But I have given to you—generously," he protested, surprised that he would feel compelled to defend himself to her.

"Things, my lord. You have given me things. You cannot trade objects for affection. You cannot buy what I offer."

His voice very low and his eyes deep glassy seas, he asked, "What is it you can offer, Tempest?"

"Only myself, that's all. What can a woman give but the love of her heart, the fruit of her body, and the strength of her will. The man I love would be companion, protector, faithful lover, and trusted counsel. Those things cannot be bought elsewhere and prettily wrapped. Could you freely give me those things, my lord?"

"I wish I could," he answered in quiet regret.

"Then do not ask me to love you."

His fingers crooked behind her neck to bring her to him. His kiss was tender, twisting her emotions with a claiming demand. She surrendered to it with a helpless ecstasy, then lay breathless in his embrace.

How strange and wonderful it was to enjoy the closeness of a woman without being pressured to demand more. Oh, he still wanted her. That longing was like an endless simmer on baking coals. But this was good too, and that puzzled him. To hold her, to look upon her, listen to her low, crooning voice was enough to satisfy him, and he didn't know why it should.

"Thank you, sweet, for being a comfort to me. You eased the bitter sting of an old painful wound, and I will do the same for you. I promise. You will love me, Tempest. As sure as day falls into night, you will be mine, and I will not hurt you. Be careful lest you break my heart."

He kissed the top of her head and released her, but she was reluctant to go. Her hands pressed to his face, rubbing the prominent cheekbones. His quiet eyes were cool tranquil ponds in sharp contrast to the thick black lashes.

"Connor, if I was Holly Amberson, I would love you fiercely, but as Tempest Swift, I cannot." Her kiss was a shock of passion; then she sprang from his bed and was gone.

Tyler looked up with a welcoming smile from his breakfast plate. He had no time to utter a sound of surprise as a fist caught him hard and well-placed on the jaw.

Jonathan smiled as his granddaughter swept into his study. The sight of her revitalized his tired spirits.

"Good morning, child. I am happy to see you. Sit. We have some things to discuss concerning you and Amberly."

Tempest took a chair. The fondness in her expression was no affectation for she was genuinely devoted to the older man. For all his bluster, he was a dear

239

kind soul. And he had raised Connor.

"Holly, it is my wish that my estate go to you. I had thought to place it with Connor until you are twenty-one or wed if you've no objection to his serving as your guardian."

"I have none. Connor loves Amberly. He will see well to its interests and mine. If I might suggest—"

"What, child?" he prompted gently, watching the slim fingers knead together on her lap.

"I would prefer you leave Amberly to Connor."

Jonathan sat back, dumbfounded. "Why would you ask that?"

Tempest answered slowly, measuring her every word. She knew she was dangerously overstepping Connor's directives and would have to be very careful. "I have been gone a long time. Amberly is but a fond memory to me. To Connor, it is everything. I could easily exist on an allowance, but he needs the responsibility of having all this."

"Does Connor know of this?" the old man asked shrewdly.

"No, and I daresay he would be quite angry if he did." That was true enough. "I only want what is fair."

"And what of Tyler?"

"I have had no use for Tyler since he broke my Jilly," she pouted.

Jonathan chuckled, remembering that row as if it had been a week past and not half a score of years. "Ah, yes, Jilly."

"I have never forgiven him," she declared flatly. "He was mean then and still is."

240

"Connor always was your favorite," he mused. Then the jowled face drooped. "Holly, Connor is not the same boy who once championed your fights. That is why I didn't deed all to him. He is—different."

"How so?"

"Disillusioned, hard, uncaring. Are you in love with him?"

The question caught her by surprise. "Of course. He's my cousin."

"Is that why you spent the night with him?"

Tempest felt the heat rush to her face. "But we did nothing. I mean—he was—I merely—"

Jonathan raised a hand to halt her stammering and repeated firmly, "Do you love Connor?"

"Yes," was the small reply.

"And what of him?"

"I don't know. I mean he doesn't know how I feel," she mumbled awkwardly. "He would not take me seriously."

"Even with Amberly in the balance?" At her blank look, he smiled. "You are wise not to involve yourself there. Connor has many things to discover for himself before he is going to be of any use to you or Amberly."

"I know," she confided sadly. "He told me about his father."

"He told you?" Jonathan was frankly stunned. "Connor? What did he tell you?"

"That he was responsible for Uncle Samuel's death. Is it true? What he said was quite dreadful."

Jonathan's eyes grew heavy with grief as he remembered back. "Dreadful? Yes, it was. Senseless. Tragic."

She waited for him to go on but seeing his difficulty refrained from any urging. She let it come slowly and was still while the details were laid out. Painfully, he related the story of how Samuel had taken Connor and Tyler out shooting. Always jealous rivals, the boys had made a competition of it, eager to best one another. They had rushed ahead flushed with a reckless excitement, leaving Samuel to follow more prudently. Hungry for his father's attention, Connor had been desperate to impress him. A bird flew up in a thicket, and he fired before it cleared the brush. When the boys hurried back to the site, they found Samuel Amberson. He had been killed instantly by a shot through the temple. Panicked, Tyler had run back to Amberly, but by the time riders had returned, they could find no sign of boy or father. The darkness had prevented them from searching the brush. At dawn, they had discovered Connor cradling his father's ruined head in his arms on the front steps of Amberly. He was freezing cold and in such deep shock he couldn't be convinced that the stiffened body he had dragged through the long night had no life left in it.

"He was fourteen years old. He never shed one tear, not then and not at the funeral. I remember how angry that made me at the time, for he had sobbed for days over his mother. I guess he had nothing left by then."

"What happened to Aunt Jilly?"

"A double tragedy there. Her child was due to arrive in less than a month. It was just a chill, but she was gone in less than three days. By the time we realized how serious it was, we couldn't get a doctor in time to save her or the child. Connor was inconsolable. It was to lift his spirits that Samuel took them out shooting. I sent the boy back to school. I thought it would be best for him to get away from here, but I think I was wrong. Perhaps if he had stayed, he could have dealt with his guilt. He never has. He's never spoken of his parents since then; that's why I was so surprised to hear he had told you. I heard of Tyler's cruelty, and I mean to deal harshly with him."

"I already have," she said smoothly.

Jonathan smiled. How good it was to have her back. How good she might be for Connor. Perhaps she could curb his idle restlessness. "I shall think on what you've asked. Do not say anything of our conversation to anyone else, especially Connor."

"I won't. Thank you." She went and put her arms impulsively about his shoulders. Her quick kiss on the fleshy cheek made him chuckle.

"None of that, puss. You'll not make up my mind for me."

"Why, Grandfather, I would not do such a thing," she teased.

Tempest paused in the foyer, arrested by the sight of Connor Amberson as he descended the grand staircase, every inch the stately lord, his features clear and composed. There was no sign of the drunken mourner who had clung to her in wretched grief. The sleepy eyes warmed when they touched on her.

"Good morning, Cousin. I was about to take in

243

some air. Would you care to join me for a stroll?"

"I would like that," she answered as their eyes caressed one another.

"First, I've some business to attend to."

Tempest followed him into the dining room. He recoiled as Tyler glanced up in surly humor. His fine jaw sported a large purplish lump.

Connor tossed a handful of bills atop his empty plate. "Your winings, Tyler. You earned it. Perhaps we'll play for higher stakes some day, just you and I, if you are not too timid to go out with me alone."

Tyler sneered as he scooped up the money, but the fierce brilliance in the pale eyes prevented him from commenting. He knew he had done well to escape with only a bruise from his titian-haired cousin. Now he knew where her loyalty lay, and that, too, was displeasing.

Taking Tempest's arm in tense fingers, Connor led her out into the cool peace of the morning. He paused on the damp lawn to draw a deep breath, his eyes closing until he had expelled it slowly. He smiled down at her and patted the hand tucked in his crooked arm.

"What do you think of all this?" he asked, the sweep of his arm encompassing the vast acres spreading far beyond what the eye could see.

"It's all foreign to me," she replied. "I feel I am in some dream, a captive princess awaiting her rescue. Are you my Sir Galahad?"

Connor took a step back, his expression odd. "Why would you call me that?" he demanded tersely.

"It was a jest, my lord. I did not mean to put you

out of countenance."

"Where did you hear that name?" His grip on her arm tightened unintentionally.

"From a story read to me as a child. Good heavens, whatever is wrong?"

He forced himself to relax, not wondering until later who would read to her in the illiterate Swift family. He managed to smile, though the strange shaky feeling persisted. "It's nothing. Forgive me for startling you."

Tempest eyed him uneasily. His stare was too bright as if looking through her. "Perhaps we should go back in. You have guests to see to."

"Let them tend themselves," he grumbled uncharitably, then relented at her pointed frown. "I suppose I should. I'm supposed to be on my best behavior." He looked away from her unable to dispel the chill of déjà vu.

Tempest went to change her sodden slippers, then hurried along the hall, hoping not to be apprehended by one of their company. She was too uncomfortable with the frivolous talk to seek it out, always fearing some slip would betray her and Connor. She slowed her steps when she heard the pleasant cadence of his voice from one of the salons and, before she realized it, was privy to his conversation with Loretta Martel.

"How long are you going to closet yourself away from London, Connie? It is dreadfully boring without you there."

"If all goes well, the wait will seem insignificant,

245

sweet."

Tempest flinched at that. She had assumed the endearment was one he held for her. She was about to withdraw in upset when the lady's next phrase stunned her.

"When we marry, will we have to spend much time here? It is so isolated from everything I enjoy."

"You no longer enjoy my company?" was the smooth reply.

"Oh, Connie, don't vex me so. You know perfectly well what I mean."

"Indeed I do. Be forewarned. When Amberly is mine, it will be my home."

"And for your little urchin as well?"

"Pull in your claws, Loretta. She will be gone as soon as her part is done."

That statement weighted heavily on Connor's thoughts. It was hard to envision Amberly without Tempest or, in fact, his life without her. Loretta Martel would never be a part of either. When he looked into the slanted green eyes, there was no warming spark in his soul. Her whining complaints were an irritant to his ears. He couldn't dismiss her too quickly, aware that Jonathan had sought her out the previous day for a battery of questions, very discreet but probing. To spurn her now would risk too much. He would have to endure as best he could, though the thought of intimacy with her left him with an awkward distastefulness. Ah well, it could not be helped and would not be for much longer. Her loathing of the country life would discourage her from pursuing him.

After a rather extensive search, Connor found his pseudo-cousin in the solarium. In her muslin gown and with her reedlike figure, she could well have been one of the fragile stemmed blossoms that thrived in the hothouse year around. She was one exotic variety he wished to see permanently transplanted to Amberly.

"I've been looking for you, sweet," he said warmly when she glanced up from her concentrated musings. She seemed to wince.

"I was hiding from our guests. Rather cowardly of me, I confess." She managed a smile to hold the sting behind her eyes. She stood so he wouldn't be tempted to join her on the bench. Instead, he came to stand so close she had to crane her neck to read his expression. His presence was engulfing and exciting despite her wish to remain unaffected.

"I must go to London for a few days to see to several tedious duties my title forces upon me. It would not seem such a chore if you were with me. I could show you Hyde Park, Almack's, and Vauxhall. Or we wouldn't have to go out at all." His tone was rich with suggestion and a preference for the latter choice. In truth, it didn't matter as long as he had her company.

Tempest thanked him prettily but declined. "I think I could better serve your purpose if I remain here. The sooner I convince your Grandfather, the sooner I can return to my own life."

Connor frowned, disappointed and piqued. "You

247

say that as though you are anxious to leave. Do you find it that unpleasant?"

"I am out of water here. What you take for granted is frightfully abnormal to me. I don't wish to live a dream. I miss being myself and being with those I love. The luxuries of wealth are a pleasing distraction but not for daily consumption."

"Like me?" he asked shortly.

"You are an extravagant fare I could never develop a taste for, my lord. My palate is too simple. The man I spend my life with will be of coarse cloth, not silk. I will work beside him, not be a slave to him."

That brought a protest to his lips, but he held it back, saying instead, "I have given my word. You may go when all is done. Hurry it if you wish, but the sight of you here does not displease me."

"You will find other more pleasing sights, my lord, and will forget my plain face."

"Plain, no. Forget, never." He took another step bringing them almost flush. "I wish you would reconsider and come with me."

"No, my lord. It is better this way." He would not be alone, she was ruefully reminded herself.

"Have I made you angry?" he asked suddenly, warned by the glitter in her bright blue eyes.

"Of course not. When do you go?"

"After lunch. George and I are riding in with several of the guests."

How convenient, she thought cynically. "Have a safe journey," was all she said, her voice sweet and well-meaning, belying the snap of her eyes.

"I will miss you, sweet Tempest. Think of me

often," he urged huskily.

"Conceited lout," she pronounced, invoking a chuckle, then a response she wasn't prepared for.

His arms closing about her tiny waist, he smashed her to his chest, his mouth descending on her up-turned lips with a desperate hunger, twisting and demanding. She held to him just as frantically, her slender arms twining about his neck and stretching up on tiptoes to savor his kiss more completely. Still clinging to him, she laid her head on his chest, hypnotized by the rapid tempo of his heart beneath the fine cut of his coat and the quick rushes of his breath in her tossled hair. Slowly, her arms uncurled, her fingers kneading his hair, then sliding along the hard muscled line of his shoulders and arms until they enmeshed with his.

"Connor—"

"What is it, sweet?"

"Enjoy your trip. Good-bye."

She pushed away and fled before the wetness on her cheeks betrayed her.

Watching the earl's fancy coach pull away with a heaviness she couldn't dispel, Tempest was startled by a soft footfall behind her. She turned to see Katherine Amberson regarding her with a wry smile.

"I'm surprised you would let your protector leave without you," she said caustically. Tempest felt intimidated by the cold stare. The woman meant her no good, and alone, she was vulnerable to the larger woman's acid tongue.

"Connor? Why would you say that?" She tried to match the other's composure with an airy disregard.

Katherine let all pretenses drop, her expression hardening into a threatening malice. "Don't bother trying to fob me off, Missy. I don't know what brothel my devious nephew found you in, but I know you are not Holly Amberson. I don't care to know what your name is, but be advised, you scheming chit, you will not succeed. Connor is clever, and you are a convincing little piece, but I will expose your plot for the deception it is. Don't rest too easily in this house, jade. You are about to find yourself back in the streets and Connor with you. Do not mistake me for a fool like that idiot, Jonathan. I will dig and keep digging until I can prove all you say is a lie. My son will have the Amberson fortune, not Connor, and you will never see a penny."

Tempest stood agog as the woman marched off with a frosty dignity. Once alone, she collapsed upon a low chaise. Her first thought was to run for Connor, for the safety he offered in the strength of his arms. But those arms would not be waiting or empty. She could seek out Jonathan, but what could she tell him? That Katherine was accusing her of being an impostor? Why plant the idea in his mind? She would have to continue the pretense and avoid the woman until Connor returned. Then what? What could he do if his aunt found such proof? What would prevent him from claiming he was a victim as well? Would he be so heartless as to turn on her to save himself, making the whole plot seem her doing?

Confused and upset, Tempest barricaded herself in

her room and began to pace. Her thoughts were wild and fearful, building up until she was certain she would face the full blame and go to prison. Why would an arrogant lord about to inherit a fortune risk it for the sake of a backstreet thief? She knew there was no honor among robbers. Was that true of liars as well, for Connor Amberson was a prince of liars, wooing her with tender words while planning to marry his mistress. He didn't care about her. He was only courting her cooperation.

A tap on her window made her gasp and whirl about. Then her startled surprise became a joyous weeping. She opened the casement and pulled in her brother from his teetering position on the trellis, hugging him until he squirmed in protest. When she released him and stepped away, his grin froze.

Eddie looked at the woman before him and saw a stranger. Only the vaguest hint of his sister lingered in the bright teary eyes, the rest had vanished, swallowed by this regal, sophisticated beauty with coiffed hair, perfumed skin, and stylish garb. He hung back, his eyes wide and uncertain with this unfamiliar lady.

"Eddie? What is it?" she asked in alarm.

"You look so different, is all. Here I've gone and got you all grubby with my hands."

He looked so unhappy, she couldn't help but laugh and hug him again in spite of his reluctance. "It's me, you goose. Still the same under all this nonsense. Why are you here? How did you find me?"

Eddie complied with her gesture that he join her on the foot of the bed, painfully conscious of his griminess in the posh setting. "Just wanted to see for myself that you was all right and that his lordship was doing right by you. Este, what is it? Has the blackguard harmed you?"

Tempest leaned against the narrow shoulder and surrendered to the consuming sobs. Inside, she ached with an empty hurt that would never heal as long as its cause was near.

"I want to go home," she wept miserably. "I'm tired of playing someone I'm not and pretending to be what I'm not. I want to leave this place. I want my family."

"He won't let you go?" Eddie growled in outrage.

"I gave my word. I signed my name. Papa's counting on me. I cannot disappoint him."

"To hell with fancy face. Papa will understand. He wouldn't want you unhappy."

"But the money—"

"We'll get it somehow. We wasn't doing so bad before he come along." His dark eyes cast about in avarice. "Cor, lookit all this. If we took all we could carry—"

"No." Her reply was sharp and final. "We take nothing from here. Do you hear me, Eddie? Nothing."

He scowled but nodded. " The horse is tied up a ways away. Come on. What's to keep you? You don't owe his lordship anything. We can take care of ourselves. What say, Este?"

"But if he comes after me?"

"He won't find you, and he won't look for long. Come on home."

Tempest chewed her lip, then said determinedly,

"Give me a minute to change. I can't ride like this."

While she was gone, Eddie was busy filling his pockets. He met her return with a smile. "Say good-bye to the good life, Este."

"Let's just go," she answered gruffly.

Chapter Seventeen

Connor stared long into his wineglass, telling himself as he had on every evening for the past three weeks that he didn't care, that it didn't matter, and that it was time to go on. And as on each occasion, he could not convince himself. The anger that had driven him for the first days had given way to a listless apathy. He hadn't moped or brooded. He had done nothing. He had been able to find no motive for even the simplest task, locking himself up in Grosvenor Square with orders to Rogers to keep everyone out. George had finally gotten past him to stare in mute horror at the unshaven, hollowed-eyed man in rumpled, obviously slept in clothes. Tentatively, George had suggested he see a physician for something to help him sleep, prompting the first amusement Connor had had for some time. Would the doctor be able to diagnosis a broken heart, he had wondered wryly.

When he had found Tempest gone, he had been

bewildered, but when he had discovered a scruffy boy had been asking after her and all the jewels had been missing, he had become enraged. But the surly lad would tell him nothing, cheeky enough to laugh at his threats. Even when he had vowed that Will Swift would never see the color of his money, father and son had been indifferent. He could search the sewers for years, they had warned, but he would never find her. He had known they were right. The streets she knew would swallow her up without a trace.

He hadn't returned to Amberly. He couldn't bear that. He had lost too many he cared for there to face its emptiness. It would also mean explaining to his grandfather, and he had been able to find no courage for that task. Let him believe whatever lies Katherine and Tyler conceived. It no longer mattered.

Connor looked up at the elegant surroundings, having heard scarcely a jot of what his hostess was saying. Lady Jersey may have been one of the most influential women of ton, but to him she didn't exist. Nor did any of the other milling socialites on this overly warm evening. It had been a mistake for him to let George convince him to attend this flat rout. He managed another lackluster smile and nodded in response to whatever the lady was going on about.

"Lord Amberson," a footman announced stiffly. "There is a 'person' here to see you. He would not be put off so I showed him into a back salon."

Vaguely curious, Connor followed him to the small, discreetly tucked away room where his caller waited. His surprise was monumental, but it never showed in his suave features.

"What business do you have with me?" he asked

255

crisply, closing the doors behind him. "I told you I'd give you no money."

Eddie Swift turned his sullen expression on him, but the dark eyes were bright with agitation. He tried to adopt a humble manner, but the sight of the coolly superior Connor Amberson made his teeth grind. "I don't want nothing to do with your fat purse, my lord. I ain't here to beg."

"Then why?" The sharp command brought their eyes together in hostile challenge.

"Not for me. I'd never come to the likes of you. It's for Este."

"Why should I care about anything to do with her?"

"She needs your help."

Connor drew a quick breath. "Is she with child?"

Eddie's face blanked with shock, then fused a hot crimson of embarrassed fury. "No. She's in Newgate." His look clearly said he wasn't sure which was worse. "Without your generosity, we had to take back to the roads to keep off the leeches. We was doing real fine too until we had a bad turn of luck. Got the drop on us, the fine noble and his fancy whore. Este couldn't get loose, and he took her away in his coach at gunpoint. She was taken afore the magistrate. The blackguard didn't have no care for her being just a girl and so young and all. He locked her up in that foul place like she done murdered the fat prig instead of trying to help herself to his small change. She's in that place, locked up tight like the meanest of criminals, and I can't get her out."

"Is she all right?" The question was terse and quietly asked.

256

"She's in prison. How do you think she is?" He was wrong to have thought this haughty nobleman would show any interest or concern. Feeling desperate and angry at having to come to this man, he began to pace.

Connor's smile was cold, and his acidic comment cutting. "Still leaving her behind? She should find a braver partner. Again, why should I want to help her? What are you to me?"

Eddie's face was flushed with the heat of temper. Only his frantic reason kept him from striking the pompous bastard. His words shook with anger and upset. "Este said she trusted you. She should have listened to me. I told her you was up to no good."

"If you listened to your own advice, why come to me?"

"I didn't have nowheres else to go." His eyes dropped in a trapped frustration, his jaw working fiercely to hold back the frightened pleas that were building up to demand he swallow his pride. Connor's searing words dashed any hope.

"Your sister can rot in prison. I will not help her."

The dark eyes flashed up all shiny black and filled with hate. "She won't. They're going to hang her."

Even the stark, oppressive room Tempest was led to could not dim the aura of elegant importance that exuded from the man who waited for her. She had taken a quick step forward with the intention of rushing into his arms when the chill of his pale eyes froze her. Confused and uncertain, she waited for some sign from him that would explain why he had come when his look was so unyielding.

"My lord, what brings you here?" she asked with a brittle calm.

Even in the drab, shapeless prison garb, her beauty held him for a long, constrictive moment before the aloof stare of her bright blue eyes reminded him of her desertion. That killed his mounting ardor with a swift stroke.

"Your brother."

"Eddie? Eddie went to you?" she gasped in disbelief.

"He asked me to save your life." He paused, letting the hopes and desperation build in her expression. His gaze dropped to rake down her shabby appearance as if gauging her worth. It hesitated briefly on the heavy manacles that circled her chafed wrists like bold, dirty bracelets. "I can do so, but first, there are some things you must understand."

Her tired spirit gave a proud rumbling at his sneering tone, the drooping shoulders squared in the sacky dress, and the determined chin came up so her eyes met his directly. "What things, sir?"

"I own you, Tempest. Your life is mine, bought and paid for at a great personal expense and sacrifice to me. You will come with me and do whatever I tell you. I will brook no complaint or disobedience."

"Or what?" she asked tightly.

"Or you'll be back here awaiting the completion of your sentence."

"Not much of a choice," she said sarcastically, but her mind was reeling with shock. Surely he was not serious.

"But it is yours to make. Come with me now or

stay. I will not make a second offer." He waited, his heavy eyes assessing her cynically. He could almost hear the panicked working of her thoughts, but he had her, and he knew it. Strangely, that gave him no joy.

"I will go with you," she said quietly. Her voice was firm with no trace of submission or anger as if she accepted his proposal without reservation.

"Take those off," he instructed the matron, gesturing to her cuffed hands. "Perhaps I should save them lest you be tempted to flee from me again."

The carriage ride was ominously silent. Tempest sat stiffly on her seat, staring down at her hands beneath Connor's unwavering stare. She didn't dare ask any questions of him or betray any curiosity when they stopped at their puzzling destination.

The Swan With Two Necks was a large inn and coach stop. Its two stories overlooked a huge yard filled with all nature of conveyances from small carriages bearing weary travelers to the grand mail coaches of maroon and black with scarlet wheels and a royal coat of arms emblazoned on its door. Brass horns sounded from the boot by a guard in royal scarlet livery to clear a path for the lathered team.

Without a word, Connor draped his Garrick about her and stepped down. When he offered no assistance, she hopped to the ground in an awkward tangle of broadcloth and hurried after him. After claiming a room for George Morely and ordering up a bath, he climbed the stairs, sparing no backward glance to assure himself that she was following.

Their room was of a good size with a large inviting bed and windows overlooking the gallery and courtyard. When Tempest sat wearily on the turned-back bed, delighting in its promising softness, the crack of Connor's voice was as sharp as a slap.

"Get up. Don't foul my bed with those offensive rags. If you must sit, do it by the open window where the stench can air out. I am going down for something to eat. Since you obviously cannot join me dressed like that, you will stay here until the hot water is delivered, then scrub every trace of that smell from you before I return." His pale heavy-eyed stare was piercing. "Think of your pretty neck before you consider running from me again." With that dire warning, he strode from the room.

Thankfully, Tempest didn't have long to wait for the gallons of steaming water to be carried up. She didn't need Connor's command to scour her skin with a vengeance, but even that could not take the stench from her nostrils. She refused to think about that nightmare or her present circumstances. Being a slave to Connor Amberson might be bruising to her pride, but it held no comparison to the horrors she had experienced. Nothing he could do to her could be that terrible. Connor might be angry and unkind, but he would never mistreat her. For the first time in weeks, she felt safe.

Her stomach rumbling in empty complaint, she looked about. There was nothing for her to put on save the gown she had discarded and nothing could persuade her to let its coarse cloth touch her body. Hungry and cold, she finally slipped between the fresh sheets to await Connor's return. She was sure his tense silence would not be of long duration and was not anticipating the tirade to come. And then there was the fact of only one bed. Worry could not hold her mind attentive. She never heard the chambermaid remove the rancid tub with a cocked brow, nor did she hear, some hours later, his lordship's arrival.

When Connor first entered the darkened room, for a panicked instant he thought it to be empty. Then he heard the quiet sound of breathing from the bed. He went to sit on the edge and stared glumly at her delicate profile. Now what was he to do? He had purposefully stayed down in the taproom until his senses grew fuzzy under the pretense that he was teaching her a lesson. But he knew it was because the sight of her was more than his wavering control could manage. Seeing her in the dreadful gaol, filthy and unkempt, had nearly broken him. It had cost him every fragment of his will to hold himself from scooping her up in a protective crush. But then she was the one who had left him. She had chosen crime over his gifts and poverty over luxury. She hadn't appealed to him for help. She hadn't even looked pleased to see him. She was only here because of his bold conditions, and now he was held from any tenderness toward her because of those harsh words.

Sighing heavily, he touched a light hand to her cheek and was sent sprawling to the floor.

The feel of his hand had woken Tempest with a jarring protest. "No," she snarled, striking out at the shadowy figure with all her might, then rolled up on hands and knees, crouching and panting, ready to launch a new defensive.

"Do you plan to murder me?"

The aggrieved voice brought awareness of time and place back to her with a jolt. She lit the lamp and looked down to see Connor sitting on the floor, his hand covering his eye.

"You startled me, my lord. I am truly sorry. It has been a time since I've rested easy."

When his hand lowered gingerly, she gave a gasp of dismay.

"Oh, I have hurt you."

"I believe you meant to," he grumbled as he glanced up. The hurt in his eye was instantly forgotten as other cauterizing agonies awoke. In her alarm, Tempest had forgotten she wore nothing but the lingering scent of the bath oil. Connor sat in numb paralysis as she bent down to apply a damp cloth from the washbasin to his already swelling lid.

His lust was shocked from him by another sight, one that brought a deep angry frown. Marring the smooth creaminess of Tempest's back and buttocks were long ugly welts and bruises, the likes of which he had seen at the hand of an irate schoolmaster with a heavy rod.

Noticing his concentrated stare, Tempest pulled the covers up around her nakedness with a challenging glare.

"Who beat you?" he demanded in a low growl.

"Some are not as tolerant of my rebelliousness as you, my lord," she remarked with a wry smile.

"For what offense were you taken to task?"

"It was not necessary for one to do anything. Newgate is not a very pleasant place." Her eyes dropped evasively, her will struggling to suppress the flood of memory that would support that claim. Her sudden quiet only deepened Connor's look of fury.

"Why were you beaten like that?" he repeated again.

"All men are not as well bred as you, sir. They do not ask if you mind or like to be told no."

Even before the first tear slipped unwanted down her pale face, his arms were about her so tight she had no room to tremble.

"Ah, damme, Tempest, did the vile beasts hurt you? I swear to God I'll see any man who touched you in irons." His voice was rough with emotion, growing even lower when he asked gruffly. "Were you forced against your will?"

"No, my lord," she said softly to calm the tension she could feel coiling dangerously in him. "I'm too handy with my fives, and there were too many others who hadn't as much fight."

Too relieved to speak, he simply held her, his face buried in the soft curls. Finally, he asked in frustration, "Why didn't you send word to me? I would have seen you free of that place in less than a day."

Her answer was very small and fragilely spoken. "To know you did not come because you did not know was easier for me to bear than to know you did not come because you did not care."

"Why didn't your brother come to me first? Why did he wait until you had suffered such abuse?"

Tempest stiffened at his condemning tone. "Do not find fault with Eddie. He would never have thought to seek you out if he hadn't tried all else."

"At least he had the sense to, even as a last resort. I hate to think of you in such a place."

263

"It was where I deserved to be, my lord. I was fairly tried and convicted."

"Of your own foolishness. Now you have me to see to your interests, and there will be no more foolishness. Is that understood?"

"Yes, my lord," she murmured meekly, content to be in the safe haven of his arms.

"You are mine, Tempest Swift, for as long as I want you. And this moment, I want you. Would you say no to my taking my rightful thanks?"

The bright head gave a slight shake. He tipped up her chin with a gentle hand, his eyes consuming and fired with desire.

"I would have done anything to save you. But only for myself," he told her. Then he was kissing her, deeply as one who had felt the gnawing of starvation and was eager to be fed. She sat quietly as his kisses scattered urgently over her face, hearing his breath quicken with impatient passion. His weight pressed her down on her back, the sheet swept away by the brush of his hand. His touch brought a flush of heat to the supple flesh it sought to conquer.

Panting with the struggle to slow his eagerness, Connor reluctantly sat back to look into the sapphire eyes that regarded him so candidly. There was no desire in that stare, but no objection either. She was simply waiting for him to take his pleasure docilely, almost in resignation. That was not what he wished, but his need for her would allow for no wait. She would come to him willingly soon enough.

As he worked down the row of shirt buttons, he said softly, "You are mine, Tempest. It is a yoke you'll not find difficult to carry. I will see you want

264

for nothing. You will never know cold or hunger or abuse again. I will be so good to you."

Tempest said nothing. She was too tired to protest, too weak in spirit to find reason to. She loved him, and he had saved her life. The more complicated aspects of that could wait until tomorrow. For now, all she needed was for him to push away the nightmare of the past weeks, for his loving to soothe those fears even if she couldn't claim his love.

Though the white-hot urgency in his loins demanded he take her quickly, it was a moment he had dreamed of for too long to let insistent lust rush him through it. He bent down to fasten his mouth on her warm fragrant flesh, covering the puckered scar, the memento of their first meeting. His hands cupped her small breasts, kneading them gently until the points rose hard and aching against his palms, encouraging him to draw on the tight pinnacles and tease them with quick darts of his tongue.

Suddenly with a moaning sob, her resistance was gone. "Connor, please come to me. I want you so. Now, Connor, please."

"You have me, sweet," he murmured, his lips coming up to take hers victoriously. He couldn't fathom why she would deny him so hotly, then beg for him as if he was her every desire. He would make it so. No woman could hold such passion if there was no emotion behind it. She had to care for him, or her kisses wouldn't burn in harmony with his, she wouldn't hold to him so desperately as if molding them into one, she wouldn't say his name with such sighing bliss or receive him with such hungry need. If

265

she cared, why didn't she tell him? Didn't she know how he longed to hear such words from her?

Tempest cried out softly at his first deep thrust, filling her to an exacting degree where more would bring discomfort and less dissatisfaction. It was this moment that had tortured her thoughts while she lay in prison waiting to die, this magical joining of one with another, the only time Connor Amberson was truly hers. Every inch of her body tingled in anticipation of his touch, its inner pulse growing quick and urgent as his sleek, hard body moved above her. Greedily, her lips parted for his kiss, seeking to devour him. But still it wasn't enough. She wanted more of him, all of him with a frantic excitement she had known only those few times in his embrace. She surged up to greet him with all the vigor in her young body, holding tightly to the rippling swells of his shoulders, her hands plying his taut flesh in encouraging caresses.

Then he was still, causing her eyes to open in objecting question. His were staring down at her intensely with a glassy fire, reflecting lights that seemed to glimmer endlessly deep into the soul of him, drawing her into them helplessly. She stretched up to kiss him, but he held himself away, imprisoning her in that brilliant prismed gaze.

"Tempest, tell me that you love me," he crooned in a low hushed voice that was a tantalizing caress to her senses.

She tore her eyes away from his probing stare, all atremble with urgency but retaining enough reason to know she couldn't surrender all to him. He would be too ruthless with such knowledge.

"No, Connor. Please," she whispered as his hot mouth burned upon the tender flesh of her neck, flaming her passion with a heat to sear all sanity. Her fingers clenched in the midnight hair, and her trembling form arched up against him.

"Tell me, sweet," he coaxed, tormenting her with the sensuous flicker of his tongue over the soft, yielding fullness of her lips. "A simple matter. Yes or no. Do you love me?"

"Please," she moaned in anguish, panting and writhing as he began a slow, agonizing rhythm, taunting and frustrating the impatient demands of her body. He trapped her tossing head between his hands, stilling it so she could not turn away from his plunging stare and the warm brush of his breath against her flushed face.

"Tell me."

"Connor, don't," she pleaded, tears glistening in her vulnerable eyes while her body strained for its own answer in traitorous need.

"Do you love me, Tempest? Do you love me?" he repeated hypnotically, his stare penetrating her resistance to read her heart.

"Yes," she wailed as if the confession had broken her will and done some terrible hurt. While she sobbed miserably, he covered her face with kisses, his leisurely movements quickening to a hard, driving pulse to bring their already sharpened senses to a sudden soaring spectacular end.

In that quiet aftermath, Connor touched her wet face and asked tenderly, "Tell me again."

No strength left to deny what he already knew, Tempest squeezed her eyes shut to blot out his pleased smile. "I love you, Connor. I love you." Her voice was but a constricted whisper. She felt his shaky laugh and let him kiss her deeply, but his words twisted her heart.

"I knew you would. Oh, sweet, you've made me so happy. Now I truly have you. You won't be sorry. I'll cherish what you've given me."

Her reply was low and hoarse with painful certainty. "No, you won't, my lord." With that, she rolled away from him and cried bitter tears while he lay silent and bewildered.

It was very late, but Tempest lay awake half listening to the irregular influx of travelers to and from the busy inn. Though her tears had long since dried, her heart ached with a heavy sadness, knowing she had lost something dear to her, the freedom of her will. Connor Amberson had bought her body and now possessed her soul as well. Her fragile spirit was at his mercy in hands that could show great tenderness or crush destructively.

Connor muttered in his sleep and rolled against her. He was warm and virile, and wretchedly, she adored the closeness of him. His arm looped about the curve of her waist in what could have been an innocent gesture had it not been for the errant thumb's maddening circle about the tight peak of her breast. Tiny nips along her shoulder and neck extracted an exquisite shiver, but she forced herself to lie still and unresponsive.

"Are you awake, my sweet?"

"Would it inconvenience you if I was not?"

Her tart reply brought a low chuckle of appreciation. "Some, but I would not be discouraged. I find it hard to rest near so tempting a distraction." His hand had become bolder, stroking down her smooth stomach to steal between creamy thighs.

" 'Twas not my intent to be so, my lord. If you wish to sleep, perhaps I can find another room." Her voice was strained and breathless in her struggle to remain aloof, but, oh, what delightfully wicked things he was doing.

"That is not my wish at all," he purred silkily. "You'll not leave me again, Tempest. I want you always within my reach, day or night, whenever I desire you. You are too important to roam free. You will be at my side when I seek your company and beneath me when I seek other pleasures, and I will treat you royally."

"Whatever you wish, my lord. You own me now." Her flat despondent vow went undetected as he made a pleased sound.

"You are mine, sweet Tempest, and I mean to use you well."

At that promise, his touch prepared the way for the hard press of his body, piercing her with a claiming thrust. Closing her eyes, she lay stiffly while his ragged breath panted against her neck. An insistent touch urged her to a quickening of the sensation she sought to deny. She bit her lip until tears came to her eyes, but still she couldn't hold off that sudden push that burst her restraint with a flaring shower of ecstasy.

Then she was moving with him in eager harmony until his embrace squeezed her tightly, threatening to crush her. With a contented murmur, he held her to his slack, spent frame, a light kiss brushing her shoulder before he buried his face in her fragrant curls and let sleep take him once more.

Chapter Eighteen

Connor woke with a start, finding no comforting warmth at his side. His eyes snapped open to be greeted with a rewarding sight. Limp with relief, he let himself doze a moment longer until the enticing picture of Tempest poised on the window sill clad only in his coat teased him back to wakefulness.

Lying silently, he watched her for some time, marveling over her profile, the tossled crown of burnished copper, the clear, china blue eyes with their fringe of inky lashes, the impudent tilt of her nose, the pair of red lips that pouted and smiled with equal fascination, the determined chin that contrasted with her deceivingly helpless appeal and the supple contours of her body hidden in the folds of his jacket. He had never been so captivated by a single set of features and continued to gaze in rapt attention as he hoped to every morning hence.

A brusque knock was followed by the bright intrusion of an orange-topped head.

"Good morning," George called cheerily. He strode in quite unembarrassed to deposit several bulky boxes

271

on the bed. His gaze scarcely touched on his friend as covetous eyes lingered on a pair of trim legs. Connor had exquisite taste in all things. "Clothes for the lady and good news for you, Conn. I've managed to arrange everything at no little cost just as you wanted it. We're expected in two hours. Is that time enough?"

"Time for what?" Tempest asked suspiciously at Connor's warning signal George didn't see in time. "What have you arranged, George?"

Smiling apologetically, George stammered, "Breakfast. I'll meet you downstairs."

After his hasty retreat, Tempest stood down from the casement, her eyes narrowing. "What ceremony, my lord?"

"Get dressed. We haven't much time, and I am famished," he said in rapid evasion, swinging off the bed and pulling on his clothes.

Frowning warily, Tempest opened the first large box and gave a small exclamation as she drew out the white satin gown. It was a beautiful piece of work encrusted with pearls and touches of fragile lace. She held it up before her. "This could almost be a—" Bright eyes flashed up in alarm.

"It will suit very nicely," Connor remarked with feigned ease. "Though I had hoped to be a little better dressed for my own wedding. I guess it cannot be helped. Such short notice and all."

When he ran out of words, she was still staring at him in open-mouthed disbelief. "Wedding?" she echoed faintly. "Whom are you marrying?"

"By noontime, you will be an Amberson in truth," he said softly. His head jerked to one side at the force

272

of her slap.

"How dare you!" she shrieked at him. "How dare you make such plans! How dare you assume—without even asking me! No! Never! I wouldn't marry you if my life depended on it!"

"But it does, my sweet," he said quietly, a slow anger beginning to build. This wasn't how he had planned it. His lust for her momentarily sated, it was easy to indulge in a sullen pique. What on earth was she objecting so strenuously for? Hadn't she professed to loving him? His cheek stinging and his eye aching dully, his ill-humor mounted. After all he had done, how dare she be ungrateful.

"I won't have you," she stated hotly, throwing down the lovely gown and kicking it with a bare foot. "Did you think to threaten me into marriage? It was vile enough to be forced to be your mistress, but your wife—never."

Connor grabbed her by the shoulders and gave her a furious shake. For a moment, the unplanned reaction stunned them both; then her jaw squared in belligerent fury, arresting his intent to beg her pardon. Instead, he launched into a harsh fierce attack with words that were more damaging than his hands.

"You have no say in this. I did not ask, because there was no need. You will do exactly as I say. I own you. I bought your miserable life. What you want or think does not matter to me in the least."

"But why must we marry? It cannot be your wish to have me for a wife," she cried frantically.

"It's not wish to have any wife and certainly not one with no breeding or pleasing manner. Do you think I went to the prison officials and said, 'Excuse me but I'd like you to release my mistress'? Do you think they would be impressed by my title or touched by the plight of separated lovers? How do you think I gained your freedom?"

"I—I do not know," she stuttered, quite taken back by the passion of his anger.

"I begged, I swallowed my pride, I crawled to a man I despise." Connor flushed hotly at the remembered humiliation of that desperate scene. "I convinced the judge that you were my new bride, that we'd had a tiff and you were out on a prank to even a score with me. He was amused but insisted I make restitution with the victim and get him to withdraw charges. Imagine my delight to discover you'd robbed my old friend, Dicken Waterston. He made me plead with him, the bastard, and only relented when I agreed to pay his losses plus throw in my best pair of horses and supply him with a copy of my marriage papers. It seems his wife had been eyeing my inseam, and he wanted to be certain I was safely snagged." His teeth ground fiercely as he spun away, his posture tense and unyielding. "So you see, your little escapade cost me more than possibly my estate, so forgive me if I am not more charitable toward you. Why couldn't you have stayed to see our plan through? Why did you have to betray me and force us into this disagreeable position?"

"I did not mean to cause you such trouble," she whispered meekly, intimidated by his towering rage, but he only sneered at her.

"Trouble? You have been nothing but a curse to me since I laid eyes on you. I should have let you bleed to death on that roadside. No more pleasantries. I am done trying to win your favor when you have turned on me at every chance. No more playing the fool. You will marry me and secure me my fortune, and you will do so without complaint or resistance. Put on those clothes now, and come down to breakfast, or go back to your noose and be damned."

With that ultimatum, he stormed from the room, ignoring the very pale face he loved so dearly.

"Good lord, Conn," George exclaimed as the surly gentleman joined his table. "Did she do all that damage this morning?"

Touching his tender eye, he scowled. "This was a misunderstanding." He gestured to his flushed cheek. "This was over her joy at the approaching nuptials."

"I had no idea you hadn't told her. I am sorry if it caused a row."

Connor shrugged. "Don't concern yourself. You couldn't have known I'd be such a coward. There was no time for it last night." He sighed regretfully. There was no hope to return to those blissful moments. "I've ruined it all. Imagine a little nobody refusing me, me a wealthy lord who's stepped over prostrate women for better than ten years."

"Don't marry her then."

"I have to, George. I've no choice in it."

George smiled knowingly. "Conn, you never do anything you're opposed to. You are not fighting this match very hard."

Connor glared; then his expression lost its harsh edge. "Perhaps not. Perhaps it would be the best thing for me if she wasn't so set against it. She won't go through with it. I'll have to let her go."

"I think not, my friend."

Connor half-turned to follow George's gaze and drew a shaky breath. He had always thought her beautiful even in the oversized mannish garb, but this vision sent his heart cartwheeling.

Tempest slowly descended the staircase, drawing all eyes with her elegant poise. Though her dress was highly inappropriate, none would argue that she was stunning. The high-waisted gown was drawn beneath the bosom by a string of pearls, another circling the neck of sheer lace that rose from a ruched bodice to a slender throat and tiny capped sleeves. Lace gloves covered hands that clutched a closed fan, that tight grip the only sign of her upset. More pearls wove through the bright ringlets and dotted her ears. Her features shone with a serenity, soft, untouched, as virginal as the gown.

Silently they breakfasted on cold pigeon pie, grilled kidneys and bacon, buttered toast and coffee, then proceeded to the municipal hall where the well-paid magistrate waited to perform the marriage in a small antechamber.

Tempest was in a daze standing at the side of the man she longed to wed with all her heart had circumstance been different. The words they vowed and repeated were a meaningless hum as she stood stiffly, trying to hold back her tears, beautiful words of love and commitment that were as false as the name she claimed. She maintained her composure until Connor tugged the gold signet ring off his little finger to place on the third of her left hand. Nothing was unusual about a young bride weeping at the exchange of vows or turning her face demurely to receive her new husband's kiss on the cheek instead of the lips.

It was done. Tempest Swift was now Lady Amberson.

Outside the hall, George kissed a very cold, pale cheek in congratulations, then shook Connor's hand.

Not waiting for well-wishes, Connor said briskly, "Close up my house for me, George. We've a stop to make, and then we go to Amberly. I don't care to fuel any rumors just yet, and Waterston pledged his silence. I want no announcements until all is settled at home."

With a fearful Tempest in tow, Connor strode into Swift's tavern, pushing by several patrons who stared after them in open-mouthed awe. After looking at the angelic beauty without recognition for a brief second, Dolly Swift rushed to embrace her daughter with a glad cry. The tearful reunion among the family failed to soften the glowering lord's disposition. After hugs were exchanged with Will and the thin, weathered Dolly, Connor pulled her away and held her at his side to heel.

From out of his coat, Connor lifted a weighty purse and placed it in Will Swift's hand. It was obviously much more than their bargain had called for. The gnarled innkeeper looked up in question.

"Our accounts are settled, Swift. Your daughter is now Lady Amberson." Ignoring their startled gasps, he continued coolly. "You can understand why I'll allow no more visits between you."

Tempest's eyes came up, bright and wide with a frantic disbelief, but he showed her no compassion.

277

"If you need more money, or if you have to get a message to your daughter, leave word with George Morley, but do not attempt to contact her directly. That I will not have."

"No!"

All eyes turned to a panicked Eddie Swift. "You can't have married him, Este. Not him. I didn't have him save you from one prison to go to another." Hot, angry eyes rose to the haughty nobleman. "Had I known what you planned, I never would have asked your help."

"You think she'd be better off dead than with me? No matter. You did not specify how when you came to beg from me."

The calm voice so heavy with contempt snapped Eddie's control. He ventured a hasty ill-timed swing only to have his wrist easily caught and twisted up high behind his back. As he squirmed awkwardly, low words of warning were spoken next to his ear.

"Hear me, boy. I don't wish to see your grubby little face anywhere near my wife. If I do, I'll have you horsewhipped and in gaol. She does not exist in your world any longer, and you best remember that."

A hard push sent Eddie sprawling to the uneven floor boards, and Tempest was instantly crouched at his side. The blue eyes that met his were dark with hatred.

Coldly, Connor told her, "Say your fare-the-wells. You have five minutes."

Connor waited in the taproom, his agitation unapparent in his imperious stance or in the hard eyes that swept the slovenly room. What a mistake he had made, he bemoaned to himself. He had her now, but what was the purpose when she would not come to him? The fierce look in her lovely eyes told him that plainly enough. His anger had forced him into an awkward corner, and her fury held him there. They would start their marriage off as combatants, not lovers, and her rigid distance was a constant reminder that the situation was not to her liking.

At the end of the five minutes' grace, Tempest swept by him without a glance, her face white and her eyes puffed. There was a determined set to her features that kept him from relenting his severe declaration, and together they left in a stony silence.

It was well after midnight when the weary, ill-tempered travelers reached Amberly. Stiff from the long ride, they were anxious for rest and thankful the house was quiet.

At the top of the stairs, Tempest paused, uncertain of where she was to spend this wedding night. She was still far too angry to willingly proceed to his room.

Connor resolved her indecision with curt finality. "It's too late to have the suite next to mine aired and ready for you, so you might as well use your former one until it can be seen to tomorrow." He turned away only to be halted by her soft cry of his name. "Yes, what is it?"

Tempest looked at him in confusion, this arrogant stranger who had made her such pretty promises and now seemed eager to be rid of her. "You do not wish me in your room?" she asked quietly.

Connor's dark brows lowered in a distasteful frown.

"Madam, you are my wife, not my lover. You should have accepted my offer to become the latter."

Hurt and bruised by his stinging summation, she railed at him, "It was not my wish to be bound to you."

"That bond need not be permanent," he clipped out icily. "An unconsumated marriage is easily dissolved. When I am done with you, you are free to go. But until then, you will play the part. Is that understood?"

For a moment, large crystal droplets trembled on the tips of her lashes, then with a quick blink that weakness was gone. "Perfectly, my lord," she said coolly as she swept away from him to her solitary apartment.

In the soft glow of the morning light, the gold ring looked warm and fitting on the small hand resting atop the coverlet. Connor frowned as he stared at it from the foot of the bed; then his gaze rose to the relaxed face still deep in sleep. His wife. It didn't seem real to him, just another part of the game they were playing to win Amberly. How had it gone so wrong? Why had he said such stupid, hurtful things to her? He supposed it didn't really matter. He couldn't take them back unsaid.

His brooding was interrupted by bright questioning eyes.

"Good morning, madam. I wish you to come down with me to face the waiting brood. I'm sure they've all heard of our arrival by now."

"Yes, of course. I'll be but a moment." She

paused, then frowned when he made no effort to leave the room. She threw back the covers with a flip of annoyance and climbed out of the bed under his piercing scrutiny. As nonchalantly as possible, she selected a gown from her ample wardrobe and let her night dress slip to the floor to don her undergarments. A covert glance at Connor confirmed he was not unaffected by the sight. When she sat at her dressing table, he came to stand behind her, his expression sharp and—ravenous. She began brushing her curls, ignoring his presence while acutely aware of him.

Connor looked at the reflection of them together, man and wife. They did make an uncommonly handsome couple. He studied his own image with a critical vanity, seeing no faults there that would displease her. Self-consciously, he raised a hand to his eye. The swelling had gone, leaving in its wake deep shades of blue, black, and purple from lid to lash, darkening it like the painting of an overdramatic harlot. He observed the discoloration from several angles, deciding his looks didn't suffer too greatly from it.

He glanced down to see Tempest smiling in wry amusement to catch him preening so raptly. "Never fear, my lord, I doubt if it's permanently disfiguring," she assured him sarcastically.

"I suppose I should be grateful you did not break my nose."

They shared a brief smile in the glass, the tension easing until Connor's hand came up to rest on her shoulder. She stiffened.

Gently, a long forefinger traced one of the marks that mottled her fair skin. "Do they pain you,

281

sweet?" His voice was deep and a bit husky.

"Concerned, my lord?" Her nervousness made her reply tart, and the tenderness in his gaze hardened.

"I do not like to see my property abused."

"I shall strive to take better care of it, sir." The brush slammed down as she stood and gave a gasp of surprise as strong arms stole about her slightly clad body, drawing her to a hardened frame. Her heart beating so fast she feared she would faint, she pried his hands away, her voice sharp. "We should not keep your family waiting."

Connor stepped back, his eyes a chill of pale blue ice. "You are right, my sweet. I shall await you in the hall."

The family was indeed waiting with expressions ranging from relief to hatred. They paused inside the door to the dining room, Connor's hand a light support on the small of Tempest's back, lending a stiffening to her spine.

"It is good to have you children home," Jonathan welcomed them smoothly. His eyes assessed them both without betraying any feeling. "Please sit and have your breakfast. No one should face an inquisition on an empty stomach."

"Thank you, sir," Connor responded in a subdued tone, immediately kindling suspicion.

Tempest forced down the boiled beef and ham under Katherine's stabbing stare, remembering well her threats. Had she been able to uncover anything to harm her case? She would never feel comfortable under those cold, reptilian eyes. Cautiously, she kept her left hand in her lap. She would let Connor spring that news. This was truly her family now, but it still felt a pretense, her being at this table, sharing a meal with the aristocrats. She wondered what her own family was doing a world away and how long it would be before she would see them again. She blinked quickly to halt the prickling behind her eyes and concentrated on her plate.

The food eaten and the table cleared, Jonathan led the procession into his study. Seated in his commanding position behind his huge desk, he looked at his family, one member at a time. Katherine looked smug and waiting, a cat at the open door of a canary cage. Tyler's usual languid boredom was replaced by an eager anticipation, for his mother to make a meal, he supposed. Connor's calm was edged with a defensive tension, and at his side, Holly was pale but composed, her fingers knotted in her skirt.

"Holly, your disappearance has brought some very ugly supposition to the surface, and I would have this all in the open now. Then I will listen to no more of it." He took a deep breath as he looked at the apprehensive girl, praying her explanation would be conclusive.

"Katherine tells me you are not Holly at all but an imposter supplied by Connor." He raised a hand to still the young lord's objection. "She has yet to show me any proof to support her belief. She tells me you fled from Amberly after she threatened to expose your masquerade. Well?"

Connor turned to her in question. It was the first he had heard of it. Was his shrewish aunt the reason for her desertion? He realized he never asked why she

283

had gone; he had been too busy moaning and cursing because she had left him.

Tempest gave a small laugh and blushed deeply. "I assure you, my leaving had nothing to do with what passed between Aunt Kate and me. I prefer not to think of the things that were said." She let her eyes fall as if embarrassed. "I left because Connor and I had a bit of a misunderstanding over a lady of his acquaintance. I followed him to London to demand the truth of it. With a bit of discussion, we managed to come to terms." With a devilish smile, she touched the corner of his colorful eye, turning the tale over to him.

Grinning in appreciation of her creativity, he took her hand to his lips, making a display of the bold ring on her finger.

"Holly and I were wed in London. We are man and wife."

For a long moment the room was silent. Casually, Connor's arm passed about Tempest's shoulders, bringing her protectively to his side.

"Why would you do such a thing?" Jonathan demanded, his tone heavy with shock.

"Because I love her."

It was said with such candor that Tempest almost believed him. She tensed under the circle of his arm.

"And because she inherits Amberly?" the old man prodded cynically.

Connor's expression tightened, his voice low and angry as if with insult. "Amberly had no part in my reasoning. It had nothing to do with you and your kingdom, old man, only Holly and myself."

His outrage was sufficient, for Jonathan smiled.

"Congratulations, my boy. You've at last chosen to do something right."

"I think so too," he replied easily.

"How terribly convenient this all is," Katherine jabbed in nasty insinuation. "How long have the two of you been lovers?"

Connor went rigid, but Tempest's hand closed gently over his. Her words were filled with a quiet sincerity that gave even the hostile woman pause. "I have always loved Connor. Always. He is the only man I've ever wanted, and our relationship beyond that point is no one else's concern. I cannot force you to believe I am Holly. Believe what you will, but I am Lady Amberson and due some respect for that at least."

"Well spoken, child," Jonathan applauded fondly. His eyes narrowed as they turned to his daughter-in-law. "No more of this vile talk, Katherine. You are under my roof and will behave as a member of this family, or you are free to find other quarters. You would be wise not to antagonize your nephew unfairly, for it is his charity you will have to rely on when I am in the ground."

Katherine was deathly pale, her lips thinned and her eyes murderous, but she held her tongue. When she looked at the newlyweds, Connor had the audacity to gloat.

"All of you be about your business. I have work to do," Jonathan dismissed them grandly and began to shuffle papers.

Tempest took her leave quickly, escaping before she had to exchange more words with Connor. She was startled to find her room empty of her effects and proceeded to the door next to her new husband's.

The room was sumptuous, done in hues of mauve, rose, and palest pink. It was obviously a lady's boudoir with its ruffles and froths of lace. The delicate dressing table was adorned with her toiletry items, and all her gowns were neatly stored in the huge armoire. Plump pillows invited a rest on the chaise arranged to catch the morning sun.

Her eyes were drawn from the luxurious comforts to the door that linked her with Connor, so close but yet as distant as the moon. Sighing wistfully, she went to the window. Her home, Amberly. Gone was the crowded dirty room above a noisy tavern. All this magnificent space and grandeur was hers, and she couldn't have been more miserable in this elegant gaol. Or more alone.

Chapter Nineteen

She saw little of Connor during the next weeks. Had it not been for the heavy piece of gold on her finger, she could have believed it all to be a fleeting dream. During the day, he was out on horseback touring the vast estate, talking with its countless agents and bailiffs. At the evening meal, he was polite and good-natured, all of which pleased his grandfather inordinately, seeing him as a miraculously transformed being. His demeanor was icily tolerant of his aunt and cousin, and with her he was civil. He never touched her, taking great pains when seating her for dinner that they had no occasion to brush against one another. At night, she could hear him moving restlessly about his room, pausing often at the joining door, but the knob never turned. And Tempest lay in her pretty room alone in the yielding bed, staring at the ring on her hand.

Most of her daytime hours were taken up by Jonathan Amberson, who was left adrift now that Connor was taking all his duties to heart. The name Grandfather came easily as did their lengthy talks.

The time spent with the elderly man was always comfortable and pleasant. Though she sensed he often wanted to ask about her relationship with Connor, he never did. It was common knowledge through the staff that they both kept their own rooms. Jonathan was puzzled, but he had seen the way they looked at one another, sneaking long heated glances. He wasn't worried that he would long be without great-grandchildren. Whatever held them so stubbornly apart, it was not a lack of feeling, and he would not pry beyond that.

This afternoon as all others began with a walk through the fragrant autumn gardens. Tempest found it difficult to keep her thoughts from the darkening horizon as the old gentleman chatted cheerfully about fondly kept memories. Lost in his reverie, he failed to notice how tightly she clung to his arm.

By mealtime, the air was heavy with moisture and the charged scent of the approaching storm. Nervous and apprehensive, she glanced to Connor, but he seemed as distant as ever. Apparently, he had no care for her discomfort, leaving at the end of the meal to disappear upstairs.

She endured a strained evening listening to Tyler go on about Edmund Kean, a fiery new actor in Drury Lane he was planning to see. She politely fended off his subtle suggestion that she be his escort, leaving him even more petulant than usual. Finally, the first growls of thunder reached her ears, urging a hasty good night and a desperate scramble for the safety of her room. Breathless and trembling, she huddled against the closed door and hesitated with surprise.

The joining door stood open.

Anxiously, she glanced from it to the open drapes. A fork of sizzling light shocked across the dark heavens, prompting her decision. Tempest fled for the hopeful security of the next room, pausing in the door to wet her lips in agitation.

"Good evening, my lord," she called with what she hoped was a reasonable calm.

Connor was standing at the window before tightly closed curtains. He turned, a long absent smile softening his features.

"Come in, sweet. I could use some company tonight."

Slowly, he extended his hand to her, offering all that she sought with that simple gesture. Her small, cold fingers safe in his grasp, he led her to the settee, though another destination was foremost in his thoughts. She settled close to him, kneading his hand convulsively and struggling to keep a brave front.

"How are you, Tempest? I have seen you little of late."

She responded with an edgy tartness to his casual speech. "I thought that was by your design, my lord."

Refusing to be goaded, he replied frankly, "I thought it would be easier for us both, but let's not talk of that. I would like to take you to London to introduce you. When could you be ready?"

A low rumble from without halted her answer as she tensed, her fingers tightening about his. When she spoke, her tone was shaky. "Whenever you wish, my lord."

"It is a bit late in the season, but there are still entertainments available. I'll wager all of Mayfair is eager for a look at the lucky chit who landed Connor

Amberson. It's all right, sweet. I'm here. You needn't be afraid." This was said as a low, soothing assurance as she twisted and cringed beside him. Her breath came in light, frantic gasps, and the eyes that rose to his were wide and pleading.

"Connor, would you hold me?"

He enfolded her easily in his arms, letting her lie limp and shivering upon his chest until a sudden crack awoke a stronger terror. Her arms flew up about his neck in a choking desperation, bringing the full press of her body against him. He wasn't prepared for the fierce shock that contact gave his system, spurring a rush of desirous need that made his head swim with a flood of hot, shaky emotion. He didn't dare touch her until he could turn his sharpened focus from the soft rounded breasts and curve of her hips back to the quaking girl who clung to him in panic. With an unsteady breath, he held her close with unthreatening care.

"What is it, Tempest? What do you fear? It's more than the storm. What is it?"

"Connor, hold me."

"I have you, sweet. Let me help you. Tell me, please."

"It's so cold. I'm so cold."

Connor frowned slightly. The night was actually quite warm. Or was it the fever her nearness woke in him. She was shivering fitfully, and her hands were like ice.

"I'll build a fire to nip the chill," he offered. He tried to stand, but she was wound tightly about him. "Release me, my love. I promise I won't leave you."

Her arms dropped away, her eyes following him

anxiously as he knelt before the firegrate. A gurgle of thunder brought her down next to him on the floor, burrowing into the folds of his coat. Smiling, he let her remain while he kindled a blaze, its small cheery glow softening the harsh lamplight and emitting a radiant heat.

"Oh, that feels good," Tempest sighed, her hand venturing out to test the warmth only to dart back to the safety of Connor's jacket to cling as another rumble sounded.

Connor settled on the hard wood floor and leaned his back against the fireplace. When he patted his chest invitingly, she curled up gratefully against it, lying between his straddled updrawn knees like a housecat.

"The thunder, it's like gunshots, and it makes me afraid," she confessed quietly.

"Who is doing the shooting?" he urged softly, careful not to jar her from her deep thought.

"I don't know."

"Is this a dream you have?"

"No."

No? His brows lowered in puzzlement. "Where are you, Tempest? What do you see?" he prompted, stroking the wayward curls with a soothing rhythm.

Speaking between gulping breaths, she said brokenly, "It's dark and wet and cold. I can't see. I don't want to see. Sometimes it's almost clear, but then I close my eyes to make it go away. If I keep my eyes closed, I'll be safe."

"You are safe now. Open your eyes. Tell me what you see."

Her head shook violently. "No," she sobbed. "I

291

don't want to look. Please don't make me look." Her voice was tiny, like a small frightened child, and Connor's protective instincts surged up.

"Hush, now, sweet. I won't make you. Keep them closed. I know how hard it is to look back. I know." As he rocked her slowly, his eyes stared into the flames. At least his own nightmares had a face. Was he wrong to try to give hers one?

Gradually Connor dozed off, but suddenly he straightened up with a jerk. The sharp movement woke Tempest, who had also been drifting in a light slumber. She looked at him in a moment of confusion, searching the handsome face that was lean and shadowed in the dying firelight. He released her reluctantly, trying to ease the awkward tension between them.

"It seems the storm is played out. It must be late. Let me help you up. It's deuced uncomfortable down here."

Their hands touched, and Connor knew he couldn't let her go even if he had to beg her forgiveness on his knees. If the door closed between them again, he feared he could find no reason to open it a second time. But before he could speak, Tempest's gaze lifted, the polished sapphires glowing with an inner luster.

"May I stay with you tonight?" she asked almost timidly, but her eyes were unwavering.

"If you do, be warned. I mean to have you," he murmured with a strange hoarseness.

She took a step closer, craning her head to retain his stare. "Do what you will, only let me stay."

She gave a tug on the cord behind her neck, and

her gown fell in a sighing whisper to pool at her feet. Connor swallowed the massive lump in his throat as his gaze dropped. The sight of the rose-tipped breasts trapped in the gauzy chemise and the even more tempting shadow of her thighs flushed him with a hot dizziness, fueling sweet longings and lustful passion. He couldn't move. Gently, she pulled at his hands, leading him to the bed they had yet to sample as man and wife. She climbed atop the covers, kneeling there like a seductive temptress. Slowly she pushed off his coat. Neither of them heard it fall. As she unbuttoned his fine shirt, her lips caressed each inch of flesh as it was laid bare from warm throat to taut, furred navel.

The bold definition beneath the skin-tight trousers displayed the height of his passion, burning so hot and trembling on the edge of control. That teetering became perilous when the trousers followed the way of his coat. Her eyes never leaving his, she touched him, teasing that throbbing pulse of him until his teeth ground and a sweat broke out on his face and chest in his struggle to contain the flashing darts, pressuring for a release.

Just when he was certain he couldn't draw another breath, the exquisite torment ended. He blinked away the fog of desire that clouded his senses and looked at the woman before him. She stretched up languidly, all supple satin, her wrists locking behind his neck and the impudent points of her vaguely covered breasts grazing his chest.

"Make love to me, Connor," she purred throatily. "For this night, pretend I am your willing mistress."

He took her lips with a greedy savagery, his twisting mouth hot and hungry. She was immediately lost in a swirl of vibrant sensation, for there was nothing on earth she had experienced as purely sensual as his deep, demanding kiss, the way it changed from bruising insistence to a tender caress, his tongue a hot plunging probe retreating for a tantalizing featherlike dance along her parted lips, all so compelling and exciting and devastating to her will. With one kiss, she had no hope, a captive of her love and his expert loving.

Connor laid her down on the coverlet, straddling her thighs as he leisurely parted her undergarments. His avid gaze was followed by a claiming touch.

"You are so beautiful," he expounded, his words a bit labored. "Why have we so foolishly denied each other what we both want, what we both can give?"

"I did not think you wanted me," she replied quietly.

"Not—? I may have wanted to throttle you, but I have never not wanted you, not since the first time I saw you. You have been a fever in my blood that I cannot cool."

"Take some relief of it now, my lord."

Her arms reached up for him, and he sank into their silken embrace.

"Good morning."

Connor mumbled what might have been a response and buried his face in the pillow. He was content to seek sleep once more until fingers teased through his hair, but it was the warm kiss at the base of his ear that brought one sleepy blue eye open.

Looking unseemingly alert and fetching, Tempest

smiled down at him. "Would you care to join me for breakfast, my lord?"

"Would you care to join me under these covers?"

She laughed at his bleary, half-hearted entreaty, for he was already dozing. "I am already dressed and quite hungry. Are you certain I cannot tempt you to come down with me?"

"You can tempt me to many things, my love, but not to putting food in my stomach at this indecent hour," he muttered.

Tempest's cheeks warmed at his new, more frequent endearment. "I shall see you at a more civil hour then. Enjoy your rest."

He grumbled something and burrowed back under the covers. Still smiling, Tempest touched the dark head lightly.

Jonathan Amberson was the only one in the dining room. He looked up at her, his eyes sparked with a satisfied amusement. "Good morning, child. How did you fare the night?" He seemed to be laughing behind the question with unexplained mirth.

"Very well, thank you," she returned with a lift of her brow.

"And Connor as well?"

Then she understood and blushed with an almost maidenly embarrassment. "He has decided to lie in this morning," she said primly, trying miserably to sound offhanded about the matter while the old man chuckled wickedly.

"Has he now? Quite done in by his duty to provide me with heirs, I trust. Good for him and for you, my dear. I am very pleased."

"How scandalous of you," Tempest charged, her face fiery but her lips twitching in a smile. "Listening to the servants' gossip like an old hen."

"An old hen who has had an empty nest for too long."

"I would be happy to fill the nursery for you, Grandfather."

"With a little Amberson every year until I die," he ordered.

Tempest laughed heartily at that. "What if you live to be one hundred?"

"Then you and Connor should consider closer sleeping arrangements."

Tempest shifted uncomfortably, studying the ring on her hand. Then a warm hand cupped under her chin, turning it up and around to meet a long, thorough kiss. Taken quite by surprise, she sat in wide-eyed astonishment; then her eyes languidly closed, and her hand came up to rest against the unshaven cheek.

"Are you two seeking to make an old man's heart fail with this impassioned display?"

The jovial complaint brought them apart, both breathless and glassy-eyed while Jonathan smiled in approval.

Connor shot the elderly man a surly pout, then brushed Tempest's temple with his lips, whispering loudly, "You should have come back to bed rather than suffer this nosy bird's quizzing."

"Nosy?" Jonathan squawked indignantly. "It is my right to see my family propagated."

"A duty I shall undertake in great earnest, sir. You

shall have your half-dozen Ambersons creeping about underfoot, if you are in agreement, my love."

Tempest merely nodded, unable to trust her voice as he sat near her, one arm about her shoulders while his other hand covered hers. The courtly attentions had her unsettled. Was there any truth in the caressing gaze that lingered on her face in such rapt fascination? She wished she could believe so. The words he spoke were not those of a man who planned to coldly set aside his wife when her purpose was served. They spoke of a permanence she longed for. But knowing him, she wasn't sure. It would take more than words to convince her.

"Holly and I leave for London this morning, a sort of belated postnuptial celebration." The sleepy eyes were dark with promise.

"This morning?" Tempest cried in alarm, casting a glance outside at the cold drizzle. "But the weather—"

"Will not hamper us. Pack lightly. We will buy whatever you need when we arrive. You should have a full wardrobe in both places. All that travel back and forth wrinkles things so and is tiresome. Hurry, love. I want to be off in an hour."

Once she had scurried off, Connor exchanged a long look with his grandfather.

"I am pleased, Connor."

"About what, old man?" he asked quietly.

"About the way you've changed or seem to have."

"Married life must agree with me."

"I would not have said so before this morning, but now I would say yes. She is good for you. Treat her well."

The flippant pose had left Connor and Jonathan had a glimpse of the grandson he had always hoped would emerge from beneath the protective guise of the indifferent libertine, one of deep character and sincerity. "I know she is, and I plan to."

"When you return from London, we will discuss Amberly again."

Connor's eyes dropped with an unwitting pang of conscience as he replied faintly, "As you wish, Grandfather."

With Connor holding the hood of her pelisse over the bright riot of curls, they dashed through the misty rain to the waiting carriage. Tempest scrambled in, shaking out her skirts before taking a seat. Connor came in after, settling opposite. He shook the moisture from his rain-slicked hair and the folds of his Garrick.

"Blast inconvenient, the weather this time of year," he grumbled, at which Tempest made an acquiescent response. "Your poor feet are drenched. Let me warm them."

Without waiting for leave, he scooped them up, stripping off her shoes and stockings. His hands were warm. With a roguish smile, he tucked the bare feet into his lap beneath the heavy coat, close to the heat of his body.

"Better?" he asked with a sultry droop of his lids.

"Much, thank you, my lord," she answered meekly. How strange it felt to be alone with him like this, just two people sharing a moment not of passion but of quiet companionship. Most of their time together was spent in heated argument or heated love-making. The choppy waters of their relationship rarely knew a calm.

Connor was thinking much the same thing as he observed the woman across from him. His wife. A stranger to him. What did he know of her other than she had a famous temper, was a tireless lover, and was a complete enigma? He had been so hurried to change her, he had seen too little of the fresh, puzzling girl who had captivated him without a struggle. With all his flair for flirtation, he had little practice in conversing with a woman. He never considered they might have anything of interest to say. But Tempest was so different, so unique. And he never found her dull.

"We have a long ride ahead of us. What say we entertain each other with sordid tales from our pasts?"

Tempest raised a delicate brow. "Do you plan to amuse me with anecdotes of past lovers?"

Connor supplied that wide flash of uneven teeth, delighted by her miffed pout. "Gad, no. How fatiguing that would be. None of them were interesting enough to warrant canonizing. You must have some daring escapades that cry for telling."

She flushed beneath his warm, animated gaze and stammered, "Please, my lord. I do not wish to bore you."

"Oh, come, come," he protested eagerly. "I'm sure I'll be quite intrigued. I've never known a criminal before." He was quick to cajole her out of the ill-tempered frown he saw gathering. "A fair exchange. You tell me of your exploits, and I'll tell you of my run through Hyde Park in nothing but my boots."

"No. Really?" She leaned forward, her blue eyes bright with an indecent mirth. "Oh, you must tell me. But then I thought we weren't going to discuss your lovers."

"Oh, I don't even recall her name, but I will never forget her father. Chased me for a better part of a mile, he did. I was quite fleet of foot back then, so the only part of me he could identify was not of much help in a drawing room. George was supposed to have been keeping watch but fell asleep. By the time he caught up with me, I was blue and furious. Thrashed him a good one for that."

Tempest collapsed back in her seat, wiping away tears of laughter. "That must have been a humbling experience."

"A cold one, I own." He settled back with a smile, admiring the color in her face and the sparkle of her eyes. "Now, you tell me."

"What do you want to hear about? Not my past lovers, I trust."

Connor's voice was curt. "Have there been any?"

The pretty blush relaxed his features. "You know better, my lord."

"Waterston. How did he take to being robbed? The odious popinjay was probably pasty. I wish I could have seen it. I quite hate the fellow."

"Oh, he was very sweaty but not, I think, at the thought of losing his purse. Is his wife a blushing girl with tow hair and sixteen summers?"

"Ho! No wonder he was so put out. Lady Waterston looks like a bulldog, jowls and all. How did he manage to catch hold of you?"

"He didn't. The girl tripped me and shot at Eddie. I had no chance to run. I am not as fleet of foot as I used to be either."

"Was it awful?" he asked quietly with a morbid interest, his eyes shiny and rapt.

Her humor faded, her expression becoming very solemn, and he regretted the question. "It was prison," she stated stiffly. "A sewer with rats of all sizes. I was praying they would hang me quickly."

"It's over and done, Tempest. I'm sorry—"

"We are supposed to be entertaining each other," she reminded him with forced gaiety, her toes tickling him beneath his coat.

"So had it not been for me, would you still be haunting the roadsides? Or the gaols?"

She made a face and was once again his genial companion.

"What of your father and mother?" he asked curiously. "If they knew, didn't they object?"

"Oh, heavens, they knew nothing of it. Papa would have skinned us both. Eddie always had some convenient tale to explain my absences."

"But the money?"

"Papa owed so much, what we managed to take in only kept the money lenders at bay." Her eyes lowered, her voice growing rough. "They threatened to hurt him and Mama and take him away the inn. That's when Eddie and I took to the roads. We vowed never to hurt anyone or to take from those who couldn't afford to lose."

"Noble sentiments," he remarked wryly.

With a glower, she started to pull her feet away, but he held on tightly. "What do you know, my pampered lord? Have you ever been hungry or cold? Have you ever feared you'd have no roof to sleep under? Have you ever been so afraid of losing something you would do anything to keep it?"

"Only once," he answered quietly. The hooded eyes held hers with an intensity that had her pulses fluttering nervously. Did he mean her or Amberly? Then he smiled, releasing her from his gaze. "It helps to have married a wealthy man. With your beauty, you should have thought of that sooner." His hands had risen to her knees in a distracting message, his interest becoming more apparent beneath the soles of her feet. Annoyed and alarmed by her own mounting ardor, Tempest snatched them back, dropping her skirts over the much warmed limbs.

"I told you, I would not sell myself to better my cause," she snapped. "Have I ever asked anything of you or your fat purse for my own benefit?"

"No. Is it because you feared I would say no or because you feared I would ask of you in return?"

She refused to reply, and their gazes fenced in challenge for several seconds. Tempest finally relented. She was enjoying his company too much to spoil it with a clash of haughty wills.

"Tell me something about you, my lord. I know all the facts and details of your family but little of you. What were you like as a boy when Holly knew you?"

Connor fell silent, a sundry of mixed emotions flickering through the pale eyes from feelings pushed away for years. Surprisingly, he wanted to talk to her, wanted to share his jealously guarded memories with this warm, compassionate girl who had heard his bitter confession and had not judged or held him in

302

contempt.

"Come sit with me," he offered, and she nestled comfortably against his side. She put her chin atop laced fingers on a broad shoulder to gaze up into his cool, clear blue eyes. His arm about her pliant figure, he let his fingers toy with her burnished curls with an absent restlessness.

"I didn't know my father. I was too young when he died. My mother was a special kind of lady, pretty, not glamorous but pleasant to look at with a smile that warmed you and a way of making you feel important and good inside. She spoiled me outrageously, letting me think the universe revolved about me. She meant no harm in it. I think it was because there was just the two of us, but I loved it, the pampering, being treated like an adult. She waited four years to go back into the social whirl. I remember when she and Samuel Amberson came to sit with me, I was five years old and telling me all serious and proper that they needed my permission to marry. Imagine." He smiled, a soft, wistful gesture that made her chest tighten with a constrictive ache.

"He was a fine man, my father but he worked too hard and smiled too little. He thought I was too undisciplined but was unwilling to push between Mother and me, so off to school I went." He gave a faint shudder and hugged Tempest to him. "It was a different sort of prison. I didn't want to go. I begged, I cried for weeks. It was a horrible place, the schoolmasters rigid and fierce and the older boys terrorizing the younger and weaker. I thought I was in some dreadful nightmare. After being so coddled, suddenly there was no one who cared for me. I didn't know what to do. I'd never been around other children and didn't know how cruel they could be. They didn't like me. I don't know why. I don't know if there was a reason. I tried to fit in, but the more I pushed, the more they forced me out. So I started pretending I didn't care what they thought of me, that I didn't need them as friends, that I was too above their cloddishness. I must have started believing it. But I had a lot of money so there were always those who would overlook me in hopes of touching it. George made it bearable. He was the only one who saw me, the only one I trusted. The holidays were so far between I would get into scrapes to get sent home. They could never stay angry with me long. When they died—"

He paused, drawing a slow, cleansing breath before he looked at her with that small, endearing smile. "They would have liked you, Tempest," he said quietly.

The shimmering sapphire eyes gently closed as his head bent for a long, searching kiss.

It was close to nightfall when Connor shepherded Tempest into his house to be met by an unsettled Rogers.

"I wasn't expecting you, my lord," he rattled out, noting the disheveled appearance of his lordship and his companion. Her arrival was a surprise that registered in the usually impassive face.

Tempest looked at her bags hesitantly. After the long, delightful ride of conversation amid much touching and kissing, she was not looking forward to separate rooms. She lifted her eyes to Connor's in a silent plea.

Very calmly, Connor told his manservant, "Rogers, see my wife's bags to my room." After his man gasped in unabashed shock, he scooped his bride in a tight embrace and added huskily, his gaze plunging into hers, "In the morning."

Chapter Twenty

Rogers was sufficiently recovered from his shock by the time he announced the arrival of a guest to the newlyweds as they breakfasted together. Word of Lord Amberson's nuptials was an unprecedented secret to all but their early-morning visitor.

George bent to press a quick kiss to Tempest's cheek, then grasped Connor's hand for a firm shake. "I didn't expect anyone to be about," he began, joining them for a cup of tea. "When did you get in? Not fleeing trouble, I hope."

"Last night, and everything is fine," Connor assured him, his glance slipping across the table to flare and simmer.

Tempest colored prettily at the heated appraisal, then took stock of her own state of dress. Clutching her dressing gown to her modestly, she rose and excused herself.

George smiled to himself as he observed his friend, wondering if Connor knew his eyes followed the retreating woman like a moonstruck boy, all large and glassy.

Connor shook himself to scatter the warming feelings urging him to pursue his absent love and turned to George with a sheepish grin. "It's good to see you, George," he pronounced a bit overstatedly.

"Really?" he questioned wryly with a cocked brow. "If there are other things you'd rather be attending, I could return later."

Connor laughed, a strange giddy sound, then shook his head. "Don't be silly, George. You know you're welcome."

Casting a glance toward the door, he said, "I vouchsafe things have changed since I last saw the two of you. Is this an example of wedded bliss before my eyes?"

"Don't roast me, George," he warned in fond humor. "Do I look all that foolish?"

"You mean besides drooling on the tabletop?"

Connor's hand rose self-consciously, then he grinned at the teasing gibe. "If not bliss, then somewhere close to heaven," he confided. "At least for the moment. I married her against her will, and I am determined to make her change her opinion of having me."

"You mean she doubts her good fortune?"

"She knows me too well for that, almost as well as you do, and I confess, I'm not sure I like a woman knowing my mind." He mused in silence for a moment until George pushed a small box toward him.

"A wedding gift. Just a little token to immortalize the occasion," George explained.

"Why, thank you. That's awfully good of you," Connor vowed with a pleased and touched smile. He opened the box, his expression growing oddly pensive.

"Do you remember the occasion?"

Connor nodded, lifting out a china cup. Its pieces had been carefully glued to make a whole. A memento or a reminder? The light eyes rose after a time and with a very quiet voice, he said, "Thank you, George. I shan't forget."

It wouldn't do for Connor Amberson to simply announce his marriage. He wanted to tease the gossips by dangling juicy hints to whet their appetites and tantalize their snoopy noses with the scent of scandal. Let them think the worst, then choke on their own sly thoughts.

Tempest was happily oblivious to his reasoning as he escorted her about Leicester Square and Covent Garden where the West End's most exclusive dressmakers, haberdashers, milliners, corsetiers, and silk mercers were situated. He had fabrics ordered through Clark and Debenham of Cavendish House and visited W.H. Botibol of Oxford Street, the plumassier, for a selection of fetching confections for her hair. With each purchase, he made a point of charging all to his name and delivered to his address.

Done in from the countless measurings, fittings, and decisions, Tempest was pleased at the thought of a leisurely drive through the leafy glades of Hyde Park. At the fashionable hour of five, the lanes were crowded with those wishing to be seen, from highbred ladies of ton to high-priced demi-reps. The sight of Lord Amberson being chauffered in a carriage while cuddling a pretty young thing began a buzz of whispers that heightened as the two appeared later at the King's Theatre in Haymarket to sit shockingly close in a secluded box, laughing together and boldly share a kiss before all quizzing glances.

To Tempest, sitting in the Italian Opera House was as much a fantasy as the one the performers on stage tiers below them were acting out. The huge horseshoe auditorium with its five tiers of boxes, a gallery, and a pit was nearly to its capacity of some three thousand plus to hear Catalani, the reknowned and highest paid prima donna, sing in "Semiramide." As one of the most fashionable centers of entertainment, the audience maintained a show almost rivaling that on stage. While the exclusives such as the Duchesses of Richmond and Argyle and the Ladies Melbourne and Jersey looked haughtily down from boxes costing as much as £2,500 per season, fops and dandies with their 10s 6d admissions to the pit minced and posed to display their fancy raiment. Tempest found it all exciting and amusing, watching both spectacles with equal interest from her vantage point.

As she sat dreamily caught up in the rich, powerful voice of the smiling prima donna, she turned at the soft call of her name to be soundly and masterfully kissed. Breathless and tingling, she leaned into the circle of Connor's arm, mindless of those who ogled and whispered, lost in this wonderful fantasy she feared would not last.

The following morning Connor gave a crow of delight as Rogers presented him with an overflowing tray of cards left at the door at such an early hour. Tempest rolled onto her side, watching in puzzlement as he sorted the cards into piles, tossing some aside with casual indifference and grinning at others with a calculated amusement.

"What is all that?" she asked finally, sitting up with the sheet clutched at her bosom to look over his shoulder. She was unable to resist the temptation to nibble along the warm, firm line of nicely tanned flesh, exhorting a distracted shiver.

"The wages of sin," he mused cynically. He gestured to the fan of cards. "All these fine, well-bred families are trying to lure me into their drawing rooms to beg me to divulge the particulars of my new affair of the heart."

Tempest gaped at him; then her color warmed. "You mean all that sweet attention was to make them think I was your mistress. You were using me so you could laugh at them."

"Now, my love, don't be angry," he cautioned warily.

"Of course, I'm angry. Why didn't you tell me so I could share the joke? No wonder I was getting such cross-eyed looks."

Connor turned and toppled her to the mattress, the cards spilling every which way while he kissed her thoroughly. His elbows propped on either side of her unruly head, he smiled down, his eyes warm and appreciative. "I beg your pardon. I'd forgotten you like to tease as much as I do. We shall play our games together from now on."

"All games," she emphasized, drawing his head down to capture his mobile mouth. "Now, which of these gossipmongers would best serve our purpose?"

In the end, they decided to show no preference and go to Almack's, the stylish assembly room on King Street. The hum was immediate as Lord Amberson appeared in his finest evening attire with an uncommon beauty on his arm. It was odd enough to see him at such a regulated affair, but for the hardened rake to be so enthralled with his lovely escort was intriguing.

The lady was soon identified as his long-estranged cousin Holly, but that only fueled the fires for it was heard that she was staying at his house. Unchaperoned. And the kiss at the opera. She was certainly enough to catch a man's eye with the gaminish hair, lively eyes, and shy demeanor. She was dressed out in rich gold and palest daffodil, the bodice and puffed sleeves held by bands of the darker shade. The flared skirt was decorated with puffs and swags of fabric about its floaty hem. It was simple but stunning as was the lady. Her pretty smile encompassed the entire assembly as she was whisked about on a proud arm.

They hadn't been enjoying brewing mischief long when they were seized by Loretta Martel, her slanted cat's eyes raking down Tempest, then caressing the man at her side.

"Connie, I would have a word with you," she stated bluntly.

Connor's eyes drooped lazily, the only sign of his annoyance. He could feel Tempest's fingers bite into his arm as Loretta waited.

Teeth all but gnashing, Tempest decided the ploy had gone far enough. It was time to lay her claim and warn off all trespassers. "I do not wish to excuse him, Lady Martel," she said smoothly.

Green and blue eyes shot daggers back and forth while Connor wished some part of the sky would fall on him. Loretta whirled, glaring up in ill-concealed fury.

"Who does this poor-mannered chit think she's addressing? What right has she to answer for you?" the lady fumed indignantly.

"She has the right," Connor said coolly. "She is my wife."

"Your what?"

The piercing shriek brought a hush to the room. Her face deathly pale, Loretta seemed unaware of the stir she was creating.

"You married the little tart?" she ranted on, panting wildly as her maddened eyes darted back and forth between them. "You married her? You deceiving bastard."

Her hand swung up viciously but was stilled in mid-air by a hard, unyielding grip, the nails marring the creamy flesh of her arm.

In a low, coldly calm voice, Tempest spoke to the seething woman as she pulled down her arm. "Don't you ever touch him. Go back to your own husband and leave me mine." She pushed the other woman's hand free and turned to Connor, a possessing hand falling on his shirtfront. "I believe this is our waltz, my lord."

As she marched off on the elegant arm, her chin uplifted and poise unshakable, her message was clear. Connor Amberson was a married man, and his wife would brook no nonsense from any quarter.

Gliding her through the graceful steps of the waltz, Connor struggled to control his suave features. He wanted to throw back his head and laugh uproariously and crush the charming little minx to him. He couldn't control the glimmer of amusement that flick-

312

ered quicksilver in the pale eyes.

"If we wanted to create an outrageous on-dit, sir, I believe we have succeeded," Tempest remarked glibly. When he had no comment, she was meek. "Are you angry with me?"

"Whatever for?"

"For being rude to Lady Martel." The blue eyes lowered uncertainly. "I know you held her in great affection."

He chuckled softly to bring her stare back up with a grievous flash. "You know no such thing. I don't care a jot for Loretta. I never have."

"But she was your—"

"You said affection, not attraction. Oh, I desired her once, but it was not a long-lived flame. That's why they are termed affairs of passion, not love affairs."

"And which am I, my lord?" Her question was quiet but deep.

"A bit of both, sweet." He whirled her through a combination of quick steps to still her retort.

Flushed and out of breath, Tempest continued to beleaguer him. "How can you take a woman to your bed when you don't love her?"

Connor's smile teased her. "What a prudish miss you are. I would have lost ten good prime years had I been waiting for true love to find me, or hold me at gunpoint."

Pursing her lips, she persisted. "But I thought you and Lady Martel had an understanding."

"Of what sort?"

"I thought she was to become Lady Amberson," she finished with an uncomfortable flush.

"So did she, but that was never my intention. Where did you hear of that?"

"I heard you both talking at Amberly," she murmured, shying away from his darkening stare.

"Did you? And my little mouse, do you always believe everything you hear? Is that why you ran from me?"

She wouldn't answer, her eyes miserably downcast and her tender lips trembling.

"Tempest, I am being mean. Forgive me. I was not going to marry Loretta. I didn't even like her much, but I needed her help so I gave her a promise."

"A promise you never planned to keep. I am wondering how much more secure are the vows you take."

"Tempest—"

"My lord, the dance is finished."

The music had stopped, and she stepped quickly away. Though she went docilely with him, she refused to speak or look at him, and he was confused by the power of her cool rebuff to disturb his emotions.

"Why, good evening, Amberson. So this is your new bride."

Connor felt Tempest's recoil of shock and surprise and Dicken Waterston sneered at them in the guise of pleasantry. His hand tightened about her in support as she faltered.

"My wife, Holly. Lord and Lady Waterston."

Tempest recognized Waterston as a man who loved to prod and twist when he felt in control, and his odious look told her he was certain he had the Ambersons beneath his grinding thumb. Time to correct that misconception.

"How familiar you look, my lord," she began innocently. "Have we met before? But no, the man I was thinking of was with a mere slip of a girl. I would not have mistaken her for a lady of your wife's gracious standing. I must have you confused with another."

"Indeed, Lady Amberson. I'm certain I have not had the pleasure before." His reply was icily civil, but the angry squint of his eyes conceded the point well taken. "What are you driving now, Amberson? Have you replaced your pair with another ride?"

His teeth grinding at the snide remark, Connor managed a curt, "Not yet."

"When you do, I am always ready for a challenge."

Connor bowed stiffly as the other couple took their leave.

With Connor out of sorts, Tempest was adrift in the strange social whirl as the evening labored on with little enjoyment. Refreshments consisted of lemonade, tea, bread and butter, and stale cake, a venue as unexciting as the decorous dancing spiced with an occasional waltz and the tedious chitchat. Bored and unhappy, she hung back with her glass of tepid lemonade while Connor spoke with an acquaintance. She started when her hand was taken up for a brief squeeze, and she looked at the regal lady at her side.

"Good evening, my dear. You look quite lost. Has your lord abandoned you?"

"For the moment, it seems," she replied, warmed by the lady's kind manner.

"Fie on him then, but it gives us a chance to chat. How do you find your first visit to Almack's?"

"A trifle dull, I'm afraid. Is it always so pompous

315

and proper?"

"Usually," she chuckled in quiet amusement. "Your entrance was by far the liveliest bit of entertainment I can recall."

"Oh dear, I've embarrassed everyone. I shan't think I'll ever be asked anywhere again," she mourned in honest dismay. Her first social introduction was a disaster.

"No, no, my dear. I find you a delightful change. I would like you to attend a small rout at my home. I shall have a card sent by. I am Lady Cowper. I have enjoyed our meeting."

Connor took her elbow lightly after the other lady had gone. "What did you two talk of, sweet?"

"Of how boring this affair is," she answered frankly.

Connor choked. "Did you? Do you know who she is? Or should I say what she is?" At Tempest's shake of her head, he supplied, "She is Lord Melbourne's sister and one of the Ladies of Almack, one of the High Seven. She and her cronies lord over who is granted permission to the subscription balls here on Wednesday evenings. And what did she say when you told her you thought Almack's flat?"

Tempest was pale with upset. "I've done something awful, haven't I? Why would she invite me to her home after I insulted her so?"

Connor traced her jaw with his fingertips and said soothingly, "Probably because you're the only chit with enough courage not to toad-eat and tell the truth. Everyone knows how fatiguing these things are, but they come anyway to be seen and be fashionable."

"I am sorry if I've failed you," she said quietly.

"I've been a curse and now an embarrassment as well."

"How could you possibly tarnish my reputation?" he laughed kindly. "You are good for me, sweet, and I am glad to have your company. Let us indulge in some more of this horrid fare, then sneak off and find our pleasure elsewhere."

The morning brought double the number of cards, all begging Lady Amberson's presence. As they sorted through them over breakfast, George Morley breezed in full of the latest talk on a familiar subject. Pouring himself a cup of tea, he took a seat and chuckled.

"I wish I had been there to see it. Loretta must have been hysterical to have caused such a whisper."

"You should have come, George. We could have used some witty conversation," Tempest decried. "Next time you'll go with us. Now, I must get dressed, if you'll excuse me."

Halfway up the stairs, she realized she didn't know Connor's plans for the day in order to choose a proper wardrobe. With the intent of asking, she returned to the breakfast parlor and heard the two of them talking casually.

"She gave Waterston a proper trimming. He'll try no blackmail now," Connor was saying.

"Hiding behind a lady's skirts, Conn, first with Loretta, then Dicken?" George teased.

"One of the advantages of being wed."

"The only one?"

"I must own, I enjoy a willing toss whenever I've the mood."

Polished coxcomb, Tempest thought in rankled annoyance. She paused to hear more of his bragging.

"She does look well upon your arm, Conn."

"I like to show her off, but deuced if I don't feel smothered. I'm too restless to play the beau while in my mind I'm still a bachelor."

"It seems odd to me as well after coming and going in your house as if it were my own and taking your company for granted. Being odd man wears hard."

"Oh, fiddle, George."

Both men gave a guilty start as she swept into the room.

Tempest bent to give George a quick embrace. "You are no third wheel," she declared fondly. "As Connor's friend, the door is always open to you at any hour." She turned to Connor, her eyes cool and steady. "And as for your freedom, my lord, it was not my intent to restrict it. Do as you will. I will hold no objections. You have been kind enough to see my way into the social set, but you needn't hover over me. I shall do nicely on my own. As a married woman, I need no chaperon, nor do you need a millstone about your neck. I will not interrupt your singular pursuits, and you needn't concern yourself over my entertainment. I wanted to tell you your time is your own today for my schedule is quite full. Good day, George, my lord."

They looked after her regal exit in astonishment, then at one another.

"Do you think she means it?" George asked.

"I don't know. I vouchsafe we will soon see."

Tempest sat despondently on the edge of their bed. A burden, a clinging vine, that was how he saw her. Even while he professed to enjoy her company, he had been chafing under the yoke of husband, pining for the roving liberties of his former state. Well, she would not force him into the mold. She had seen many of the grand dames functioning independently of their spouses, and that was what she would do. She would play the part of Lady Amberson, flaunting the title if not the man, and she would make him proud of her success, proud of the woman he had married, perhaps proud enough to keep her.

And so her plan was launched. Lady Amberson soon dominated the social set. Debutantes marveled over her ease at conquering the Almack Seven, wooing the well-bred ladies with her honest charm and earning her voucher in unprecedented time. Her name was on every noted guest list for balls and private parties, the evening dismally disappointing if the vibrant Lady Amberson failed to appear. The ladies liked her for her unaffected admiration of them and for her endearing innocence. It was her often shocking disregard for opinion that drew a bevy of followers on her heels. She flirted easily with the married men without being a threat and teased the swains with a care for their hearts. They marveled at her courage for wedding a notorious rake and at her confidence for giving him rein to roam out of her sight. The handsome couple was rarely seen together, and whispers of speculation rose that she had married him to add to her wealth and he to have a buffer behind which to continue his affairs.

It was not only in public that they were seldom

together for in the house on Grosvenor Square, they often but passed in the hall. Connor slid back into his habit of frequenting the clubs, gaming until the wee hours of the morning. Having returned hours earlier, Tempest never awakened at his return and was busy entertaining company or out on morning calls by the time he awoke. She had hired a horse from Mr. Tilsbury, whose high-class livery was on Mount Street, and wheeled about the park in her two-person vis-à-vis often in the company of one of the smitten cubs who sought her favor.

Knowing he should be thankful for a wife who would give him such rope, Connor was oddly out of sorts. He brooded over his solitary meals and shifted restlessly beside the slumbering figure of his wife at night. The evenings of cards and dice in the exclusive men's clubs became a boring routine, and even George's amiable company failed to lift his spirits, which seemed to gladden only at the brief encounters with the woman he lived with but never saw.

Tempest had become everything he had schooled her to be, gracious, well-bred, outgoing, fashionable, and immensely popular. The transformation from bulky caterpillar to flitting social moth had pushed them apart. She no longer seemed to need his guidance or, in fact, his presence. She never even asked him for money. She was polite to him when they had occasion to speak but maintained a careful distance save for a reserved brush of her lips against his cheek in public. When he would linger with her, she hurried him away or was herself rushing to some appointment. How he wished for the return of his awkward, uncertain, loving Tempest in place of the cool, self-possessed Lady Amberson.

Even though they never graced the same events, Connor was always well informed of Tempest's doings. It was hard to avoid hearing of the quaint colorful Holly Amberson, impossible even. She was always in the center of conversation for her candor and almost outrageous behavior. People enjoyed making excuses for her often shocking manners. Connor grimaced as he listened to fondly told tales of her exploits, of his wife's dutiful entourage, of the boldly independent way she conducted herself. He frowned at the stories of her gaming in private rooms with gentlemen of title to earn her pin money and of the high opinion the Jockey Club held for her hunches at Newmarket. The lady could eye a horse with the best of them. Lady Amberson had them all charmed.

After listening for the fifth time in the same evening about his wife's latest conquests, Connor tossed down his cards to the baize tabletop and stalked out in ill-humor.

Chapter Twenty-one

Tempest woke early as she was wont to and blinked back tears at the sight of the empty sheets beside her. He hadn't even come home. How callous he had become in his indifference to her. Perhaps they weren't just spiteful whispers, these rumors she had heard that he had taken a new mistress. Was that the reason he had seen no need to touch her for—how many weeks had it been?

With a sigh of resignation, she donned her silk dressing gown and made her way down to breakfast to see what the day would bring. Would it be another tiresome tea, a morning call to endure catty gossip, a drive in the park while tactfully fending off amorous advances? How nice it would be to just stay in and ignore the world outside the door. But she had obligations and was bound to them in this role of the highborn lady, a role she wore easily now but failed to relish.

Tempest stopped in the doorway to the parlor, her composure failing her. Then she asked coolly, "Are you just getting in, my lord?"

The haunting pale eyes regarded her closely for a long beat before he answered. "No. I brought an early end to the evening so I could rise to breakfast with you. Will you join me, sweet?"

When he stood, she was held by the magnificence of him, her eyes hungry with longing and desire. Even casually attired, he was unquestionably elegant. He wore a loose, shawl-collared dressing gown over his shirt, waistcoat, and trousers. The deep crimson damask was a compelling compliment to his dark intense looks, and Tempest was suddenly awed by this beautiful man whose name she shared. As he seated her, he leaned close to breathe in the fragrance of her hair, leaving her clammy with agitation when he returned to his own chair.

"What are your plans for today, madam? Can you spare some time for a neglected husband?"

"Whose, my lord? Do you know of one?" she answered saucily with a flash of her old banter; then the reserve returned. "My schedule is quite impossible today."

"Then free it this evening," he insisted.

"For what purpose, sir?" His attitude that she would cast away all plans at his sudden whim had her hackled and defensive.

"George and I are attending a ball given by Countess Lieven. George was saying it's been long since he's had your company and begged me to ask if you would let us escort you."

Tempest was silent. So it was George who had the interest in her company, not Connor. Careful to betray no pique or hurt, she replied coolly, "Tell George I would be delighted to see him again."

After she had departed, Connor moaned to himself. Why had he concocted that foolish tale? He had started to tell her he was lonely for her smile when that bit of fantasy burst forth like a cheap wine. But she was going with him or rather with him and George, and that was all that mattered.

The wife of the Russian ambassador, the countess was one of London's leading hostesses. Tempest had occasion to meet her in her position as one of the Ladies of Almack but privately had no liking for the woman. Obsessed with her own sway in political affairs and English society, she was quite caught up in herself and used only those who would sustain her ambitions with haughty exclusiveness. Tempest had never been to Ashburnham House and was enthralled by its splendor.

Whispers followed the odd-looking trio as they moved through the crowd. Ensconced between George Morley and Lord Amberson, Lady Amberson was dazzling in her plain high-waisted gown of bottle-green satin. The lustrous fabric was overlaid by aerophanes of blue. Bands of silk emphasized her bust and shoulders and created a sash at the waist, and the long, full sleeves ended with a frill to match the chemisette that peeped modestly to keep the neckline from showing a scandalous display. Whenever she moved, the blue net shimmered over the green, creating an illusion of light playing on water that held the eye in fascination on her superb figure.

Tempest was immediately surrounded by her admirers, who, even in the presence of her rather forbidding husband, begged for dances and the honor of serving her refreshments. It had been months since Connor and George had seen her in the guise they had taught her, but it was obvious she had learned far beyond their meager instruction. She flirted like a polished coquette, drinking in the silly talk with pinked cheeks and fluttering fan while teasing eyes encouraged until Connor was tempted to shake her.

As soon as the music started, her hand was claimed by George Augustus, the prince of Wales. Since Connor could hardly object to the Prince Regent, he watched in stony silence as she was turned about in the arms of a man well known for his lust for music, dancing, and amorous entanglements. Even though the elegant figure, handsome high color, and shapely legs of his youth had settled to a caricature, the Regent was still charming with his bright blue eyes, impeccable manners, and intelligence, and Connor fidgeted unhappily as she enjoyed his company.

The moment she was free, Connor started forward to claim her, but she was caught up by her league of prancing dandies, and he saw little of her for the next two hours. At his side, George's snickering did little to soothe his aggrieved pride.

"Won't come to heel, eh, Conn?" he gibed unwisely, bringing about a cold icy stare that only widened his grin.

As the preening puppies begged for her hand, Connor pushed among them to seize the tiny fingers. When the deposed suitors had the gall to protest his intrusion, he leveled a glare that sent them shivering.

"I have a higher claim to the lady," he stated with a bold warning, then tugged her arm roughly. "Come, sweet. Let us take a turn in the garden."

Tempest couldn't have pulled free of the steely grip, but she didn't care to try. She hurried at his side, happiness disguised by a sedate expression. His very anger filled her with a hopeful excitement. Did he care then? Had her meaningless dalliances provoked him to jealousy?

The garden at Ashburnham House was like being transported among the stars. Colorful lamps twinkled from concealed spots in the flowers where they rose up the slope of Hay Hill to blend into the heavens. Water cascades gurgled in sultry promise between the mossy paths and arrangements of scented shrubs, in all creating an intimate perfumed Arcadia for lovers to lose themselves from the crowds within.

"That was rude of you, my lord, to tear me from my company," she protested in false upset.

"Let the panting jackanapes cool their heels for a time as I have had to do these last months," he growled.

They stopped beneath an arched trellis where the delicate scent of roses hung sweet and poignant. It reminded her of the bath in his house when she had been his unwilling guest. He released her arm but continued to stand close, using his body as a formidable threat. Whether a threat of violence or passion, she wasn't sure.

"Oh, la, my lord. Would you have me believe you prefer my insipid company to that of the gaming tables and your other ladies?" Her eyes flashed hotly to contest the silly banter of her words.

"What other ladies? What nonsense are you speaking? I am not the one who receives a drawing room of

326

bouquets every morning. I feel as though I'm closeted in a mortuary."

Tempest's lips twitched with mirth. So the gifts had annoyed him as well as embarrassed her. She made her voice indignant. "I did not design to have them sent."

"No? No? Indeed. Then what was all that fluttering of the lashes and giggling about if not to encourage those poor calf-eyed boys?" He looked magnetic when angered, his dark brows sweeping down over the hot blue ice of his eyes, his nostrils flared and his full mouth pulled in a tight pout. She would have been intimidated had she not been so flushed with impassioned appreciation.

"I have done nothing but behave as the proper, fashionable Lady Amberson. Was that not what you wished, my lord? Was that not why you bought me?"

"It is not my wish that every buck in Mayfair be lusting after my wife with her giving every indication that she enjoys it from every corner but mine."

All pretense of calm fled her as her fierce bright eyes glared up at the pridefully outraged features. "Never fear, my lord. I have not let your property be abused."

His expression wavering between anger and frustration, he snarled, "You are not my property."

"Then what is this if not a slave band?" she flung at him. Light flashed with molten richness on the broad band of gold as she flaunted her hand before his taut face. "Tell me what it means to you, my lord."

He gripped her hand in both of his, bringing it to his lips. With his eyes tightly closed, he kissed each knuckle in turn until his breath had grown so hard and fast it fairly scorched her skin. When his eyes opened, they were a pale flame consuming her with a quick, hungry desire. His deep voice made her quiver. "You are my wife, mine to hold and cherish and protect, whose company I prefer above all else. Sweet Tempest, I wish to own your heart, but only if you give it freely. You told me once that it was so. Is it still?"

Instead, she answered gruffly, "Do you mind terribly if we shorten this evening? I believe I have matters at home that require urgent attention."

"I have no objection," he replied softly. He tucked her hand into the crook of his arm and escorted her back inside to seek out their hostess. Those who observed them could not help but admire their striking contrast, she the lively essence of sun and sky and he dark, seductive midnight. It was just as apparent that, at least on this night, Lord and Lady Amberson were very much together. The gentlemen slumped to see all her vivacious charm center in serious intent on one man, her eyes so filled with his handsome face she saw no others while the ladies who knew sighed to recognize the simmer of explosive passion in the face of the cool, elegant lord so usually preoccupied with self-indulgent ennui.

George looked between them with a raised brow, feeling the heated current before either spoke.

"We've leaving now, George," Connor said in an oddly rough voice. "Be a good fellow and say you don't mind."

"Of course I don't, but I do plan to hold you to your promise to stop for a taste of that French brandy

328

I had brought over."

Connor was about to groan in protest when a small hand touched his, shocking him with its warmth and his own keen desires until he could find no words.

"We wouldn't think of begging off, George," Tempest assured him with a gracious smile.

In the carriage, snuggled close to her husband's side, Tempest murmured naughtily, "I want to thank you for insisting I come with you tonight, George. I'm touched that you would consider me."

George looked so blank Connor was on the verge of kicking him before he said smoothly, "The pleasure was all mine. It was worth canceling two appointments at the last minute to see the thunderclouds gone from over Conn's head."

Connor's glare softened in an instant as the woman at his side pressed a warm kiss to his cheek. Annoyance with his friend forgotten, he was able to concentrate on the prickly warmth that began to radiate through him, nudging emotions that made all else pale in comparison.

While George went to fetch his prize brandy, Connor sat beside Tempest on the couch. He searched for some way to tell her of his urgent feelings of need and those that lay deeper when she spoke his name softly. When he turned in question, her lips were upon his. It was the striking of flint and stone, sparks snapping at the contact to become quick heated flames. His coat was pushed from yielding shoulders, followed by his waistcoat. As her fingers tore at his starched cravat and worked down the buttons of his shirt, Tempest's mouth blazed a path to his throat where she could feel his blood pulse beneath her burning

329

kisses in a fervor to match her own.

Moaning softly, Connor struggled to gather his wits. Leadened arms rose to her fair shoulders, but he couldn't decide if he should pull her back or hold her closer. His dazed eyes lit on George's amused countenance.

"I think I'll retire," George announced with a feigned yawn. "Since you don't seem to need any of this fine liquor to heat you, I shan't waste it. You might find it more comfortable upstairs, but suit yourselves. Turn off the lights behind you."

"Good night, George," Tempest called huskily from her ravenous feast on the warm throbbing neck. She lifted up to look into the swirling blue eyes, her own as bright as flaring stars. "Shall we continue this, my lord?" At his vague nod, she stood, shaking out her gown and smiled seductively. "See to the lights, sir. I'll await you upstairs."

She was already between the sheets when Connor closed the door behind him. While she watched in frank appraisal, he shed the rest of his clothes and came to join her. Lips and hands and breaths and bodies met and merged as fires forged a more consuming heat. Matching longings and passions had free rein in those endless moments of shared perfection. And as that frantic rush burst into a shower of glory, Tempest clung to her lover-husband with a helpless cry.

"Oh, Connor. Connor, I love you."

George looked up from his cup of tea to find them once again indulging in a lingering kiss. With a

330

harrumph of displeasure, he let his cup drop noisily to complain, "I say, couldn't you find enough hours in the night to see to your lusting without turning my breakfast table into Covent Gardens after dark?"

"Ignore him, sweet," Connor whispered against the moist encouraging lips. "He's jealous, poor miserable sot."

"Indeed," their host snorted, making Tempest giggle and breaking the romantic interlude.

"Don't tease George, my lord. He's been very tolerant of us. Now apologize, you obnoxious brute."

In all sincerity, Connor murmured, "Do forgive me, George. My lady is right. I am a mean fellow." George had his answer on who would teach whom manners.

A small hand turned his face back for a deep, searching kiss. "But a wonderful lover," she sighed. Her fingertips caressed his lean cheeks, kindling those deep fires in the sleepy eyes.

"Enough," George grumbled. "If you are going to start shedding your clothes again, go to your own home. I grow weary of picking up after you. Exhaust your own staff. They are paid to put up with you."

Connor shot him a pouty glower before asking his wife, "How does your schedule look today, my love?"

"Miraculously cleared, my lord, for whatever your pleasure might be."

"Come to Vauxhall with me this afternoon; then tomorrow we'll return to Amberly." He frowned at her sudden hesitation. "Has London charmed you so that you do not wish to leave it?"

"London holds only one charm for me," she vowed softly, touching a forefinger to the full mouth pursed in displeasure. "I will go with you gladly. I only wish—"

"What?" he urged, anxious to do anything to hold her favor.

"I would like to see my family."

Connor sat back, his expression losing its warmth to caution. "That would not be wise at this time, Tempest. Perhaps later, after the holidays we can arrange something."

Her eyes dropped so he would not see her misery. "As you wish, my lord. I would like to purchase some things before we go. I will meet you at the Gardens."

He lifted her chin to warn gently, "Do not go to them. I want your word on that."

Her willful mouth firmed. "You have it."

Connor searched her expression warily, then nodded. "I believe you."

Tempest's low spirits began to lift as her attention turned to the gifts she would need to buy for Christmas, though still better than two months away. She would buy them in case she didn't get back to London and leave the ones for her family with George. For her sister, she found an exquisite porcelain doll that drew her eye and more practically a warm pelisse and furry muff. For her mother, she purchased a white muslin gown with an apron front fastening with ties at the waist and an Indian shawl in a fashionable pinecone pattern. She smiled to herself thinking of the dreams she had had as an unwilling prisoner of Lord Amberson. Now she could make them more than wistful fancies. For the three men in the family, she ordered boots from Hoby's and a fine beaver hat for Will from Lock's. Her tour down St. James's Street took her to Berry Brothers to be lost in the rich heady aromas of choice tea, coffee, and tobacco from the New World and pungent spices from the Far East. Departing with a laden basket, she turned into Gunther's, the celebrated confectioner, to find a box of sugar plums to delight the elder Amberson.

Feeling elated and pleased with her purchases, she continued down St. James's puzzling over what to give Connor. The odds and ends she had bought would hardly signify. Her thoughts kept returning to the pair of horses he had lost to free her from Newgate. Tattersall's had a reputation as the finest auctioneer, but a Thoroughbred went for 1,000 guineas and her reticule had been nearly emptied. There had to be some way to make up for his sacrifice for her.

Her musings were interrupted by a hail from a carriage. She glanced up to see an unfamiliar woman with bright auburn curls, tiny hands and waist, and ample bosom waving her over.

"My dear Lady Amberson, it is hardly proper for a lady of your standing to walk Bond or St. James's in the afternoon, let alone the morning, without an escort. Please allow me to convey you somewhere."

"Thank you for your concern over my reputation," she answered in some amusement. "Since my feet are weary, I will accept your kind offer."

Tempest was aided into the carriage and eyed the other woman curiously. "How is it you know me, madam?"

"I do not. I—um—know your husband and

thought, as a friend, I could not help but rescue you from idle gossip."

"Again, thank you, Miss Wilson."

"I see you know me as well."

Who in London did not know of the famed courtesan. As she drove through Hyde Park in her carriage lined with pale blue satin, she was always surrounded by a crowd of horsemen hoping she would bestow some sign of recognition on them. That Connor would know her came as no surprise, and Tempest harbored no ill-will toward the openly friendly woman.

They chatted companionably until they reached Grosvenor Square, at which time the woman extended a small gloved hand.

"It has been a pleasure speaking with you. A pity we do not frequent the same circles, for I should enjoy renewing our acquaintance."

"If I were not leaving London tomorrow, I would make a point of it. When I return, I will send you a card."

Harriette Wilson lifted an arched brow, then smiled to see the lady was sincere. "My best to your husband."

"I shall enjoy relaying the message."

As Tempest hurried along one of the many avenues in Vauxhall Gardens, she saw Dicken Waterston and was reminded again of her earlier thoughts. Casting aside any misgivings, she approached the man boldly.

"Good day, Lord Waterston. May I have a word with you?"

Dicken Waterston was a man who appreciated many things, fine foods, exorbitant wagers, and beautiful women. Holly Amberson was definitely the last so he paused to hear her out. She was an uncommon woman and, as he already knew, not what she seemed. Her proposal was outrageous, and he knew better than to give it heed. But she was Connor Amberson's wife, and the possibilities were intriguing.

George looked about in alarm at Connor's sudden gasp. He had the presence of mind to grip his friend's arm firmly to hold him in check as they watched Lord Waterston bow low over Tempest's hand, pressing avid lips to it. Feeling the muscles tense beneath his breath, George advised him quietly, "Go easy, Conn."

"What is she doing with that person?" Connor snarled fiercely, his eyes narrowing into dangerous slits.

"Let her explain it to you," George said calmly. "Don't charge her unfairly."

"As you say, George." He brushed his sleeve smooth when released and waited for his wife to spot them. His suspicious thoughts gave him a guilty pause when her fair face warmed with joy as their eyes met. She hurried to his side and hugged happily to his arm.

"I have missed you, my lord," she said in quiet earnest.

"Did you have an eventful day, sweet?" She didn't note the cool edge to his question.

"Oh, yes. I met an old acquaintance of yours." Her eyes danced wickedly, assuring him she wasn't speaking of Waterston. "Harriette Wilson was saucy enough to ask me to relay her regards."

Connor laughed in surprise and gave her a hard squeeze, anger and doubts dismissed. "I trust you didn't come to fisticuffs with her, you jealous termagant."

"Of course I didn't. I found her quite amusing. Do I have reason to be jealous?"

"No, my love."

"Then I am content."

She smiled up at him, holding tightly to his arm while her glowing eyes warmed his heat.

"So am I, sweet."

Connor had procured them a small supper box in one of the Gardens' leafy arbors where they dined on powdered beef, custards, and syllabubs laced with wine while sipping Arrack punch. As darkness began to creep in on the cool evening breeze, the thousand lamps that illuminated the grounds were lit, and the musicians played in the orchestra pavilion while couples strolled the long avenues of trees in the setting of fountains, cascades, and Roubiliac's statue of Handel.

Wandering along those shadowed paths, Tempest was blessed with a glimpse of pure happiness. George was rambling on amiably, ignoring the fact that he had no audience while Connor kept her hand tucked close against the warmth of his body. His manner was attentive and courtly, but his eyes were a smolder of anticipation. Why couldn't it always be like this between them, defenses relaxed and emotions free to explore and experience?

Connor basked in his role as gallant. Looking down into the limpid pools of blue, his thoughts raced ahead to Amberly where he planned to concentrate on producing an Amberson heir. Perhaps when she was round with his child, he could be comfortable with her as his wife, not fearing she could be gone from him in an instant. Having her sport his heavy ring and name and hearing her declare her love in moments of blinding passion did not convince him to trust and build on what he had taken by trickery and threat. Once they were at Amberly away from distraction and frivolity, perhaps he would relent and let himself be convinced.

"Evening, Missy. Remember me?"

Tempest regarded the painted woman who clutched her arm with curiosity, but Connor's reaction was much more aggressive. He pulled the calloused hand away, his voice gruff with warning.

"How could she possibly know you? You are mistaken, madam."

The woman glared at the haughty gentleman, then back at the girl. "I ain't either. You be Will Swift's girl though you shorely do look different. Done well for yourself, eh? I like to see one of us step up."

Tempest remembered the coarse-voiced woman then. She had worked the tavern for several months before moving to a Covent Garden brothel to take advantage of her still youthful face. People had begun to stop on the path, wondering what business such a creature had with Lady Amberson.

"My wife does not associate with your kind, so please step away," the steely-eyed gentleman was saying.

"The Swifts ain't no better'n me, and watch who you're shoving there."

Her loud voice had begun to attract more attention. Very calmly, George steered his friend to one side and urged quietly, "Take Tempest out of here. I'll see to the vulgar tart."

While Connor walked quickly away with an apprehensive Tempest clinging to his arm, George turned to the woman with a charming smile.

"Obviously you've confused Lady Amberson with someone else. I apologize for my friend's rudeness. I trust this will settle the matter. Good evening, madam."

The Cyprian looked down at the fistful of notes that had been pressed into her hand, and her smile became one of scheming. She hadn't been sure it was the Swift girl until the cold-eyed man had insisted so adamantly she was wrong. She had no doubt now, and if it was worth so much to protect that information, how much would it bring her if she was to seek out whom they were trying to hide it from?

Badly shaken by the encounter, Tempest shivered in Connor's tight embrace in the concealing darkness of their carriage.

"Oh, Connor, let's go. Please. Let's leave for Amberly tonight. Now."

"No, sweet. We cannot run, or we'd make it all the worse. What we will do is go to Melbourne House as planned and act as though nothing is amiss. Come now, where is your famous pluck? Don't let it desert you now."

With a wan smile, she leaned away. He returned

the smile softly and looked so wondrously fair, she wanted to weep anew out of love for him.

"Would you kiss me, Connor?" she asked quietly, trembling as he complied.

"I see the two of you are not suffering unduly over this," George remarked wryly as he climbed in.

"We have complete faith in you, George," Connor returned with a grin before he placed another quick kiss on the softly parted lips. "Is all taken care of?"

"I paid her well so the matter should lie silent."

"Thank you for your quick thinking. I confess I was at a loss. Let's go on and forget the whole affair."

It would not prove that simple.

Chapter Twenty-two

Melbourne House, situated in Whitehall was a grand dwelling, its ample portico leading into a circular domed vestibule lit by lantern light. Its gracious painted ballroom had a vista of windows overlooking St. James's Park. Along with her sister-in-law, Lady Cowper, Lady Melbourne was by far Tempest's favorite among the Mayfair hostesses. She was beautiful and feminine with clear, practical dark eyes and was a confidante sought for her worldly judgment and caustic humor. Her sitting room saw the solution to many a troubled, broken heart, and her counsel sought even by former lovers she had the wisdom to keep as friends. Connor Amberson had never been more to her than a passionate thought. She found him too intense, too wrought with uncertain recklessness, but she envied his wife so fine-looking a man who, in spite of rumors she seldom heeded, she recognized was totally devoted to her.

While Connor and George were drawn into a game of hazard, Tempest sought out a game of her own.

Alone with Waterston in a secluded parlor, she spread the cards on the table.

"One game, my lord," she stated coolly. "If my hand proves better, you will see the horses delivered to Grosvenor Square day after tomorrow."

"And if you lose, my lady?"

"Name your stake, sir."

The dark eyes roamed greedily down her trim figure. She was a spectacular-looking woman, and the fact that she was Connor Amberson's only increased the allure. For the vain rakehell to have begged him for her freedom with such sincerity, she must be a prize worth any stake. "You will leave with me this evening."

Tempest was very still. She had been playing cards since childhood and knew her own skill, but this was a dangerous bet. If she lost Connor, nothing would matter. The chance meeting with the courtesan haunted her. If she chose to be indiscreet, her deception would be over. Would that spell an end to her marriage as well? She had to make Connor want and care for her enough not to make that choice. The return of her price for release from prison would go far toward accomplishing that goal.

"As you wish, my lord," she agreed, cutting the pack toward him with a snap.

Tempest went down the first rubber but not disastrously. Waterston was an experienced hand, calculating odds neatly and judging his cards well. She took the second by a slim margin.

"You play well for a lady," Waterston said begrudingly, his gaze lingering on the shadow of her bosom.

"You, too, sir, though your discards are weak."

"Shall we decide all with this hand?"

Tempest nodded. She felt very cold, but her mind continued to work smoothly to her advantage. She gauged what had been played: a quint, a tierce, fourteen aces, three kings, and eleven cards played.

Waterston frowned at the galaxy of face cards the lady displayed and at his single card. Boldly, he slapped it down.

A diamond, she cried to herself in weak relief, then set down her club. "I win, my lord."

Unwilling to graciously accept such a coveted loss, Waterson frowned with menace. "You deal a pretty hand, Lady Amberson. So smooth and sure. One would think you knew the cards in advance."

"Are you accusing me of trickery, sir?" Her voice was crisp. "You will not writhe out of our wager by making so outrageous a claim. I won fairly."

"Then perhaps you could be a little more conciliatory to your opponent."

Tempest gave a squeak of surprise as she was crushed to the broad chest, too stunned at first to avoid the hungered press of his mouth. Before she could deal him an angry slap, she was released abruptly. Waterston was rigid, his wide eyes drawing her gaze around to where Connor and George stood in the doorway.

Finding his wife in another's arms was shock enough, but the identity of the man she chose to betray him with was a cruel thrust home. The bright blue eyes looked at him in relieved entreaty, then chilled to an objection of his presence. Very softly, he asked, "Swords or pistols, sir?"

342

She had been so glad to see him, Tempest forgot to think of how the scene must have appeared. When the heavy-lidded eyes stared through her in bitter accusation, she was dumbfounded. Then furious. How dare he believe the worst.

"The thought of running my blade through you has been a wish of long standing," Waterston answered coolly.

"No," Tempest cried fearfully. She recalled the scars that marked his arms and shoulders. Waterston would not be satisfied to pink him. He would kill him. "I won't allow it. Please, my lord. It was a misunderstanding. It was my fault. Connor, please. If someone is to be punished, it should be me." When the hard eyes remained unmoved, she pleaded, "George, do something. Dissuade him, please. Stop it now before someone is hurt."

"Conn, back down," George advised him. "You'll accomplish nothing but a scandal. You've too much to lose. Kill him later if you must but not now. Conn, do you hear me?"

"Your pleasure, sir," Connor clipped out frigidly to the other man.

"Another time, Amberson."

Connor turned and strode from the room, George giving Tempest a long, harsh look before hurrying after him.

Waterston gave a laugh of relief. He knew, where Tempest didn't, that Connor was the far superior swordsman. "You save me from much, my lady," he began.

"But not all." Her fist struck him a rattling blow to the chin that dropped him to his chair. "I am no lady.

You'd do well to remember that, sir. Have the horses delivered, and never, never cross me again."

Tempest rushed across the dance floor as rapidly as decorum would allow to find and placate her husband. He turned to her with a stony countenance that she could have melted with a pleading word, but then they saw the sapphires.

Lady Martel had made few appearances since the scene at Almack's, but tonight she was in her glory. She was on the arm of a pretty-looking young dandy, and about her sparkled a wealth of blue stones.

Without a word, Tempest fled Melbourne House. She ran several blocks before the painful cut of her stays and the flimsy shoes forced her to slow to a sedate pace. No tears fell until she was safe in her room; then they burst forth in a torrent.

He had given them to her. Her jewels. His gifts. She had wondered what had happened to them but had assumed she had overlooked them in packing. Connor had taken them from her to give to his former mistress. Or did the term "former" apply?

As the hours passed, her thoughts cleared, and her tears dried as anger replaced hurt. She paced in fury, readying her words for the return of her husband, but he didn't return. As evening became predawn, she called for a carriage in a burst of panic.

George Morley regarded his visitor through groggy eyes.

"George, is Connor here with you?"

The small, frightened voice brought him fully awake. "Come in, Tempest. It's too deuced cold to have to stand on my steps." He shepherded the shivering figure into his parlor and poured her an ample brandy. She took the glass in unsteady hands and repeated her question.

"Is Connor here? He didn't come home, and I thought maybe he was with you."

Very gently, George said, "No, Tempest. He's not here. He didn't leave with me."

"Who—who did he leave with?"

George shifted uncomfortably. She was bound to hear it anyway, so better it came from him in private. How he hated the whole business.

"He left with Lady Martel."

"I see. Thank you, George. I'm sorry to have disturbed you. Good night." Carefully, she set down the glass. Her expression stiff and pale but strangely calm, she turned to leave, but her step faltered and in a wavering voice cried, "What am I to do, George? I know you warned me not to, but it can't be helped. I love him so very much."

"Come and sit down and drink your brandy," was his advice.

After the fourth glass, Tempest had finished telling of the wager and the sapphires and was too weary to cry. George refilled her glass.

"It's the first I've heard of the jewels," he confided. "I cannot fathom Conn's doing such a thing. He cares the world for you and not a groat for Loretta."

"He cares for no one, George, least of all me," she mourned, sagging against his supportive shoulder.

Putting a fond arm about her, George smiled. "You'd be surprised."

"He cares so much for me, he goes to lie with

345

another woman?" she cried miserably.

"I said he cared, I didn't say he was overly bright. In fact, right now I think he's being incredibly thick. I don't know what to say. If you can tolerate him, stay by him because you are the one he wants."

Tempest only muttered vaguely and settled her head more comfortably as she let the brandy soothe her exhausted nerves and ease her to sleep.

Connor was very drunk and very angry, and he needed both those qualities to get him through the night he had planned. Even so, his senses recoiled as Loretta's thin fingers threaded through his hair. Steeling himself for the sight of a face other than the one he longed to see, he opened his eyes. The features blurred, almost taking the desired shape, but his dulled mind wouldn't allow that blissful deception long.

"Why should I believe you, Connie? You've proven to be a terrible liar."

"Believe what you like. I didn't think honesty was one of the qualities you most admired in me."

Loretta gave a low chuckle. "You know exactly what I admire about you, and it has nothing to do with character." She stretched languidly and rolled up against him on the thick fur rug. Her clothing was tangled in passion-inspired disarray, but he was still fully dressed and looking too calm and detached to suit her. "Make yourself more comfortable, Connie," she purred, tugging at his coat impatiently.

"One would think your new paramour is useless," he remarked unkindly, resisting her hurried fingers.

"He is young, and frankly, I've found no one half as pleasing as you. Come now. Why the delay? This was your idea. Have you changed your mind?" The green eyes grew more slanted with pique.

"There is something I want first. I have conditions, too. You are the one who taught me about conditions."

"What is it you want?" Her hand stroked along the strong line of his jaw. He was a magnificent looking man.

Connor reached into the tangle of her discarded clothes and held up the winking blue stones.

Loretta's gaze hardened, but her fingers still caressed his cheek and neck. "You see yourself as quite expensive, Connie."

"You put the worth on me, not I." He was so cool, so sure, so smug.

"And what will she have to do to get them back?"

"Nothing," he said smoothly. "She'll have them because I love her."

A trio of sharp pains went from ear to collar, bringing Connor up to catch the flailing hands before more skin was lost to the taloned fingers. His hard push tumbled her head over heels on the rug until she rose to her knees, panting with savage anger.

"Take the stones, you bastard. I only bought them from the hawker to make the little tart simmer. Take them and get out. Go back to your precious whore, and enjoy what time you have left with her. You are going to pay for this with a price far dearer than your pretty face and much-used physique. Get out and be damned."

The walk back to Grosvenor Square was a long

one, giving him time to think a slow, stumbling process in his state. He wasn't sure of anything except that he loved Tempest. No matter what she had done, those feelings hadn't changed. That was the one constant in the whirl of confusion. He couldn't lose her.

His house was dark. She wasn't there. Where could she be at the break of dawn? He didn't want to consider the only answer that came to mind, nor would she find him anxiously waiting her return, bearing gifts.

After an hour of faro at one of the clubs, he wasn't certain which, he was too weary and distracted to concentrate on his cards and was losing so badly, the dealer advised him to go home.

Tempest was waiting for him in the parlor. With aching head and spirit, he was willing to forget all and go straight into her arms, but her piercing stare checked him.

"Where have you been?"

The cold demand bristled his rebelliousness. "Out."

"With whom?" She regarded him fiercely, her hands on her hips and her back rigid. How exciting she looked.

"With George if it matters."

"Liar," she spat, the words crackling like a slap.

"Ask him then," he challenged belligerently.

"I did. Next you'll be telling me it was some wild animal that attacked you on your walk home and left its mark on your neck and the stench of its perfume clinging to you."

He had forgotten the scratches. His mind was

348

moving too slowly for a proper defense, so he turned to a quick attack. "And where were you? Finishing your business with Waterston perhaps?"

"I was at George's and fell asleep without intending to."

A look of incredulous hurt flashed across his features as he took a pained breath. "You and George?" he stammered in shock, taking a wobbly step back. "Oh God, what kind of fool have I been?"

"No bigger one than you are being right now. How dare you think such a thing of George? He's the only one who cares a snap of his fingers for you, yet you'd condemn him as fast as you would me. You are a poor excuse for a friend."

That hurt, and in retaliation, he growled, "At least I'm not a cheap whore."

"What kind of whore are you, my lord?" She was almost past him when his amazement ended. She gasped at the hurting grip that caught her arm.

"Don't you ever speak to me like that. Not ever. You are a nobody. A nothing. I found you. I created you. I made you a lady from the lowest form of life. If it hadn't been for me, you'd be swinging from a rope and your precious family would be starving. I took you out of that filth. I let you share my life and my name. Don't you ever act as though it was something you earned or deserved. I gave it to you, and I can throw you back any time I choose. Do you want to take off those fine silks and put on your ragged sack cloth? Do you want to trade the taste of brandy for swill? My touch for the coarse hands of a stinking pauper?"

She swung at him then, her eyes blinded by tears.

He blocked her hand easily and pulled her close so his harsh breath scorched her face.

"You are mine. And even though you don't care for me, I've no mind to share you with another. You'll not shame my family by acting the gutter tart you are. London has seen enough of you, my sweet, and so have I. You are going to Amberly. Gather your things and be ready in ten minutes. You will stay there until I want you or I wish to come home, and neither is very appealing to me at the moment. Enjoy the hospitality of my home because that's all you'll have of me."

He pushed her away and watched her flee up the stairs through a haze of rage. Feeling wildly hurt and even guilty, he didn't want her close to confuse things more. Better she go to Amberly where he could keep her safe for him and from him until the violent eddies of passionate emotion could be sorted through. Then he could go to her. But not now.

"Connor?"

He turned to find her dressed and ready. Time for her to leave so soon? He was about to utter a quiet word to ease their parting when her palm smote his cheek, rocking him back.

"I hate you. Make your stay in London a long one, my lord."

His hand closing about the back of her neck, he jerked her up to his chest, his mouth plummeting down to seize hers, twisting, hurting, but governed by an uncontrollable passion that could not let her go without tasting her kiss, even if it was by force. And it was. She fought against him, dealing him another hard slap when he released her.

350

His voice coldly confident, he vowed, "You'll be begging me to come to you."

"You'll wait forever to hear me beg," she spat, hating him, loving him.

"Not so long as that. Good-bye, sweet."

Then she was gone.

Connor returned to the parlor to lie on the settee, closing his eyes and letting the draining ebb of emotions and tension wash over him. What was left was a loneliness so great it was like a pain. When he heard a quiet step some time later, he bolted up with the hopeful cry of her name.

George hesitated in the door, taken back by the sight of his usually impeccably groomed friend in his crumpled eveningwear. "The door was open so I came in. Are you all right, Conn? You look dreadful."

He lay back with a miserable groan. "I feel worse."

"Where's Tempest?" He could tell they had met by the welt on the side of his face, then began to frown at the sight of the nail marks. Had it been as bad as that?

"Gone," he said flatly, his eyes closing.

"Gone? What do you mean? Gone where?"

"To Amberly. I sent her to Amberly."

George let out his breath in a gush of relief. "Are you going as well?"

"No. Let her stew there alone; then perhaps she will appreciate me."

George threw up widespread hands in disbelief. "Appreciate you? Appreciate the fact that she was bullied into a marriage with a man who ignores her, treats her with contempt, flaunts his mistresses, then

351

demands respect? You are a fool."

Connor glared up sullenly through murky, tired eyes. "It wouldn't hurt your cause to treat me a little better after all I do for you."

"I never asked you to do anything for me, and if you think to attach strings, I shall sever all ties. I am no maid you can push about with your haughty threats. I don't deserve it from you, and neither does she. Good day, Lord Amberson."

"Dammit, George, are you her friend or mine?"

"Yours, but at this moment I don't know why. I will speak with you later, for I don't like you much this morning." He turned and began to walk out, his posture rigid with indignation.

Connor came up with a chill of alarm, his words quick and anxious. "George? I'm sorry. Please. I didn't mean it."

George Morley paused at the door, running a hand through the shock of orange hair, then giving a heavy sigh. "I know, Conn, and I can forget and forgive, but will she?"

Amberly was more comfortable than Newgate but in many ways much the same. She was a prisoner within its walls, awaiting Connor's judgment when and if he returned. Days went by, and her depression deepened into a woeful melancholy that even Jonathan could not lift. In the waning days of November, he came upon her in a flood of tears and demanded to know if his grandson was the cause, threatening to send bailiffs to London to drag him home if that would ease her pain.

"Please you mustn't interfere," she begged as he drew her head to his shoulder.

"I will not have that insolent cub treat you so shabbily. You are my granddaughter, and I'll not have it," he proclaimed angrily.

"But I'm not," she sobbed, forgetting all in her upset. "Don't you see? I'm not Holly." With a gasp, she sat back, her hand to her mouth in horror, but Jonathan only smiled.

"I know, child. I've known for some time. A wretched creature came to ply me for money saying she knew you to be the daughter of some tavern keeper in Southwark. I paid her enough to keep her silent."

"But—but why have you said nothing before this?" she uttered, her thoughts sluggish with shock.

"Because I wanted to see if you or Connor would come to me with the truth. I had hoped Connor would." He sighed heavily.

Tempest sat very still, her eyes downcast and her lip trembling. "I am so very sorry to have deceived you. You have been so kind to me."

"And you have made my Holly alive again. Not an unfair trade."

"I will gather my things."

The gnarled hand caught hers as she began to rise, and he said sternly, "You will do no such thing. Even if you are not Holly, you are Connor's wife, and as such this is your home."

"I fear he will not want me here once he finds that you know the truth."

"Have I said I would tell him?"

The teary eyes flashed up wide and nonplussed. He

chuckled at her look of bewilderment.

"Connor is not the only one who can play these games. And as for secrets, when will you tell him yours?"

"Mine?"

"Come, come child. I had three sons. I know an expectant mother when I see one. Connor cannot know of it, or he would be here at your side."

Tempest bit her lip, struggling to hold in her torment. It would not do to let him know how bad things were. "I had no chance to tell him in London. I was going to tell him when he came home, but he stays away. I won't use a child to bring him to me. He has to want to come on his own."

The old man spoke gently, kneading her trembling hands. "Connor can be stubborn and difficult. What if he stays in London?"

"I plan to return to my family after the holidays," she said with hard-fought determination.

"You have a family here as well, child. This will be my great-grandchild after all, and I'll want a hand in spoiling it."

Tempest hugged him tightly and cried in fond emotion, "I would not deny you that."

"Now," he said firmly, setting her away, his face serious, "what to do about Connor?"

"Oh, please, I know what he did was wrong, but it was only because he was afraid he would lose Amberly. He saw no other choice. He didn't want to hurt you. He only wanted what was his. Please don't take it from him now. He has tried so hard to earn it fairly this time."

Jonathan put a hand to the damp cheek and shook

his head. "How could he not know how much you love him? You cannot answer for Connor. It is something he will have to do. Until then, I see no need to share our secrets with anyone else, do you?"

Chapter Twenty-three

As it was, what brought Connor home could not be foreseen. Laid flat by a chill that took an ominous turn, Jonathan Amberson was used to opening his eyes to faces of doctors and clergy but to wake and see anxious blue-gray eyes set in a darkly handsome face made him smile weakly.

"So you've come home," he wheezed.

"How do you feel, old man?" Connor asked worriedly.

"Not like dying today. Have you seen your wife?"

"Not yet." The eyes lowered uncomfortably.

"Go, talk to her. I'm an old man. What could you have to say to me?" He gave the covering hand a push. "Go on. We'll speak later. And Connor—I'm glad you've come."

"Did you think I wouldn't?" he chastised in mild reproach. "I love you, old man. Where else would I be?"

"With a woman who loves you. Go."

She was sitting in the garden, warmly dressed against the chill of the afternoon in a deep blue pelisse, which closely followed the lines of her gown. A long shawl was knotted about her hunched shoulders, and a ribbon-trimmed hat framed the delicate features. For a moment, Connor stayed silent so he could study that beloved profile, the same impudently tilted nose, tender mouth, and determined chin. Looking upon her, he found the same deep calming peace that stirred his soul as when first glimpsing the rose-red brick. She was as much a part of him as his home, and he couldn't be without either.

"Tempest?"

The low voice brought a stiffening to the lone figure. She turned very slowly, her large eyes, the color of the summer sky, swinging up to meet his. She stared at him for a long moment with a steady regard, no emotion betrayed in her lovely face. It would have been an easy thing for them to seek each other's arms, but the longer the silence lay between them, the more impossible the distance became. Finally, she spoke, her husky voice warming him pleasantly.

"Thank you for responding so quickly, my lord. It will do him much good to have you here."

"I'm glad you thought to write me. He doesn't look well. How long has he been down?"

"Almost a week. The doctors tut-tut and shake their heads so I thought you should know of it in case of the worst."

Connor nodded. "He is a tough old bird. It would take a great deal to persuade him to go quietly. You look well. How go things with you?"

"I am comfortable here, my lord. How is George?"

All this was said with the formality of two strangers.

"He sends his regards. I have seen too little of him. He's been keeping company with some green girl and neglecting our friendship dreadfully."

"An affair of passion or the heart?"

"The latter, I fear."

"Oh, good for him," she cried in delight, animation pinking her cheeks most becomingly.

Chafed that she would display such fondness for his friend and not inquire after his own state, Connor grumbled, "He would not heed my warnings about matrimony."

"As well he should not," she scoffed. "What do you know of the state, sir?" She stood so their gaze was more direct, fired by a flare of past hurt and deeper emotions. Then her stare was cool once more. "I've had your room readied in anticipation of your arrival. It is a long journey, and you look very weary, my lord. Rest yourself before dinner, and I shall have a bath sent up."

She spoke crisply, like an efficient, dutiful wife. Or servant—and that thought annoyed him. The lazy eyes grew heavy, and his tone silken.

"What, no proper greeting for your husband?"

"What sort of greeting would you like, sir?"

"A kiss would please me if you could manage it."

His haughty words kindled a brief snap in her eyes; then she responded civilly. "I think I can."

She came to him slowly, putting small hands on his shoulders to bend him down. Cool, passionless lips brushed his warm cheek; then she stepped back.

"Welcome home, my lord. I will go see to your comfort. Unless there is something else you wish."

"No." It was brittlely spoken, and Tempest almost

358

smiled before proceeding with a simple grace to the house.

Connor gave his Garrick a careless toss and went to drop heavily on his bed. After a moment of uncomfortable fidgeting, his coat, waistcoat, and boots were discarded with similar ill-humored abruptness. He stared at the ceiling, pouting unhappily. None of this was as he had planned. His stay in London had been torture, so sure was he at first that she would relent and beg him to come to her. But as the weeks went by and no word came, he grew more and more agitated, beginning to fear he had made a terrible error. And when the missive came, its contents were not what he had wished for, but it didn't matter. It was the excuse he needed for his pride to allow him to go home.

He had prepared for two kinds of welcome, the fierce anger of a wronged wife, which he planned to quell after an exciting match of wills, or one of passionate apology, which he would have accepted without reserve. But she had outflanked him with this cool, indifferent demeanor that held him at bay without giving him reason to protest. And then there was the matter of the closed door between their rooms. He rolled onto his stomach, eyeing that offensive door with a jaundiced eye. He could demand she move into his room. He had the right, but his pride rebelled against resorting to force, and more truthfully, he had no wish to push her into something disagreeable to her.

If one good thing had come from his hermitage in London, it was the realization that Tempest Swift

Amberson was permanent. She was the only woman he would want or need for the rest of his life. She was the one he wanted to share his home with, bring his children into the world with, grow old beside. He knew how to seduce a mistress, but how did one woo his own wife? She was not going to make it easy. The challenge was hot in her eyes. He had hurt her, and she had yet to forgive him. If she ever would.

The bathwater cooled, and his supper went back to the kitchen as Connor slept straight through the night to awake stale and rumpled in his clothing. Once refreshed, he found all but his grandfather at the breakfast table. His spirits sank when Tempest flinched beneath his touch as he pressed a kiss to her temple.

"Good morning, sweet."

"My lord."

"Ah, the vultures have begun to circle," Tyler mused dryly. "Did the scent of the kill bring you home, Connie?"

Connor gave him an icy smile as he buttered his toast. "The greatest pleasure of my life is going to be throwing you off this property, bags and baggage." His gaze shifted pointedly to his aunt.

"Hold to that dream, Cousin, for that's all it is. Amberly won't be yours, I guarantee it. But then it would be deuced inconvenient for you to bring all your mistresses out here, wouldn't it?"

His face flushed with fury, Connor started out of his chair when his hand was gently taken to distract his anger and return him to his seat.

"Ignore him, my lord. He is a little wind that blows with occasional gusts."

Connor tried to capture the tiny hand, but her fingers slid coolly from his. Her stormy glance stated clearly that though her words made Tyler's insinuations seem of no importance, she still believed them.

"We shall soon see," Connor decided finally. "Until we know who's to be named heir, can we try to behave with minimal bloodletting for Grandfather's sake?"

"You act as though we were savages," Katherine criticized in irritation.

"Some of us just conceal it better, that's all," her nephew replied.

Tempest had finished her small, forced meal and stood, bringing the pale eyes up at her movement. "Connor, Grandfather wanted to see you when you'd finished your breakfast."

Tossing aside his napkin, he rose with her. "I've not much appetite, anyway."

Once they were alone in the hall, Connor caught her arm to bring the calm eyes up to his. "Tempest, Tyler was not speaking the truth. He only said that to hurt you."

She regarded him levelly, then said, "I was not hurt by it. It is not uncommon for your set to banish their wives to the country so they can play the rutting stag in London. As long as you've been discreet, I see no humiliation in that. You would not be foolish enough to flaunt any of your dalliances here beneath my nose for fear I would do worse than blacken your eye. I will not be mocked in my home, as long as I can call this my home. Other than that, do what you will."

She turned with a regal poise and continued on,

smiling to herself as she heard him trot to catch up to her.

"Then it would bother you to hear I was with other women?" he pressed, falling in beside her and trying not to look as encouraged as he felt.

"I am not thin-skinned, but I am not cased in armor either. I can bear the knowledge but not the evidence."

He took hold of her by the shoulders, bringing her about so she could not evade his searching gaze. "Does that mean you still love me?"

Her voice flat and resigned, she answered, "I have never stopped loving you, Connor. I don't know if I ever will. Love is a silly emotion. It doesn't respond to hurt or betrayal or even common sense. It's independent of reason, and since I have not been able to stamp it out, I have learned to bear it with a minimum of discomfort, like an ingrown nail. It only hurts when stepped upon, and I shall be careful to stay out from under your feet."

Connor frowned at that as she hurried on. At least he knew she still cared, but he wasn't sure he liked being thought of as an illness of an extremity to be borne as best one could.

The massive bedroom was dark, stuffy, and silent except for the raspy breathing of the withered figure on the bed. Connor drew a chair close to the bedside and took up a thin, veined hand, pressing the cold shriveled flesh to his lips. The old man muttered vaguely; then his fingers tightened.

"Connor?" he asked himself, then smiled. "Hello, cub."

"Good morning, old man. How are you feeling?"

"Old, but I guess that cannot be helped. Are you anxious to rush me to glory so you can make Amberly yours?" He gave a slight pleased smile when Connor gave an appalled gasp, his pale eyes growing bright and shiny.

"How can you say that even in jest?" he cried in anguish, clutching the shrunken, birdlike hand to his cheek. "I don't want it that way."

"Where do you draw the line, boy? I thought these walls were the most important thing in your life." His thin voice was gently chiding.

Connor's eyes lowered as he twisted in guilty shame and grief. The old man could well be dying. If he said nothing now, he would be safe and secure at Amberly. "I thought so, too. Once," he added quietly.

"You've changed your mind, then?"

"About Amberly? No. You know how much it means to me. I just don't want to live here alone."

"Then find a woman to share it with you."

"I have, and she's here, but I'm not sure she'll stay, and I don't want one without the other any more."

"Why wouldn't she want to stay?"

"There are so many lies. I've made so many mistakes. It may be too late to make amends—for a lot of things."

"Those who love you won't judge you too harshly."

"How can you say that? You don't know. You don't know what I've done."

"Tell me."

Connor sat back in his chair, his emotions in a crazy cartwheel tumbling out of control, his hopes, the lies, the guilt, his love, the fear he would lose it all. Then he took a long deep breath and began tonelessly.

"I've lied to you, Grandfather. I've used your love for Holly and for me for my own purpose. I've exploited the woman I love more than my life. I made promises to you I couldn't—no, never planned to keep because I was greedy and selfish and scared I couldn't get by on my own merit. I meant to take Amberly any way I could, and I didn't care what I had to do, only it's gotten too bitter to swallow, and I'm choking on it. I wanted it so much. Too much."

"All you had to do was come to me."

Connor laughed tersely at the soft suggestion. "How? You didn't have a jot of respect for me, and why should you? I behaved like seven kinds of fool, thinking consequence would never catch me."

"And now it has."

The dark head nodded miserably.

"Connor, you should have come to me. I should have made it easier for you, but I was enjoying your scrapes too much to want you to turn about." He chuckled at the blank stare. "Do you know how hard it was for me not to laugh while giving you a trimming? I didn't gave a straw about any of those pranks. It was the reason behind them. You never did things because you enjoyed them. You did them out of anger and lack of respect for yourself. That's what angered me. I never wanted Amberly to go to anyone save you, but you made it difficult. You always make things harder than they need be."

"Please don't hate me. Holly isn't—"

"I know. I wanted to hear you tell me. I was praying you would tell me. I own I was hurt you would go to such lengths, but hate you, no."

Connor sagged in the chair. It was gone, everything lost, but there was a relief that made it possible to bear. At last he could look into the tired, old eyes without shame. "Please don't blame Tempest. I forced her into being my accomplice. She didn't like any of it. I beg you not to bear her any ill. I will accept the punishment alone, whatever you see fit."

"Was marrying her part of this scheme?"

"No. It had nothing to do with Amberly, as I said before. I was afraid she would escape me. I loved her. I do love her." He slowly straightened, readying for the judgment, be it gaol or banishment, but he was thrown by his grandfather's next statement.

"No matter what your purpose, I do owe you for bringing Holly home."

"But she isn't Holly. She isn't even a real lady. Her name is Tempest Swift and I found her—"

"You don't understand. Listen to me. She is Holly. Tempest is Holly."

"No. You're confused. I paid her to act the part."

"It has nothing to do with you. They are one and the same. Holly is Tempest. Tempest is Holly. You did find Holly, Connor, and didn't even know it."

Numb with shock and disbelief, he could only shake his head. "How could you think that? I've met her family."

"But how long have they been her family? Since birth or since she was six years old? Could it be your inventive tale was more truth than fiction?" Jonathan's eyes were bright and hot with excitement, bringing a ruddy flush back to the sagging jowls. His withered hand clenched the fine-clad knee to increase the impact of his words.

"No."

"Connor, think. Think. She knows things, things she and I shared that you couldn't have known to tell her. Did you remember that she called your mother Aunt Jilly or that she gave her that doll, her dear Jilly doll that Tyler broke?"

"I'd forgotten," he muttered in a daze.

"But she didn't. Part of her remembered. And there are other things, too many for coincidence."

"Galahad," he whispered.

"What's that?"

He shook himself vigorously. "Nothing. You're just guessing, old man. You don't know she's Holly."

"And you don't know that she's not. Find out which of us is right, Connor."

In sudden alarm, he cried, "Does she know of any of this?"

"No. I wanted to wait until I knew for sure. Then you should tell her. It should come from you."

The old gentleman lay back on his pillows. The excitement had left him drained and weakly trembling. He looked very old and very sick, and Connor took up the frail hand that had known such strength with great care.

"I will find out for you," he promised. "Rest now, old man. Get well. I don't want to lose you."

Tempest sat beside the silent figure hunched up on an unyielding pew in the small chapel. Whether he prayed or merely sought privacy for his thoughts, she didn't know. His fingers curled quickly and tightly about the ones she offered, but he didn't look at her.

"It's so hard to see him like that," he told her quietly. "I guess you let yourself believe some people will live forever. I cannot imagine what it will be like when he's gone."

"I know, Connor. You must have faith. He may yet recover."

"This time, but he's old, and time is no friend to him." He brought her hand up to rub his cheek against the soft knuckles, remembering how rough they had once been. He had forgotten their antagonism, seeking comfort from her the way he would from no other, and feeling his hurt, she didn't deny it. They sat together in silent empathy for long minutes, until he lightly kissed her hand and said softly, "Thank you for being here for me. I've lost too many to count you among them now. Please promise you'll stay with me to see this through."

"I will be here as long as you need me, my lord."

He looked at her then, his eyes searching and intense as if looking for something important he hoped to find. "I truly never thought to see you again."

He said it so strangely, she felt he was speaking to someone else; then he leaned forward and kissed her, not on the lips but gently on the cheek as if with great affection. And then he left her with no word of explanation.

Jonathan did recover and, though weak and confined to a chair, was able to be on hand for the opening of the gifts on Christmas Eve as was their tradition. For once, they seemed almost a family, still wary but not openly hostile, and they enjoyed a truce over a succulent stuffed turkey and goblets of cheer.

Tempest and Connor had come to a truce of their own. They were considerate of each other when together but carefully formal to keep any emotion from threatening. They behaved like polite acquaintances with kind, passionless manners while in their private rooms, though both burned for more than the occasional chaste brush of their hands.

Cautiously, Connor had begun to probe into Tempest's past, which was surprisingly easy since they did little but exchange surface conversation. Slowly, he found growing inconsistencies, an unexplained number of blanks concerning the Swifts prior to her sixth year. She could read, but she couldn't explain how. She knew nursery rhymes and church hymns but didn't know where she had learned them. She couldn't remember Eddie as a baby. And she didn't know what frightened her in the darkness of the storm. But Connor was beginning to think he knew the answers.

For Tempest, time proved a constant threat, unsure how long she could conceal the gradual expansion of her figure. Already she had to forgo stays for the sake of comfort and adopt more loosely cut gowns. Thankfully, her health remained excellent, her pregnancy causing no ill-effects with her body. Not so with her mind.

Knowing she would soon have no choice but to tell Connor of her state, Tempest was in a quandary. Their relationship was tenuous at best without her secret. His absence had created a throbbing ache of loneliness, but knowing him to be so near, on the other side of the closed door, across the table, or apt to appear in the cavernous halls at any moment, was an agony to bear. To see him and not have him was a denial of all the vital, urgent yearnings of her young body. To have his cool, veiled stare touch on her in indifference was a stabbing blade to her uncertain heart. Her precarious position in his house and future left her emotionally adrift. If only she could believe he cared for her, but there was never a word or a sign. For all she knew, she was still a pawn in his charade, the name she bore as fictitious as the part she played.

She spent long, melancholy hours in Amberly's empty nursery, torn between the urge to plan excitedly or to weep in helpless misery. Connor's husky suggestions concerning the room haunted her relentlessly. But that was before she brought that look of hurtful accusation to his eyes, that shadow of betrayal she caught in his expression before it was quickly masked. Would he want this child? Would he accept it with the same devotion she already knew, or would he refuse his name? Even if he didn't cast the slur of bastard on the innocent, would he be willing to claim the child of a nameless pauper, a thief he dressed as a lady? Would he make a child of no social pedigree his heir? Would her thickening figure and the pull of responsibility drive him back to the arms of his ever-present mistresses?

Her heart heavy, her eyes lingered over him as the family celebrated the holiday. He was so beautiful, so tantalizingly male. The memories of his tenderness and passion, of waking with him beside her and falling asleep in the aftermath of their loving made her sigh in futile longing.

Gifts exchanged and dutifully admired, Tempest was finally able to escape the strained festivities to the silent seclusion of her room. A short time later, she was startled by a tap on the adjoining door, surprised because Connor hadn't set foot in her room since his return.

At the faint call to enter, Connor advanced tentatively, but when she looked up and he saw the glistening of tears, he forgot his caution and went to her quickly. Kneeling down beside her chaise, he asked in quiet concern, "What is it, sweet? What's wrong? Please tell me."

She sniffed loudly and looked away, finding it difficult to express the hollow ache in her breast. "Nothing's wrong, my lord. I'm just being a goose. I was thinking of past holidays with my family; oh, none so grand as this but nice, you know. I had my gifts sent, but it's not the same as being with those you love on Christmas day."

His fingertips brushed the damp cheek in a tender caress, bringing the unhappy eyes around to meet his. "Dry your eyes, my love. Pack some things. We can be there by morning."

She stared at him as if he was making some terrible joke, then with a joyful wail cast her arms tightly about his neck. "Oh, Connor. Connor, thank you."

She had meant it to be a brief embrace, but she couldn't release him. It was so wonderful to be in his arms, to have the lean strength of his body against her, to breathe in the clean masculine scent of him. Just to be able to touch him was heaven. Her fingers lost themselves in the midnight hair and plied the muscled shoulder with a desperate longing. Her thoughts were too filled with him to think beyond the moment.

Connor pushed away from her and stood, his voice slightly strained. "I'd better go wake up a driver. You dress warmly."

"Connor," she said softly, "you don't know how much this means to me."

"It's Christmas," he explained with a small smile.

Under the pretext of going to visit George and his newly bethrothed, they were on their way to London within the hour It took only a suggestion for her to nestle close to his side to share the warmth and comfort on the cold December night. Beneath the heavy lap robe, Tempest was pleasantly snug, the heat from Connor's body serving more as a balm to the spirit. With his arm about her shoulders in a protective circle and the slow steady rhythm of his heart beneath her cheek, she settled happily to sleep. He was taking her home.

But Connor didn't sleep. The disturbing tension of her nearness in tandem with his apprehension over what this visit with the Swifts would yield kept him wakeful and restless. What if she would not leave the bosom of her family to return with him? What if he indeed found Holly in the person he loved? He hugged her pliant figure close in the darkness of the coach and stared into the night. All too soon, he became aware of the sour, marshy scent of South London made fouler by the stink of tanning and glue factories. Through the cold, rising mists of dawn, he could see the huddle of ancient houses and inns, crumbling, stark, and uninviting. How could he let her remain in such a decaying place?

371

Frowning moodily, he gave her a gentle shake. "Wake up, love. We're almost there."

When she mumbled and stretched, he opened his arm to let her sit back, glumly realizing he might never have the chance to hold her again.

Chapter Twenty-four

The Swifts swarmed the carriage like a denizen of eager robbers, pulling Tempest into their midst with floods of tears and joyous weeping. Connor followed them inside, excluded from the emotional welcome and feeling very much the outsider. Being Christmas, the tavern was empty but still bore signs of the previous night's revelry. They passed through and into the kitchen, their only truly private family space other than the shared bedrooms overhead. It was a large spotlessly clean room smelling pleasantly of spitted fowl and the pungent simmer of grog spices. While the family settled on benches about a huge trestle table, Connor lingered back in the doorway.

"What a surprise and a blessing to see you," Dolly Swift was sobbing happily, dabbing streaming eyes on the corner of her apron. "Can you stay? For how long?"

"I'm not certain, Mama." The large blue eyes rose in question, drawing attention to the presence of her elegant husband.

"For as long as you like," he answered quietly.

Tempest looked away quickly, her heart in her eyes. Did he mean to leave her here? Was that the purpose of his generous offer? Was he ready to release her from her part? Was that all being his wife had ever been?

"You'll have to stay for supper at least," Dolly continued. "It's all your favorites. We opened your gifts last eve. So generous and unnecessary after all his lordship's already done for us." She cast a shy glance at the aloof nobleman and tendered a grateful smile.

"What things?" Tempest demanded in confusion.

"The new bedding for the children, the hogshead of rum for Will, the crockery so I can finally set a matching table, the fine brace of pistols for Eddie. And then there was mending the roof and a new front glass and oh, I don't remember what all before that. But always the extra shillings for whatever was needed. We are blessed to have a daughter who so remembers her family."

Tempest was very still; then she looked again at Connor. It was the first she had heard of any of these deeds. The pale eyes regarded her unwaveringly until once again she turned away in uncertainty.

"Here, my lord. Warm your insides. It's a cold one outside today."

Connor took the mug of steaming grog with a nod of thanks, then said, "I would like a word with you, Swift, when it's convenient."

"It best be now then. We gots company coming this evening."

Will led them back into the taproom and drew up

two chairs. Out of sight of the kitchen, he produced a bottle of tolerable rum and laced their cups stiffly. "What's on your mind, my lord?"

"Tempest. You say she's your daughter."

"Well, a man should know that, shouldn't he? Of course, she's my girl." Will stared deeply into his mug, his shoulders squared and defensive.

"Why didn't you tell her who she really was?"

Will Swift looked up then, his eyes black with torment. "Because I didn't know. Honest to God, I had no name to put to her until you'd already married her. Do you think I would have agreed if I knew you meant for her to masquerade as herself? She was supposed to be dead. I was paid to see that she was killed."

Both men took long drafts from their cups; then Will labored over his tale while the cool-eyed gentleman sat unmoving.

In his younger days, Will Swift had been a desperate man. With a wife and young son he could barely provide food and lodgings for, he took little exception to any work he could find. When the chance availed to make more money than he ever dreamed of, he asked no questions, and on a stormy Christmas night, he and five others set upon a designated carriage on its way out of London.

"I didn't know the plan was to kill them all," Will swore fervently. "I'd have had no part in that, no matter what the payoff. I thought it was just a holdup until the shooting started. The driver and the man in the coach were killed. The tongue of the carriage broke, and it went into the river. The water was fast because of the rains and so cold no one but me would venture in. The lady had hit her head and drowned. That's when I saw Tempest. She was a little tiny thing so scared and barely hanging on. Them others, they would have killed her, a little tyke like that, but I—I just couldn't be party to that. I took her up under my coat and hid her until I could leave the others. Dolly, she took to her right off."

"A couple of days later, Johnny, one of the others, came by and said there'd be £10,000 to the man who could prove the little girl from the carriage was dead. It was a lot of money, and I'd been dreaming of buying this place so Dolly and the boy would have a proper home. I took Johnny the shoes and coat and told him I'd found her washed up on the bank of the river. No one was the wiser. I got the inn, and they quit looking for her."

"And Holly?"

"She was real sick for a long time. I thought we'd lose her, but when she got better, she'd forgotten all of it, who she was, everything. Dolly and me decided to take her in as ours. Saw no harm in it, her folks dead and all and somebody wanting her that way too. We named her because of the storms. She was so afraid of them. I thought she would remember, but she never did, and pretty soon she was our girl, and that's what she still believes."

"Who hired you?" Connor asked quietly.

"I don't know. Johnny took care of the money and all. He's been dead, hanged for five years now."

They sat in silence for a long time, each with his own deep thoughts. Finally, Will ventured, "What's it to be, my lord? Gaol for me?"

Connor sat back heavily, thinking of his grandfather's mercy, and shrugged. "I don't see the point of it now. You raised her well enough. Your hand didn't take the life of my aunt or uncle. It wouldn't change anything that's happened. Holly thinks you're her father. I couldn't very well put you in irons."

"What about Tempest—Holly? Will you tell her?"

"I don't know," he admitted flatly.

Will hesitated, then asked bluntly, "You being her husband and all, I ain't got the right to ask, but do you care for the girl?"

"I love her. That's why I'll do nothing that would hurt her."

Will nodded, satisfied by that.

"I would appreciate it if this matter would stay silent between us."

"Done, my lord."

Seeing Connor leave with her father, then having them both return with long, somber faces, Tempest's hopes were crushed. He was leaving her. She loved her family, but she had made her life with the handsome arrogant lord who had wed her. She wouldn't grieve over the loss of the lavish lifestyle he had given her. She couldn't deny she had enjoyed it, but she had always seen it as play acting and refused to take it seriously. Connor she took seriously. Her marriage to him was no act on her part. She wanted more than anything to live the vows she had spoken. And then there was the child to consider.

Finding Tempest, for she would always be Tempest to him, in a speculative mood, Connor resigned himself to a day of uncomfortable isolation. Eddie's fierce stare followed his every movement, Will was too full of his own torments, Dolly was friendly but painfully shy, and the children ogled him as if he were some foreign creature that might yet devour them. When they sat down to the meal, the sight of them all eating with their fingers set his stomach on edge.

It was a family custom to join hands at the table to give thanks, one Dolly insisted upon with uncharacteristic stubbornness. With Tempest's cool fingers on one side and Eddie's roughened paw on the other, Connor was awed by the quiet eloquence of Will Swift's words, so sincere and humble as he listed their meager fortunes. When his name was given among them, he felt Tempest's hand squeeze his almost imperceptibly.

It might not have been elaborately displayed, but his first meal with the Swifts was as good as any he had sampled, and the conversation far superior. They may have had no flair for manners, but their table was easy to sit to, abundant with relaxed, animated talk and the warmth of a family's love. Keeping quietly to himself, Connor enjoyed watching the rapid, noisy exchanges. How different from the table they had been to the previous night.

As the dishes were cleared away, Dolly blushed fiercely at Connor's heartfelt compliments and thanks. Then the guests began to arrive. There were cousins, aunts, uncles, nieces, nephews, brothers, fathers until Connor was sure the entire East End was somehow related to the Swifts. The tavern filled with the company, and casks were tapped and generously sampled. They all skirted Tempest's new husband with a respectful discomfort until he began to feel his presence was dampening the spirit of the day. After deciding it would be best for him to travel on to George's, then Grosvenor Square on his own, he went to find Tempest to say good-bye.

They met under an arched doorway, and before he could utter a word, Tempest grinned teasingly and pointed overhead.

"Mistletoe, my lord. I'm afraid you are compromised."

Locking her wrists behind his neck, Tempest stretched up to give him a quick kiss, but he had other intentions. One hand pressed to the small of her back and the other clenching in the riot of curls, he brought her up hard against him. His hot mouth devoured hers as if it was a delectable fare that had teased his appetite long enough, and now he meant to have his fill. And while the room of gawking relatives grew silent in their staring, he did just that. He drank of the sweet taste of her lips until he was lightheaded with it, yet agonized that this sample only whetted his hunger for the rest of the dish he had been held from for so long. Hot and shivery with desire, he let her go.

"What's wrong with the lot of you?" Dolly Swift scolded, flapping her apron at the ogling group. "Ain't you ever seen a man kiss his wife before?"

"Not his own like that, we ain't," one man called, and the silence gave way to ribald laughter.

Dolly seized Connor's hand and gave him an encouraging tug. "I'd like a dance with my son-in-law. Nothing fancy, mind you. I'm just a simple maid."

379

"Not so simple," Connor vowed with a wide, warming smile as he led her out into the area cleared for dancing and now teeming with couples.

Tempest sagged gratefully into the chair she was steered to and gulped down the ale that filled her hand. Her heart was pounding much too fast, pushing crazy careening tremors of confused emotion through her until every inch of her trembled with it. Oh, what that man could do to her with the simplest of touches. But his kiss had never been a simple matter, always reducing her to a weak, malleable form that wanted to be shaped by his hand alone. His mouth had conveyed a wealth of fiery promise, of want, of need, of urgent desire. For her. She shook nervelessly. He still wanted her. But was it for this night alone when she was accessible, and he was adrift in her element? If she went to him now, how could she let him go tomorrow?

Sobered by that reflection, she watched him move among her family with an accepted ease. After all, how could they fail to like a man who could take the starch out of Will Swift's little fireeater? Before her composure was firmly in hand, he was lifting her up and drawing her into his arms for a dance. His steps would have shocked the naughtiest Mayfair hostess, and those who thought the waltz a scandalous excuse to fondle in public would have been mortified. His feet moved in a side-to-side shuffle out of sync with the music but full of a rhythm they knew and shared. With her crushed close, his body rubbed hers with a seductive invitation that grew impossible to ignore. When his head lowered to whisper hoarsely in her ear, she clutched to him in a rapturous panic.

"Oh, sweet, I'm on fire for you. Please say you still love me. Tell me that you want me. Love me, Tempest."

She couldn't force an answer, her will engulfed by the heat and strength of him and her own frailty working against her with a traitorous insistence. You want him, take him, it urged. Make him want you. Make him love you.

Without awaiting her decision, Connor stopped before Will and Dolly, Tempest still very much in his arms. "Please forgive us, but it was an exhausting journey here, and we should find lodgings."

"Nonsense. You'll stay here. Dolly, fix them our best room."

"No," Tempest protested in panic. How could she bear the shame of their knowing she and her husband had separate rooms and solitary beds. "We should go across the river and find a fitting place for his lordship."

"Really, my love. What a snob you've become. A room here will be more than adequate for us. I swear I'm weary enough to sleep on one of the tables down here." He grinned, but the pale blue fire of his eyes warned that if she didn't get him upstairs quickly, she might find herself taken across the top of one.

"As you wish, my lord," she assented nervously. "Don't bother yourself, Mama. I'll see to the room. Good night."

She fairly ran up the stairs, her heart an anxious flutter as she heard Connor's light tread behind her. When he stepped into the room and closed the door to the world apart from the two of them, she was smothered by his presence and trapped by her own surging desires. In an attempt to calm the frantic rush of emotion, she began to putter about the room, turning up the lights, pulling back the covers, fluffing pillows while lazy eyes hungered over her every move. When he advanced into the room, all dark, sleek grace and male magnetism, she scurried back to put as much possible distance between her and the narrow, intimate bed.

Connor sat on the edge of the bed, raising a soaring brow at the loud groan it uttered. When he gave a testing bounce, the rattles and creaks made him chuckle wickedly. "A good thing your family is noisy. I quite like them, you know. They remind me of the Morleys, more of them turning up all the time, jumping at you like friendly, untrained pups. Tempest, come here."

She shied away as if she hadn't heard, crossing to the window to look out the hazy glass. "I want to thank you for what you've done for my family. Why didn't you tell me you were seeing to them? Why would you want to?"

"Because they're your family. I told you I was a good and generous fellow. Didn't you believe me?"

"Forgive me for pointing out how little truth comes from much of what you say. And as for your good and generous nature, I have not seen it of late."

Her prickling attack brought a pout to his fine mouth, but his glittering eyes only grew heavier. "I want to recompense you for that now. Come here."

Still she held back, eyeing him with jaundice. "Is

that a command, my lord? Are you merely taking inventory of your properties? Will not my word that I have seen to them well suffice?"

"I would prefer to see to them well myself. Tempest, come here to me. Now."

She hesitated. She could balk and try to force him into making pretty speeches about how much he wanted her, not sure she could believe him anyway, or she could go to him and show him how much she wanted him. She looked at him narrowly, the smug, patient master who had given an order and waited for compliance, the cool color of his eyes masking the inner fire. If she delayed too long, those sleepy eyes could harden and she would lose him. Nothing was worth that risk, no amount of pride. So she went to him.

With hands on the lithesome curve of her waist, he drew her close between his knees, then surprised her. Resting his head against her soft bosom, his arms circled her in a tight, almost desperate embrace. His voice was low and rough with emotion.

"Promise me that, no matter what happens, you won't stop loving me. Promise me."

Tempest closed her eyes, her heart clutching in pain. He was going to leave her. Slowly, her hands rose to touch, then tangle in the dark satin of his hair. "I will always love you, Connor," she said almost sadly, but he was placated, heaving a sigh of satisfied relief. When he looked up, his perfect features were cast in an uneven light, creating an intriguing pattern of contours along the strong, clean jaw, finely cut cheekbones, and thin aristocratic nose.

"Then love me now."

It was a deep powerful command that met with no resistance. She went down on the complaining mattress with him, accepting and returning his claiming kisses while the barrier of their clothing was breached in careless urgency. Shoes and boots and whispers of silk and the scatter of buttons all fell to the floor as they hurried to find with each other the pyres of passion with its blissful aftermath of shared peace.

But Tempest could find no peace even though the desires of her body had been well met and exhausted. Tears slipped unnoticed to wet her pillow as she lay in the darkness studying the shadowed face of the man who slept beside her. Would their child look like him? She hoped so, imagining he was wondrously fair even as a babe. How unfair it would be for this child not to know its father.

Her hand caressed the warm cheek, bringing a soft mutter as he nudged into her palm. With a helpless cry, she kissed him, feeling his response waken as he did to the greedy, panicked searching of her mouth and hot splash of her tears. As his hands came up to hold her, she burrowed her face into the hollow of his throat, sobbing quietly.

"Tempest? Sweet, what is it?"

"Oh, Connor, even if you don't care for me, tell me how I can make you want me enough to take me with you. I will do anything, be anything you wish, only please don't leave me behind."

"What? I'm sorry, love. I fear I'm not completely awake. What is this about my leaving you?"

"I know you plan to leave me here with my family.

384

Please take me back to Amberly with you. I promise I will be no trouble for you. I won't be tiresome or make demands."

"My sweet, you were born to be troublesome, but that's why I care for you so. I don't want to leave you here. Listen to me." He took her wet face in the spread of his long, cool fingers. "I thought you wanted to remain. I've done so little to make you happy, I feared you wouldn't want to leave with me."

"But I love you," she protested. "Of course I want to be with you. You are my husband. My place is wherever you are."

"I haven't wanted to be apart from you since the first time I looked into your beautiful eyes. You foolish creature, how could you believe I'd ever tire of you? I married you, didn't I?"

"But that was against your will. You were so very angry."

"Because you scared me so badly. You left me, and I feared I couldn't get you back. Come home with me, and we shall work on being man and wife."

With a soft cry, she hugged him about the neck. Then they were kissing, and she forgot her tears and her worries as he rolled above her, fanning the fires of passion.

A soft click brought Connor's eyes open with a snap to see the dark bore of a pistol an inch from his nose and over it the sullen black eyes of Eddie Swift. He hazarded a glance to the side, but Tempest wasn't next to him.

"Are you going to make my sister happy?" the boy growled.

"Has she complained to you that I haven't?" he replied with a nonchalant ease.

"She didn't have to say nothing. You may come from that fancy set, but you ain't going to do no better than Este."

"No argument there. Now either shoot me or get that out of my face before I break your wrist."

Eddie gave a rare grin and lifted the muzzle. "It weren't loaded anyways. I was meaning to ask if you'd show me how to use one."

In one smooth motion, Connor sat up, snatched the pistol from his hand, and leveled it between the dark eyes. Eddie swallowed hard. Knowing it was empty didn't lessen the deadly threat in the cool blue eyes that had become a flash of steel.

"First lesson, never aim unless you mean to shoot, ever. Don't rely on a bluff. Be prepared to kill any time you draw a weapon."

The gun dropped, and Eddie gave a relieved breath. It took only a moment for his bluster to return. "You ever use that on anybody?"

"I've been in a dozen or so duels, some with pistols, some with swords." He said it casually, not bragging, but as simple fact as if not proud of what Eddie saw as an accomplishment.

The black eyes widened as the boy struggled not to seem too impressed. "Is them from your duels?" he asked with feigned indifference, gesturing to the scars that marred the broad chest and well-developed arms. When Connor nodded, he pursed his lips. "You must not be too good at it to get so marked up."

"That's because I let them fire first."

"Well, that don't sound too smart."

"Nothing about duels is smart, boy. Only a fool toys with matters of life and death. I let them shoot first because I was the fool at fault and should be the one to meet the punishment."

"Were they all poor shots?" Eddie was sitting on the bed now, giving up the pose of boredom, his eyes rapt and shining.

"There's a difference between shooting at targets and looking down a barrel at a man you could kill or be killed by. When that man looks you straight in the eye, it's hard to hold onto your steady hand."

"Were you ever scared?" That question was soft, echoing his own feelings of inadequacy and man-hood.

"Always. Right down to my boots every time."

"Did you ever kill any of them?"

"Two. One in anger. One by mistake."

The terse reply made the boy take stock anew of the gentleman. "What did you fight over?"

Connor's lip curled sardonically. "Are you thinking it was some noble cause? I was caught with the careless wives of neglectful men, whose only fault was to trust the flirting chits they married with men like me."

"And is this something you plan to keep doing?"

Connor smiled ruefully at the scowling face. "Any duels I'm involved in in the future will most likely be over my wife's honor. An ironic turn, wouldn't you say?" But he didn't want to think of that, not today, and forced his thoughts elsewhere. He looked toward the window, squinting at the brightness of the day. "Why is it you are here instead of my wife?"

"She's been up and about for hours. She sent me to fetch you down for breakfast."

"Fetch me? Indeed."

"If you want to eat. We don't coddle to the lazy here. Ain't nobody got the time to bring you breakfast in bed."

"What a rude little child you are," he grumbled with the twitch of a smile. "I will be down directly if you can find a shirt for me to wear."

"We ain't got no fancy linen."

"Anything with sleeves will do nicely. Now get out of my sight before I box your ears."

Eddie grinned and hopped up. He appraised the bristle-haired man who sat naked and bleary-eyed between his sister's sheets for a long second. "You ain't half so fancy first thing in the morning," he begrudged.

"But you are just as boorish. Go on with you."

Tempest paused in her conversation with her mother at the arresting sight of her husband. She had seen him in all his court finery, yet here in this poor kitchen, sleekly groomed and clad in one of her father's coarse-weave shirts worn open at the neck and pushed up over his forearms, Connor Amberson looked capable, earthy, and ruggedly handsome. She didn't see him as some far superior, wealthy lord, but as a man whom, on that basic level alone, none could equal.

"Good morning, ladies. I have been duly fetched," he called easily, but controlling the sudden flare of his ardor was no easy matter. Tempest was dressed in the same type of baggy trousers and shapeless shirt as the highwayman of old, perched on the countertop. Her lovely face was flushed from the heat of the kitchen, but the warmth in her eyes was from an inner fire. This was the woman he had fallen in love with, not the artificial puppet he had forced her to become, and he would never mistake the two again.

He walked up to where she sat, their eyes locked in that deep communion lovers share. Forgetting Dolly in that world where only the two of them existed, Tempest leaned down to accept his kiss of greeting, her arms slipping about his neck and her legs twining around his lean waist as he drew her to him. He lifted her from the counter and carried her, wrapped about him and still feasting on his mouth into the empty taproom where he settled into a chair with her in his lap.

After several minutes of contented touching and savoring, Tempest leaned away only slightly so his face filled her entire field of vision. "Good morning, my lord. You are looking particularly manly today. What happened to your own fine attire?"

"There didn't seem to be any buttons on my shirt. So you think this rather brutish image suits me?"

" 'Tis not the image that suits me, sir," she murmured sassily, her fingers following the angles of his face in a loving caress until his pale crystal eyes drooped in sultry pleasure.

389

"And you suit me, my love, just as I see you now. Don't ever let me try to change you. Everything I desire is before me."

"Are you through with the charade then?" she asked, puzzled but pleased.

"It's not important to me anymore. You are all that matters and making a home for us at Amberly. Are you certain you want to come with me? I am not a very good fellow, and you could do much better."

"Perhaps," she teased. "But I want you."

When their leisurely kiss ended, Connor said, "I'm going to visit George this morning. Will you go with me, or would you like to see more of your family?"

"I don't plan to let you out of my sight. My family will understand. You are one of us too."

"I don't know why, but that thought pleases me."

Chapter Twenty-five

The last thing George Morley expected while sharing a quiet, intimate breakfast with the woman who had just recently agreed to marry him was a sudden joyful cry from another woman as she flung her arms about his neck and smothered his face with kisses. As Miss Sarah Norwich sat stiffly in shocked dismay, George cast a helpless glance to Connor, begging for rescue.

"Let poor George breathe, my love," Connor scolded with a chuckle. "You are putting him in a deuced dangerous position with his lady. Hello, Miss Norwich. This wayward chit is my wife, Tempest, so never fear that she is attempting to steal away your betrothed. I wouldn't allow it."

Both George and Tempest looked at him in surprise at the casual use of her name; then Tempest blushed fiercely, remembering herself.

"Oh, I do beg your pardon, Miss Norwich. I must

seem the shameless hussy, but George is my dearest friend, and it's been so long since I was banished from London." She shot Connor a naughty glance, rewarded by his wince.

Sarah Norwich, while not a great beauty, was petite and quiet with light brown curls and a set of lively dark eyes that warmed with a gentle humor. Tempest liked her immediately and snatched her away to leave George to the mercy of Connor's teasing. As the women chatted away in an easy budding friendship, the two men withdrew to the parlor to toast over a brandy.

"To your happiness, George. May it be as rich and full as mine promises to be."

As they drank to that, George regarded his friend closely. "Conn, what is it? What's wrong?"

"Wrong? What could be wrong? I'm married to a woman I care for, who loves me. I'm about to inherit Amberly." He slid George a sidelong look to verify that he believed none of his cheery assurances. With a heavy sigh, he mourned, "Oh, George, why does everything have to be so hard and confused?"

Standing at the window watching Sarah and his wife in the garden jungle, Connor related his discovery about Tempest's past.

Recovering from his amazement, George said calmly, "I fail to see a problem, Conn. She's your wife. You should be pleased it worked out this way. Now there can be no threat to Amberly. She has clear title to it."

"But what if after finding out who she is, she decides she wants Amberly and no longer needs me?"

"What nonsense are you spouting?" George chided

kindly. "Do you think she loves you only because of what you can give her? You do, don't you?"

"Why else?"

George stared at him in disbelief, then shook his head. "You are an idiot, Conn. You just cannot believe there is anything good about you that people might like. Do you think I've stayed your friend for all these years just because you pay me well to be?"

"Have you, George?" he asked in quiet misery, afraid to look up until he was sharply cuffed. George looked indignant, exasperated but also amused. "Sometimes I do not know why I tolerate you except that you are the best friend a man could have, and I guard that jealously. Conn, Tempest loves you not because of your circumstances but in spite of them, just as I do. Perhaps if you didn't have all that wealth to hide behind, you'd be forced to act yourself instead of the snobbish aristocrat that steers people away. You might even like what you see."

"I can never like what I see," he cried in an low anguish, sure that if George knew the truth, he would share his loathing.

"Why? Because of a careless accident that happened to a boy more than ten years ago? Yes, Tempest told me. Why are you punishing yourself for something that was not your fault? Let go of it. No one blames you."

"Someone has to. Someone should have. I cannot let it go."

"Cannot or will not? Is playing the martyr a role you relish?"

"Enough," he snapped fiercely, then in a softer tone asked, "As my friend, please, George, no more of this."

"As you wish." He clasped the tensed shoulder and squeezed tightly until the rigid stance loosened.

His eyes once again on the titian-haired sprite, Connor murmured, "I don't have to tell her. In truth, she'd come to no harm never knowing. She'll still have her rightful inheritance. Her children will be Ambersons. She's happy as she is. What good could come of her knowing the man she believes is her father helped kill her parents? She doesn't remember any of it. Isn't it better that she be spared that confusion?"

"Better for whom? For you, certainly. That way you won't have to take a risk or trust your wife. For her? I don't know. I won't advise you on this, Conn. That decision's yours. But be warned, if you don't tell her and she finds out—well, you know her temper."

"I know I'm being a beggarly coward but, damme, George, I can't lose her."

Almack's was hardly prepared for the arrival of Lord and Lady Amberson accompanied by George and Sarah. After Tempest's abrupt disappearance from Mayfair and his lordship's angry solitude in his haunting of the gaming clubs thereafter, no one expected them to arrive together and so obviously reconciled. Especially one lady.

After the immediate crush of admirers had been endured, Tempest looked up at her elegant husband with a mixture of pride and anxiety. Love and hurt played cruelly upon her heart until she was forced to ask in feigned gaiety, "Are there any new mistresses I should be warned of so there will be no unnecessary tearing of hair and costly silks?"

"Do you think I hopped guiltlessly from bed to bed after I sent you away? Look about this assembly. Do you see another that could come close to replacing you in my bed or in my heart? Look at me." The vulnerable eyes lifted slowly, unwilling to trust but begging to be convinced. "There was no one. There has been no one for me since our marriage. No mistresses, no consorts, no demi-reps, no flirtations, not even any secret longings. Just you. Ask George if you must. He'll tell you I was such wretched company while you were apart from me that even he was hard-pressed to bear my presence."

"Oh," was all she said, her eyes dropping. Why should she believe him? Why would he stay faithful to her when he had yet to name a reason? While these thoughts tormented her, he laid a light hand on her arm to draw her attention.

"I love you."

He said it without looking at her, in a casual manner with the same inflection as "Good evening." She glanced about to see if he was speaking to someone else.

"What did you say?" she demanded tightly.

"Well you needn't look as though I was insulting you," he replied a bit huffily, his handsome face drawn in haughty lines.

"I would hear it from you again, my lord." Her voice was trembling. The huge, china blue eyes were intent on his.

"I merely said I love you."

"Oh!"

Her joyous cry was followed by a crush about his neck and a flood of weeping that drew many curious stares.

"Calm yourself, sweet. Why so surprised?"

"Because I am," she sobbed, hugging him fiercely and never wanting to let go. "You've never said that to me before."

"Of course, I have," he protested in mild indignation. "I've said it to you often, but you've never thrown yourself at my head in hysterics."

"But you haven't. I've never known it until this minute." She came down off her tiptoes, her large eyes bright and shimmering with happiness.

He brushed the dampness from her cheeks and smiled faintly, pleased but also a bit shy. "How could you not know? Why else would I have done so much to keep you safe and at my side?"

Her soft lips quivering slightly, she whispered, "I wish I had known. So much would have been different. At last I can tell you that I'm—"

Suddenly a voice said, "May I have the pleasure of this dance, Lady Amberson?"

Tempest swung about with the intention of giving the interloper a crisp dressing down, but dropped into a curtsy at the sight of the Prince Regent. She cast Connor an apologetic glance as she was whisked out onto the floor to be spun about in the arms of countless eager partners until Connor was able to claim her hand once again.

Holding her possessively as they moved through the waltz, Connor pouted sulkily as if in a high dungeon. She did little to soothe his aggrieved condition, looking smug and teasing him with her eyes.

Finally, nettled by her amusement, he complained, "Why is it these prancing ninnies pay court to no one else's wife but mine?"

"It could be because in order to be of the highest fashion, I am wearing nothing under this gown."

Connor misstepped, trodding heavily on her slippered foot as his eyes dropped to scrutinize the emerald taffeta until convinced it betrayed none of her charms. To make matters worse, she pressed against him to let him feel the truth of her statement.

"I'm on fire for you," she whispered roughly in his ear. "Connor, kiss me. Take me now."

His breath was a raspy rattle, his arms growing so tight she feared he would crush her. Then with a groan, he gave her a push away. "Shameless creature. Do not tease me so in public."

He was unaware of the magnitude of his reaction until she giggled naughtily. "My lord, you should be more concerned with your own shocking lack of modesty."

He followed her saucy stare to the front of his skintight trousers and grimaced. "You wicked jade. Look what you've done to me. Is it your wish that all these simple maids be enlightened at your expense?"

"If they dare ogle you, I'll tear the eyes from their milksop faces," she growled crossly, moving nearer to conceal the front of his bulging attire.

"Well, my love, you created the situation, you'd best tend to it." Now he was teasing, and her cheeks warmed with anticipation.

With Connor walking close behind her, Tempest made her way to the door, saying pretty, polite good evenings while keenly aware of the heat of the hands that rested lightly upon her waist. Their darkened coach was only slightly warmer than the frigid night, but when Connor pulled her into his lap, its interior heated rapidly.

Tempest squeezed her eyes closed with a shaky breath of excitement as his lips burned hotly through the crisp fabric of her bodice. The long taffeta skirts crunched noisily as they were ruched up about her knees that rested on either side of his thighs on the cold seat cushions. His warm hand slipped up that length of creamy leg to meet with the urgent welcoming heat of her body. His mouth moved up to take hers, breathing in her hurried gasps with a claiming strength while his purposeful touch made her writhe and tremble at his control.

All was hot and swirling, passion, love, desire all merging and blending and mounting until Tempest was panting frantically into his kisses. Her body seemed more his than her own, responding to his every touch with an instinctive fervor divorced from thought or emotion to be used and shaped by his will and command.

Connor felt her pleasure build and boil through the pressure of her clinging lips and clenching fingers until it was all he could do to restrain herself. Finally, she sobbed into his kiss, the tension of her body becoming liquid, melting against him in grateful surrender. He held her close, shivering with the cold of the night and the heat of his own desire, kissing her gently before shifting her head to his shoulder.

"Oh, Tempest, how I love you," he said with heavy emotion. His eyes shut with an agony of need as she nibbled along his neck, shaking his passions to the limit.

There was a rattle of the coach's doorknob and an impatient call from without.

"Conn, it's freezing out here."

George grinned at the colorful expletive and hurried to scramble away before the door was kicked open. He handed Sarah up, then climbed in to smirk at the rather flushed and crumpled pair. Tempest lay languidly upon Connor's chest, her eyes heavy and expression dreamy while Connor was all tense, sharp edges and fierce glowers, looking so hostile that Sarah was quite intimidated. George patted her hand and met his friend's stare with little sympathy.

"Is it your wish that we walk?"

"Yes," Connor snapped in angry frustration, his insides a tight, knotted ache.

"Of course not, George. Connor is just being testy," Tempest purred silkily. Her fingers ran up and down the firm thigh until his hands clenched the edge of the seat, his knuckles white and well defined. When that tantalizing touch slipped under his coat to stroke from chest to taut middle, it was all he could do not to groan in torment. Unmindful of Sarah's discomfort and George's amusement, his eyes closed and his breath grew labored. Her lips moved upon his throat in a tempting combination of nips and wet kisses until the heels of his boots scraped the floor of the coach and his toes curled up tightly. Giving a low growl, he snatched the teasing minx up for a firm masterful kiss.

"Don't think too badly of them, Sarah," George chuckled. "They're always lusting after one another in public. It's shockingly poor behavior, but do try to ignore it."

Having overcome her embarrassed blushes, Sarah slid him a sidelong glance. "Do you think we might behave as badly."

George raised a speculative brow. "I'm sure they won't notice," he said, drawing her into his arms.

The driver finally had to rap on the roof after waiting several minutes outside the Morley house to draw a response from within.

"It seems we've stopped," Tempest murmured huskily.

"Good. Get out, George," was the blunt reply.

"Thank you for your hospitality," his friend said sarcastically.

"I will be charming and hospitable next time we meet," he promised. "But right now, I am impatient, so be good enough to leave my coach."

Laughing, George extended a hand to him. "You're not staying?"

"No, we're for Amberly. At least there will be no interruptions for a decent amount of time. A happy holiday to you and your lady." He pressed an envelope into Sarah's hand, then kissed it gently. "I am not really a terrible fellow."

She smiled as if she wasn't sure she believed it, then exclaimed over the passes to see Joseph Grimaldi in Drury Lane's Christmas pantomime. She was a great fan of the gentle clown and was heartbroken to find the performances had been sold out. How had he managed? She looked across at the magnetic, intense man and decided there was little that he could not obtain if he wanted it. George's friend was overpowering and scary to her timid nature, alarming her with his dramatic swings of mood and untamed boldness. She had dreaded his presence and frequent company and resented George's fondness for him. But the appearance of his wife had altered that. Tempest, who had completely charmed her, managed the brutish lord with ease, changing the volatile temperament into a subdued energy that simmered and flared according to her whims. Connor Amberson presented a glossy, attractive splendor in face and form but always with a threatening hint of something dangerous beneath it. Apparently, Tempest had more courage than she. Sarah preferred her George and was frankly grateful that Connor was leashed and distracted.

"Thank you, my lord. This is very kind of you."

"Please, not so formal. If you marry George, you'll be like family." He took up her hand again, his pale eyes warm and compelling as he leaned forward and kissed her lightly on trembling lips. "My wife isn't the only shameless one. I thought I'd steal that while I had the chance."

"You've the last one," George warned with a smile and a wary look as his arm passed about Sarah's shivering shoulders. He, too, was glad his friend was safely netted.

"Yes," Tempest seconded.

"Now, get out. My good humor is at an end."

Alone in the darkened coach, rushing on its way to Amberly, Connor turned and whispered thickly, "Now, where were we?"

Much later, Tempest sighed in contentment. She

401

no longer felt the chill of the night, snug between Connor's half-reclined figure and covered by his Garrick from neck to bare toes. Rubbing her cheek against the warmth of his hard chest, she murmured, "Tell me again."

"Tell you what, sweet?"

"Connor."

"Oh, you mean that I love you? All right if I must. I love you. I love you. I love you."

"Don't tease, you vile beast," she reprimanded crisply.

"Vile am I? You were not of that mind during the last few hours."

"They were wonderful, weren't they?" she crooned throatily, tipping up her head to nuzzle his neck. "We should always travel in this manner."

"As you wish, my love," he agreed. He shifted slightly so she rested full against him, the soft rounded contours stirring a lazy simmer of unhurried desire.

"Your love," she mused dreamily. "How long have you loved me?"

"If you need an exact day or hour, I do not know. It just took me by surprise, the way you always do."

"Was it when you first kissed me?"

"That was lust, sweet, pure, and simple," he chuckled, wincing when she twisted a piece of flesh over his ribs. His voice deepening, he told her, "I think it was when I knew I could have you for the taking but waited, knowing it would be better if you came to me. I've never waited on anything I wanted before, and oh, how I wanted you, how I still want

402

you."

She kissed his shoulder and nestled more closely into his embrace.

"And when did you decide you loved me?" There was a touch of hesitance in his voice, just a touch, but it made her smile.

"That first kiss. Your kisses always ruin me. They make up for all else."

She fell silent for a moment, and he took that time to fumble about the heap of clothing on the floor of the coach.

"I've something for you. I want it to please you, but I think I must first ask your forgiveness."

"For what, my lord?"

The sapphires sparkled in the dimness as he held them up. He watched her expression closely to gauge her reaction. She was very pale, her eyes soon shimmering as brightly as the stones.

"Please take them, Tempest. They only do justice to you."

Very quietly she asked, "Then why did you give them to someone else?"

"Give them? I don't understand. I gave them to you. It hurt me quite deeply that you would pawn them, but I do not blame you, love. Those were desperate times between us."

"I didn't sell them. I thought you gave them to Lady Martel. How else would she come by them?"

"She said it was from a streethawker to make you angry."

"A— Eddie." She came up on her elbows, her eyes hot and angry. "He must have taken them from my room and sold them to try to get me out of Newgate.

403

The little thief. I told him to take nothing."

In sheer relief Connor was laughing at her for calling her partner in crime a robber. But it was short-lived.

"How did you get them back, Connor?"

The soft question gave him pause. A dozen convenient tales raced through his quick mind, but he dismissed them, saying heavily, "Through the meanest of intentions. Please forgive me."

"You made love to her to get them back for me?"

"I didn't have to. She threw them in my face when I told her I loved you." He held his breath, waiting for anger or tears, but the calm, quiet voice surprised him.

"Take them away, Connor. I don't want them. You paid too much for them."

He opened his fingers and let the stones trickle to the floor. "Please forgive me, Tempest," he asked eloquently. "It's a mistake I won't make again, I prom—"

Her fingers touched to his lips. "Don't promise. Prove it to me."

Connor hugged her tightly, the memories of that night waking a turbulent mix of emotions. "I know I've no excuse. You hurt me, and I wanted to strike back. When I saw you with that roué, Waterston, at the Gardens then found you in his arms, what was I to think? I wanted so much to believe we were going to be happy; then I have your affair with that odious bastard pushed into my face."

"My what? You thought— Connor, how could you believe I'd be interested in that person when I had you?"

"I saw you kissing him?" he challenged in a wounded tone.

"You saw him kissing me. In another second, you would have seen me kissing him with my fist."

"But you tried to protect him."

"You. I didn't want you to be hurt, not over such foolishness as that. I couldn't risk the thought of any more scars on this beautiful body. I wouldn't have cared a whit if you killed him, once our business was through."

"What business was that?"

She explained the wager and her reasons, and he gave a wry chuckle.

"I thought he sent me the horses for sparing his miserable life. What a ridiculous situation. Let's be truthful with one another from this point on, so we've no reason to quarrel."

"Agreed."

It would have been the perfect time to tell him of the child, but selfishly, she wanted to savor the time with him alone before a third party was included. She would tell him at Amberly.

For his part, it would have been the perfect time to tell her of her identity, but once her lips touched his, all thoughts dissolved into that blissful pool of sensation. He would tell her at Amberly.

But when their coach slipped before the massive rose-red mansion in the gray misty dawn, they both forgot their pledges.

Looking out the window, Connor gave a short, choking cry of desperate disbelief. "No. Oh, God, no. It can't be."

Then he was gone, leaping down and running to

the house as if she was forgotten. In puzzlement, Tempest stepped out of the carriage. Then she understood.

On the heavy door of Amberly hung a large, black wreath.

Chapter Twenty-six

The service was small and simple, held in Amberly's chapel. George and Sharah attended as well as several neighbors and long-time friends of the deceased patriarch. Connor accepted their solicitations stoically, while clinging to Tempest's small hand. He promised George he would visit London soon and stood stonily during his brief, hard embrace, his eyes never blinking.

Later, the Ambersons gathered in the drawing room, a dim somber place, as Julius Chambers, the family's solicitor, unrolled the heavy parchment will of Jonathan Amberson. He looked briefly at the four people in the room, then affixed his spectacles.

"Dispense with the fine print, Julius, and tell us the fate of Amberly," Katherine insisted. Dressed in black crepe and perched on the edge of her chair with eyes brightened by avarice, she looked frightfully like a giant bird of prey about to swoop down on the carrion of her father-in-law.

"If that's all right with Connor and Holly."

Connor gave a brief, jerky nod.

Julius cleared his throat. "I, Jonathan Amberson, and so on and so forth, name as my heir, my grandson, Connor Garret Amberson. Under his care, I place Amberly, its surrounding properties, and their income, the net worth of my holdings as well as my love and respect."

Connor relaxed in his chair, his eyes closing and one hand crossing over them quickly.

"To my grandson, Tyler, I bequeath an annual allowance to be determined by Connor according to his needs." That brought a sputter of protest quickly quelled by a piercing glance over the thick lens. "The rest concerns small bequests to staff and the like."

"That's it then," Connor concluded heavily.

"No, not quite," Julius interjected. "Jonathan insisted I add a clause, a strange one but all very proper. In short, it states that Connor's inheritance is dependent on the continuation of his marriage to Holly. Should he default, all reverts to Holly. If the validity of her claim proves false, all goes to Tyler immediately."

"What?" Connor shouted in outrage. "That old meddling tyrant. He can't force these kinds of conditions on me."

"He can and he has. All binding. He was quite specific. Is there any other discussion?"

Katherine settled back, her cold eyes hooded and speculative. "Does that mean if Holly proves not to be Holly at all, Connor gets nothing and Tyler all of Amberly?"

"Yes."

Katherine looked at Tempest with a cold smile. "That woman is not Holly. Her name is Tempest

Swift, a common thief Connor hired to fool Jonathan. I have here a paper signed by them both agreeing to the terms and exchange of monies. I also have the sworn word of Lady Loretta Martel that Connor deceived her into aiding his scheme."

Tempest sat very still, her face white and her eyes riveted to the gold band on her hand, but Connor laughed, a deep rich sound of enjoyment.

"You've outdone yourself, Aunt Kate. You must be quite pleased that all your efforts finally puts Tyler as head of Amberly and your greedy hands deep in its pockets. I shall have to get a better lock for my private papers. That agreement looks damming, and I'm sure Loretta is angry enough to swear on a stack of Bibles. But dear Aunt, I hate to disappoint you. I admit to it all just as I did to Grandfather. I engineered the deception with Tempest and Loretta, but you see, it doesn't matter because Tempest *is* Holly. Nothing will change that."

"Another pretty tale, Connor," Katherine sneered. "Holly is dead."

"So everyone was supposed to believe. Will Swift was one of the men that robbed her parents' coach that night. He saved Holly and raised her in the guise of his own daughter. Will told me as much and will swear to it."

"No." That was from Tempest. She looked badly shaken. "Don't lie about that. Connor, that's not true."

He took up her trembling hand, pressing it gently. "Yes, it is. It is the truth. Will told me."

She searched his eyes frantically looking for some sign that he was creating yet another piece of fiction.

His gaze was steady, sincere, and full of tender concern. She didn't want to believe, but she knew he was telling the truth.

"I don't believe it," Katherine gasped. "I'll fight this, Connor. You've won nothing yet."

Julius stood slowly. "The matter of who has what is still open until I have time to study all this. Connor, you can produce this person?"

"Yes."

"My office, first of the week."

Tyler gave a cynical chuckle. "You still lose, Connie. Amberly's yours only as long as you can keep your wife. How long do you think that will last when she can have it all without you? Unless of course you can talk her into going shooting with you. That's a convenient way to dispose of those in your way."

The force of Connor's punch knocked him from the chair, and Connor was atop him before he measured his length on the floor. His face stark with rage, he dealt out a punishing rain of blows before Julius and Katherine could try to pull him off. The only thing that stopped the savage beating was the sight of Tempest slipping from the room, and he forgot all else to follow her.

"Tempest?"

She turned from the window at his quiet voice, her arms hugged about her and her eyes huge with numbing shock. "Is it true?"

"Yes."

"Why didn't you tell me?"

"I didn't have a chance to. No, I was afraid to."

She looked even blanker. "Afraid? Of what? How long have you known?" Her eyes said, how long have you kept it from me.

"Day before yesterday when I asked Will about you. Are you all right, my love? I know this must be a shock to you."

"A shock?" She laughed hysterically. "You tell me my whole life has been a lie, that I am not who I thought I was. No, I'm not all right. No, stay away from me." She withdrew in confusion when he moved to take her into his arms. "No, I have to think."

"Tempest, I'm sorry you found out this way."

"You weren't going to tell me, were you? If it hadn't come up in the will, I never would have known." When he made no reply, her suspicions sharpened in distraught anger. "When did you really find out? Did you marry me just to secure your precious Amberly? Was that why you were so reluctant to let me go?"

"No. I told you. I just found out."

"You've told me a lot of things, things I believed because I wanted to. Is that what you were afraid of? That if I found out I was Holly, I would take Amberly for myself? Is that why the forced marriage and all the pretty sweet talk? It must have been quite a shock for you to learn you had to stay tied to me or lose it all. Had your plan been to keep me ignorant of who I am until you could get control of Amberly, then rid yourself of me?"

"Tempest, please. You're upset, and all of this is nonsense. Come here to me, please."

His words were low and soothing, but they made her all the more distressed. He reached out to take her hand, and she slapped it away.

"No. You think you have it all, don't you, Lord

411

Amberson, so smug and clever? So you saw me as a scheming jade who would step over you to steal your hoarded pennies. I'm a thief, what else would you believe? If that's what you think I am, I'll not disappoint you. How dare you not trust me. How dare you lie to me about this."

George had been right about her temper. It flared wildly out of control and reason amid her hurt confusion. Seeing one lie, all became lies, and with a fierce gesture, she pulled the ring from her finger and shoved it at him.

"There. You wanted your freedom, take it. Get out of my house. Get out of my life. I don't need you to bring me more grief. I would have given it all to you, but you couldn't believe that, could you? You just couldn't trust me. It's all mine now, and you'll have to beg me to let you come back. Get out of my sight, you narrow, greedy fool."

As she ranted, Connor's blood had slowly chilled until his eyes burned with a frozen fire. His intention of comforting her had fallen away beneath her biting accusations, leaving him cut and bleeding from the sharpness of her tongue.

"No, I won't beg you. I won't plead with you to believe me, not when you push trust in my face. Take it. Take the whole damn lot. I wish to God I'd never laid eyes on you." The heavy gold ring clutched in his hand, Connor turned on his heel and stalked out.

Tempest swayed dizzily and collapsed on the chaise. Holly. She was Holly. She tried to force that knowledge into her mind, but it met with solid resistance. No. She had a family. Her name was Swift, not Amberson, and her father was Will Swift, not some faceless name. There were no memories here, no familiar specters of her past. Was that true? She had often wondered why it was so easy to talk to Jonathan. She had assumed she drew on the information Connor had given her, but thinking back she saw a wealth of tiny bits and pieces, scraps of fact that she just knew without being told. It was true. She was Holly. Amberly was her home. She knew it even if it was still all an empty haze. Of course Connor had known. She remembered his strangeness toward her when he returned from London, his intent gazes, the probing questions. Had he known or just suspected?

She had to talk to him. If anyone could help her with this jumble, Connor could.

"What do you mean, gone?"

"Like I said, my lady, he asked for a horse, and he rode off."

"How long ago, Bridget?"

The housekeeper was alarmed by the usually gentle lady's fervor. "Several hours ago, ma'am."

"Thank you."

Tempest lay awake on her bed, staring up into the darkness. The only thing that seemed real to her was the fact that Connor had left her. No, that wasn't right. She had driven him away. She had refused to listen to him, had refused to believe him, had accused him of vile ugly things, but now none of those doubts mattered. All that mattered was that she was alone. Holly or Tempest, rich or poor, the only thing she

413

really wanted was Connor. Why hadn't she told him that?

Dressed in trousers and an engulfing coat, Tempest strode down to the stables before the dew had been burned away by the winter sun. She was going to bring her husband home. She wouldn't let him hide in London a second time while so much went unresolved. She would not give him up that easily.

"Where is he?"

Rogers looked nonplused at the dusty, bizarre figure that he had come to accept as Lady Amberson. "I beg your pardon?"

"Connor, where is he? I have to speak to him now, and it cannot wait. Rogers, for once please be my friend. I love him. He is my husband. Tell me where he is."

Harriet Wilson raised a delicate brow in delighted surprise. "Lady Amberson, is it? I hardly recognized you in that—interesting ensemble."

"I've been told that Lord Amberson is here. I wish to see him."

The courtesan pursed her lips. "Even if that were so, I could not allow you in. There is a rather exclusive guest list for this ball."

"Don't dance about with me, Miss Wilson. I know all the fine, well-bred gentlemen are here looking to be indulged and flattered by your pretty demi-reps."

"So you see my predicament. I cannot just let unattached wives wander in. It would be unprofessional and, I suspect, dangerous."

"Please. I promise to be discreet. It is a most urgent matter. Oh, damme, I didn't want to cry."

Harriet provided a lacy handkerchief and a sympathetic shoulder. Patting the sniffling girl's back, she relented. "All right. But you must be discreet."

Tempest opened the door to the private salon and all her promises were forgotten. Half-dressed and half-reclined on a gaudy chaise, Connor was kissing a lovely dark-haired woman who was wearing even less than he. The piercing shriek brought them up and apart in confusion. The wide-eyed Cyprian was tossed bodily from the room in her corset and drawers to the appreciation of the gathering crowd. They whistled and catcalled as the girl scrambled for a hiding place from the blazing-eyed demon that had set upon her. The onlookers leaned near the closed doors, hoping to hear what passed between the volatile Ambersons.

"What is the meaning of this?" Connor demanded, recovering from his surprise at seeing his wife appear and so outrageously attired.

"I wish a word with you, sir, but not here while you are still warm from your whore." Her hand wiped roughly across his mouth to erase the smear of bright lip rouge. "Get your clothes on. I will see you at home."

The curious scattered as the doors jerked open, and the always elegant Lady Amberson stalked out like a fuming dockhand. They had barely time to speculate before she was followed by Lord Amberson who tried

415

to look calm and unconcerned while rushing after her, tugging on his boots. He glared murderously at the hidden smiles, his back stiffening at the sniggers that ensued in his wake.

"I demand an explanation," Connor began hotly as he strode into the parlor.

Tempest whirled, her tiny balled fist catching him smartly on the jaw. Before he could react, she followed that attack with several stinging slaps. He caught her wrists tightly and shook her.

"Enough. Stop it, I say," he snapped. "Just what the hell do you mean by marching in like some street brawler and creating such an on-dit? What right do you have—"

"Right? I am your wife. I've come all the way here to fetch you back only to find you in a rutting lust with some painted baggage. And as for my appearance, you did claim to want me as I am. Well, this is what I am, be my name Holly or Tempest."

"Fetch me? You toss me out, then demand such a thing? And as for being my wife, is that something you plan to claim only when it suits you? If you don't want me, why protest when others do?"

"Is that what you mean to replace me with? Paid bedmates?"

"Why not? I paid dearly enough for you."

She managed to exact another slap before he imprisoned her in his grip once more.

"Now, what is it you have to tell me, my love?" He made the tender endearment a sneering insult, his face all taut lines and arrogant angles.

Tempest pulled free of him, panting and blinking back tears. "I came to tell you that I love you and I want you. I came to ask you to come back with me to Amberly. You made me your wife. Either I am or I'm not. Come back with me."

"No," he growled.

She took a shaky breath, trying to cling to her resolve when all was crumbling about her. "I will go back alone then, and I will wait there for two days. Then you will never see me again. I will not divorce you. I would not take Amberly from you. If it is all you care for, live there alone."

As she turned and walked away, he shouted after her, "Don't you threaten me. I'll be back when I'm ready, and if you are not there, so be it. Do you hear me?"

When the door closed softly behind her, he gave a roar of frustrated rage, his hand flashing out to clear the mantelpiece of its knickknacks. Then his anger was gone as he stared down at the pieces of a china cup.

Some time later, a quiet voice disturbed his tranced state.

"Conn?"

Connor looked up from where he knelt on the floor, his eyes bright and frenzied. In his hands, he held tiny fragments of fine china. "I've broken it, George, and I cannot mend it," he cried softly. "What am I going to do?"

"So you've finally found something you cannot repair with bullying words and a fat purse," George stated. "I tried to warn you, Conn, but you wouldn't hear my words. Will you now?"

"George, please. No lectures."

"No lectures. You're not a schoolboy to be dressed down for behaving badly. Just some plain truth. You've a heavy hand, Conn, and when you swing it thoughtlessly, things get broken. A man who values objects to be cherished can have things of a fragile nature, things made of china." He lifted a fragment from the extended hands and examined it pensively. "People are like this cup, especially women who are pretty to look at, useful, and of service but easily damaged. Emotions and spirits are delicate pieces. To handle them, you need a soft touch, an appreciation of what you have, and a responsibility to see to their care. But you—" His thumb and forefinger snapped the fragment between them, and Connor winced, "You don't see the worth of what you have. If it breaks, you toss it away and get something new. You've never learned to be responsible for what you hold in your hands."

"I don't mean to break them," came a quiet voice from the man bowed over the crushed dreams he held so gently now.

"I know that, Connor."

The glimmering eyes rose in puzzlement. "How is it that after all the abuse you've taken from my rough touch, I've never cracked our friendship?"

George smiled, placing a hand on the slumped shoulder. "Because I am made of metal, coarse and not pretty but very durable."

Connor managed a ghost of a laugh; then the unhappy eyes surveyed the destruction in his hands.

418

"Oh, George, I love her so very much, but look what I've done. So many, many pieces. I cannot continue trying to fit them back together. I've made an awful mess of it."

"So you have, but do you know why? Conn, are you listening to me?"

"Tell me, George. Please tell me how this pitiful shambles I hold can be made whole again. I swear I'll be more careful. I'll be so very careful."

"No, you won't, Conn. It's not in your nature to be considerate all the time. If this poor cup were whole again, it would only leak and displease you until in a fit of temper, you destroyed it."

Connor looked aghast, his desperate gaze searching his friend's somber face for some reason to hope. "I cannot just toss it aside. I love her. Even broken and imperfect, I would have her."

"I'm not speaking of Tempest. This cup is the marriage you've made with her. It was pretty to look at, a source of pride to own and serviceable if taken out only on special occasions and gently used. But it was fragile and couldn't stand the stress of daily use in clumsy hands."

"But I want her, George. Is there nothing I can do?"

George gestured to the shards he held. "Throw them away."

Connor's fingers closed convulsively, but that protective gesture only made the breakage worse.

"Do you really want the marriage you have?" George challenged him gently, reaching down to pry open the shaking hands. Blood glistened from where the fragments had bitten into the flesh. "What you

419

have is based on a lie, a paper-thin showpiece that lacks strength. Like this cup, it's easily damaged by misunderstanding and mistrust. It cannot sustain the rigors you've put it through. It wasn't made to last, Conn. It will keep coming apart and hurting you, as it is right now."

Connor made a soft sound of denial, but the tiny cuts in his fingers bled as fiercely as the wounds in his heart.

"Replace it with something stronger. Tempest is no piece of fragile porcelain. She's of polished pewter that can take many a dent and scratch without losing shape. Buff out the marks, and the piece is perfect again."

"What if she won't let me?"

"She will. She loves you. Give her a real marriage, not this delicate bit of nonsense, one that can take a dent and careless tip and retain its value. China is cold and stiff, but pewter is warm and conforms to the hand that holds it. In time, it only fits that one hand."

"I've hurt her, George."

"That you can smooth with a lot of careful attention. I'm not saying it will be easy, but then you never liked things to be made easy for you."

There was a flash of uneven white teeth. "True enough. Sarah is lucky to have you, George. I wish I could be more like you for Tempest's sake."

"Tempest likes you just as you are, Conn. She likes the challenge of pounding out dents, too. If you hadn't noticed, she doesn't really care much for china cups either."

That brought a low, full-bodied laugh and a smile

of warm gratitude. "Thank you, George."

"Make her happy, Conn, and she'll reward you every day of your life together. I've a feeling that first reward is soon forthcoming. Have I congratulated you yet?"

Connor looked at him blankly. "For what? Being a thick-headed fool?"

"No, for bringing in another generation of thick-headed fools."

"What? Speak plainly, George."

George blurted awkwardly, "She hasn't told you?"

The dark brows lowered. "Told me what? What are you babbling about, George? You sound as though I'm about to become a—father?" He sat down heavily, his eyes round with amazement. "Tempest—she's—she didn't tell me. Why would she tell you and not me?"

"She didn't have to tell me. I come from a large family with lots of nieces and nephews. I had only to count the months and the gradual loss of her fashionably slim figure."

"Of course she didn't tell me. I've been such a complete idiot of late, she must have been afraid to. Oh, the things I've said to her. It can't be too late. A father." He gave a crazy little laugh and bounded up to seize George in a crushing hug. "I'll name the first one after you, boy or girl."

"You'd better ask Tempest first."

"Tempest. Damme, George, I've got to fly. Here, hold these."

George looked down at the handful of shards and smiled as Connor rushed about madly yelling for a horse.

"Conn, you'd better take a carriage. It's going to rain soon."

"No time. I'll go cross-country and save a couple of hours. Good-bye, George. My best to Sarah."

"And mine to your lady."

"A baby," he shouted to the dark heavens from his front steps, which he followed with a loud whoop that echoed down the empty street. Looking a bit abashed, he grinned at his friend. "Marry that woman. I don't like to be a fool alone. Then I can laugh at you." Giving him another rib-creaking embrace, he turned and dashed down the walk, vaulting into the saddle. With a wave and a huge smile, he was off.

Chapter Twenty-seven

The last hour of the ride was wet, cold, and miserable, but it urged Connor to greater speed, fearing Tempest would be alone when the fury of the storm broke loose. Both horse and rider were spent by the time Amberly appeared in dark majesty against the dramatic play of light in the distant sky.

Dripping and shivering, Connor raced up the stairs only to draw up short at the door of his wife's room. "She's left me," he moaned aloud, surveying the empty armoire and dresser top in an agony of loss. Slowly, mechanically, he turned to his own room and again was given pause. The bed had been invitingly pulled down, a wisp of ivory silk draped over its foot. On his bureau tucked intimately between his brushes and toiletries were her dainty combs and bottles.

With a gush of relief, Connor tossed his sodden topcoat over a chair and chafed blue-fingered hands together. "Tempest? Tempest, where are you?" He found her in the nursery.

The wall of windows opened on a breathtaking

view of the approaching gale. Lightning creased the sky with its demonic forks while thunder sounded upon the horizon. Tempest had sought comfort in that hopeful room to soothe her worries and had fallen asleep on a chair she had drawn in from another room. But now that rest was far from peaceful as the violence of the night intruded upon her subconscious. She moaned as the sound reached her and shifted uneasily.

Moved by the image of vulnerable innocence she created, Connor bent and shook her gently. "Tempest? Tempest, love, wake up. It's Connor. I'm here, and I love you." When she made a small sound and turned her face away in denial, he gathered her up to his chest and turned into the chair so she was cradled in his lap. Holding her close, he urged, "Tempest, wake up. It's Connor. There's nothing to be afraid of. Come back to me."

"No," she protested faintly, her undirected hands rising to meet some unseen danger. "Please don't hurt me."

Frowning, Connor hugged her protectively while he struggled with indecision. Could he let her wander in the unremembered dream without trying to force her to see its meaning? Had she been right? Was he afraid to let her find her past, afraid it would leave him no place in her future? If she loved him, knowing would change nothing between them. He would know of that now.

The flashing of the heavens created an erratic pulse of light, the sound that followed making Tempest shrink into the circling haven in a fit of trembling.

Her hands tangled in his clothes seeking safety. A low, insistent voice penetrated the fog of shrouding fear, drawing her slowly to the brink of awareness, but the terrible dream wouldn't release her, its threatening shadow clinging to give all a hazy quality. Still dazed by sleep, she muttered into the wilted shirt-front, "Connor, hold me. Don't let go."

"I won't. I promise. Keep your eyes closed, sweet. Let me help you."

Weeping softly, she clutched at him, her fingers anxiously kneading the dark coat. The ominous growl of the storm was like a threatening predator, stalking her, bringing danger and terror from an unknown source. She shivered for some time in that private horror, her tenuous link to the present in the gentle hand that stroked her hair.

"It's all right, my love. I'll never let anything harm you. Keep your eyes closed and listen to my voice." He spoke slowly, hypnotically so not to jar her from her subliminal trance. "We're at Amberly, in the nursery. I want you to forget all else and concentrate on that. It's empty now, but I want you to imagine how it would look when there were children playing in it, when there was laughter."

"All bright with sunshine and lace at the windows and yellow like spring daffodils," she murmured hopefully, grateful to turn to a soothing oasis in the surrounding confusion. "There's a rocking horse and a doll, like the one I bought Jesse. And there's a boy at the window." A frown creased her brow. "He has dark hair and tears in his eyes, but he makes no sound. I don't understand. He is so familiar. Do I

425

know him? Who is he?"

"Me, a long time ago," he said softly, his eyes going to the wide expanse of glass, remembering the boy who watched his cousin and father ride off without him. He sighed and pressed a kiss to the fragrant curls to distract his own gloomy thoughts. "There's a little girl in the room, a pretty thing with a bright riot of hair. Can you see her?"

There was a pause and a hesitant, "No."

"Let me tell you about her. It's Christmas, and she and her parents are coming home to Amberly. It's dark outside of their carriage and raining. And cold. Feel how cold." He touched his icy cheek to hers, and she trembled. He began to rock her, the movement a rhythmic sway. Tempest's breath had quickened into short gasps, but she was still in his arms, listening. "It's very late, and the little girl is tired, but something keeps her awake. At first it's the thunder, then something else. And the child is afraid of those sounds and of the voices she hears in the darkness. What are those sounds, Tempest? Look into the darkness, and tell me what waits there, what frightens the little girl in the carriage."

"I—I don't know. Please, Connor. I don't want to look." Her voice was high and thin, a child's voice. The sound, the rocking movement, the smell of rain that lingered mustily in Connor's clothing combined in a growing catalyst to prod the barriers that forbade remembrance. Subtly, they changed in her panicked thoughts, becoming the roar of gunshots, the pitch of a careening carriage, the smell of the river and storm, cold and crisp on the winter night. With that sense of altered time and place, the slow trickle of images became a surging pressure in her head. Dizzily, she gripped Connor to hold herself safe from the sweeping rush of that cold, dark tide, but it was too strong, carrying her into that frightening abyss of her forgotten dreams.

"It's safe to look now. You know you must. I'm right here with you. I'll bring you back safe."

Her fingers kneaded his convulsively. "Can you keep them safe, too?"

"Who, my love? Who is with us?"

"Mama and Papa. Can you keep them safe too? Please, Connor."

"I wish I could, Holly. I wish I could, but no. What do you see now? Open your eyes and tell me."

Thunder crashed against a sizzle of brightness, and Tempest sat bolt upright, her body rigid and her round eyes staring blankly at the rain-streaked panes. Sound burst from her in a shrill scream.

"Papa! Papa!"

Connor clenched his teeth to stop himself from calling her back from the nightmare she was living. Her hands were tearing at his forearms as if struggling not to fall. Then that high-pitched little voice began again, weak and strained in panic.

"Mama. Wake up, Mama. There's water in here. It's so cold. Mama, wake up. Papa, where are you? Help me. I'm scared. Don't let those men in. I'm cold. So cold." She broke off into hoarse sobs, sagging in his arms like a limp doll, like the precious Jilly she was never without.

"Holly, wake up," he said firmly, shaking her until

427

her head bobbed loosely, spilling a tumble of curls and tears in a random scatter. "Come on, Holly. Come back to me. It's over. It's just a dream now. It can't hurt you."

Gradually, he felt her return, her breath growing steady and deep as the lolling head came up. Her expression was momentarily dazed with confusion, seeing him without recognition.

"Holly, look at me. Holly, who am I?"

The huge glistening eyes stared long and hard, then shaking fingers touched the planes of his face wonderingly. "Connor," she said with heavy meaning. "Oh, Connor."

He held her tight as her arms encircled his neck. "Welcome home, Holly."

"They killed Mama and Papa," she wept softly.

"I know, sweet."

"I thought they were going to kill me, too."

"They would have if Will hadn't been there. He saved your life by hiding you with his family. Do you remember now?"

She nodded into his shoulder. "It's all vague like a dream, but mostly, yes." He was silent, letting the tremors of shock and knowledge shiver through her. She needed those lengthy minutes to piece together the jigsaw of her past. When she was calmer, he could ask her if she still had a place for him. But he didn't have to.

Tempest leaned away from him, looking up through large teary eyes, seeing a strange double image of boy and man. "I've always loved you, Connor, and you came back to me."

428

"How could I not? All I love is here," he said softly, cupping her face in his palm. "Forgive me, Tempest. Amberly means nothing if you're not here with me. Let me come home. It's all I've ever wanted."

Smiling tenderly, she said, "Welcome home, my lord."

Their kiss was brief, Tempest pushing back with an exclamation of dismay. "You're all wet and cold. Get out of those clothes before you catch your death."

"Sound advice," he agreed huskily.

Curled close beneath warm covers, Connor sighed as Tempest vigorously rubbed his cold flesh to restore its heat. After a few minutes of blissful enjoyment, he rolled onto his back and caught her hands.

"It meant nothing, Tempest."

"I know," she replied without having to ask what he spoke of.

"I love only you. I want only you."

"I know."

She sounded so sure and smug that he pouted, "If you knew, then why weren't you a little more understanding in London?"

"You didn't need understanding. You needed a good thrashing."

He touched his tender chin with a lopsided smile. "I suppose I should thank you then."

"Oh, you will, my lord. You will."

Ignoring her sultry promise with difficulty, he insisted gruffly, "We've one other matter to settle first. Is there something I should know that you've not told me?"

Her cheeks pinked, and the sapphire eyes glowed warmly. "You mean about the first of our half-dozen little Ambersons that will be underfoot in about five months? Are you pleased?"

Connor put his hand almost timidly on her slightly rounded belly, and hers covered it with a squeeze. "My child."

"Our child," she corrected with a smile.

He brought her hand to his lips and looked quickly down so she wouldn't see how shiny his eyes had become. "Our children will play in Amberly's nursery. I am more than pleased. I am grateful. I wish Grandfather could have known of this. He would have been so excited."

"He was."

His expression sullen, he glowered and grumbled, "Was I the only one who didn't know of this? The last to know after I did all the work?"

"Not quite, my lord," she chided.

His kiss was deep and thorough, and she was lost to it in a willing rapture. No more holding back. This was her husband, father of her child, the man she loved above all, the man who loved her. She gave a murmur of objection as he sat up suddenly and pulled on his trousers.

"Connor?"

"I'll be right back, love. There is something I must do."

"Now?" she nearly wailed. "Can't it wait?"

He flashed that broad, imperfect grin. "Patience,

430

sweet. We've at least four and a half months to indulge ourselves outrageously. I'll be but a moment."

The willful mouth pursed reluctantly. "Just for a moment."

Connor hesitated in the doorway, waiting for the rushing waves of guilt and torment, but the chapel was quiet, peaceful. His bare feet made no sound on the cool marble as he went gingerly to kneel at the rail. His voice was low and hushed in the reverent silence.

"I have everything now, a wife to love who loves in return, the miracle of a child, a home for my family, yet in the face of all this fortune, I still have nothing. I'm still afraid to ask. Please forgive me. It was an accident. I loved you, Papa. It wasn't my fault. Please forgive me and let me go."

He cringed, waiting in dread, but his soul and conscience lay silent. The terrible vision and twisting recriminations were no longer dwelling there. His breath rattled out in a shaky gush of relief. "Thank you. I've needed that peace for so very long. I will make you proud of me, I prom— No. I will make you proud."

Tempest was awaiting him at his door, the ivory silk glowing against her fair skin and bright curls. The sight moved him to a tenderness, warming him with a deep, unshakable love. Taking her in his arms, he held her close, reveling in the welcoming feel and scent of her.

"Is all well, my lord?" she asked him, puzzled but touched by this sudden shift of mood.

"All is well," he answered contentedly.

"To bed then. You must be all in."

He nuzzled her neck with a lusty vow. "I hope to be."

Tempest gave a giggle as he lifted her up and deposited her on the bed. Then the teasing manner was gone, and her arms raised up for him.

"Come to me, my lord husband."

They had barely begun to renew their acquaintance when there was a hasty tap at the door.

"What is it?" Connor snarled in ill-humor.

A timid voice called, "I'm sorry for the intrusion, my lord, but there's a boy downstairs asking for her ladyship. He's badly hurt."

"Eddie," Tempest cried in alarm. She sent Connor tumbling and leaped from the bed, racing out in a flutter of silk.

Eddie had collapsed in a chair in the front parlor, water pooling on the expensive carpet from his soggy clothing. He tried to struggle to his feet when Tempest and Connor appeared but had no strength. Tempest caught him as he staggered, and he clung to her with hard, breathless sobs.

"Eddie, what is it? What's happened? What are you doing way out here? Eddie?"

"Tempest, let the boy rest a minute," Connor ordered calmly, taking quick control of the situation. Eddie let out a yelp of hurt when he was steered by the shoulders back down on the chair. Connor poured

432

a glass of brandy and held it up to the blue, trembling lips. "Drink this down."

Eddie complied, then gasped hoarsely, "Can I have another?"

"Certainly."

When the glass was emptied, Connor knelt down, frowning over the sight of the boy's battered face. "Who did this to you?"

"Some men came to the inn. I didn't know them, but Papa did. He was afraid of them. He had me take the children and hide them and told us not to come back until he came for us. He wanted Mama to go too, but she wouldn't leave him. I saw Jack and Jesse safe at Mumphrey's Livery, then went back. They set fire to the inn. No one came out. One of them caught me and knocked me about, but I got away and came here. Nobody came out of the fire, Este. I think they killed them."

The dark eyes welled up, spilling over in grief and hurt as he looked up at his sister. The long hard ride had taken all his strength, and he couldn't stop the flood of tears. "Jack and Jesse'll be so scared," he muttered brokenly.

"I'll go get them," Connor assured him as he carefully opened the tattered coat. Eddie gave a wail of complaint when he pressed lightly. Smiling encouragingly, he clasped the boy's wrist. "Eddie, I want you to grab hold of my arm tight as you can. Good. Now take a deep breath and hold it. Good. Now, close your eyes and take another deep, deep breath. Hold it." Bracing his hand against the boy's collarbone, Connor gave his arm a quick hard jerk, then caught the boy as he swooned.

"Connor?"

The worried voice made his gaze lift. "It's all right, sweet. He just had his shoulder pulled out. I popped it back. He'll be fine, just deuced sore for a while. Happened to me once when I took a tumble from a second-floor window."

"In just your boots, I suppose."

He grinned at her brave attempt at humor. "As I recall, I was twelve and sneaking off to go boating instead of tending my studies. Sit with him while I go get dressed. Don't let him move that arm."

Connor returned shortly, warmly dressed in a woolen Garrick and topboots. When Tempest saw him tuck a pistol into the generous folds of his coat, she hurried to him in alarm.

"Connor, please be careful," she cried, hugging to him tightly.

"I will, my love. I'll bring them here safe and sound. Can I get a carriage at this Mumphrey's? I'll ride there then and save some time. When he comes round, fill him with brandy and keep him quiet. I'll be back by next evening. And Tempest, say nothing about having your memory back."

She nodded at his somber warning, asking no question, then pulled his head down. Her kiss was hard and desperate. "I love you, Connor."

"That, alone, will bring me back." He chucked her under the chin and strode out into the rainy night with a squaring of his shoulders.

434

The coach stopped at Amberly just before dusk, and Tempest ran to meet it. Inside, a sleepy child on either side, Connor straightened from his dozing. The eyes that met hers were heavy with sorrow and fatigue. Her breath caught, and it was a moment before she could swallow the hard knot of tears.

"I'll take the children up to the room next to ours and see they're fed. What of you, my lord?"

"I'm just cold and tired. I think I'll go to bed" She pressed his hand briefly. "Thank you."

His nod was slight and weary as he watched her gather the babes and shepherd them up to the house. He followed more slowly, stiff and aching from three back-to-back rides to and from London. He paused in the hall, coming face to face with Eddie Swift. The boy's face was a rainbow of bruises and lumpy swellings, his arm rendered useless in a snug sling. What held him was the boy's stare. He had seen that look of hollow-eyed grief many times staring back at him from the mirror.

"I'm sorry," he said simply.

For a moment, Eddie didn't move, then he asked huskily, "You sure?"

"I wouldn't have come back until I was."

The boy's composure crumpled, and for several minutes he sobbed noisily while Connor held him in an easy embrace. Then the tears stopped. No more of them would follow. Eddie pushed away with a mature dignity, the dark, swimming eyes calm and steady.

"Thank you for what you done for us, my lord. You been the most kind."

"You're family now. You owe me no thanks."

435

Eddie looked doubtful, then said gruffly, "I best see to the little ones. They'll be needing me."

Connor watched him climb the stairs with a faint smile. A plucky bunch, the lot of them. They would be all right.

Tempest closed the adjoining door quietly and smiled to see Connor already asleep beneath the covers. Bending down, she brushed a kiss upon his warm cheek and went to sit at the window to watch the drizzly rain streak down the mullioned panes. Soon that image blurred as the ache in her heart found its release.

"Tempest? Come to bed, sweet."

She took a shaky breath and replied, "I'd just like to sit here by myself for a time."

"Mourning alone only makes the grief deeper. Come and let me hold you."

A soft sob was his only response.

Very quietly, he said, "When my mother died, it was as if someone had cut a great hole in me, but the wound was clean and healed. When I lost my father, the scars were deep and ugly. It took your love to take those marks from my soul. Let me help you now. Let me love you, Tempest."

He engulfed her in a tight protective circle, drawing the covers about them both. She wept quietly for some time, soothed by his silent support. Then she lifted her head, and he was kissing her. He made love to her tenderly, his every move a lingering caress. There was no flare of urgent passion, but a slow, gentle tide that grew ever stronger, its pull calming but inevitable to draw her from her misery into the swirling eddies of bliss. Adrift on the buoyant ebb of his sweet loving, Tempest closed her eyes as Connor's mouth moved leisurely upon hers and surrendered herself to sleep.

The low, quiet voice played through her memories with an elusive tease, so familiar yet different enough to provoke her curiosity. Tempest opened her eyes and smiled, content for a moment to silently observe the scene of her husband sitting in an armchair with six-year-old Jesse curled in his lap. The words of the story he was reading she knew by heart, read to her over and over in the same soothing voice with a slightly higher pitch by a gruff, snobbish boy whose generous heart she had captured. The rapt, attentive look on the child's face had been mirrored in her own those many years ago. She began to recite the words with him. Connor glanced up but continued through to the "happily ever after."

"Jesse, go to bed now and let his lordship get some sleep," Tempest admonished gently.

With a shy smile, the child hugged Connor about the neck and hurried into the next room with a patter of tiny bare feet.

"The little one woke up crying and frightened," Connor explained. "I remembered how well a knee and a fairy tale worked to quiet a little girl's fears."

"So do I," she mused, smiling fondly.

"I didn't mean to wake you, sweet."

"Come back to bed."

"I'm so tired, I can't sleep," he mumbled unhappily.

Tempest patted the sheet beside her, finally luring him out of the enveloping chair to seek the inviting warmth of her body. She turned him onto his stomach to knead the bunched, sore muscles, eliciting a moan.

"You will make a wonderful father, my lord," she told him as she plied the firm swells, not unaffected by the supple, satiny feel of him.

"And you make a wonderful wife. The first truly brilliant thing I've ever done was to fall in love with you."

"And the second?" she prompted sassily.

Connor rolled over and pressed kisses to her hands. His expression was searching and oddly vulnerable. "I know I had to force you, but would you have married me had I simply asked?"

"No."

He blinked. "No? But you said you loved me."

She kissed him lightly to soothe his ruffled vanity. "But you had not said the same to me. I wanted to marry you more than anything but for the right reasons."

"And now?"

"Now I am Lady Amberson, your wife, and most content to remain so."

He drew the heavy signet ring off his hand and slipped it on her finger. "Make sure that remains where it belongs then."

"Yes, my lord," she conceded meekly. Her eyes held a tart sparkle. "And you see you remain where you belong."

"Yes, my love. Besides, I would never be able to find a mistress in London willing to tangle with the infamous Lady Amberson."

"Then I shall have to serve as both wife and mistress. Now, go to sleep, my lusty lord."

"Are you sure that is what you want of me?" He put a hand behind her head, bringing her down to meet his parted lips. That was all the convincing she needed.

Chapter Twenty-eight

"Connor?"

Connor gave an irate grumble at the disturbance, unwilling to be pulled from sleep even by his loving wife. "What? Again? If you wish to enjoy another four months of conjugal bliss, you best let me get some rest. You abuse me sorely, madam."

"Connor."

That crisp tone brought his eyes open to stare in surprise at three youthful faces. Jesse was smiling naively, Jack was blushing fiercely, and Eddie didn't bother to conceal his smirk.

"Oh," he muttered, rubbing his eyes. "Visitors this early." He looked to Tempest in puzzlement. She sat beside him, the sheet drawn up over her bosom, apparently not in the least embarrassed by the intrusion of the youngsters while they lay naked in bed.

"We was wondering what was going to become of us now that we's orphans and all," Eddie said bluntly. His forthright speech started Jesse crying and Jack's lip trembling.

"Here now," Connor began, and the little girl was

instantly upon the bed, her arms tight about his neck.

"She's all upset about Ma and Pa being burned up in the fire and all," Jack explained in a tiny voice. "It's the idea of 'em roasting like that."

"Don't cry, sweet. The fire didn't hurt them. They'd been shot. It was quick and painless. They didn't suffer," he explained gently.

The huge, trusting eyes lifted. "You mean they went straight to God?"

He smiled softly. "I'm sure they did. And as for what's to happen to you, you cannot be orphans when you have family. You'll stay here, of course."

Jack's eyes popped in disbelief. "Here? In this palace?"

"This is my home now, Jack," Tempest told him, sensing his awe with remembered sympathy. "It shall be yours, too. Would you like that?"

"You mean we'd be the only ones living here?" he gaped.

"For now we share it with an unpleasant pair, but soon we will be alone."

Jack bounced on the bed to hug his sister excitedly.

Eddie hung back, his expression sullen as he observed them. The fancy lord had taken first Este and now the children. As man of the family, the task of provider should have fallen to him, young as he was, but the wealthy Lord Amberson had stolen that from him, had stolen his family.

"Well," he said harshly. "I ain't no babe what needs your charity. I can look after myself. I don't need no handouts."

Tempest looked at him imploringly, but it was

441

Connor who spoke first.

"It's not charity when between family or friends."

"Well, you ain't neither to me," he growled.

"Eddie Swift, that will be enough from you. You will treat my husband with respect, or I'll add more pretty colors to that palette on your face."

The dark eyes dropped, but the line of his shoulders were still tense with rebellion.

"All right, you ragamuffins, out. Give us some privacy."

Alone with him, Tempest turned and placed a lingering kiss on Connor's mouth. "Good morning," she cooed, snuggling against him protectively. "Since when have my attentions placed an undue burden on your manhood, my lord?"

"Since this morning," he admitted, falling back on his pillow with a groan. "I feel terrible. A month's sleep would be too short."

"Then I won't overtax you in your feeble state."

He grinned and pulled her down on top of his chest. "A kiss would not strain me overmuch."

From the kiss, time lost all meaning to lovers aware only of one another. Some half-hour later, Tempest peered into the next room to find her brothers and sister dressed and patiently waiting. She hugged and kissed each in turn, but Eddie wouldn't accept her touch, ducking his head with a scowl.

"I don't want you hanging on me after being with him," he muttered. "Maybe you can stand having his hands all over you, but I can't."

Tempest slapped him. She hadn't meant to, but it was done. With a choked-back cry, Eddie fled the room.

"Let him go, Tempest," Connor said firmly from where he stood in the door.

She turned large, pleading eyes up to him. "Oh, Connor, what are we going to do with him?"

"Love him," was his simple solution. Hoisting Jesse up in one arm and putting the other about Jack's thin shoulders, he called cheerfully, "Come on, you waifs. I'll introduce you to Bridget. She loves to spoil little children."

"Connor, what are we going to do?" Tempest asked again as they sat together over their breakfast alone.

"The best we can by them. They can't be left to think they're alone. George is going to have Sarah pick up some things for them to wear and bring them out. Until then, we make do."

"Connor, I do love you."

"You always seemed surprised to find I'm a decent fellow. I ought to be insulted."

She pressed his hand, then sobered. "What about Eddie? He'll make things difficult."

"I'll see to him, sweet. I know all about brash swaggering boys."

"Why did it happen?"

Connor sighed and shook his head. "I don't know. Swift ran with a rough bunch and very deep. I thought he'd paid them, but it could have been something else."

"Me?" Her eyes shimmered.

Connor kissed her hand gently. "I won't gudgeon you. That's the most likely turn. I want you and the children here until I find out. I've already set the Bow

443

Street Runners on it. If there's a tie between this and you, it will surface."

He fell silent as Katherine, dressed in mourning black from head to foot in a caricature of grief, swept in. The chill was immediate.

"What are those dreadful-looking pauper children doing here feeding off our table? Friends of yours, my dear?"

Tempest's back stiffened, and her eyes glittered in dangerous warning. "Those paupers, as you call them, are my brothers and sister."

"It certainly didn't take them long to surface at your rise in circumstance," was the snide reply.

Connor stood slowly, his towering height and the cold steel of his gaze giving even the outspoken woman pause. "The Swifts are here because I brought them and will remain at my table for as long as I choose. Your opinion of them is of no consequence."

"Good morning, Connie," Tyler announced dryly. "Trying on the marquis's crown so soon? Need I remind you that nothing has been decided."

"It will be soon enough for you to think about where you'll be staying. Remember your livelihood is to come from my generosity, and you seldom leave me feeling very generous."

"And how generous are you being with the Swifts so they'll agree to tell your lies?" Katherine bit out coldly. "Are they going to move here too? Will you make them into fine gentry the way you have this little tart?"

"They are dead," Tempest stated flatly.

Katherine hesitated, then pursed her lips. She

444

looked more like a dark angel of death than a respectful mourner in her black garb. "So there is no one to back your claim of being Holly, is there? Perhaps you should consider where you'll go, dear nephew."

His features set in confident lines, Connor lifted Tempest up by the elbow. "Come, sweet. The air is very stagnant in here." Though his expression betrayed none of it, his thoughts were working frantically over his aunt's words.

A smile of remembrance touched Connor's lips as he came upon Eddie Swift. The boy stood on Amberly's lawn, looking abandoned and lonely. That lost expression became one of hardened hostility the minute he saw his host.

"Beautiful, isn't it?"

"If you say so, my lord." He always managed to make that title drip with insult.

"Come on, boy. Take a ride with me. Unless you have something more pressing to do with your time." He walked toward the stables, hearing Eddie follow after a brief hesitation. "Can you handle your own reins, or do you want to double with me?"

"I can ride as good as you, fancy face," came the expected retort.

After saddling his own leggy bay hunter, Connor found a mare with a gentle mouth. Eddie had tossed off his sling, but lifting his arm above his head brought a tight grimace. Without waiting to be asked, Connor gave him a firm boost up.

They traversed the estate in an easy lope. Seeing it all would take the better part of three days. Connor stayed on open ground where he could keep a watchful eye on his injured companion without seeming to. The boy did sit a good horse and, though a bit awkward at first, managed well.

Connor reined in at the top of a gradual incline and looked down like a proud ruler over his kingdom. Amberly's main house stood below with its flanking outbuildings. Eddie gazed about, appearing bored and restless.

"This is all mine. I've dreamed of owning it since I came here at about Jesse's age. I have loved every inch of it for more than twenty years, but I would surrender it all without hesitation for your sister. Or for any one of you because she loves you so."

"You expect me to believe you?"

"No. Why should you? You see me as idle and rich."

"No. I see you as a lying schemer."

Connor laughed, taking no offense. "I'm all of that. But I do love Tempest, and she is my wife."

"Well, we ain't married to you. You can't make us stay here. You're nothing to us."

Holding his temper with difficulty, he said, "No, but like it or not, you are my responsibility. I don't know who murdered your parents or why, but until I find out, the best place for you is here."

"Says you."

"I'll be straight with you, boy. You don't like me, and I don't have much use for you. We both see the other as coming between those we love. If it was just you, I'd say go. You're old enough to tend to your own affairs. But the little ones are tied up in this too, and you know how much they depend on you. I'm asking you, man to man, for their sakes to stay and not fight me until we discover why your parents died. When that's done, you can go, no argument. I'll see Tempest abides by that. I know you put your family before your pride as any man would. What do you say?"

Eddie glared at him. He was outmaneuvered, and he resented it. As much as he disliked the alternative, he didn't want to appear too selfish to consider the welfare of the children. "Just till it's settled then," he growled reluctantly.

Holding back his smile, Connor looked away, mentioned casually, "A pity the little one Tempest carries won't have a sensible uncle about to balance out the flightiness of its father."

"Este is—"

Connor chuckled. "It seems I wasn't the last to be told.

Eddie digested this silently. A baby. His baby. That was a tie he couldn't, no, wouldn't break. His Este was Lady Amberson, and that would not change. He glanced sullenly at the man beside him, wanting to still view him as the vain, arrogant dandy that he had hated so. But he couldn't. In the heavy woolen great coat and scuffed top boots, black hair bristled untidily by the crisp breeze, he didn't see a haughty lord but the man who had ridden to London to get his brother and sister, the silent comforter who had held him in his grief, and the father of Este's child. And unwillingly, in spite of the conceit and snobbery, Eddie liked him.

"You have no brothers or sisters, my lord?"

"I would have had one about your age," Connor

replied quietly.

"Off at some fine school or something?"

"No, my mother died before giving birth."

"Oh."

With a long, cleansing breath, Connor looked over Amberly, forcing his concentration to focus there. "There's a lot involved in running an estate like this. It's not just sitting pretty on a horse or playing about in London. I'm going to need some good men with me to make it good."

"Meaning what?"

"Meaning whatever you want to make it."

Eddie looked at the clean profile in a turmoil. "I don't know nothing about this kind of thing. I wouldn't be no good to you."

The cool blue eyes flashed about in challenge. "Learn, boy. You're not stupid. Do you want to live in the London sewers? Do you want the little ones to? What kind of life could they have or you? Stealing? Ending at the end of a rope?"

"No, that ain't what I want."

"You have a chance, boy, for you and them. It won't be charity, and it won't be easy. I'm a difficult fellow to work with. I'm temperamental, pushy, opinionated, and those, Tempest will tell you, are my better qualities. I'm just making an offer in my own interest. You make of it what you will, boy."

"Eddie. My name is Eddie, not boy, my lord."

"And mine is not my lord."

"I will think on it, Connor," he said coolly, then touched his heels to the mare's flanks, setting it off in a canter.

For Tempest, the day was a strange mixture of sadness and joy. The happiness of having the rambunctious children about her lessened the pain of loss. They raced about the stately halls of Amberly in wild abandon just as she once had. The memories came flooding back like a sweet, cherished dream, images of her family, her real family seen through the eyes of a child, and of Connor, mostly Connor. How she had adored him. At his vast age of thirteen, he had seemed so worldly and aloof when he returned from school. To have him pay her any heed brought a rapturous glee. In the presence of adults, he had ignored her with an adolescent's scorn, but alone, he had been her Galahad, teasing but always mindful of the fragile moods of a five year old.

The children had been tucked in, the younger still in the adjoining room, and Eddie, pretending not to be awed, in Connor's old room. Pampered and smothered by a loving Bridget, Jesse and Jack fell into untroubled sleep, having forgotten the nightmares of the night before. Eddie had been quiet and thoughtful since returning from his ride and was wandering about in the soft shadow of dusk. Of Connor she hadn't a glimpse all day until he sought her out in the parlor in the peaceful still of the evening.

"Oh, my lord, you look dreadful."

"Thank you, sweet. Prick my vanity when my spirits are low," he bemoaned, then blew his nose loudly. He frowned into a small cheval mirror. Miserable features looked back through cloudy eyes over a sore, red nose. "I hate sickness. It wears so cruelly on the appearance."

Tempest laughed at his aggrieved pride and taunted unkindly, "Even the rich and beautiful suffer the indignities of a cold."

His sensuous mouth pulling into a pout, he sulked and sniffed until she showed some sympathy.

"Come here, my poor love, and let me make it better," she crooned, the words enticing him to sit at her feet, his dark head lying back on her knees. When she stroked a hand down his face, she frowned in concern. "You aren't well, are you?"

"I'm warm and lightheaded, but I think that's because of you," he murmured silkily, his sleepy eyes sparking with a cool blue flame. His head turned so he could place a kiss on her hand.

"It's odd the things I'm remembering, like the time when I made you play hide and seek with me, and I hid, and you never looked for me."

"It was a joke, and you made me feel so awful with all your tears. Three year olds have such big tears."

"You gave me that locket, by way of apology. I still have it."

"Do you?"

"I never took it off. I was so in love with you."

"You were just a baby."

"And you were my tall, handsome cousin, a bold, brave hero. You made my heart pound whenever I saw you. You still do," she added softly.

He smiled. "Even with a drippy nose?"

"Even so." She rubbed his cheek with her knuckles to affirm it tenderly, then gave a surprised, "Oh," and put a hand to her middle. At Connor's expectant look, she said excitedly, "That's the first time I've felt it move."

"I envy you that," Connor sighed. "I shall have to wait a good month or so for the pleasure."

"I thought you knew nothing of children."

"Of children, no, of babies, a great deal. I used to sit and wait to see a tiny hand or foot move across my mother's stomach. I was forever pestering her with questions. When you're fourteen, you're full of the most outrageous notions. It must be a wonderful feeling to know you have life inside you. All I get is the pleasure of putting it there." He turned slightly to pillow his head on her knees. "I can live with the thought of losing Amberly but not of losing you. Swear to me that I'll never lose you. Swear to me that you'll never leave me. Swear it, Tempest."

"I swear it, my lord. Nothing could make me leave you." She tipped up his chin and bent to kiss him. Their tender exchange was cut short when he wrenched away to blow his nose noisily.

"I apologize for being so unromantic," he sniffed wretchedly.

"Calm yourself, husband. I shall weather your infirmity without complaint." She rumpled the glossy black hair, then asked somberly, "Are we going to lose Amberly?"

"It appears so, my love. We've no way to prove you're Holly, and they have much to say you're not."

"You're wrong there."

They looked up in surprise to see Eddie, who had been a silent witness to their intimate scene. Whatever doubts the boy held were dismissed.

"Eddie, how dare you eavesdrop on us," Tempest began, but Connor cut her off impatiently.

451

"What do you know of this?" he asked brusquely.

"Only that Papa had some papers drawn up to see that Este was provided for should anything happen to him. It was right after your visit."

"Where are these papers?"

"Safe in London."

Connor gave a shaky laugh. "We might get out of this yet as winners."

Tyler stopped the courier as he was about to leave the house. "Where are you off to at this hour, Toby?"

"His lordship bade me to take a note to Mr. Morley."

"Tonight? In this beastly weather?" Tyler sounded appalled as he eyed the clutched missive. "That's terribly inconsiderate of Connie. I'll tell you what. I've a coach going to London in the morning. Give me the note, and I'll see it's delivered. You can go to bed nice and warm, and no one need know."

"Why, that's right good of you, sir," the relieved Toby gushed, passing him the letter.

"Yes, I'll see everything's taken care of."

Chapter Twenty-nine

The sound of Connor's hard, dry cough woke Tempest early with a touch of alarm. He lay beside her shifting in a restless sleep. When she put a hand to his forehead, the hot blue eyes opened.

"You've quite a fever, my lord. I'm going to send for a doctor."

"Don't be—" He broke off with a spell of hoarse coughs. "Nonsense," he wheezed. "I'll be fine. My throat's a bit dry, is all. I could use something to drink."

"I'll get it for you. You just lie still and rest."

"Yes, madam," he murmured faintly and was dozing fitfully before she left the room.

Tempest was surprised to find Katherine up having a cup of tea, her eyes baggy and unfocused.

"Up so early, Aunt Kate?"

"Who could sleep?" she grumbled. "Is Connor ill? He sounds terrible."

"Just a touch of a cold."

"I'll have cook send up a tray. No sense his coming

down and exposing us all."

"That's not really necessary."

"Colds have a way of turning nasty. You'd best have a care for him."

Tempest eyed her warily, but she seemed to have no ulterior motive for her mild concern. "I will. Thank you for the tray."

Katherine dismissed her with a wave of her hand and groggily returned to her tea.

Connor had managed to get himself half-dressed before an abrupt queaziness sent him stumbling to the chamberpot to empty his rolling stomach. He curled back into bed and was shivering miserably when Tempest returned. When she lay close and tried to hold him, he gave a mutter of complaint and pushed away.

"Don't. Leave me alone," he rumbled gruffly, drawing the blankets into a tight singular cocoon about himself.

Feeling slighted and at a loss, Tempest sat up.

"Sweet, I'm sorry. I feel poorly. Please have patience with me. I am a wretched sick person," he moaned regretfully.

"Just tell me what I can do for you."

"Stay by me. Is there something to drink?"

The tray Katherine ordered was delivered. Connor drank down the juice greedily but groaned at the sight of food, begging it be taken away. She sat with him through the day, forcing liquids between the short naps his worsening cough would allow. They tore through him with a harsh, painful rattle until he clutched his chest in discomfort. Finally, by evening, he was ready to concede.

"Tempest, I am most unwell. You best send for someone."

"I have, Connor. Lie back. He'll be here soon."

When he opened his eyes again, it was to stare into an intense glare. His throat was prodded and peered down, his chest thumped, his body turned this way and that until he shouted for the annoyance to end.

"Just a mild inflamation of the lungs, Lady Amberson," the doctor assured her, leaving powders to ease his breathing and instructions to be called if his condition worsened.

He was back the following day, and his prognosis was bleak. Lord Amberson was acutely ill. His fever had shot up accompanied by fierce chills. The dry coughs had begun to produce a rust-colored sputum and severe chest pain. Restless and disoriented much of the time, he suffered from a rapid pulse and respiration.

"My lady, the inflamation is widespread. I'll not lie to you. There is every chance he won't recover."

"I see," Tempest said very calmly. "What can I do for him?"

"Keep him comfortable and quiet and pray. That's his best hope."

And so she did, stationing herself at his bedside day and night, speaking to him quietly when the bright, vague eyes were open, and bathing his face with cool water while he slept in brief snatches. When he was aware of her, he would smile, but talking brought on the racking coughs so he stayed silent. Mostly, he drifted, his eyes wandering in an unfocused daze while the fever consumed his strength.

All the while she watched him suffering, Tempest remained serene and quiet, soothing his restlessness with her presence, unruffled by the children's fears and forbidding any of her own from surfacing. As long as she was busy, she didn't have time to think, and that kept her from slipping into despair.

Katherine became an unlikely ally, bringing food and drink and spelling her for short periods of rest. As she watched the older woman lift the dark, damp head to give him the nourishing beef stock she had made, Tempest wondered if she had judged her too harshly. Perhaps when the matter of Amberly was settled, they could arrange a truce. After all, they were family.

An unexpected visitor interrupted her regimented schedule and brought reality home for the first time. When she came down the wide sweeping stairs to see George Morley standing there, her composure fled. With a heartrending wail, she dashed across the foyer to cast herself upon his chest in a flood of weeping.

"Here now. What's this? That dog hasn't left you again, has he?"

"I fear he will," she sobbed. "Oh, George, he can't die. He can't."

The feel of a cool hand on his cheek opened the blurry eyes. They wavered, then settled on a bright thatch of orange hair above the smile etched on

George's face. The unsteady hand he lifted was taken firmly.

"Hello, George. How good of you to come visit me on my deathbed," he said in a raspy whisper.

"Stuff and nonsense. I wouldn't have wasted the trip just to watch you expire. How do you feel? Worse than the time you took the spill from the curricle onto your head? Thought I'd lost you then, too."

"You may this time, George."

His fingers squeezed tight as a spasm of coughing ripped through his chest. After a long moment, the pale eyes opened again, sharp and glittering with pain and fever. He forced a dry swallow and began to speak again, his voice even rougher.

"I don't think I'll mind dying so very much. I have finally made my peace here."

"No!"

That came from Tempest as she happened into the room. She dropped down on the bed, seizing his shoulder with a desperate, angry shake to emphasize her words. "Don't you say that! Don't you dare say that! If you give up and leave me, I will never forgive you. Ever. Do you hear?" Her fierceness dissolved into tears, the first she had shed in his sight, but she was too tired and despondent to hold them in. "Connor, please. Please don't leave me. Please."

He drew her to his chest, holding her there while he breathed in the fragrance of her hair. "Oh, sweet, I love you so. Don't cry. I will do my best."

The wheezing rattle of his breath beneath her cheek made her weep all the harder. She was unprotesting as he pulled her down beside him, cuddling her in the curve of his arm as he had often done to soothe her fears. Had it not been for that vibration in his chest and the incredible scorching heat from his body, she might have been convinced that all would be well. Determinedly, she tried to push her anxieties away. She should be tending to him, not the opposite. When she tried to rise, his arm tightened with surprising strength.

"No, stay by me," he urged hoarsely. "Rest yourself. George can nursemaid me while you sleep. Please, my love. Think of yourself and the child. Do not argue with me."

She bit her lip in anguish. How could she tell him she feared to close her eyes, afraid she would cheat herself out of a single second of looking upon him? But he knew.

"I will be here when you wake," he vowed softly. "Please, sweet. It will make me feel better."

With a resigned sigh, she relaxed against him, putting a superstitious hand over his heart to feel the comforting reassurance of its quick steady pulse. Her eyes closed to the gentle caress of his fingertips along her cheek and jaw, that tender touch easing her way into sleep.

Once assured of her slumber, Connor looked at George, his expression quiet and warmed with the affection of their long friendship. "I'm glad you're here, George. I wanted to talk to you."

Alarmed by the dry scratchy voice and labored breathing, George insisted softly, "Later, Conn. You should rest yourself now."

Connor shook his head in denial. "No, might not

458

be a later." He gave a wan smile as George crushed his hand between his, his hazel eyes filled with upset and protest, but he said nothing. "George, if I don't see this through, I want you to have my Garrett fortune as a posthumous wedding gift."

"Conn, no, I—"

"Please, George. It hurts me so to talk, so please just listen. Tempest has all she'll need from the Ambersons, and she'll agree to it. Over these past years, you have seen me through the highs and lows and have been more brother than friend to me. You and Tempest and the old man are the only ones who cared enough for me to ignore my monumental faults. This is a way I can show my appreciation, not a payment, for your companionship. That way when you try to talk Sarah into letting you spend it foolishly, you will think of me. You see, I'm just being selfish."

George averted his eyes, blinking quickly. His voice was low and unsteady. "You shouldn't do this, Conn."

"I rarely do the things I should. You know that, George. I would ask a favor, that you see to Tempest, that she is well and happy." He felt better now, his mind and heart resting easier and surrounded by those he loved. He was content to give in to the pull of exhaustion that lapped up in insistent waves. "The papers should see to that. Do you have them?"

"What papers do you mean?"

Connor tried to bring his thoughts back into focus, but the struggle was too much. His breath was growing painfully short, rasping noisily in quickly shallow pants.

"It can wait, Conn. We'll talk of it later. Rest now. I'll be right here. Don't be so stubborn."

Connor nodded, his concentration ebbing rapidly. Turning his face into the soft titian curls, he let his senses drift on the heavy fog of fever.

It was a pleasant waking. The room was in velvety darkness, and all was warm and secure. She was about to dismiss all as a most delightful dream when it happened again, the tender perusal of her lips. She was fully awake then.

"Connor?"

"Shh, sweet. Don't wake George.

He kissed her again, as deeply as his shortened breath would allow. It was an effort for Tempest to pull back and grasp her control firmly, admonishing him like a haughty boy.

"Really, my lord. You are not well enough for this kind of play."

His fingers rubbed her cheek, then slipped further to tangle in her hair, bringing her face close to his. "I am not playing, sweet. I am quite delirious so I cannot be expected to behave rationally. Humor me, love. I am a sick man."

Traitorously yielding to his weak touch, she moaned softly and caught his transgressing hand. "Connor, enough," she whispered with a shaky conviction.

"For now, I'm afraid it will have to be," he agreed reluctantly, nuzzling her gleaming shoulder. "Willingness of the heart and mind is not enough to overcome a useless body. I cannot offer more than to lie here and let you ravish me as you will."

Her soft chuckle was low music against his ear. "A most tempting proposition, my lord. You must be feeling more yourself." Her hand brushed his cheek and forehead for confirmation, finding him damp and cool. The fever had broken.

"If I were myself, we would not be spending this time talking," he vowed. He shifted uncomfortably on the sticky sheets and wrinkled his aristocratic nose. "I need a bath."

"I will see to it myself in the morning," she promised gladly, burrowing against his side. She closed her eyes in brief thankful prayer that they could discuss tomorrow and the future with a certainty. Resting in the crook of his arm, she wanted to think about those tomorrows together to convince herself that his mortality was not in question, that their love would continue past these last tentative days, and that she would have her vital, passionate husband back.

"I love you, Connor. Forgive me for being so foolishly afraid."

"Of what, sweet?"

"Of a life without you. I couldn't have borne it."

"Stuff," he chided, but his embrace tightened. "I'd have been quickly forgotten in the face of all my wealth. You'd not have worn widow's weeds long."

"Connor, what a dreadful thing to say," she gasped in outrage until his rough, rumbling laugh made her scowl. "You tease me most unkindly, my lord. Pray

461

who would I find to replace such a paragon as yourself? I have just gotten used to your many vices. Don't force me to go through that again. You will not rid yourself of me so easily."

"Good," he concluded.

At the bedside, George gave a grumbling mutter as he twisted in the rigid chair, sound asleep.

"Looks deuced uncomfortable, doesn't he?" Connor mused, then reached out a hand, his knuckles rapping George sharply on the knee to startle him awake.

"Are you all right, Conn?" he asked in groggy concern, running a hand through the bright beacon of his hair.

"A fine nursemaid you proved to be, snoring at my bedside. Find yourself a room, and give us some privacy."

George snorted at the two of them curled so cozily beneath the covers while he sat stiff and sore. "I can see you're in good hands. Forgive me for thinking you too ill to indulge in such things."

"Lust is a powerful cure. Good night, George."

"Good night. Don't murder him with good intentions, Tempest."

When the door closed, Connor rolled toward her, his voice husky. "If I'm to die in bed, I would prefer no other circumstance. Or company."

"Connor!" she chastened in dismay.

His fingertips sought her in the dimness, spreading wide over her delicate cheekbones. His voice was no longer raspy with the gurgle of his illness but was a hushed whisper, the timbre rich with emotion.

"Remember our first night together? I thought I would burst with wanting you. I didn't believe I would ever know passion such as that again. How wrong I was. And the night before we married, I was sure I could never experience love so deeply. Again, I was wrong. I wish I could make love to you now and prove myself wrong when I say I've never had such happiness before."

"There will be many, many more chances for you to prove that, my lord. For now, be content with having my love, for you do, and that will never change."

Slowly, carefully, tenderly she came to him, her kisses a cool rain on his face, her light touch a soothing breeze against his skin. She sat up to wriggle out of her crumpled gown, then slid up against him all warm, supple, and painfully inviting. As his hand glided familiarly down the smooth satin contours, she sought his mouth, savoring its warmth and sensuous shape, tasting and delighting in all it would yield with a tender longing.

"I love you, Connor," she said softly, stroking the dark head that nestled into the curve of her shoulder. His reply was a vague mutter, and the caressing hand ceased its wandering, lying still on her rounded hip. "Connor?"

When there was no response, Tempest smiled and closed her eyes, letting the strength of her relief and the cool peace of the night draw her deep into the embrace of slumber they found together in each other's arms.

There was a giggle and a sharp shush.

"Be quiet. Don't wake them," came a voice full of dire consequence.

"I'm not. I just wanted to see if he was better." That was a petulant, little girl whine.

"You can see he is, or Este wouldn't be sleeping. Now, come on before you cause trouble."

"I'm not. I want to see for myself."

A tiny hand gingerly touched the warm cheek bringing open one gray-blue eye and a welcoming smile.

"Good morning, sweet, and I feel much better, thank you. Well enough for a hug at least."

Jesse blushed with pleasure and climbed up to embrace him shyly about the neck. She thought Connor Amberson was the most beautiful thing alive.

"Do you think you and Jack could talk cook into sending up some breakfast?"

Jesse nodded and scampered off with Jack in tow.

"Another six-year-old conquest, my lord?"

Connor grinned and kissed his wife thoroughly.

"How are you this morning?"

"Better than terrible," he assessed. "Today, I think I've improved to awful." He did look better, his color not so high and his eyes a cooler shade of blue. Though still feverish, he had a greater clarity of mind, and the binding crush in his chest was not so severe.

"Does this mean I get no more pampering?" he pouted, his eyes heavy and inviting.

"What kind of pampering do you need, my lord?" she purred. Her lips teased over his lightly until he was panting in quick labored gasps. When she leaned away, he lay still, his eyes closed and his moist mouth parted. "Enough, sir?"

"I am quite at your mercy," he gasped faintly. "Take advantage of me. I won't put up much of a struggle."

"Calm yourself, my lord. Speak those bold words when we've no danger of being interrupted."

"Then quit torturing me and clothe yourself," he groaned. But watching her dress was a greater torment yet, his eyes hungering over the lithesome figure. Lusts simmered helplessly while she moved about, full of supple seduction and mischievous glee while he ogled her sullenly.

The harsh, rasping cough brought Tempest to the bedside, her eyes soft with concern. "Connor? Are you all right?"

Her forearms were grasped, and a sharp jerk brought her down upon his chest. He rolled with her until his weight held her prisoner.

"Tease me, will you, you vexing chit! If I could manage it, I would teach you a sound lesson, but since I am already exhausted, you shall have to settle for a mere sample of your punishment."

Tempest gave a murmur of pleasure as his mouth covered hers. Her arms came up about his shoulders in a possessive circle, content to accept as much of this punishment as he could mete out.

The noisy arrival of company halted their play. Katherine came in with a breakfast tray followed by George and the three Swifts.

"Look what Uncle George brought us," Jesse

465

trilled in delight, dumping an armload of boxes on the bed.

"How good of Uncle George," Connor remarked dryly, settling back on the less pleasant softness of his bed and prop of pillows. "Let's see what we have here."

Connor ate heartily while the children tore open their boxes, exclaiming in awe at the contents. As Jesse whirled about the floor with a white muslin shift held like a dance partner, Tempest snuggled close to her husband with a smile. Even dour Eddie seemed pleased with the sturdy nankeens and caped topcoat found among his parcels.

In a low aside, George told his friend, "I didn't spend it all. I thought when you are better recovered, you might send them down to stay with me for a time. They can purchase some things of their own liking, and you and Tempest can indulge in some time to yourselves alone."

"You are truly brilliant, George. A most thoughtful uncle," Connor proclaimed with a grin.

"Oh, I agree," Tempest seconded, nuzzling the warm throat.

To take his wandering mind off the tempting things his wife was doing with her lips and sharp little teeth, Connor asked a bit unsteadily, "Did you find the papers, George?"

"What papers do you mean, Conn?"

"The ones I wrote you about."

"Wrote me? When?"

"Several days ago. I sent a courier to London. You received no message from me?"

"None. Conn? What is it, Conn? Are you all right?"

George's voice echoed with a tiny echo through Connor's head and grew fainter and more distant until it was an annoying buzz. Connor shook his head to rid it of the buzzing clamor, only to arouse a dizzy sickness and flush of heat. When his eyes opened, all had doubled and were out of focus.

"George? Tempest?" His voice was a vague whisper as he sank into blackness.

Chapter Thirty

By evening, Connor's condition had deteriorated so severely that they once again feared for his life. Thrashing with a weak violence upon the bed, he did not respond to Tempest's voice. When his nearly black eyes were open, they showed no recognition. His fever raged out of control, and his pulse beneath hot, dry skin was alarmingly rapid and weak.

While Eddie kept the children quiet and distracted, Tempest and George kept a worried vigil.

"I don't understand it, George," Tempest wept softly. "He seemed so much better. I was so sure he would recover. Oh, George, I'm going to lose him, aren't I? What am I going to do without him?"

Holding her in a gentle embrace, George kept his own doubts to himself. He made his words firm and reassuring. "Conn's a tough, stubborn man, and he's never had more reason to want to live than now. That will make the difference. He loves you too much to let you go. You must believe that."

"I'm trying to. I want to." Tears slipped down her

cheeks as she turned back to watch her husband writhe in the private torment she was helpless to ease.

Connor was confused. Before, he had been sick and his body suffered from the weakening consequences, but this was more like madness. His mind was afire, the flames of fever feeding off images of wild distortion that ran amok whether his eyes were open or shut. Crazy snatches of past recollections wove about the present until he wasn't sure what was real. He would hear his mother's voice calling to him low and soft and forced his eyes open, eager to see her again, but the voice was Tempest's and her features were a vague blur until a cool chill on his forehead eased the vision away. Occasionally, he would see George and try to reach out to him, but he could promote no response from his leadened arms. He tried to call out to him, but his mouth and throat were so dry he could form no words. He twisted in frustration until George bent down to take up his hand.

"Tempest. See to her, George," he croaked with difficulty.

"I will. My word on it, Conn."

Satisfied, he let awareness slip away and fell back into the fearful swirl of delirium. Some of the images were so clear and so real he felt himself transported to another time and place.

He was kneeling. The painful dryness in his throat was from weeping. Strong hands clutched his shoulders, and his father's voice was low and shaken with emotion.

"Connor, come away. There is nothing more we can do. We've lost them, son."

469

"No," he wailed, his eyes rising to the cold waxen face on the pillow. He gave a choking cry. It was not his mother he saw but Tempest.

"No."

The hoarse moan brought Tempest close, to still the tossing head with a gentle hand. Thin trails of wetness penciled down his flushed cheeks. As she wiped them away, the dark eyes opened. She kissed him lightly, only to be crushed to his chest in a sudden strong embrace as he sobbed, "Oh, Tempest, please don't leave me. I love you. Please."

Then his arms fell away and his eyes closed, leaving her to weep in silent anguish.

The smell of the pungent fall grasses was sharp and fresh. As he brought his gun to his shoulder, he could hear Tyler's voice behind him but not the words. The recoil shocked his shoulder and gunpowder burned his nose. Down a long distant tunnel, he saw the quail plummet down, hit by his single shot.

"Connor, here. Drink this."

It was a woman's voice, not Tempest's. His head was lifted, and a cup placed at his lips. Obediently he swallowed, the process difficult and uncomfortable. When he paused to catch his breath, the voice grew more insistent.

"Hurry now. All of it. Take it all. You won't suffer long. It will be quick as it was with your mother."

The hot eyes snapped open. Katherine was bent over him, holding a goblet. Her features were wildly misshapen. With a cry, his arm struck out blindly,

470

knocking aside the cup and spilling its contents. The abrupt movement brought on a paroxysm of coughing. As Katherine scrambled to pick up the cup, he struggled to sit up.

"What in heaven's name goes on here?" George demanded. He had just managed to convince Tempest to eat something and rest, and all the commotion endangered his efforts.

"I don't know, Mr. Morley. I was giving him a drink, and he just became violent. He tried to strike me. I fear he's not in his right mind."

George frowned and sat on the side of the bed. Carefully, he raised Connor up to ease his breathing, surprised by his friend's sudden burst of strength as he clung to him desperately, trying to speak between frantic gulps for air.

"George—George, help me. Get her out of here. Out of here."

"Go," he told the bewildered woman.

"But I've done nothing," she protested.

With Connor scrabbling nearly over the top of him like a drowning man, gurgling with the heavy fluids that choked him, he said simply, "Just go. I'll tend him. Go now."

"George, help me. Don't let me die," came the sobbing gasps as Connor sagged against him, his fingers twisting convulsively in George's coat. "Trying to kill me—poison in the cup—like my mother—please, George—"

George hugged him fiercely, chilled by the ranting voice. "It's all right, Conn. She's gone. Quiet now," he soothed, patting his shoulder and trying to ease him back down. The panicked grip only tightened.

"George—George, keep her away from me," he panted.

"It's all right. It's just the fever, Conn. No one is trying to harm you."

The dark head shook jerkily. "No. No. Listen—to me. Please."

With a soft moan, Connor lay limp against him, and the desperate grasp loosened. George laid him back and drew up a cover, evading the weak attempts to catch hold of his sleeve as the huge dilated eyes stared up blankly.

"I'm right here, Conn. Quiet now. I'll stay with you. Don't try to talk. It's all right."

"George, listen." But it was only a faint whisper as his eyes closed.

Shifting restlessly, Connor couldn't hold onto the vague awareness. Was the poison even now coursing through him? How long had he been taking it? In his food? In his drink? In the breakfast he ate before he fell ill once more? Katherine had brought that too. Had she been impatient because the pneumonia had failed to serve its purpose?

Swallowing painfully, he looked for George in the blur all around him. How frustrating to have so clear a mind trapped in this useless body. He had to talk to George. He had to convince him of the danger. But he couldn't find him in the distorted jumble, and his throat had closed too tightly for the passage of sound. Helpless, he closed his eyes.

The water was cool, trickling down his cracked lips and down the parched desert of his throat. He took several greedy swallows before realizing what he was doing. What was in the water? Whose hand held the cup?

As Connor thrust her hand away, Tempest gave a gasp. Damp circles splotched the sheet that covered him as the water sloshed out. His mutter of protest was insensible. The disoriented gaze was bright with panic but never settled on her face. When she touched his dry, hot cheek, he cringed back and grew so agitated she withdrew her hand.

"George, what's wrong with him? He has to drink. The fever's burning him up inside. He won't take anything from me." When George told her what had happened that morning, she pondered over it, then went quickly to see to her plan.

She returned with a tray and sat down at the bedside. She bent close, taking the flushed face between her hands and holding him still as he tried to twist away.

"Connor," she called steadily, her voice low and authoritative. "Connor, it's Tempest. Look at me. Concentrate. It's Tempest."

His breathing only quickened, and his efforts to escape became more purposeful. Holding him immobile, she kissed him. He tried to recoil, then the frantic gasps slowed, and his lips slackened with lack of resistance.

"Connor, it's Tempest. Do you know me? Can you hear me?"

The glazed eyes ceased their wandering, fixing on

her face for a long moment. Then he nodded.

"Good. I've brought you some tea and some soup." When she felt him stiffen in denial, she added, "I made it myself. I made it for you with my own hands. Will you take it from me?"

Again, the faint nod. "Thank God, you believe me," he whispered.

The food served to strengthen him, and as he lay back fairly comfortable, his thoughts were racing at a frantic pace. Katherine was trying to kill him. She had killed his mother. Was that fact or part of his delirium? Had he heard her speak to him, or were those damming words spoken only in his fevered mind? His mother had died of influenza. He, himself, was deathly ill. Could he trust the tangled workings of his own reasoning? Would all appear an embarrassing amusement when he recovered? If she let him recover. Was it madness or cold, clear fact? His aunt and uncle and supposedly Holly were murdered. His mother died. Was she poisoned? His grandfather died. Old age or had he been hurried along? The Swifts had been killed. All coincidence? Or pieces of the same dangerous puzzle. When all the parts fell in place, would that picture be of Katherine and Tyler reigning at Amberly? If he died, what stood in the way?

Holly. Tempest.

Tempest was gently sponging his hot face with a cool cloth when she found him staring at her intently. She smiled encouragingly. When he struggled to speak, she wet his lips obligingly.

"Tempest, they're trying to kill me," he began, his

474

words slow and labored.

"Hush, my lord. I would never let any one harm you."

Her gentle reassurances only increased his fervor. His hand closed about her wrist. His touch burned. "Listen to me. They killed them all, everyone in their way. Can't you see it? Don't let them kill me as they did my mother. Tempest, please. Please listen to me."

The desperate rantings made her bite her lip. She had to remain calm. She had to quiet him before he did himself more harm. "Connor, I love you. Things will be clearer when you get better. Trust me, my love. The only danger is in your own mind. I would never let any harm come to you. I would die to protect you, but there is no danger here. Please, Connor, believe me, please. You are very ill. You're confused now, but that will pass. You have to rest. You have to get stronger. Please, my lord. I could not bear to be without you. Try to rest. I will stay here with you. You are safe, Connor. Trust me, please."

Connor closed his eyes to the tender expression of concern. She was going to sit at his side, loving him, caring for him while they poisoned him right before her. With him disposed of, what would happen to her? They would murder her as well if she blocked their way to Amberly. But he could change that. He had to change that.

"George. I need to talk to George."

"Connor, you need to rest," she began, but his hand tightened convulsively on her wrist, making her wince.

"No. Now. Now."

"All right, I'll get him. Only please don't upset yourself."

He raised her hand slowly to touch to his lips, then released her, his strength waning all at once. After drifting in and out of awareness, he felt his hand pressed warmly and fought to focus on that contact.

"What is it, Conn? Anything I can do for you, it's yours."

Connor gathered all his shaken control, trying hard to appear totally rational. "George, take Tempest with you to London." He heard her quick objection but closed his eyes and continued forcefully. "Tell Rogers to guard her with his life. Find those papers and bring them to me along with Julius. I'm forfeiting Amberly and will need him to do it properly."

"Conn—"

"George, please. If I'm dead when you return, leave me in the chapel and burn the house over me. There can be nothing left. Sell the lands as quickly as you can, everything. There must be nothing left that they would want. You have to keep Tempest safe."

"Connor, this is madness. You must realize that. Wait until your mind clears and ask again."

Angry and desperate, Connor raged at him fiercely. "There is no time. Do it now. For God's sake, if you won't do it for our friendship, then do it for the money. Take it now. Take it, George. Just do as I ask. Please. Please, George. Do this for me. I beg you." His words dwindled off. The violent rifts of emotion had sparked that burning in his lungs. He clutched his chest while panting rapidly to ease the distress. His other hand clung to George's, but his grip was weak as a child's. "Please, George."

"Conn, no amount of money could make me do something so adverse to my better judgment, but I will do it because you asked me. Anything to put your mind at rest."

"Thank you, George. Thank you, George," was the relieved whisper.

"Now, you promise me something" George insisted firmly, squeezing his hand hard. "You be here when I return. All right? Don't you die on me, Conn. I saw you through your wedding. I need you to do the same for me."

"I promise, George." There was the faintest shadow of a smile. "You are a good friend, George. Take care of her. She's all that matters to me."

"My word on it."

Tempest had stayed silent during their exchange, standing in the background with an unreadable expression. After George had gone, she sat beside her husband and embraced him tightly. How hot he felt and so very weak. She kissed his mouth, his cheeks, his eyelids, his forehead, and then his mouth again, lingering there. His hand curled against her cheek in tender possession.

"I love you, Tempest. Don't look back. Don't remember me this way. Tell our child how good it was between us, how good it could have been."

She smiled, her fingertips brushing through the wet, lackluster hair. "Never fear, my lord. You are still the most fabulous-looking man I've ever seen. As for our child, that should come from you and it will. I will not give you up so easily. How could I ever

477

replace you, my arrogant, sweet love? How could you think any force on heaven or earth would make me leave you now? You are mine, Connor Amberson, and I plan to see to the care of my property myself."

His damp cheek rubbed into her palm, and he spoke with rough emotion. "Tempest, please. I beg you go with George. You and the baby have to be safe. Please—"

Her fingers covered his lips to halt the passionate words. "No argument, my lord. Stop being so selfish and overbearing. This time, it will be as I say. I stay here. I've no desire to sleep in a bed without you in it. Rest, my love, while I see George out."

Connor closed his eyes weakly, no strength left to debate his reasoning. He made no move as soft lips touched his forehead. They had beaten him. They would have everything at the cost of all he held dear. How could he protect them now?

"Did you mean what you said about giving up this place?"

Connor slitted his eyes. Eddie sat on the edge on the bed. "It doesn't matter now. It's too late," he answered dully. Without hope to sustain him, he sagged on the bed, hot and aching and strangely giddy. "You'd just think I'm crazy too."

"I think you're crazy to toss away all this with no reason. Is it because of Este?"

He sighed heavily, crushed and defeated. What did it matter if the boy thought him delirious. Haltingly, he told of his suspicions.

"You going to hand it over to 'em? Do you think they'd just leave you go? What a greenling you are. So what are we going to do?"

"You believe me!"

"Why not? What you got here is worth killing a dozen people over. I don't fancy the two of them stepping into your shoes over my sister and my folks. You got a plan?"

Connor's laugh turned into a harsh cough, and it was a moment before he could respond. With broken words, he gasped, "Get your pistols. Don't let them give me anything. If they come near me, kill them. We have to get Tempest out of here. It's up to you, Eddie. I can't manage it."

The dark eyes held his steadily. "I'll handle things. You weren't my pick as a brother-in-law, but I'll be damned, you've grown on me. If Este wants you, I mean to see she keeps you."

Connor smiled faintly and let his attention ebb. All was not lost. He had a capable ally in the boy.

"Hello, Connie."

His eyes flew open with a gasp of alarm to see Tyler at his bedside. A silky smile curved upon the sharply handsome face as he observed his cousin dispassionately.

"You don't look at all well, Cousin. I don't think you'll live through the night. In fact, I know you won't."

When Connor made a feeble effort to roll away, Tyler leaned a knee upon his chest, crushing out his already restricted breath. His hand shot out to grip Connor by the jaw, holding his head still while he slowly swirled the contents of the cup he held. He smiled at Connor's ineffectual struggles to pull free.

"Here you go, Connie. Bottoms up."

The bitter draft was forced between his lips, and it was swallow or strangle. When the liquid was gone, he was released.

Tyler gave a low chuckle and patted Connor's cheek smartly. "Good-bye, Connie, and thank you for all you're about to give me."

Chapter Thirty-one

"Step away from him."

The harsh command was reinforced by the click of a hammer being cocked.

Tyler turned, his voice cold with disdain. "What is the meaning of this? Are you out of your mind threatening me?"

"No, but I'll leave you no space to store yours in if you don't get out of this room. His lordship needs his rest, and I intend to see he gets it." Eddie motioned toward the door with the barrel of his pistol. "Get out, and if I see your face again, it won't be so pretty to look at."

Tyler looked from the menacing boy to his cousin who lay thrashing weakly on the bed, then smiled. "I just came in to pay my respects. Rest easy, Connie. As for you, boy, I intend to make you very sorry for this. Soon."

The moment the door closed, Eddie set the pistol aside and caught Connor's tossing head.

"Are you all right, my lord? Can you hear me?"

Connor's glazed eyes stared up blankly. He couldn't focus or force words through his constricted throat, his thoughts spinning in a dizzying reel.

"Did he give you anything? Did he make you swallow anything?" Eddie shook him until he received a jerky nod in answer.

Determinedly, the boy dragged the heavy unresponsive figure until the lolling head hung over the side of the bed. When the stubby fingers jabbed down his throat, Connor gagged and began to struggle in protest, but Eddie's grip was firm on the back of his neck.

"Don't fight me. You've got to get that up before it's too late."

"What are you doing?" Tempest shrieked as she stared in confusion at the sight of her brother apparently trying to choke her husband.

"Don't interfere, Este," Eddie snapped and went back to his grim purpose. When Tempest pulled at his arm in angry objection, he gave her a hard push that sent her sprawling to the floor. This time, he was able to complete what he had started, and with a hoarse, strangling cough, Connor emptied the poisons from his stomach.

Tempest's fist caught Eddie unaware, splitting his lip and tumbling him over. While he blinked and held his bloodied mouth, Tempest pulled Connor into a protective embrace. Her words to him were a tender murmur as she tried to quiet him and stop his shivering and gasping weakly for air. The bright fiercesome eyes flashed up as she stroked the dark head she hugged to her breast and raged at her brother in low, hissing fury.

"Are you mad? You might have killed him!"

"Me or them, what makes the difference?" the boy mumbled with difficulty. His lip was already ballooning hugely.

"What are you saying? Don't tell me you listened to Connor's ramblings? Eddie, he's sick. His mind has been touched by the fever."

"Has yours been as well? Are you going to do nothing while they push poisons down him? He's not crazy. He's trying to save his own life since you won't do it for him. Those people murdered my Ma and Pa and you're going to let them kill him as well. You're a damned fool, Este."

"Eddie, enough!" Connor broke in softly, his senses restored.

While the boy wept in silent upset, Tempest laid Connor back carefully on the bed and sponged the sweat from his face. Her voice trembled.

"Are you all right, Connor?"

He swallowed to ease his raw throat and rasped, "I think I will be now. Your brother saved my life."

Tempest was silent for a long pause studying his haggard face, then touched it with a tentative hand. "Connor, is all that you've been saying true?"

"Yes."

She searched his expression for any betraying sign but could find none to suggest he wasn't completely lucid.

"Aunt Kate and Tyler are trying to poison you?"

"Yes."

"They killed my parents and Eddie's?"

483

"And my mother and most likely Grandfather."

"And almost you." It took a moment for her to digest all this; then she was hugging him tightly, frantically. "Oh, Connor, I could have lost you through my own stubborn ignorance. Can you ever forgive me for allowing such things to happen?"

"Hush, sweet. There is nothing to forgive," he vowed softly into the coppery curls.

"But I've been so stupid. Eddie believed you. Why couldn't I?"

"He hasn't been up every night for the past week half-mad with worry either. No words of blame. Just hold me and tell me you love me."

"Love me? Oh, God, how I love you," she cried vehemently. She sat back, her bright eyes hard and angry. "How dare they! How dare they try to take you from me! How dare they try to take Amberly from us and our children!"

"Let them have it!"

She stared at him. His soft-spoken words were so unlike the fiercely possessive lord she knew. "But, Connor, it's yours. Ours."

"It's not important. Only you and our child matter now, and surrendering Amberly is a small price to pay to keep you safe."

Those words gladdened her heart, but her pride rebelled hotly. "No. We will not give in. They'll not have Amberly as a reward for murdering our loved ones."

"Tempest—"

"Connor, no."

"Please." It was a quiet entreaty, simple yet heavy

with pain. "Tempest, I watched my mother die with her unborn child. I couldn't endure that again. Nothing matters if I don't have you. I would live on the street, labor with my hands, anything so long as I have you and your love. Don't take that from me. Don't ask me to risk it all. I cannot. I will not."

She kissed him, slowly, deeply, tenderly with great feeling, knowing his words spoke for her heart as well.

"First, we must get away from here; then we will talk of what to do. We still have no proof. Can you travel, my lord?"

"Not on foot."

She returned his smile, her fingertips caressing his flushed face. Their gazes held for a timeless moment; then she stood, all brisk efficiency.

"Eddie, stay with him. No one but me comes in this room."

The boy nodded, his eyes downcast. His glum expression lifted when her arms wrapped about him.

"Go on now," he growled. "I'll see to your fancy face husband."

Tempest slipped quietly into the children's room to find them sleeping soundly. Securing the latch on their outside door, she ran lightly down the stairs. She would have Bridget get them ready while she went for a carriage. They could steal away from Amberly and take shelter with George until their scheming relations could be justly dealt with. The kitchen was empty, but so was Bridget's room. Frowning, she hurried along the servants' wing, but all was uncommonly silent.

"Looking for someone?"

Tempest nearly screamed as she turned to face Katherine. In the dimness of the hall, she cast a large frightening shadow, all dark and engulfing. Tempest's thoughts scrambled in a panic that didn't show on her face. She couldn't let the cold-blooded creature know she was suspect.

"Oh, Aunt Kate, Connor is so very ill, I was going to have someone ride for the doctor, but there's no one about. Where are the servants?" Her voice trembled with just the right amount of alarm.

"They've gone. Knowing how badly Connor needed quiet, I sent them away. No one will disturb him now." Her black viper eyes said no one would be witness to what she planned.

"But what am I going to do about Connor?"

"Do?" a quiet voice behind her said.

She jumped, startled, and her arms were caught in a tight hold.

"We're going to do nothing, dear Holly. Sadly enough, Connor is going to die tonight," Tyler said with a low chuckle. "The question is what to do with you."

With a fierce snarl, Tempest kicked back at the same time her elbow found his ribs. His grip slackened, and she wiggled free to dash for the stairs, her only thought to reach Connor, to warn him. Then there was a sharp pain at the back of her head. Then nothing.

Man and boy waited together for what stretched into an hour. Finally, in edgy anxiety, Connor asked, "Go see about your sister, Eddie, but quietly."

Eddie returned in less than a minute, his face pale and his manner fearful. "They have her in the study, all tied up. One of them must have tricked her."

His voice very calm and assured, Connor instructed him, "Eddie, I want you to go after George Morley. If you take my horse, you should catch him halfway to London. Bring him back here at gunpoint if necessary. Can you get to the stables without being seen?"

The boy gave a confident grin. "If I don't want to be seen, I won't be."

Connor sat up. It took an absurd amount of effort. The illness had sapped his strength just as the poison had misshapen his senses. He gave a wan smile at Eddie's pinched look as he sat sucking air noisily.

"What do you plan, my lord?"

"Whatever it takes. Give me one of your pistols." With the primed piece in hand, he looked more capable. "Go on, boy."

"Be careful, Connor."

Connor took the hand extended to him and shook it firmly. "Hurry."

It was a terrible effort just to move. An echoing cannon-fire roar resounded through her temples. Her position was awkward and restrictive. Then she realized she was bound with her hands behind her back. The firelight wavered before her eyes, flaring and waning, then becoming constant.

"I'm so sorry that was necessary, dear Holly. I had no real wish to hurt you," Tyler said as he observed her narrowly from the opposite settee. Katherine stood by the fire, her shrewd eyes pensive.

"You won't get away with this," she told them firmly.

Katherine smiled condescendingly. "But we already have. Many times. It has been a long wait, but finally we'll have what we deserve."

"I hope to see you'll get just that."

The woman laughed at the quiet threat. "I do admire your courage. You are the one thing I didn't count on. I was certain you were dead. But no matter, you soon will be, and everything will belong to me and my son. All those years of suffering that squandering fool who thought penny-pinching a virtue and the humiliation of toad-eating to that wretched old man will finally yield us our due. I was so patient. I took my time, and no one suspected a thing."

Tempest shivered to herself. They were going to die, she and Connor and probably the children. She had to forestall it by some miracle. If she could keep the bitter woman talking, perhaps she could find a way.

"But why all this? Why the killing? Did you plan it that way from the start?"

Katherine gave her a gauging look, then felt like boasting. "No, not at first. Afterward. I was poor. Almost as poor as you. The Ambersons were my way out too. I wanted things their money could buy me. Thomas married me when I told him I was pregnant. So honorable, that man. What a dreadful mistake that was. He wouldn't live here in luxury, no. He had to make his own way, the proud fool. He took me to this drafty hovel and made me act the servant. Me! I couldn't bear it. In anger, I told him how I tricked him into marrying me. How furious he was. He vowed I would never get another penny, and I shot him. It was easy to blame some drunken fool for the deed. No one would have been the wiser. Except then your father came nosing about with his questions and suspicious looks. I don't know how he found out about my secret, but he did and was going to see I was cut out of the family."

"What secret?" Tempest prompted.

"Me," Tyler put in smoothly. "I'm no Amberson. Your uncle wasn't my father."

While Tempest gasped in astonishment, Katherine continued easily. "You see what would have happened if that got out. Jeffrey was going to tell the old man. Then I would have no claim. The old man hated me anyway. So I had to get rid of him, and in doing so, I thought, why not all of them? I took my time and took care of them one by one. All we had to do was wait for the old man to cut Connor out, and Connor was obliging us so well by being such a rakehell. But then you almost ruined it all. Almost, my dear. I will see to you myself, just as I did dear Jillian and that bastard Jonathan and—"

"My father!"

They all turned at the unexpected voice. Connor stood in the doorway, pistol in hand, his eyes a frigid fire.

"You killed him, didn't you? It wasn't my shot at

all."

"I arranged for it to be done," Katherine admitted coolly. She made a brief gesture to Tyler, who began to ease to one side, drawing the barrel of the gun with him.

"And all these years you let me think I had done it. You let me think I had killed my father. It must have provided you great amusement to see what that did to me." His voice faltered slightly, his other hand rising to steady the pistol.

"Oh, yes. A brilliant plan, really. I almost succeeded in eliminating you both at one time."

"You made my life hell, and that's where I'm going to send you." His eyes flashed between mother and son, his breath growing short and difficult. He took an awkward step to one side so he could lean against the jamb for support. Everything had begun to tip as an insistent heat rose to his head in a swirl of dizzy weakness. Knowing he was about to faint, Connor struggled to aim the gun. He had to kill them before he lost consciousness. But which target should he fire at? There were two Tylers advancing slowly, two smugly smiling Katherines. Slowly, his ankles and knees turned to liquid, spilling him down into a deep, unpleasant darkness.

Tyler caught the limp figure in one arm, wresting away the pistol before tossing him facedown on the sofa beside Tempest. As he secured the slack wrists with a length of drapery cord, Katherine called out a curt warning.

"Not too tightly. We can have no marks on either of them. It must appear as though poor Connor suc-

490

cumbed to his illness, and in a fit of despair, his devoted wife took her own life."

"No," Tempest cried urgently. "There is no need for this. Connor sent George to bring Julius back. He's going to forfeit Amberly. He's going to give it to you. It's all yours. Please just let us go. We'll make no trouble for you."

"I'm sorry, my dear, but I know Connor too well to believe he'd ever keep his word. No, better we dispose of you now. I want no loose ends. The two little ones are no problem, but the older boy might make trouble. Bring him here, Tyler."

Tempest sat very still on the sofa, maintaining a calm facade. She could feel Connor's breath brushing her arm, so she knew for the moment that he was all right. Looking at the harsh features of Katherine Amberson, she knew it would do no good to beg for their lives.

"I can't find him."

Katherine turned on her son fiercely. "What do you mean?"

"He's not upstairs. There's no sign of him."

Katherine clenched her hands into impotent fists and snapped, "Check the stables. I'll look upstairs again. We have to find him. Hurry."

The minute they were alone, Tempest twisted around to grasp a heavy decanter and smashed it on the edge of the settee. She wedged the broken neck between the cushions and sawed the ropes across the jagged crystal, wincing as they slashed at her tender flesh. With a hard pull, the frayed bonds gave way.

On her knees, she untied Connor and rolled him

toward her, shaking him and calling his name in a compelling whisper. Finally, the foggy blue eyes flickered open.

"Connor, can you hear me? Where's Eddie?"

"Gone after George," he mumbled thickly, trying to steady his tenuous concentration. "Be hours before they get here."

"Then we'll just have to keep ourselves safe until then. Can you stand, my lord? We've not much time."

With Tempest's help, Connor staggered to his feet. He had no sense of balance or direction in his wavering world of double images, and what little strength he had was used on the arduous journey downstairs.

Very quietly, he said, "Sit me down, my love. I cannot make it. Go on, Tempest. Think of the child, not me."

Taking his beloved face between her hands, she kissed him quickly. "No, Connor. I'll not leave you. You come with me, or I stay with you."

"Stubborn creature," he groaned. "Lead on. I'll do my best."

Supporting as much of his weight as she could, Tempest hurried through the great hall and into the servants' quarters. Through the small panes at the rear door she could see a bobbing lantern light as Tyler returned from the stables. Without hesitation, she turned Connor into the narrow back stairwell and closed the door behind them.

By the time they had climbed halfway, Connor collapsed weakly on the steep winding steps, barely conscious. The rattle of his gasps for air echoed in the confined space. Tempest hunched down beside him, anxiously tapping his sweat-drenched face in an effort to revive him.

"Connor, please. Don't give up. It's not much farther. You have to help me."

Connor's chest was on fire. Every strangled breath scorched his throat and lungs. The ever-tightening band about his ribs allowed only brief snatches of air, and his head was giddy for the want of oxygen. Tempest's hand was cool on his face, her gentle voice the embodiment of strength. He reached out blindly to catch her capable shoulders and struggled to his feet.

Tempest didn't pause at the second floor and followed the stairs up to the massive attic. It ran the length of the great house, dotted with dormers and heavy with the musty atmosphere of disuse. Furniture was stored by rooms, squat and shrouded. Her eyes teared involuntarily at the sight of her much-traveled hobbyhorse, the one she had hoped would bear her own children on many a journey in the nursery below.

Connor sagged down, sitting on his heels, his eyes closed and his energy spent. He couldn't even lift his arms to embrace his wife as she clung to him fiercely. His thoughts were full of her, quick flashes that pricked his emotions, the sight of her huge blue eyes opening for the first time, the satiny feel of her arms entwined about his neck, the taste of sweet surrender in her kiss in the exotic garden, her cold fingers as he slid his ring on her hand, the fragile pieces of a broken cup, the sob of a broken heart, the whisper of ecstasy.

"I love you, Tempest," he said faintly.

"I know you do, my lord, as I have always loved you." Her lips pressed warm and tender to his. "Stay here, my lord. I'm going down for Jack and Jesse."

"There's a pistol in my top bureau drawer," he panted unevenly.

"I'll bring it." She started to stand, then bent down so they were eye to eye. She was smiling. "Connor, you have made me so very happy."

His unsteady fingers grazed her cheek. "Thank you, sweet."

"I want more of the same and soon. No one will cheat me from having that or from filling the nursery with your children. I want you. I need you. I will not give you up. Do you understand me?" At his nod, she kissed him, this time with a passion and desperate hunger that feared it would never be fulfilled, savoring and holding to the memory of the sensuous, pouting mouth, the warm vital heat of his body and the pleasures both had yielded. Reluctantly, she released him and ran down the stairs without a backward glance.

The sound of footsteps on the stairs woke Connor from his groggy stupor. He listened to them for a moment before he realized what was wrong. One set of footsteps was made by a man's heavy tread.

Tyler lifted his lamp high, which cast an eerie glow down the long cavern of darkness. He knew they couldn't have gone far with Connor so ill from the pneumonia and touches of belladonna, but he could see no likely hiding place. Perhaps his mother had

494

been wrong. Perhaps they had braved the harsh weather.

He was about to start back down when the lamp flickered. Slowly, he turned. The scent of rain-washed night was fragrant in the dusty air. With a wry smile, he walked the length of the attic until he came to the final dormer. He gave it a slight push, and it swung open in a betraying arc.

Chapter Thirty-two

George Morley was troubled. He hadn't felt right since leaving Amberly. He tried to tell himself it was due to worry over his friend, but it was something more, something nagging. He couldn't dismiss Connor's eyes, so dark and wild with desperate panic, or the frantic clutch of his hands. Of course it was the fever. There was no other explanation for his accusations. But those eyes were begging for his help.

George shifted uncomfortably. He didn't like the errand he was on. In fact, he hated it, stealing from his dearest friend the one thing he had coveted for so long. But Connor wouldn't give up Amberly in a fit of delirium. To keep Tempest safe, he had said. Burn the house. Sell the land. So there would be nothing left they would want. They.

The rapid pounding on the roof halted the coach. When the trap opened, George called up to his driver, "Back to Amberly as fast as you can, and pray we're not too late."

Tempest pulled open the drawer in the darkened room and fumbled about through Connor's neatly arranged cravats, gloves, and handkerchiefs until her hand bumped against something solid.

"So here you are."

She stiffened at the low, dangerous voice, her fingers tightening about the solid strength of the pistol. She turned, brandishing it with a cold smile that too quickly faded. Katherine stood in the joining door, a wide-eyed child on either side of her and a glittering blade at Jesse's throat.

"How resourceful of you, my dear, but you won't be needing that," Katherine purred, her knife nudging upward. "Hand it to me, butt first."

With a shaky breath of frustration, Tempest passed her the weapon.

"Now I don't suppose you'd tell me where your errant husband is. No? No matter. Tyler will find him. Let's wait where it's more comfortable."

Sitting on the settee, once more hugging a weeping child in either arm, Tempest held her calm so as not to frighten them further, but her panicked thoughts were two stories above.

"You won't get away with this. Eddie's ridden for the sheriff. If you were wise, you and Tyler would flee with everything you can carry. Killing us will get you nothing now."

"On the contrary. It will grant me a great deal of satisfaction. The high and mighty Ambersons. How I've hated all of you." The woman was quite mad, her eyes taking on a hard brilliance and her lips a strange twist.

"If we are harmed, George and Eddie will never let you escape. Go now, and no one will look for you. You have my promise."

Katherine laughed. "You lie almost as convincingly as your husband. You know very well that Connor would never rest until we were punished. That's why it must end here. Morley will never be able to prove anything."

The sudden shot brought Tempest to her feet. Her face was pale as death.

"So much for your husband."

The rain slashed down with a cold brutal indifference on Connor as he huddled in the partial shelter of the dormer. With no coat to ease the chill of the winter night, he was trembling uncontrollably and soaked through. He didn't consider what the exposure would do to his fragile health. It was doubtful that he would survive anyway.

That fatalistic thought was reinforced when the casement swung open and Tyler grinned up at him. "Hello, Connie. Devil of a night to be out in your condition. Give me your hand. I'll bring you back in."

Connor scuttled backward, his boots scrambling on the steeply slanted roof until he was out of reach. He lay back against the wet tiles, panting softly as the twin images of his cousin seesawed below.

"Come down, Connie. If you make me come up after you, I'm not going to trouble myself with bringing you in. I'll just say poor Cousin Connor in a crazy hallucination jumped from the roof before I could save him."

Connor edged even further away. The rain-slicked tiles were treacherous.

Tyler frowned and came out on the narrow sill. He looked down, but the ground was cloaked in a misty darkness.

Connor knew he had to stall for time. He was no match for Tyler. "How could you let them kill my father? He took you in. He treated you like a son."

"I didn't know about that until much later, and I do feel badly but that won't change things. I'll feel badly about Holly too." He had inched away from the window until he was below his cousin. All he had to do was reach up and catch his foot. Dragging him over the edge would be easy. Connor's weak raspy breaths could be heard even over the noise of the wind. Slowly, he stretched up and seized the toe of his boot.

Connor lunged back, kicking and rolling. He heard Tyler's curse. Clawing with fingers and toes, he skidded several feet before he was able to halt his descent. He crawled upward on hands and knees until he came to one of Amberly's tall chimneys. He clung to the warm brick, shivering and gasping for each tortuous breath. Everything spun about him, roof and sky blending into one dark cloudy mass. Out of that swirling fog, he saw movement. With a harsh cry, he threw himself up over the peak of the roof.

The rain made the steep pitch into a fast-moving slide. Plunging down face first, Connor flung his arms and legs wide, pinwheeling several times before stopping. He lay still, his face pressed to the cold tiles and his eyes squeezed shut.

Breathing hard and shaking with cold, Tyler climbed over the crest. Connor lay spread-eagled halfway down the roof. He always made things so difficult. Tyler began to edge down the slick incline until he was above his antagonist. When the dark head lifted, Tyler grinned and kicked him in the face. There was a sudden report, too loud and quick to be thunder. A bright crimson flower burst open on Tyler's coat. His expression blank with amazement, he went down, toppling off the roof. He never felt the jarring impact of the ground.

Connor also was going over the edge. His body slid without resistance down the last few yards, then was jerked up short, his curled fingers catching a bit of broken tile. His feet swung out in the dark empty air. He lay like that for long minutes, his fingers cramped and his arms going numb with cold. He had no strength to pull himself up.

"Don't move, Conn. Stay very still," George's voice sounded.

"I can't hold on, George."

"Just a few seconds. You can do that. Come on, Conn. I'm almost there. Don't let go."

His muscles were jumping with jerky spasms from the strain; then his fingers just loosened. He gave a short gasp as the tiles slid past him, affording no buffer as the weight of his dangling legs created the momentum to draw him over the brink. His wrist was caught firmly, and for a moment, he pendulumed back and forth. Then George grasped his other hand.

With a desperate strength of will, Tempest knew she could not let this woman take the life of her child, Connor's child. Nothing else mattered. Not caution, not fear, not her own safety. She seized a burning oil lamp from the side table and swung it with all her might. The crystal base shattered as it struck Katherine's shoulder. The fluid spilled down her arm and skirt, becoming an instant trail of liquid fire. While Tempest gathered the screaming children to her, the living inferno reeled about the room, setting fire to the furnishings and drapes. Her hideous shrieking wail was ended with a single shot.

Tempest cast her arms about Eddie, her tears of panic and horror finally winning an escape. Eddie patted her briefly, then pushed away with a gruff, "Later, Este. Let's put this fire out. This is our home, after all."

The smoldering drapes were pulled down and used to smother the flames that engulfed several chairs, and the children stamped on sparks that lit on the carpet. Soon the blaze was reduced to a smelly thick smoke.

His face set in grim lines, Eddie covered the motionless figure on the floor with the charred drapes. "No one should have to suffer like that," he said softly to himself, thinking of his parents.

To air out the choking heaviness in the room, Tempest threw open the large mullioned casements. The crisp night breeze brushed in with a chilling shock, but that was not what made her cry out. Her wide eyes riveted on a dark shape sprawled on the lawn.

"No!"

The cry tore from her lips from a heart ripped asunder. Barely able to see through the blinding tears of anguish and disbelief, she stumbled over her skirts as she raced across the soggy grass to the recumbent figure. Clutching her constricted throat, she knelt in the wet, then finally summoned the courage to roll the still body over.

"Tempest."

She looked from the features of another to the source of the familiar voice to see him standing only with the support of his friend, drenched and shivering. But alive.

"Oh, Connor," she sobbed and was in his arms.

Chapter Thirty-three

Amberly was awash with the bright splotches of spring color. Signs of new life were everywhere, and Tempest smiled serenely as she felt impatient stirrings beneath the palms she rested on her mammoth belly. From her shaded chair, she fondly watched Connor and George tussle with the scores of children on the smooth green lawn, indifferent to the fact that their wedding attire was not designed for such misuse.

George Morley and Sarah Norwich had been joined in marriage beneath the stained-glass oriel of Amberly's chapel. Tempest's advanced state prevented her from traveling to London, and in spite of all George's anxious entreaties, Connor had refused to leave her side. Moved by George's misery and his insistence that Connor be at his side, Conn had brought the lot to the grand estate.

Tempest recalled Connor's comment abut the Morley clan in amusement, for there seemed to be an endless procession of them. All shockingly bright-headed and good-tempered, they made wonderful company. Several of the gangly calf-eyed girls mooned over Eddie, who was home from school and looking devilishly dapper. School had been his idea, for he said he could be no help at Amberly while dumb as a box of rocks. He surprised them all with his aptitude, and Connor, all the while grinning up his sleeve, had already taken him to task for bruising several classmates who objected to his background.

Winded and rumpled, Connor flopped down beside his wife's chair. "I'm too old for this," he complained remorsefully.

"Nonsense, my lord. They are just too young to treat you with the gentle handling befitting your vast age."

Her cajoling won an affected pout, but it was gone as soon as her hand stroked down his cheek.

"You have gotten too little exercise of late, sir."

He colored slightly at her meaning and put a careful hand on her swollen abdomen. "Not by choice, my sweet."

She covered the long shapely hand with hers and pressed it down firmly. "I am not made of glass, nor is this child. We are flesh and blood, and both are overly warm."

He drew his hand away awkwardly. "We'd best give the Morleys their gift. George looks as though he could use rescuing."

Who needed the rescue, she thought unhappily as she watched him retreat behind his solicitious manner. As soon as her figure had begun to ripen, Connor had placed her on a fragile pedestal, always loving and kind in his treatment but never with any physical closeness. He had even offered to move out of their shared bed, but her flat "no" had put an end to that.

Driven half-mad by his achingly sweet kisses and cautious, tender but impersonal touches, she eyed his tall, sleek stature with a covetous hunger. How she yearned to have him treat her with that passionate fire. She was secure in his faithfulness, knowing he hadn't cast so much as a wayward glance since the night she had fetched him from Harriet Wilson's. Had her awkward shape soured his desire, she wondered. Was she no longer attractive to him?

Sarah tucked against his side, George smiled as he took the gift Connor extended. That smile widened as he lifted out two lustrous pewter chalices.

"A little polishing will see to any scratches, I know. I've had to work quite diligently at it," Connor chuckled.

Tempest gave him a quizzing glance, for they owned no pewter, but George seemed to understand.

"Thank you, Conn. I will treasure these." When he went to replace them in the box, he found a roll of parchment. Curious, he read it, his jaw beginning to sag as his eyes moved quickly along.

"George, what is it?" Sarah asked in bewilderment.

"By God, Conn. We can't take this," he stammered, pushing it back at his friend almost in horror.

"If you don't, I'm going to force it on you," Connor remarked mildly, his pale eyes alit with mirth.

"George?"

He passed Sarah the paper, and as her eyes flew along it, they grew round and dazed. "The Garrett fortune? But, Connor, we—"

"Will accept gladly, not wanting to offend you and put an unpleasant end to a long and happy friendship," he concluded brightly. "Build her a grand estate, George. London is no place to begin a life. I love you both dearly, but you cannot stay under my roof."

George bent to kiss Tempest warmly, then hugged Connor in a crushing embrace. "I don't know what to say."

"Say thank you."

"Thank you."

"No more of it then. Just make sure you find some place close so I don't have so deuced far to ride should this termagant decide to cast me out."

"I see too little of you to wish you away," Tempest argued softly.

Seeing the sadness in her eyes, Sarah led George away with a firm tug.

"She's beautiful, isn't she?" Tempest said, wistfully admiring the trim figure.

"Beautiful."

The sultry tone brought her head up in question to find the light eyes intent upon her. "Don't tease me, my lord. You needn't pretend you find anything pleasing in this ungainly matron I've become."

Connor's laugh woke the sparks of anger in her bright eyes, and he was quick to placate her. "Not only pleasing but damned desirable."

The touch of his fingertips beneath her chin made her tremble, her lips parting softly and her eyes slipping closed in painful longing. Her breath came in a sob as his mouth slanted over hers, his kiss hot and pulsing and as urgent as the stirrings in her every fiber.

"Oh, Connor," she breathed against his greedy lips.

"I want you so."

He was panting and all ashiver when he drew her to his chest. "And I have dreamed of you until I fear I'd go mad. I cannot touch you and not want to make love to you."

"Even now?" she whispered hopefully.

"Especially now. You bear my child, the greatest gift of love a man can receive. If any harm came to you or that babe, it would crush me. Oh, sweet, my need is not as great as my fear."

Holding his dark head close, she said gently, "Is that why you've been so distant?" At his nod, she hugged him tightly. "My love, no harm could come to either of us for better than a month. There is no danger." She felt him hesitate as his mind was filled with the memory of his mother's face becoming hers on that quiet deathbed. "Connor, please love me."

Their kiss was long and filled with a desperate need. Tempest sighed as his eager lips scorched down her throat to press to the recent fullness of her bosom.

"Please, my lord. Our guests," she reminded half-heartedly. "They may take exception to you mauling your so obviously pregnant wife."

"We cannot have them upset," Connor agreed, hot, icy eyes lifting to plunge into the depthless blue seas of her own. "Let us retire inside for a time. What they cannot see cannot shock them unduly."

"As you wish, my lord," she murmured submissively.

From her place at George's side, Sarah watched Lord and Lady Amberson stroll up to the great house, his stride shortened to accommodate her cumbersome gait and a helpful hand on her elbow. When they

507

stepped inside, he swept her up in his arm, making her witness to a searing kiss before his boot kicked the heavy door shut.

Sighing, she drew George's questioning stare. He followed her gaze to the house and the empty chair and grinned. "Off lusting again, I see," was his uncharitable remark.

"Will you treat me as well?"

George looked amazed, for he had never seen Connor as one a woman would desire a role to be modeled after. "How so?"

"Will we be that happy?" she explained.

"Let us hope so," he replied and kissed her soundly.

THE BEST IN REGENCIES FROM ZEBRA

PASSION'S LADY　　　　　　　　　　　　(1545, $2.95)
by Sara Blayne

She was a charming rogue, an impish child—and a maddeningly alluring woman. If the Earl of Shayle knew little else about her, he knew she was going to marry him. As a bride, Marie found a temporary hiding place from her past, but could not escape from the Earl's shrewd questions—or the spark of passion in his eyes.

AN ELIGIBLE BRIDE　　　　　　　　　　(2020, $3.95)
by Janice Bennett

The duke of Halliford was in the country for one reason—to fulfill a promise to look after Captain Carstairs' children. This was as distasteful as finding a suitable wife. But his problems were answered when he saw the beautiful Helena Carstairs. The duke was not above resorting to some very persuasive means to get what he wanted . . .

RECKLESS HEART　　　　　　　　　　　(1679, $2.50)
by Lois Arvin Walker

Rebecca had met her match in the notorious Earl of Compton. Not only did he decline the invitation to her soiree, but he found it amusing when her horse landed her in the middle of Compton Creek. If this was another female scheme to lure him into marriage the Earl swore Rebecca would soon learn she had the wrong man, a man with a blackened reputation.

Available wherever paperbacks are sold, or order direct from the Publisher. Send cover price plus 50¢ per copy for mailing and handling to Zebra Books, Dept. 2143, 475 Park Avenue South, New York, N.Y. 10016. Residents of New York, New Jersey and Pennsylvania must include sales tax. DO NOT SEND CASH.

CHILLING GOTHICS
From Zebra Books

FIERY ROMANCE
From Zebra Books

AUTUMN'S FURY   (1763, $3.95)
by Emma Merritt

Lone Wolf had known many women, but none had captured his heart the way Catherine had . . . with her he felt a hunger he hadn't experienced with any of the maidens of his own tribe. He would make Catherine his captive, his slave of love — until she would willingly surrender to the magic of AUTUMN'S FURY.

PASSION'S PARADISE   (1618, $3.75)
by Sonya T. Pelton

When she is kidnapped by the cruel, captivating Captain Ty, fair-haired Angel Sherwood fears not for her life, but for her honor! Yet she can't help but be warmed by his manly touch, and secretly longs for PASSION'S PARADISE.

LOVE'S ELUSIVE FLAME   (1836, $3.75)
by Phoebe Conn

Golden-haired Flame was determined to find the man of her dreams even if it took forever, but she didn't have long to wait once she met the handsome rogue Joaquin. He made her respond to his ardent kisses and caresses . . . but if he wanted her completely, she would have to be his only woman — she wouldn't settle for anything less. Joaquin had always taken women as he wanted . . . but none of them was Flame. Only one night of wanton ecstasy just wasn't enough — once he was touched by LOVE'S ELUSIVE FLAME.

SAVAGE SPLENDOR   (1855, $3.95)
by Constance O'Banyon

By day Mara questioned her decision to remain in her husband's world. But by night, when Tajarez crushed her in his strong, muscular arms, taking her to the peaks of rapture, she knew she could never live without him.

Available wherever paperbacks are sold, or order direct from the Publisher. Send cover price plus 50¢ per copy for mailing and handling to Zebra Books, Dept. 2143, 475 Park Avenue South, New York, N.Y. 10016. Residents of New York, New Jersey and Pennsylvania must include sales tax. DO NOT SEND CASH.

FIERY ROMANCE
From Zebra Books

AUTUMN'S FURY   (1763, $3.95)
by Emma Merritt

Lone Wolf had known many women, but none had captured his heart the way Catherine had . . . with her he felt a hunger he hadn't experienced with any of the maidens of his own tribe. He would make Catherine his captive, his slave of love — until she would willingly surrender to the magic of AUTUMN'S FURY.

PASSION'S PARADISE   (1618, $3.75)
by Sonya T. Pelton

When she is kidnapped by the cruel, captivating Captain Ty, fair-haired Angel Sherwood fears not for her life, but for her honor! Yet she can't help but be warmed by his manly touch, and secretly longs for PASSION'S PARADISE.

LOVE'S ELUSIVE FLAME   (1836, $3.75)
by Phoebe Conn

Golden-haired Flame was determined to find the man of her dreams even if it took forever, but she didn't have long to wait once she met the handsome rogue Joaquin. He made her respond to his ardent kisses and caresses . . . but if he wanted her completely, she would have to be his only woman — she wouldn't settle for anything less. Joaquin had always taken women as he wanted . . . but none of them was Flame. Only one night of wanton ecstasy just wasn't enough — once he was touched by LOVE'S ELUSIVE FLAME.

SAVAGE SPLENDOR   (1855, $3.95)
by Constance O'Banyon

By day Mara questioned her decision to remain in her husband's world. But by night, when Tajarez crushed her in his strong, muscular arms, taking her to the peaks of rapture, she knew she could never live without him.

SATIN SURRENDER   (1861, $3.95)
by Carol Finch

Dante Folwer found innocent Erica Bennett in his bed in the most fashionable whorehouse in New Orleans. Expecting a woman of experience, Dante instead stole the innocence of the most magnificent creature he'd ever seen. He would forever make her succumb to . . . SATIN SURRENDER.

Available wherever paperbacks are sold, or order direct from the Publisher. Send cover price plus 50¢ per copy for mailing and handling to Zebra Books, Dept. 2143, 475 Park Avenue South, New York, N.Y. 10016. Residents of New York, New Jersey and Pennsylvania must include sales tax. DO NOT SEND CASH.